THE AMAZON QUEST

BOOKS BY GILBERT MORRIS

THE HOUSE OF WINSLOW SERIES

The Honorable Imposter
The Captive Bride
The Indentured Heart
The Gentle Rebel
The Saintly Buccaneer
The Holy Warrior
The Reluctant Bridegroom
The Last Confederate
The Dixie Widow
The Wounded Yankee
The Union Belle
The Final Adversary
The Crossed Sabres
The Valiant Gunman
The Gallant Outlaw
The Jeweled Spur
The Yukon Queen
The Rough Rider
The Iron Lady

The Silver Star
The Shadow Portrait
The White Hunter
The Flying Cavalier
The Glorious Prodigal
The Amazon Quest
The Golden Angel
The Heavenly Fugitive
The Fiery Ring
The Pilgrim Song
The Beloved Enemy
The Shining Badge
The Royal Handmaid
The Silent Harp
The Virtuous Woman
The Gypsy Moon
The Unlikely Allies
The High Calling
The Hesitant Hero

CHENEY DUVALL, M.D.[1]

1. The Stars for a Light
2. Shadow of the Mountains
3. A City Not Forsaken
4. Toward the Sunrising
5. Secret Place of Thunder
6. In the Twilight, in the Evening
7. Island of the Innocent
8. Driven With the Wind

CHENEY AND SHILOH: THE INHERITANCE[1]

1. Where Two Seas Met
2. The Moon by Night
3. There Is a Season

THE SPIRIT OF APPALACHIA[2]

1. Over the Misty Mountains
2. Beyond the Quiet Hills
3. Among the King's Soldiers
4. Beneath the Mockingbird's Wings
5. Around the River's Bend

LIONS OF JUDAH

1. Heart of a Lion
2. No Woman So Fair
3. The Gate of Heaven
4. Till Shiloh Comes
5. By Way of the Wilderness
6. Daughter of Deliverance

[1]with Lynn Morris   [2]with Aaron McCarver

GILBERT MORRIS

the AMAZON QUEST

BETHANYHOUSE
Minneapolis, Minnesota

The Amazon Quest
Copyright © 2001
Gilbert Morris

Cover illustration by Bill Graf
Cover design by Josh Madison

Published by Bethany House Publishers
11400 Hampshire Avenue South
Bloomington, Minnesota 55438

Bethany House Publishers is a division of
Baker Publishing Group, Grand Rapids, Michigan.

Printed in the United States of America

ISBN-13: 978-0-7642-2969-5
ISBN-10: 0-7642-2969-9

The Library of Congress has cataloged the original edition as follows:

Morris, Gilbert.
   The Amazon quest / by Gilbert Morris.
      p. cm. — (The house of Winslow ; bk. 25)
   ISBN 0-7642-2117-5
   1. Winslow family (Fictitious characters)—Fiction. 2. World War, 1914-1918—Veterans—Fiction. 3. Americans—Amazon River Region—Fiction. 4. Amazon River Region—Fiction. 5. Headhunters—Fiction. I. Title.
   PS3563.O8742   A84   2001
   813'.54—dc21   2001000879

To Terry McDowell—
my editor and my friend.

It's hard to believe that we have done all these Winslow novels, Terry. You have done a splendid job as an editor and have been a light along the way to me. Thanks for all the work and the tender love and care you've put in on these books.

GILBERT MORRIS spent ten years as a pastor before becoming Professor of English at Ouachita Baptist University in Arkansas and earning a Ph.D. at the University of Arkansas. A prolific writer, he has had over 25 scholarly articles and 200 poems published in various periodicals, and over the past years has had more than 180 novels published. His family includes three grown children. He and his wife live in Gulf Shores, Alabama.

CONTENTS

PART FOUR
Summer–Autumn 1923

THE HOUSE OF WINSLOW

★ ★ ★ ★

THE HOUSE OF WINSLOW

★ ★ ★ ★

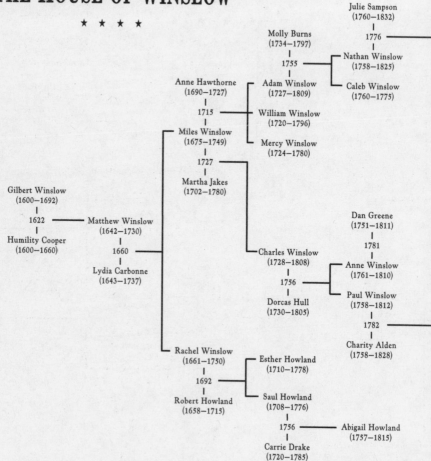

Julie Sampson
(1760–1832)
|
1776 ——

Molly Burns
(1734–1797)
|
1755
|
Anne Hawthorne   Adam Winslow
(1690–1727)   (1727–1809)

Nathan Winslow
(1758–1825)

Caleb Winslow
(1760–1775)

|
1715 ——
|
Miles Winslow
(1675–1749)
|
1727
|
Martha Jakes
(1702–1780)

William Winslow
(1720–1796)

Mercy Winslow
(1724–1780)

Gilbert Winslow
(1600–1692)
|
1622 —— Matthew Winslow
(1642–1730)
|
1660
|
Lydia Carbonne
(1643–1737)

Humility Cooper
(1600–1660)

Dan Greene
(1751–1811)
|
1781
|
Charles Winslow   Anne Winslow
(1728–1808)   (1761–1810)
|
1756
|
Dorcas Hull
(1730–1805)

Paul Winslow
(1758–1812)
|
1782 ——
|
Charity Alden
(1758–1828)

Rachel Winslow
(1661–1750)
|
1692 ——
|
Robert Howland
(1658–1715)

Esther Howland
(1710–1778)

Saul Howland
(1708–1776)
|
1756 —— Abigail Howland
(1757–1815)
|
Carrie Drake
(1720–1785)

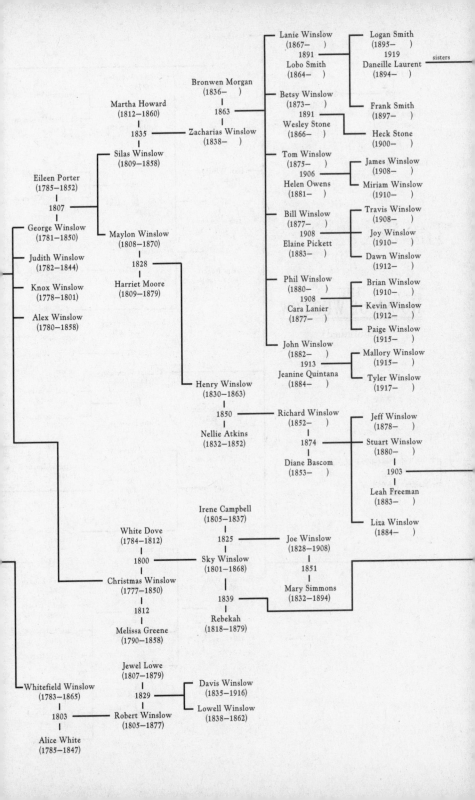

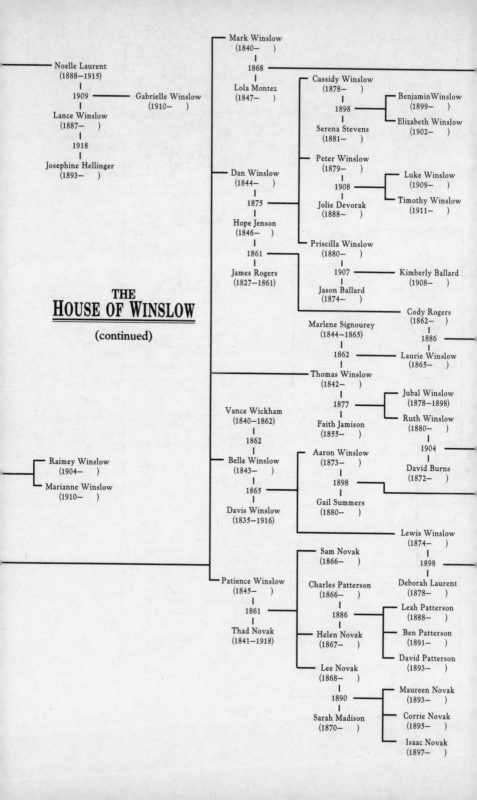

THE
HOUSE OF WINSLOW
(continued)

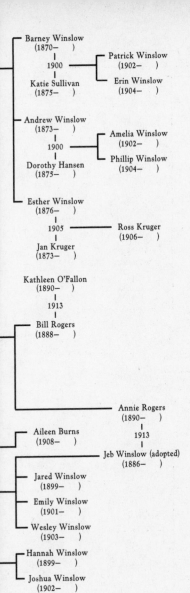

Barney Winslow
(1870—   )
|
1900 ———— Patrick Winslow
| (1902—   )
Katie Sullivan
(1875—   ) ———— Erin Winslow
                  (1904—   )

Andrew Winslow
(1873—   )
|
1900 ———— Amelia Winslow
| (1902—   )
Dorothy Hansen
(1875—   ) ———— Phillip Winslow
                  (1904—   )

Esther Winslow
(1876—   )
|
1905 ———— Ross Kruger
| (1906—   )
Jan Kruger
(1873—   )

Kathleen O'Fallon
(1890—   )
|
1913
|
Bill Rogers
(1888—   )

Annie Rogers
(1890—   )
|
1913
|
Aileen Burns
(1908—   )
Jeb Winslow (adopted)
(1886—   )

Jared Winslow
(1899—   )

Emily Winslow
(1901—   )

Wesley Winslow
(1903—   )

Hannah Winslow
(1899—   )

Joshua Winslow
(1902—   )

PART ONE

MARCH–OCTOBER 1917

★ ★ ★ ★

CHAPTER ONE

ARAB DEATH

★ ★ ★ ★

"Oh, come on, Jared—don't be such a stick-in-the-mud!"

Jared Winslow looked down at his younger sister, Emily, with irritation written across his features. At the age of eighteen he felt that the two-year advantage he had over her demanded from him a special responsibility for her safety and well-being. He himself was an even-tempered young man given to serious thought, but Emily was prone to a vitriolic temperament, although she had a kind heart. She often tested the limits of their parents' guidelines, and now as Jared studied her, he wondered where she had gotten such qualities. No longer a child, she was not yet fully a woman either but was clearly entering the mysterious and dangerous world of adulthood. She was not particularly beautiful but was so vivacious and lively that no one seemed to notice. She had a wide face, a full mouth usually turned upward in a grin, a creamy complexion that complemented her red hair, and almost electric cornflower blue eyes. Her prominent widow's peak was an attribute she hated and frequently threatened to shave off. Now as Jared observed her, he couldn't help but notice how quickly his little sister was growing up before his eyes. It seemed only last year she had been as thin as a garden rake, but now the light green crossover sweater she wore revealed her maturing feminine outline. She had on a dark

18

gray skirt, and a green ribbon tied her hair back from her face.

"We're not going to see that immoral woman and that's final!" Jared said firmly. "Everybody knows she's no good. Nothing but a vamp."

"But I want to see her, Jared. Please. Just this once."

Jared hesitated—and promptly lost the argument. When up against his sister, there was no room for hesitation, for once she had her foot in the door, she would press in until she got her way.

"It's only an old movie," Emily insisted, "and everybody's talking about Theda Bara."

"Theda Bara—what a name!" Jared groaned.

"It's an anagram for 'Arab death,' you know."

"I know that!" Jared snapped. "But it's just downright indecent!"

"You've never seen one of her movies."

"You don't have to *see* them. Everybody's talking about what kind of woman she is. James Satterfield saw her in that movie *A Fool There Was*. He said it was pretty bad and would do nothing but lead men right down to the pit."

Indeed, Theda Bara had cast quite a spell over the American public. She brought a pantherlike purring to screen characters such as Juliet, Camille, and Cleopatra. Her seductiveness was thought to be a grave threat to public morality. Ministers thundered against her from pulpits coast to coast, but apparently with little effect, for theaters continued to sell out across the country. Earlier Clara Bow and the Gibson Girl had been the symbols of womanhood, but now American young people were flocking to see Theda Bara.

Jared and Emily were walking along the sidewalk in their hometown of Richmond, Virginia. Each of them carried a paper sack, having just gone to the neighborhood grocery store. An overly large dog of questionable ancestry trotted along beside them. Seeing a squirrel, the dog lurched over toward Emily, who reached down and shoved him away. "Get away, Cap'n Brown!"

Cap'n Brown gave her a reproachful look, then lumbered off on his fruitless chase.

"There ought to be some sort of law against a dog that big," Jared remarked.

Despite Jared's teasing, all of them loved the big dog. Jared had found him abandoned in a rainstorm, half drowned and hungry, and had brought him home. All three of the Winslow children—Emily, Wesley, and Jared—had mounted an attack on their parents to keep him and had been successful. Now at the age of three, Cap'n Brown was full grown and very large. Having lost sight of his prey, he jogged back with his tongue lolling out like a red necktie.

By the time they had reached the walkway that led up to their house, a large two-story Victorian with turrets and intricate trim, Jared felt exhausted. "We're not going and that's it."

Emily's temper flared. "All right! If you won't go, I'll go by myself!"

"You can't do that."

"I will. You see if I don't. We need to know what's going on in the world," Emily insisted.

Jared rolled his eyes up and heaved a sigh of exasperation. "All right, Emily, I'll take you to the dumb movie—but if Mom and Dad find out about it, we're dead!"

★   ★   ★   ★

Emily blinked as she came out of the Rialto Theater. She and Jared had taken advantage of an early matinee, and both of them fervently hoped their parents would not ask them where they had been. Usually Jared went to ball practice, and Emily quite frequently had after-school meetings, for she was active in many of the clubs. Now as they stood outside of the theater, Emily said, "Oh, Jared, wasn't that exciting?"

Pushing his lips out in disgust, Jared shook his head. "I don't think so. I think it was downright depraved."

"Depraved! How can you say that?"

"Why, that woman's nothing but a tramp."

"That's just a role she plays. In real life, she's probably very sweet."

"Sweet! You can take one look at her and know *exactly* what she is. All you have to do is go down to the eastside right here in Richmond, and you'll see women like that hanging around bars."

Emily suddenly laughed aloud and turned toward Jared. She grabbed him by his sweater and pulled him around. "How do you know what bad women look like? Have you been hanging around bars on the eastside?"

Jared's face flushed. Being a very truthful young man, he shrugged his shoulders. "I went once with a couple of guys, but it didn't take me long to decide it wasn't for me."

Emily took his arm and held on to it as they turned to leave. They had not gone more than ten feet when a piercing whistle made them both pivot around to see where the sound had come from. Three young men were lounging outside of Benny's Pool Hall. All of them were smoking cigarettes and had their hair greased back in the current fashion. The leader of the three wore a lightweight sweater in the cool March wind.

"Hey, sweetie, how'd you like Theda Bara? Some doll, hey?"

"Don't pay any attention to them," Jared said. "Come on."

But the thickset, bulky young man in his late teens moved quickly toward them. He blocked their way and soon was flanked by the other two. All three were grinning, and the tall, lanky one with blond hair said, "What do you say, Judd? Maybe we should take the little lady out and show her the town."

Judd laughed aloud. He turned and spat on the street, then flicked his cigarette away with a careless gesture. "That might be a good idea. What's your name, babe?"

"None of your business!" Emily snapped back. "Come on, Jared."

Emily started to walk away, but Judd grabbed her arm and swung her around, pulling her away from Jared. "Let me loose!" she screamed.

"Hey, this redhead's got a temper, Mort."

"I always liked a little spirit in a woman. Come on, sweetheart, let's you and me go stepping!"

"Turn her loose!"

Jared's face was flushed as he lunged toward the man who

had grabbed Emily. He was a well-built young man of six feet and one of the best athletes Richmond had ever produced. He had starred in basketball, football, and baseball, his strong right arm making him the best pitcher in the area. Angry now, he reached out and slapped Judd's hand away. "Let go of her arm!"

Judd's face was scarred from many a brawl. Always eager for a fight, he planted his beefy hand against Jared's chest and shoved him backward. "Why don't you go for a walk, sonny? We'll take care of your lady friend here."

Emily cried out, "Don't, Jared!"

But she was too late. Jared had launched his powerful right hand, and his fist caught Judd squarely on the cheek. The blow turned the husky young man around but did nothing to hurt him. Judd instantly swung back, striking Jared's chest and forcing him off balance.

As Jared staggered backward, Emily saw the other two moving toward him, and when one of them doubled up his fist and drew it back to hit Jared from behind, she kicked him in the knee with all of her might.

"Ow!" he yelled, hopping about on one foot.

Meanwhile, the tall one named Mort reached out and grabbed at Emily, but she immediately yanked his hair back as hard as she could. The young man let out a loud howl, and Emily held on like grim death.

Judd and Jared were fairly evenly matched. Judd was heavier and stronger, but Jared was much faster with his fists. As the two exchanged blows, Judd was getting somewhat the best of it.

Emily yelled out, "You let my brother alone!" and jumped up in the air, landing on Judd's back. She threw her hands around his face, blinding him. He tried to shake her off, but she clung like a leech.

There was little doubt how the fight would have ended, for the three thugs clearly had the advantage over Jared and Emily.

But Emily heard a voice saying, "All right, you fellows. Break it up."

She turned to see the slight man who had come to their rescue. He was wearing a dark gray suit with a white shirt and a tie and looked exactly like a schoolteacher—which indeed he was. "Mr. Laurence!" Emily cried.

Ryan Laurence was the English teacher at Richmond High School. With his thin build and average height, he was not a prepossessing figure. Around thirty years old, he had blond hair, piercing blue eyes, and a lean, aristocratic face. He ordered the boys in his dignified British accent, "You fellows move along, or I'll have you run in."

Judd was shaking his head as he stared at the soft-spoken man who had interrupted their fight. "You want to get in on this?"

"No, I've designated all this kind of fighting to my dog," Mr. Laurence replied. He glanced across the street and said, "There's Officer Sullivan over there. Would you like to take it up with him?"

Judd shot a glance across the street and at once ducked his head. "Come on, guys," he said. "There's nothin' here. Let's go shoot some pool."

As the three went inside the pool hall, Emily approached Ryan Laurence. "Mr. Laurence, I'm so glad you came."

"How did this brawl start?" the teacher inquired. Seeing Jared's bloody nose, he took out his handkerchief and offered it to him. "Maybe we'd better go put some cold water on that."

"No, it's all right, Mr. Laurence," Jared said. "But I'm sure glad you came along. Another few minutes and I'd have been a goner."

"Yes, thanks a lot, Mr. Laurence." Emily's eyes glowed as she spoke to the man. She had developed a girlhood crush on Ryan Laurence that had lasted for two years now.

Avoiding her gaze, he replied, "Well, I didn't do anything really." Then, cocking his head to one side, Laurence lifted a suspicious eyebrow. "You young people haven't been to that movie, have you?"

Emily lifted her chin. "Why, yes, we have."

"Do your folks know about it?"

"No, they don't," Jared said quickly.

"It wasn't his fault, Mr. Laurence. I made Jared take me."

Laurence suddenly smiled, his eyes twinkling. "You have a

habit of getting your own way, Emily. I've noticed that."

"Why, Mr. Laurence, how can you say that?"

"I say that because last semester I gave you a B, and you came to see me about it. When you walked out the door, somehow you had an A." He reached up and removed his felt hat and ran his hand over his fine hair, which was blowing in the wind. "I never have figured out how you did that."

"I just explained some things that you didn't understand." Emily smiled.

Laurence laughed. "I suppose so. Well, you both better get home now."

"You're not going to tell our parents, are you, Mr. Laurence?" Emily pleaded.

"No, I'm not. But I would think maybe your conscience would lead you to confess it. I'll see you in class tomorrow."

"He's so good-looking," Emily sighed after the man had walked away. "And don't you just love that English accent?"

"Not as much as you do." Jared managed a grin. "Well, come on. Let's go home and tell our folks that we've fallen into the depths of depravity."

"You're going to *tell* them?" Emily said with alarm.

"I sure am. I don't want this on my conscience." He reached out and playfully punched Emily on the arm. "And since you don't *have* a conscience, I'll have to do the confessing for both of us. I'll tell them I talked you into going with me."

"They'll never believe that," Emily said. She looked up and smiled slowly, studying her brother's face. She thought he was the most handsome young man she had ever seen, with the same crisp brown hair and blue eyes as their father. The two of them were very close—more like best friends than siblings. Jared also looked a lot like their brother, Wesley. The family resemblance did not carry over into their friendship, however. Emily shared a much closer bond to Jared than to Wesley. She and Jared had always been into everything together. He was the perfect older brother. He took her with him practically everywhere, and Emily idolized him. She had never missed one of his games, be it basketball, football, or baseball. Now she took his arm and said, "Let *me* tell them, Jared. They won't be as hard on me as they would be on you."

★   ★   ★   ★

"So you went to see that horrible woman," Aaron Winslow said. At the age of forty-four he still carried no excess weight. As he looked across at his two older children, he was worried about them but did not let his concern show. He was wearing a light blue woolen jacket and gray flannel trousers. His pale blue shirt was open at the neck, and he looked tan and fit, for he spent a great deal of time hunting, fishing, and on the golf course. Now he looked over toward his wife, Gail, and shook his head. "What are we going to do with these two?"

Gail Summers Winslow was thirty-seven but looked at least ten years younger. She was one of those women who seemed not to age. Her rich brown hair was as abundant, and had the same reddish tint, as the first time Aaron had seen her. She shook her head now and said, "I think we ought to ground them for the rest of their lives."

"Oh, Mom, you don't want to do that to us," Emily countered. "It was just an old movie." She could tell by her mother's expression, however, that she was upset. Emily had learned to recognize her mother's moods, and now she tried to reason with her. "It wasn't so bad, Mom."

"It doesn't make any difference how bad the movie was," Aaron said sternly. "What disappoints your mother and me is that you did it knowing we wouldn't approve."

"It was my fault, Dad," Jared said.

"It was not," Emily cried. "I talked him into it. He did everything he could to make me change my mind. I finally told him I'd go by myself if he didn't take me."

Aaron listened as his daughter defended her brother, and finally said, "You know you're wrong, don't you, Emily?"

Emily Winslow was an honest young woman. As far as Aaron and Gail could tell, she had only lied to them once in her life, and that was when she was eight years old. She had come to them brokenhearted over deceiving them and had cried her heart out. Something in her could not stand a deviation from the truth—in herself or in anyone else. Now she admitted, "I knew it was wrong, and I'm sorry, Mom and Dad. But please don't blame Jared."

"I have to blame him," her father insisted. "He's two years older and you're his baby sister. You shouldn't have done it, Jared."

Jared shook his head and stared down at his shoes. "I know it, Dad. Just pour it on. Whatever you say, I deserve it."

Aaron suddenly broke the tense moment with a chuckle. "You two are always into something! What one of you doesn't think of, the other one does."

"But, Dad," Emily said, "if I'm going to be a writer, I've got to know what life is really like."

"Do you think Theda Bara's life is worthy of study?" Aaron demanded.

"Well, she's the one person everyone's watching these days, and I think people are what they watch."

"That's why you don't need to be watching her," Gail said at once. "I hope you don't want to become like Theda Bara."

"Oh no, Mom!" Emily shook her head. "I didn't mean that. I just want to know what's going on in the world."

"Well," Aaron said slowly, "you've had an experience you can write about. Now let me give you another one—you're grounded for a week. Write about *that*."

Emily's face fell. "You mean I can't leave the house?"

"I mean you come home right after school, and you stay in until you leave again the next day."

Emily bit her lip. "All right, Dad. Whatever you say."

"Me, too," Jared said.

"No, son. I know you have ball practice, and that's very important to you. It's important to me, too. You go to ball practice, but you stay in nights."

Jared suddenly grinned. "Wouldn't you just rather whip me with a belt?"

Aaron looked at his son's strong physique. "There was a time when I might have been able to handle that, but I have my doubts about it right now. No, you just stay in."

"It's all right, Jared," Emily said. "We'll find something to entertain us."

"Sure we will," Jared said cheerfully.

"We'll play records, and then I'll help you with your algebra."

The two turned and walked away, their voices echoing back as they ascended the stairway.

"Didn't seem to hurt them much—being grounded," Aaron muttered.

Gail came over and put her arm around her husband's shoulders. "Come on, let's have coffee. After a crisis like this, I feel I need some reinforcement." She led him into the kitchen, poured two cups of coffee from the large coffeepot, and set them on the kitchen table.

As they sat down and drank the rich brew, Aaron leaned back. "This is good," he said. Then a thought occurred to him, and he shook his head. "It's a good thing Wesley's staying overnight with Clarence, or he would have gone with them."

"Oh, I don't think either one of them would have dragged him to that awful movie," Gail said quickly. "They're both good children. You probably did worse when you were a teenager."

Aaron laughed. "I sure did. I think I was studying for the gallows when I was their age."

Gail laughed and looked with affection at her husband as he drank his coffee. Aaron Winslow worked very hard. He had become a fine writer and wrote a daily column for the Hearst papers. In addition, he was active in his church as chairman of the board of deacons, and he took every chance to go hunting or fishing, taking the children with him whenever possible.

He looked back at Gail fondly. "You know, I was thinking today about when I went off to fight in the war."

Gail's face changed as she, too, remembered her husband going off to fight in the Spanish-American War.

"That was a hard time for us, wasn't it?" Aaron said.

"It was, but God brought you back."

"Yes, He did, and I've always thanked Him for it. Lewis and I both could have died over there, along with some pretty good fellows." Aaron and his brother, Lewis, had fought all the way through the Spanish-American War, and Gail had gone as a nurse. The war had been a turning point for Aaron. Before facing the bloody charge up San Juan Hill, he had been a rather selfish individual. But that crucible of fire had changed his whole life. As he sat holding the mug of coffee in his big hands, he reminisced about that time. He shook himself finally and said, "That wasn't anything compared to this war over in Europe. At the Battle of Verdun last year seven hundred thousand men were killed. It's unbelievable."

"What's going to happen?" Gail wondered. "Do you think we'll get into it?"

"I think we're bound to. Wilson's dead set against it, but if Germany ever declares submarine warfare against our ships, President Wilson will have no choice. It's just gotten completely out of hand. Hundreds of thousands of men are dying, and for what?"

"It's terrible, Aaron."

"Countries are constantly trying to expand their control, so it just seems that wars are part of the curse that's on the world." He took another sip of his coffee and then said, "You remember last March when Pershing and his troops went down to Mexico to fight Pancho Villa? They didn't capture him, but nonetheless our country may be glad of that military experience, because right now our army doesn't have *any* experience."

After a moment of silence, Gail spoke aloud what they were both thinking. "Jared might do what Logan did. He might enlist." Logan Smith, a relative of Aaron's, had gone to France and joined a British unit and become an ace pilot. He had shot down twenty-one planes, and his picture was in all the papers.

"Yes, he might just do that," Aaron said with a sigh of resignation. "He's not impulsive, but Jared will always do what he thinks is right. We'll just have to pray that America can stay out of the war."

★　★　★　★

Emily stood in front of her English class and cleared her throat. "The name of my theme is 'Europe Is None of Our Business.'"

Mr. Ryan Laurence smiled behind his hand but said nothing. He looked out over the class and saw agreement and disagreement on the faces of his students. As a rule, the girls wanted America to stay out of the war, while the boys, always looking for adventure, would have liked nothing better than a chance to get into it. Mr. Laurence listened as Emily read her paper, which basically argued that Europe had always had wars, and that America should take care of her own business. When she finished, he asked the class, "Any comments?"

"I've got a comment," Bill Jackson piped up. He was a tall sixteen-year-old who played fullback on the football team. He had black hair and dark eyes, which now sparkled as he said, "Emily, I don't know what you're thinkin' about. You believe we can hide out over here forever? The kaiser's not going to stop with Europe. He'll come this way, too, and fight us if we don't go stop him."

"That's right," Don Daily agreed. He was a scholarly boy, the brain of the class, and he knew all about the European war. "All you have to do is look at what's happened already. The kaiser wants to dominate all of Europe. What makes you think he'll leave us alone?"

"We're too far away," Emily snapped. "He wouldn't dare cross the ocean and come way over here."

"We couldn't do anything to stop him if he did," Daily argued. "We don't have any army."

"What do you mean we don't have any army?" Emily demanded.

"I mean we cut back on spending so that we only have a few troops. We'd have to put twenty million men in uniform to stop the kaiser."

Mr. Laurence allowed the argument to go on for some time. It was his way, when his students were interested in a subject, to let the discussion go whichever way they pleased. As the bell rang and the students started filing out of the classroom, he said, "Emily, just a minute. I need to talk to you."

Emily picked up her books, held them to her chest, and walked over to him. "Yes, what is it, Mr. Laurence?"

"Here's the theme you wrote last week. I've made some observations."

Emily at once put her books down on a desk and grabbed the paper. Her eyes flew open. "Why, you've got comments written all over it in red ink. It looks like it's bleeding!"

"It's overdone, Emily. Too strident. You need to calm your writing voice down."

Emily stared at him with indignation. "But I worked for *days* on this theme."

"And you've done a good job in some ways, but you've let your heart outrun your head. You've ignored some facts that I've pointed out."

"That's not bad to let your heart rule you, is it, Mr. Laurence?" She wished she could call him Ryan, but she knew as a student she could never take that liberty.

Laurence, who had endured girlhood crushes from his students for several years, knew of Emily's feelings for him. He kept his comments on a strictly formal basis, however, as he continued. "You have a good heart, Emily, but you're too impulsive."

He went over his editorial suggestions with her on the paper. Finally Emily sighed and took it, tucking it into her notebook. "All right. I'll write it again." She looked up suddenly and said, "You think I'm right about the war, don't you? That we ought to stay out of it."

"No, as a matter of fact," Laurence said, "I'm leaving to go fight in two weeks." He saw her face fall and added quickly, "I'm joining a unit in Canada. I'll be in the trenches in France in less than two months, I would suppose."

"No, you can't do that!" Emily's face twisted in distress.

"I'm afraid I have to. You follow your heart so much, and this time I have to follow mine. I am English, you know, and it's my friends and companions who are dying now. I can no longer ignore their plight. I've got to go and do my part."

Emily felt a heavy cloud descend on her, and she wanted to reach out, take him by the lapels of his coat, and demand that he stay out of the war. That would not do, of course, and she could only say, "But what will I do without you?"

"There'll be another teacher."

"But he won't be like you."

"He may be better. Let's hope so. I'll probably tell you this again before I leave, but you've been one of those students who brings great joy to a teacher's heart. Most kids don't care about anything—especially English," he said dryly. "Not much fun diagramming a complex sentence. But it's been a pleasure to me, Emily, seeing your mind develop. You're so full of life and so impulsive," he added with a slight smile. "You're a fine writer, too. Use your gift to help people." He hesitated and then said, "And use it for the glory of God."

★   ★   ★   ★

". . . and so he's leaving to fight. He's joining the army in Canada. Mom, he shouldn't do it!" Emily was beside herself with grief as she spilled out the news to her mother.

Gail had been aware of Emily's crush on her English teacher for some time. It had caused her some concern, but she had gained a measure of relief when Mr. Laurence had once confided in her, *"Emily's at a bad age, but she's got a good spirit. Much like yours, I think, Mrs. Winslow. She'll get over this, just as she'll get over some other things in life."* Now Gail was thankful for that conversation. Still, she knew his leaving was hard for her daughter, and she tried to comfort her. "I'm sure Mr. Laurence is doing what he feels he has to do."

"But I don't want him to go," Emily wailed.

"All over this country, and I'm sure all over Europe, there are sisters and mothers and friends who are crying, 'I don't want him to go.' But they have to, I suppose. He is English, and his country's in danger."

Gail talked with Emily for some time, and when the girl left to do her homework, she went to the window and stared out. The winter of 1917 had been a mild one, and she was thankful for that as she looked out at the new spring growth budding on the trees and blanketing the distant hills of Virginia in a vivid pale green. She watched Cap'n Brown as he chased his tail and then tried to catch a mockingbird that lived in one of the hedges. The dog was unsuccessful, of course, but he never seemed to grow discouraged.

Gail thought of Jared and could not push away the fear of losing him. "If America gets into this war, he'll have to go, too," she said, shaking her head. "What will I do then?"

CHAPTER TWO

A REAL WAR HERO!

★ ★ ★ ★

Aaron looked up from the emerald green grass he was cutting and paused to take a breath. The last days of March had proved windy as always and the air was crisp, filled with the smell of fresh earth and grass clippings. He watched Gail, whose back was to him, as she plunged a spade into the dirt, and he grinned. Leaving the push mower, he walked over to her, put his arms around her, and lifted her clear off the ground.

Gail gasped, "Put me down!"

Aaron immediately obliged, then spun her around and kissed her vigorously.

Gail let the shovel drop and tried to push him away, mumbling, "Aaron, what are you doing?"

"I'm kissing you."

"The neighbors will be scandalized."

Aaron released his wife and held her at arm's length, gazing intently into her eyes. "You know, I think they probably expect that the two of us have done this before."

Gail struck his chest and said, "Go cut the grass!"

"I'd rather kiss you than cut that old grass."

A smile touched the corners of Gail's lips, and she was suddenly filled with happiness. Her married life had been wonderful, and now as she studied Aaron, bronzed and fit, she thought,

How God has blessed me! So many women don't have what I have. . . .

The two of them turned suddenly at the sound of an adolescent war whoop.

Wesley Winslow, age fourteen, was running toward them—tall, lanky, and almost skinny. His brown hair matched his father's, as did his large blue eyes. He had a white canvas bag imprinted with the words *Richmond Daily News* draped around his neck. His voice was shrill as he announced, "Look who's coming to Richmond!"

"Must be somebody important," Aaron said, grinning. "Is it Charlie Chaplin?"

"No!" Wes exclaimed indignantly, his eyes sparkling. "It's Cowboy Smith!"

Aaron held the newspaper up, and Gail moved around to study the story. A picture of a fine-looking young man adorned the front page with the large headline declaring, "Cowboy Smith Comes to Richmond."

Aaron read the first lines of the story out loud. "Lieutenant Logan Smith, known more familiarly as 'Cowboy Smith,' will make Richmond one of his stops on a speaking tour around the country. Lieutenant Smith has shot down twenty-one enemy aircraft in the European arena and has engaged in combat with the famed German ace Baron von Richthofen. Lieutenant Smith is the son of Lobo and Lanie Smith and has been furloughed to tour the United States. He has stirred the country with his aerial exploits against the Germans and alerted his hearers to the dangers of the war in Europe. Smith will speak on Saturday at the Civic Auditorium."

Wes danced around impatiently. "Dad, he's our kinfolk, isn't he?"

"Well, yes he is," Aaron nodded. "I did a story on his father once—Lobo Smith. He was a gunfighter out west and later became a marshal in the Oklahoma Territory."

"Since he's family, do you think Cowboy Smith would come see us?" Wes asked. "I'd sure like to meet him."

"I don't know," Aaron said thoughtfully. He looked up at Gail. "I would like to see him, too. He's a fine young man. Of course, when I met him years ago, I think he was only about fifteen. I like his parents very much. You met them at our last family reunion."

"Yes, I did. He was so romantic," Gail said.

"Who?" Wes demanded. "Cowboy Smith?"

"No, he was just a boy then," Gail said. "I was talking about his father, Lobo. He had a patch over one eye and looked like a pirate."

"And he was a *real* gunfighter?" Wes asked.

"Something like that," Aaron said. Then an idea seized him, and he said, "I'm going to go call Lobo and Lanie. Maybe they can put in a good word for us. I'd like to invite Logan to stay with us so we can show him around."

★　★　★　★

A small crowd had gathered at the Richmond Airport, for word had gotten out that Cowboy Smith would be landing there soon.

It was Saturday afternoon, and there being no school, the whole Winslow family was there. Wesley and Emily jumped up and down with excitement as somebody in the crowd yelled, "There's a plane! That must be him!"

Emily grabbed Jared's arm and said, "Just think, we're going to have a real war hero at our house."

"I thought you were against the war," Jared said with a grin.

"Well, that doesn't matter," Emily protested. "What counts is that we get to meet a real hero. I've never met one."

"Yes, you have. Dad was a hero in the Spanish-American War," Wesley said indignantly.

Aaron laughed. "That's ancient history, Wes."

"I don't care, Dad. You were a hero for all of that."

Aaron shook his head and smiled as they all turned to watch the dot in the sky grow larger. The plane flew through a bank of clouds, made a sweeping turn, then came in for a perfect landing. The pilot taxied up to the edge of the crowd and cut the engine. Then he climbed out of the cockpit, jumped to the ground, and spoke to the maintenance man for a few moments before turning and walking toward them.

"Isn't he good-looking?" Emily breathed.

Logan Smith was indeed an attractive young man. He was not tall, but his carriage was erect. He wore a fingertip-leather flying jacket and a pair of jodhpurs, and his feet and calves were encased in gleaming black boots. As he pulled his helmet off, the sun struck his hair, showing a faint red tinge. Emily noticed that he had the most unusual eyes—almost indigo in color—and he was smiling as he approached. He raised his arm to acknowledge the applause and cheers that broke out from the crowd.

Aaron had been selected as spokesman, since he was a relative, and he stepped forward. "Hello, Logan. Do you remember me?"

Smith stared at the tall man and grinned widely. "Why, I sure do. You're Aaron Winslow, my kinfolk."

"That's right. I don't believe you've met my wife, Gail, and these are my children, Emily, Jared, and Wes."

As the crowd surrounded the pilot, voices began to pop up. "How many planes have you shot down?"

"Did you get the Red Baron yet?"

"Are the Allies going to win the war?"

For some five minutes Logan Smith stood at ease answering the questions, some of them from a reporter with the *Richmond Daily News*.

Finally Aaron spoke up. "I know the lieutenant's bound to be tired. That was a long flight. If you'll be at the auditorium tonight, I guarantee he'll give you some question-and-answer time then. Come along, Lieutenant."

With some difficulty, Aaron got his family and the pilot through the crowd and into the Winslows' Model-T Ford and drove away carefully, cautiously avoiding several well-wishers.

"You must be hungry, Lieutenant," Gail said.

"I could sure use some good home cooking," Logan said. He was in the backseat pressed between Emily and Jared. He turned to Emily and smiled at her. "I guess I'm crowding you a little bit, Emily."

"Oh, that's all right," Emily said. "A real war hero can do anything he wants to."

A secret humor touched the eyes of Cowboy Smith, and he shook his head. "No, he can't. He's just like everybody else, Emily, except he flies an airplane."

★ ★ ★ ★

When they reached the Winslow home, Logan went at once to the guest bedroom and took a brief nap. A couple of hours later, he arose, showered and changed, then came down to dinner looking refreshed. Hungry after his long trip, he pitched into the meal that Gail had carefully prepared—a huge cut of beef roasted with potatoes and carrots, savory red beans, and fresh-baked bread. Logan remarked enthusiastically, "This is delicious, Mrs. Winslow. Just like Mom's cooking."

"How are your parents, Logan?" Aaron asked.

"They're fine. They worry about me a lot, of course."

"Well, there's no help for that," Gail said. Her eyes touched briefly on Jared, and she shook her head. "There are mothers all over the country worried sick that we might be involved in this war soon."

"Tell us about shooting down airplanes," Wes broke in, unable to contain himself any longer.

Emily hardly touched her food as she sat entranced while Logan described air combat and Wes fired questions at him. Logan was careful to stress his own shortcomings instead of his successes. Even though he had gained fame as an ace pilot, he did not want his young admirers to get a false impression of the cruel reality of war.

Finally Aaron had to put a stop to Wes's questions. "You're not giving the lieutenant time to eat, son, and your mother's baked a special blackberry cobbler for dessert."

"I picked the berries myself," Emily said.

"Did you get chiggers?" Logan asked, grinning at her.

"Yes. All over me."

"Chiggers like me, too. But even so, I still like to be out in the woods—picking blackberries or, even better, fishing."

"Well, now you're talking my language," Aaron said eagerly. "Can you stay for a while?"

"I don't have to be in North Carolina for two days."

"Good. I'll guarantee you'll catch the biggest bass you ever caught in your life."

"Can I go, Dad?" Jared spoke up at once.

"I don't see why not."

This, of course, prompted Wes and Emily to mount a campaign to be allowed to accompany their famous guest. Aaron protested at first, but Logan shook his head. "Everybody come. You, too, Mrs. Winslow."

"Just call me Gail."

"Good. You can call me Logan."

"Don't you like to be called 'Cowboy'?" Wes asked.

"It's the newspapers that call me that," Logan said, smiling.

"I wish Dad were living," Aaron said. "He passed away six months ago. He was always interested in flying and would have loved to have met you."

"I'm sorry about your father," Logan said. "I know you must miss him."

Aaron nodded. "Many of our older relatives have died recently—Mark Winslow and his wife, Lola. You remember them, Logan?"

"I sure do. My mom and dad went to their funerals last year. They died within a week of each other. My mother was real torn up about it."

"Yes, I saw them there," Aaron said, then shook his head. "For a long time we had no deaths in the family, but then Thad Novak died two years ago, and we've had a number of them since. I hear that Dan, Mark's younger brother, has been ailing."

"Let's not talk about such things," Gail said quickly. "Tell us what it's like in France, Logan."

"Well, all I see of it is the airfield, pretty much, and they're just about all alike."

"What about Paris? Have you gone there?"

"I've been a couple of times. Went up on the Eiffel Tower once. That was fun."

"I bet the girls flock around you every time you go to town," Emily said.

Logan turned and laughed at her, his teeth very white against his tanned skin. "Not so's you'd notice it. However, I've got one young lady just about talked into marrying me."

Emily blinked with disappointment. "You mean you're engaged?"

"I mean I'm trying to be engaged. Her name is Danielle Laurent. I just call her Dani."

"Where did you meet her?" Emily pressed, leaning forward, her eyes intent on the handsome flyer.

"I met her when I was wounded and in the hospital. Her father's a doctor, and I was invited to their home. One look at her, and I was a lost cause."

After dessert, they all moved into the living room, and the pilot listened with pleasure as Gail played the piano. She had taken up music late in life but had quickly learned both the piano and organ and now was the church organist. At Logan's request, she played the more popular songs of 1917, including "The Bells of Saint Mary's," "For Me and My Gal," and a ragtime melody called the "Darktown Strutters Ball."

Emily sang several solos, for she was a fine singer and knew all the latest songs. She sang "For Me and My Gal" so well that Logan went over and gave her a hug. "You have a wonderful voice, Emily Winslow."

Emily flushed with pleasure and said, "Would you come to our school tomorrow? They'd let everybody out of class for assembly if you would."

"If we can fit in both the fishing and the school, that'll be fine," Logan agreed.

★ ★ ★ ★

The next day proved to be memorable for Emily. She put on her best dress, a light blue frock with white lace around the sleeves and the hem. When her mother asked her why she was wearing such a nice dress to school, she simply replied, "Logan's going to be there."

Logan spoke to the entire student body of Richmond High School and afterward fielded the students' questions. No speaker had ever received such an enthusiastic response, and fully half of the male students were determined to become aviators and join the war effort.

Logan had smiled and informed them that the only way he had gotten into battle was to join the Foreign Legion, and from there had been fortunate enough to be accepted into the Lafayette Escadrille, a French flying unit made up of American volunteers.

Emily stood beside Logan as soon as the assembly was over and whispered, "Will you come to my class with me, Logan?"

"Sure. I'm all yours until noon, then we're going fishing, right?"

"I'll have to play hooky."

"That's all right. I used to be an expert at that."

Logan sat in on Emily's history class and once again was nearly swamped by the students. The girls especially were practically swooning over him.

As soon as the noon bell rang, Emily said, "Let's make our getaway, Logan."

Logan grinned at the young woman. "Determined to become a fugitive, I see."

"Oh, fuzz, I'm not missing anything important. Just algebra."

Logan laughed and took Emily's arm. "All right. I'll cover you. Let's get away from here."

★ ★ ★ ★

The fishing trip was an enormous success. Logan and Aaron each caught a five-pound bass, and Emily caught one almost as large. They fished until nearly dark, when Aaron said, "Let's get home. By the time we clean these whales, it'll be time to eat."

"Suits me." Logan looked out over the lake and shook his

head. "It's so different from what I've been doing. Look at how peaceful and quiet it is."

"Was it really so bad over there, Logan?" Jared asked.

"It's not bad in the air as wars go. At least it's a quick death, for the most part."

Emily shuddered a little. To think that this young man, so full of life and so attractive, could be killed in a moment brought the reality of war home to her.

"The ground war is bad, I expect," Aaron suggested. "I didn't see anything as bad in the Spanish-American War, but it was tough enough."

"The generals in this war think if you throw enough men against a position, even if it's well defended, it can be taken. That might have worked back when there were no machine guns. But you put a machine gun in a protected position and rush a hundred men at it, and a hundred men are going to get shot down. And that's what's happening. I've flown over fields where a person could almost walk across them without touching the ground. Just walking on bodies." He went on to speak of the horrors of war, and he noticed that Jared was listening carefully. *Jared can't wait to get in it*, he thought with concern. *I was the same way. I guess you can't tell anybody how bad it really is. . . .*

★　★　★　★

Logan stayed with the Winslows for two days, and all the girls at Richmond High were frantic to meet him. Emily was besieged with pleas for an introduction, but she denied them all.

"You just want him all to yourself, Emily Winslow!" Margaret Dickerson complained. She was the reigning beauty queen in Richmond, but nonetheless, she had made absolutely no impression on Logan. His thoughts were on Dani, the woman he hoped to marry, and he didn't really have any interest in schoolgirl crushes, though he found all the attention rather flattering.

Emily merely laughed at Margaret. Logan was *her* guest, after all, and she was going to enjoy their brief time together, despite the fact that he was very nearly engaged.

Logan was amused at Emily's interest in him, but he kept those thoughts to himself. When he asked her, "What are you going to do with yourself in life?" he was surprised by her response.

"I want to be a writer," Emily said proudly.

It wasn't the answer he was expecting from a young woman, but he was impressed that she would be thinking about going into a profession, not just snagging a beau. "A writer, eh? I guess that does suit you, Emily. You're a good observer of people. You ought to get in touch with Josephine Hellinger."

"You mean the lady who writes a column for all the papers? Do you know her?"

"Know her! Why, we went over to France together," Logan said. "She's a very intelligent woman. As well as beautiful, I might add. The trouble is she's fallen in love with a British flyer—a Winslow, by the way. The same as you."

Nothing would satisfy Emily more than to hear the entire story of Josephine Hellinger. Logan told her what he knew, then finally suggested, "You ought to write her a letter, and I'll take it back with me. Maybe she can give you some good advice on how to become a writer."

★　★　★　★

"I don't see any sense in diagramming compound sentences," Wes said, frowning. "It doesn't do anybody any good."

"Yes, it does," Emily said. She had been helping her younger brother, who hated English with a passion. Not only did he hate grammar lessons, but he was also having a hard time adjusting to the new English teacher at Richmond High, whose assignments, in Wes's opinion, were "boring and stupid." Like his sister, he missed Mr. Laurence, who had been a favorite teacher among the students but had joined the Canadian army and had already left Richmond for his basic training.

Emily was trying to explain to Wes why grammar was important when Jared suddenly entered the room, pale, shaking, and clearly upset. She cried out, "What is it, Jared?"

"It's . . . it's Mr. Laurence, Emily. He's dead. He was killed in a training exercise before he even had a chance to leave for France."

Emily stood stock-still. For a moment she thought she had misunderstood him. "He can't be dead," she said.

"It's true enough. Word just came."

Silently Emily got up and walked stiffly out of the room. She went to her own bedroom and fell across the bed, trying to keep back the tears. She heard a knock, and then the door opened.

"Are you all right, Emily?"

"No . . . nothing's all right. He was . . . such a wonderful man. This just can't be true."

Jared sat down and laid a hand on his sister's back. He was quiet for some time, and then he said with bitterness in his voice, "He never even had a chance to fight. It's not fair. We'll be in this war soon ourselves, Emily. We're all going to be involved."

"Not you, Jared!" Emily at once pulled herself up and took Jared's hand. "You don't have to go."

"If America goes to war, I'll have to go, too. Just like Mr. Laurence had to go to fight for his country, I'll have to fight for mine."

Emily could not speak, and when Jared left the room she again fell down, not only in grief, but now in fear as well. She tried to pray, but no words would form in her mind or on her lips. Truly, she was more afraid than she had ever been in her life.

CHAPTER THREE

THE WINDS OF WAR

★ ★ ★ ★

Aaron Winslow sat reading a newspaper in his study, pondering the events of the past few months that had been pulling the United States closer and closer to war. The year had begun well insofar as economic matters were concerned. While the war raged in Europe, prices were up but so were wages in America. Unemployment was virtually nonexistent. With more and more money to spend, Americans were investing in an array of luxuries. Prosperity had cast a spell over the country despite the carnage across the Atlantic.

In the midst of this prosperity, America received an enigmatic and terrible message from Germany. Russia was tottering toward disillusionment, and the Romanoffs had fallen from power. Czar Nicholas II discovered that the masses had turned against him. When the Bolshevik Revolution eased the burden on Germany's armed forces in the East, Germany then turned her attention to the West, planting a time bomb that exploded with such force America was drawn into the conflict.

On January ninth a message had gone out from Kaiser Wilhelm II to all vessels of the German navy: "I order that unrestricted submarine warfare be launched with the greatest vigor on February the first."

British Naval Intelligence had picked up a German wireless

message and had thought at first it was only a routine transmission. But the terrible truth was soon realized, and when the news leaked out, America was forced to acknowledge that she could no longer ignore the European war. The broad Atlantic was not enough protection from the German menace in such modern times of international shipping and submarine warfare.

Then in March 1917 German U-boats sank three American merchant ships. It had been nearly two years since the sinking of the *Lusitania*, in which 128 Americans lost their lives, setting off a national undercurrent of pressure to fight back. As a distant earthquake will set off a seismograph, so Germany's now clear intent to wage unrestricted submarine warfare, even against American ships, shook the powers-that-be in Washington. And the tremors filtered down to farmers, tradesmen, and indeed to the entire country.

Emily found her father at his desk, looking at a newspaper story detailing the recent catastrophic events that were taking place on the high seas. Knocking on the open door, she said tentatively, "Are you busy, Dad?"

"Not too busy for you." Aaron put down the paper and waved at the chair close to his desk. "Have a seat and tell your old dad everything that's going on."

Emily sat down and twisted her fingers together nervously. She had unlimited confidence in her father's wisdom, and now she asked, "Will America go to war, Dad?"

"If you'd asked me that a few weeks ago," Aaron said, "I would have said it's doubtful. But now that Germany has loosed its submarines on all ships, I think it won't be much longer before we're pushed into it."

"I hate to think about it."

"You're worried about Jared," Aaron said, nodding. "I'm concerned about him myself. He'd go like a shot if America declared war."

"That would be terrible."

Sighing heavily, Aaron went over and clasped his hands together and shook his head. "This war has been unlike other wars, Emily. The world's never seen a war that consumed men so rapidly. It's commonplace now to hear of a hundred thousand men being killed in a single battle. Before this, no war, in its entirety, ever cost that many lives."

"I don't understand how it started."

"It started because of pride, Emily. Maybe all wars start like that. Men want something that isn't theirs so they can be bigger and better and stronger. Germany started building a huge arsenal, and France, in order to defend itself, did the same. Both kept adding ships and guns, and finally the whole continent was an armed camp ready to explode. When the Austrian archduke and his wife were assassinated, their deaths were just an excuse to go to war. There's no *reason* in it, so I don't waste my time trying to ask why. It's here and that's it."

Emily had expected this answer, and now she said in an unsteady voice, "Dad, I think I would just die if anything happened to Jared."

Aaron rose and went over to her. He pulled Emily to her feet and put his arms around her, and she clung to him tightly. "He can't go, Dad—he just *can't!*"

★　★　★　★

With the prospect of war looming for the United States, Aaron and Gail Winslow allowed their children to take a few days' vacation to get away together and tour some Civil War battlefields. They knew it might not be long before Jared would be going away to war, and they wanted him to have some time alone with his younger sister and brother. Jared drove his siblings in the family car first to nearby Cold Harbor, then on to Fredericksburg and Antietam in Maryland, finally arriving in Gettysburg, Pennsylvania, their last stop before heading back home to Richmond.

Emily was walking between her two brothers as they strolled down a road lined by old cannons. She stopped to go over to one of the cannons and run her hand over the metal. "How do these things work, Jared?"

Jared came over and patted the cannon. "Why, you shove a bunch of powder in a bag down the muzzle and pound it in, then you put a cannonball in and a wad to hold it in place."

"But how does it shoot?"

"You see this hole back here? It goes to the powder. In earlier times you had to use a match and ignite it. Later on they developed fuses that exploded the powder."

Wes climbed up onto the cannon and said, "Come on, Jared, get up here. Emily, you take a picture of us."

"All right." Emily took the simple box camera, and when Jared leaped with an easy grace up on top of the cannon, the two young men put their arms around each other and waved with their free hands. Emily snapped the picture and then said, "Now you come and get one with me and Jared, Wes."

Wes was the photographer in the family, and he gladly took the camera. Jared leaned over, grasped Emily's wrists, and easily lifted her up so that the two were standing on top of the cannon. She started to lose her balance, waving her arms in big circles to keep from falling. Jared quickly grabbed on to her, getting a secure hold around her, and laughed. "I can't believe anyone who can skate as well as you can't keep her balance on a cannon."

Emily was thankful for Jared's athletic strength and agility as she held on to him to keep herself steady and called out to Wes to hurry up and take the picture. Wes began calling out commands.

"Don't just stare at the camera," he said. "That looks dumb."

Emily twisted her head around to look at Jared, and he smiled back at her. In that instant Wes snapped the picture and said, "Now *that* will be a good one."

Jared leaped to the ground, then reached up and took Emily by the waist and gently lifted her down.

"What part of the battle took place here, Jared?"

Jared looked across a sloping meadow at the low-lying hills. "You see how the country goes downhill from here, and then there are those hills over there?"

"Yes," Emily said. The early spring sunlight was bright, and the grass was as green as emerald. The earthy smell of freshly plowed fields from a nearby farm filled the air.

"Well, the main Union army was lined up on top of that hill over there. They had cannons and men packed almost solid.

Over there," he said, "was Round Top, and there's Little Round Top beside it."

"I've heard about that," Emily said.

"Well, that was the end of the Union line. So Robert E. Lee commanded his army to attack."

Wes had come to stand beside his brother and sister, and he stared in disbelief. "You mean across that open field and up that hill over there with guns pointed right at them?"

"That's the way it was. The first day of the battle Lee tried the left side over there and had no success. The second day the Alabama troops attacked Little Round Top, and they were beaten back. So on the third day Lee ordered his generals Longstreet and Pickett to attack the center of the line."

Emily stared at the beautiful green field. A flock of blackbirds flew over, making raucous cries and wheeling in the air. "I don't see how they could have charged straight at the cannons. They must have known some of them were going to get killed."

"That's what Longstreet said," Jared agreed. "He argued as best he could, but General Lee pointed up at that line of hills and said, 'The enemy is there, and I'm going to strike him.'" Jared shook his head. "It was the wrong order. Lee had been ill for several days. Everyone knew his strategy was wrong, but when Pickett started out, they all went. They had to break rank several times to get across the fences and down through gullies, but finally they started up that hill. The Federals held their fire until they were in range, and then they simply destroyed Pickett's division. Men died by the hundreds. A few of them reached the tops, but it was a devastating loss of life that day. The South never recovered from Gettysburg."

Emily stared across the field. The green grass was waving as the spring breeze moved across it. A group of brown-and-white cows grazed peacefully, lifting their heads to stare solemnly at the trio. It was one of the most tranquil scenes she had ever seen. "It's hard to believe that so many thousands of men died right here," she whispered.

"It was a terrible day," Jared repeated. He was silent for a moment and then shook his head. "But it's worse now in France. The Battle of Verdun went on for months last year, and there were over seven hundred thousand casualties. So many men just shot to pieces—and the senseless slaughter still goes on."

Emily again felt the chill of fear that came over her whenever she thought of Jared going to a battlefield somewhere in Europe. She shook her head and said, "Let's go. I've seen enough."

The three left and went back to the car. Jared shook off his soberness and was happy for the rest of the day. Later they stopped at a restaurant, where he entertained them with stories of ball games he had played in. Emily noticed that the waitress, an attractive young woman with bright red hair, was watching Jared closely.

"I think the waitress likes you, Jared," she whispered.

Jared smiled at her and said, "When I find a girl as pretty as you, Emily, I'll take out after her. Whatever man gets you is going to get a real prize."

"With a temper like hers," Wes groaned, "don't bet on it."

Jared paid the flirtatious waitress no mind as they finished their hamburgers, french fries, and cherry sodas. Then the three went outside and got back in the car. As they started off with Emily wedged between Jared and Wes, she felt a sudden fear. *I wish it could always be like this*, she thought, leaning over against Jared.

As if he had read her mind, he turned his head and winked at her. "You're still my best girl, sis, aren't you?"

"Yes, Jared. I always will be."

★　★　★　★

The noise in a classroom at Richmond High School was getting out of hand. Emily had joined a group of four other students, two boys and two girls, and they had started an impromptu game chasing one another around the room and bumping into chairs.

"Come on," Emily shouted. "Let's try to get something done here. How are we going to have a dance if we don't plan for it?"

Eric Statler came by and squeezed Emily's arm. "Don't worry.

We'll have a dance," he said. "The best one Richmond High's ever had."

Emily pulled away from Eric. "Well, sit down and let's make some plans. How are we going to decorate the room? Let's at least decide that."

The others were mostly concerned with who would take whom to the dance, and finally, after the meeting ended an hour later with very little accomplished, Emily left, saying, "Well, I guess it doesn't matter whether we have a dance or not."

"Ah, don't be mad, Emily," Eric said. "I'll give you a break. I'll dance every dance with you."

"I wouldn't dance with you, Eric Statler, if you gave me the Washington Monument!"

The group laughed, and Emily shrugged her shoulders. Leaving the room, she turned down the hallway, her mind on the upcoming school dance. She stopped abruptly to look at the bulletin board on the wall. Almost against her will, she moved closer to study the picture that was prominently displayed there. It was Mr. Laurence in his uniform. Alongside it was a story from one of the Richmond papers, which told how he had died in Canada in a training exercise. Emily tried not to look at the picture, but now she could not seem to help herself. She looked at his thin features. The photograph had caught the slight smile that was his customary expression, and he looked somehow younger in the uniform than she remembered him. A shiver went over her as she thought of the tragedy that had cut his life short before he had even achieved his goal of fighting for his country. Not only did war not make any sense, but life itself at times seemed so arbitrary and senseless. She turned and hurried away, trying to put such disconcerting thoughts out of her mind.

When she got home she started helping her mother fix dinner and set the table. They were having pork chops, mashed potatoes, green beans, homemade bread, and for dessert a chocolate cake with chocolate frosting.

"Is Dad going to be late tonight?" Emily asked.

Wes and Jared had come downstairs, and Gail said, "Yes, he is. I guess we'll have to go ahead without him."

They sat down at the table, and Gail asked Jared to say the

blessing. Jared obliged and then reached out and picked up a bowl of mashed potatoes and scooped a generous helping onto his plate.

"Don't take all the potatoes, you hog!" Wes protested.

"Mashed potatoes are good for you. I've got to keep my strength up," Jared said with a grin.

"If you eat all the stuff you've got on your plate, you'll pop," Wes argued.

Emily smiled, for her brothers argued like this almost constantly. The two had a real affection for each other, and Emily was always glad to see it. She thought suddenly, *I'll bet there aren't three kids in the world any closer than Wes and Jared and me.*

At that instant she heard the front door slam and turned expectantly. She saw her father come in and heard her mother say, "Come on in, dear. We just got started."

Aaron came over and took his place at the head of the table. He stopped long enough to kiss Gail on the cheek, then sat down and unfolded his napkin.

Emily waited for him to speak, but he did not. Finally Gail asked, "Is something wrong, Aaron?"

Aaron lifted his head and said, "I just got the news by phone. President Wilson has asked Congress to declare war on Germany. The whole country's been watching President Wilson, asking what he will do about the Germans. Will he go to war with them, or try to build a moat around the country? Now that they've sunk three of our ships, he's simply got to act—and he has. My congressman friend Gerald Grayson is very close to the president. He told me that Wilson made the greatest speech of his life, saying, 'There is one choice we cannot make, we are incapable of making—we will not choose the path of submission.' He also said that Chief Justice White, who is a Civil War veteran, raised his hands and collapsed in tears. Wilson got the greatest ovation of his life, and Gerald was there when the president said to his secretary, 'Think of what they were applauding. My message today was a message of death for our young men. How strange that they applauded that.' "

"How did the vote go, Dad?" Jared asked quietly.

"The House voted 373 to 49 to support the president. Congresswoman Jeannette Rankin of Montana was one of the dissenters. She voted no—and then fainted."

A silence had fallen across the dining room, and Emily could not keep from turning to look at Jared. She heard her father say, "It's settled. We'll fight in France."

Emily could not speak. Her throat was constricted, and she knew she was close to tears. She did not dare ask Jared the question she most feared, for she already knew the answer.

CHAPTER FOUR

WE'RE COMING OVER!

★ ★ ★ ★

April had been a lovely month in Virginia. The dogwoods had blossomed, spotting the woods with glistening white. The wild flowers had outdone themselves, filling the roadsides with bright yellows and reds, and the farmers had broken their fields into rich black earth turned over neatly in folds.

Jared's high school graduation in early May had been a high point for Emily, who was so proud of her brother's accomplishments. The family's celebration for their oldest son was a welcome relief from the worries they all shared over what the future might hold for him, and indeed for them all, with America now at war, too.

The morning after his graduation party, Jared had invited Emily to go fishing down at the pond, and for the last hour they had sat there with their poles in the water, drinking in the early-morning freshness of the day.

"I like early morning," Jared said. "I like to get up before the sun rises and go sit out in the yard. I call it the cobwebby time of the day."

"I didn't know that," Emily said. She was wearing an old dress that had once been a pale yellow but was now bleached almost white from so many washings. She wore a well-worn white hat with a broad brim to shade her eyes when the sun came up and to keep away the freckles, which she despised. Holding her pole in her hand, she watched the red-and-white cork as it bobbed up and down with the current when the wind rippled across the top of the water. "I like to stay up late."

"Scared to go to bed?" Jared teased.

"No," Emily said quickly. "I'm afraid I'll miss something."

"You always were a night owl. I can remember when you were no more than four or five. I decided to stay up all night for some reason, and you begged to stay with me. I'll be dipped if you didn't almost do it, too! You kept pinching yourself to stay awake, and every time I told you to just go on to bed you said, 'I'm going to stay awake with you, Jared.'"

"I remember that," Emily said slowly. "We were out in the backyard sitting around a fire, and we toasted marshmallows."

"I don't see how you can remember that. It's been so long ago."

"I do, though. I think it's one of the first things I do remember. It was such fun, and I was so proud that you let me sit up with you. Where was Wes, I wonder?"

"He was too little. He couldn't have been more than two. You and I have always been good buddies."

Emily turned to study Jared's profile. The summer sun had turned his skin golden, and now his crisp brown hair fell over his forehead. *He's better looking than Douglas Fairbanks*, she thought suddenly. Aloud she said, "You remember the old tire swing we had out in the woods?"

"I'll say I do. I wonder if it's still there."

"No, the rope finally rotted. We had such fun with that swing," Emily said. Her eyes half closed as she spoke of that time with pleasure. "I remember it would swing out over a big gully. When I was little it seemed like a mile to the ground, but when I went back later it was just a little gully. Not more than ten feet down."

"I guess time does things like that. You remember when we went to our relatives' home in Missouri? I thought they had the biggest house I ever saw. Then when I went back last year, why, it was just a tiny thing. I guess the past gets magnified."

"I guess so," Emily said. "Have you heard any more about getting a scholarship?"

"Oh, I've heard from a college or two. I could get a football scholarship to the University of Alabama, but Notre Dame said I could come and try out."

"Notre Dame! That would be something to play for the Fighting Irish."

"Sure would. It's always been a dream of mine."

"Why don't you do it, Jared?" Emily urged. "We could all come and see you play."

"It's a long way to Notre Dame."

"We could come, though," Emily insisted.

Jared lifted his pole, studied the bait, and then put it back in. The cork sent out a series of concentric circles into the water, and he watched them lap against the shore. After a long while, he turned to her and said quietly, "Emily, I enlisted yesterday."

Emily's throat constricted. She could neither speak nor move. His news was not unexpected, but suddenly she was terrified at what the future held for Jared. Cap'n Brown, who had come with them, had been chasing squirrels, but now he came over and sat down beside Emily, almost as if he sensed her distress. He was as tall as she was in this position, and he easily reached over and licked her face.

"Get away, Cap'n Brown," Emily whispered, shoving him back.

"You'll hurt his feelings," Jared said. He pulled the dog closer to him, caressed him roughly, then put his arm around him. "You mustn't feel bad about this, Emily. I know you don't want me to go, but it's something I have to do."

"This is a stupid war!"

"All wars are stupid," Jared nodded. "But it's the right thing for me to do. I'd like for you to see that. It would mean a lot to me to know that you're with me in this."

For the life of her, Emily could not speak the words that Jared wanted to hear. She dropped her pole suddenly and threw her arms around him, holding him fiercely. She felt his arms go around her, and finally she straightened up. The tears were running down her cheeks, and she managed to whisper, "God will bring you back."

"That's the way to talk, Emily," he said, smiling at her. "I'm sure everything will be fine."

★ ★ ★ ★

Within a week Jared and his family stood in the midst of the crowd milling about at the train station. He looked so tall and strong and handsome in his uniform. Emily had cried herself to sleep the night before. Her mother had come to her room to say, "You mustn't cry when Jared leaves. He must see nothing but smiles and good cheer from all of us."

Emily had steeled herself for this moment, and now amidst the shouts and the cheers and the playing of the band, she waited bravely to say good-bye to her big brother. He had saved her for last, and now he bent down and whispered in her ear, "You're still my best girl, right?"

"Right." It was all Emily could say. She blinked back the tears and forced a broad smile. "You be careful. You hear me?"

"I will. I'll be back in no time, and we'll go fishing and hunting in the woods."

A sergeant bellowed above the hubbub of the crowd, "All of Company C get aboard!"

Jared kissed Emily on the cheek and then turned. He shook hands one more time with his father. The two men embraced and then he kissed his mother. He turned to give Wes a brotherly punch on the shoulder and ruffled his hair. "You're the boss until I get back."

"Sure, Jared," Wes managed to say.

The soldiers, a mass of khaki, boarded the train, and then the whistle sounded as the engine gave a huge huff. Soldiers leaned out of every window, waving and smiling, most of them looking fit and eager to fight for the cause. Emily searched for Jared. She saw him in the middle of one of the cars and shouted, "There he is! Good-bye, Jared, good-bye!"

She saw his lips move as he said good-bye, and then the train moved out of the station.

Emily turned blindly, unable to keep the tears from her eyes any longer. She looked at Wes and saw that he too was fighting to keep from crying. She took his hand, and the two of them followed their parents out of the station.

"He's got to come back, Wes!" Emily whispered. "He's just got to!"

★   ★   ★   ★

America was not ready to go to war. The United States was so low in arms and matériel that draftees had to train with wooden guns. One general said, "It would be better to give them broomsticks than not to train at all." Posters sprouted up everywhere with Uncle Sam pointing his finger, saying, "I want YOU for the U.S. Army," and a sailor putting his arm on the shoulder of a civilian, saying, "The Navy needs YOU—don't read American history. Make it." In almost every city from coast to coast parades were held, and a tremendous gathering on New York's Fifth Avenue symbolized the growing emotional involvement of Americans everywhere. Speechmakers thundered their rhetoric to the crowds, bolstering morale and justifying the rightness of America's involvement.

In small towns and on farms all across America, men and women suddenly saw the Great War in a different light. As their young men left by the thousands to join the army, the world had become much smaller, and the reality of war had touched the home front as never before.

Jared's letters from boot camp were as cheerful and witty as he was himself. He made light of the hardships and commented once, "The farm boys do better than any of us. They're used to getting up before daylight and working hard all day. Us city slickers are soft, but we'll toughen up by the time we get to France."

More than once Emily asked her father what the war he had fought in was like.

"It was nothing like this one, Emily," Aaron had replied. "I thought it was rough at the time, but from what I'm reading in the papers from the frontline correspondents, life in the trenches is horrible—dirt and filth, sickness and disease of every kind. Why, measles are killing more men than enemy guns in some places."

"And Jared's always been so neat. How will he stand it?"

"He'll do all right," Aaron said.

Emily noticed something in her father's eyes that she had never seen before. *Why, Dad's afraid*, she thought. *I've never seen him afraid of anything!*

★ ★ ★ ★

Jared came home on an unexpected two-day leave before shipping out to France in the summer. Everyone was so excited to see him one last time, and they determined to show him nothing but smiles and their support. Emily, too, performed nobly and kept her doubts and fears to herself. All of her girlfriends wanted to see Jared during his leave, but Emily put them off.

"I think you're mean, Emily," Wilma Taylor said. She was the current most popular girl in high school and had practically besieged Emily, begging her to invite her to their house or to go on some of her errands with Jared.

"I'm sorry, but we want him all to ourselves," Emily said firmly. "He's only home for two days."

The family crammed every moment they could together, and at sunset on the second day, Wes, Emily, and Jared went swimming in the river. They splashed and yelled and dunked one another, and finally they came out, dried off, and sat watching the sun go down. Wes thought he saw a deer, and he grabbed his camera to try to snap a picture of it.

"He'll never catch that deer, if that's what he saw," Jared laughed.

"Don't be so sure. Wes is good at taking pictures, and it's all he cares about. He can be pretty patient about getting just the right shot."

"What about my best girl? What's she interested in?" Jared turned and studied Emily. She was no longer a child but a young woman now. He smiled and said, "Don't you be letting any of those drugstore heroes rush you into anything."

"I won't. I don't care about that sort of thing."

"I know you don't."

The two sat there quietly for a while, and Jared said, "I know you've had to put on a good front, but I can tell when you're sad, Emily."

A lump rose in Emily's throat, and she had to clear it away before she said, "I wish it were all over, and you were back home again."

"You're going to pray for me every day, aren't you?"

"Yes, every day, Jared. I promise."

"And I hope you'll write, too. You're good at that," Jared said.

"Of course I will," Emily said. "Every day."

Wes came back shortly after that, having found the deer and taken the picture, and then the three got back in the car. Jared took one last look at the river and then uttered the only words of regret Emily had heard from him: "I won't be seeing this old river for a while, but you two come every chance you get and think of your old beat-up brother over there in the trenches."

Emily put her arms around him, and Jared hugged her. Reaching out, he grabbed Wes, too, and said, "All for one and one for all. Just like the Three Musketeers."

"That's right," Wes said.

Emily could not speak, and later, when she got home and went to bed, she could not sleep. Finally she got out of bed, knelt down, and began to pray, "Oh, God, take care of my brother. Don't let anything happen to him. Please."

The next day they all rose early and accompanied Jared to the train. The station was filled with soldiers again, but there was no celebration this time. Men were loading on quickly, and Jared shook hands with his father and brother and hugged his mother. "We've done this before, Mom," he said.

Gail managed a weak smile. "Oh, son," she said, "I wish you didn't have to go, but I know you do."

"I'll be back," Jared said.

He hugged Wes, and Emily heard him say, "You take care of the folks until I get back."

"I will, Jared."

Emily then felt Jared's arms go around her. He hugged her, held her tightly, and she clung to him. He whispered, "Don't forget, you're my best girl—and you're going to pray for me every day."

"I will, Jared. I will."

They all stood there with the rest of the parents and families of the men who were leaving, and again they watched the train pull out of the station. Aaron stood between his two children and put his arms around them. "He's got to go. I pray that God will bring him back safely."

Emily bit her lower lip. She felt the tears rise in her eyes and run unbidden down her cheeks. She turned and buried her face against her father's chest, unable to speak.

CHAPTER FIVE

EMILY HAS A DISAGREEMENT

★ ★ ★ ★

Emily Winslow rose early one September morning, and before dressing, she pulled a small sheaf of letters from the top drawer of the armoire. She had worn Jared's letters thin by reading them over and over again.

Sitting on the edge of her bed in front of the window, she pulled the first letter out and ran her eyes over the writing. Jared had always had the best penmanship of the three Winslow youngsters, writing in script almost as readable as print. As she looked at the bold, square lettering, a longing rose in her breast. She read his first letter that he had sent from boot camp back in the spring. Moving her lips as she read, she could possibly have quoted it from memory:

Dear Emily,

Well, here I am in basic training, sis, and I must tell you it's kind of a joke. There are young fellows here from all over the country, but most of our boys are from the South. Some of them are right off the farm and others out of offices and quite a few like me just out of high school. We get up every morning before dawn to the sound of a bugle, and the barracks is always filled with groans— mostly from the city boys who aren't used to such early hours. I must admit I had some trouble with that myself, but now I've gotten accustomed to it.

I have a good friend here whose name is Bobby Carr. He comes from a little town on the Gulf Coast in Alabama that I've never heard of called Gulf Shores. Bobby claims there's no place like it on earth. Just nothing but heaven. He's made me promise when we get back to bring you and all the family down for a fishing trip. Says he'll guarantee we'll catch more fish in a day than I've caught in my whole life, at least as far as weight is concerned. He's a fine young man but not converted. I've been witnessing to him, and I'm hopeful. Pray for him, will you, Emily? His family's not Christian, so he doesn't have anybody to care about his soul.

We are training now with wooden guns, and it makes me feel a little bit like a kid before I started school and even for a while afterward. You remember we made rubber guns and begged the old inner tubes from all the gas stations. Those were some wars we had! I remember once I popped you right in the head by accident, and the knot raised a welt. I expected you to start crying, but you never did. You never were a weepy girl, though. I think of those days often.

I miss you a great deal already. Please write. And watch out for Cap'n Brown. I miss him more than I thought I would.

Laying that letter aside, she picked up one he had written later in the summer after he'd arrived in France. It was very brief. He had simply responded to the news she'd told him about the family and the town and ended by saying,

Your letters mean more to me than you can know. You'll be a senior in high school this year, and you're such a good-looking girl I know you'll be besieged with suitors. Do you have a favorite right now? If so, don't let him take you to see any of Theda Bara's movies!

For some time she leafed through the letters trying to read his moods, and finally she got to the one that had given her the most fear. It started out with the announcement that he had been in action:

Please excuse my writing. It's getting dark here, and all I have is a piece of candle. It's been raining for days now, and the trenches are nothing but mud. All of us have fungus between our toes. "Trench foot" they call it, and many of the fellows have gone sick

with flu or pneumonia or just plain terrible health. Thankfully trench foot has been my only problem.

The handwriting changed at this point on the letter, and she had known when she read it that something was wrong:

We had our first action today. It wasn't much, but I must confess it shook me up. We all knew that we were going over the top in an offensive, and I kept watching the old-timers—an old-timer here is someone who's survived one offense—and I saw that they weren't in much better shape than those of us who'd never been through any action at all.

You remember I told you about Bobby Carr? He's become very close to me, and he gave his heart to Christ a week ago in a service we had here. I don't think I was ever so happy, because I cared a great deal for him.

But Bobby didn't make it. The barrage began today, and everyone was pretty tight-lipped. Bobby turned to me and said, "I hate to tell you this, Jared, but I'm scared green."

I managed to grin back and said, "Every man here is as green as you are. Don't worry about it, Bobby."

"I'm glad I found Christ," Bobby said.

"I'm glad, too," I said. "So many of the fellows haven't, but you and I are safe now, no matter what happens."

At that moment the barrage began. It seemed like the whole world was blowing up. Our cannons were throwing shells as fast as the gunners could shove them into the breach. I noticed that the birds overhead scattered in erratic patterns across the sky. The air was so thick with smoke we could hardly breathe, and when I took a chance and looked over the top, I saw the shells exploding on the German lines.

The whistles started blowing, and our lieutenant was screaming, "All right. Let's go." We all managed to scramble out of the trenches. I put everything out of my mind except getting under the barbed wire and not making any mistakes. It was like nothing I'd ever experienced, but I won't go into it. When we were halfway across, I saw Bobby go down. I turned to him, but the lieutenant screamed at me, "Never mind! We'll come back later for the wounded." So I ran on with the rest. We took the position, but we lost a great many men. I went back, and Bobby hadn't made it. I

*sat beside him for a long time and thanked God that he had not
gone out to meet the Lord without being prepared.*

Emily could not read the rest of the letter. She folded it
quickly and moved on. She got to the letter that she had enjoyed
the most:

*We got a weekend leave, and a bunch of us went into Paris.
Morals are pretty bad here, and many of our fellows don't seem to
care. Even some of the married men have gone wrong. God has been
faithful and protected me from all of that. I did meet a young
woman named Marie. She reminds me a great deal of you. I met
her at a canteen where she was serving cakes and coffee to the
troops. She was so pretty she was getting a lot of attention, but I
managed to cut the other fellows out, and she and I went for a walk
outside. She spoke very little English, and I spoke little French. But
we hit it off right away. I hope I get to see her again. She said I
could see her when I come back on another leave.*

*I hope you'll continue to pray for me because I sure need it.
Temptations are strong anywhere, but out here they seem to be more
violent than any I've ever undergone. Keep yourself sweet and pure,
because when I come home I want to see the same good friend I've
always had.*

> *With all my love,*
> *Jared*

Emily sat for a moment and read the letter again. And then
her mother's voice drifted up. "Emily—Wes! Hurry up. Breakfast
is nearly ready."

Jumping off the bed, Emily stripped off her nightgown and
quickly donned cotton drawers and a chemise, over which she
slipped on an outfit she had just bought. It was a muslin midi-
dress with a blue-striped skirt and an azure-colored midi with a
white collar. She fastened the matching white belt, took a few
swipes at her hair, and then ran downstairs.

"You'd better hurry or you'll be late," Gail said.

"I meant to come down and help cook breakfast—" She
stopped, not wanting to mention Jared. They spoke carefully
about him, not bringing him up too often. They all shared the
letters he wrote to them and saw to it that the mailman often got

a plentiful stack from each of them. Sitting down at the table, Emily waited until Wes came crashing down the stairs. She smiled at him. "You're not supposed to fall down the stairs, Wes. Just walk down like everybody else."

Her little brother grinned at her and said, "I was going to show you something nice, but since you're being so mean I don't guess I will."

"Oh, come on, Wes! What is it? It's probably a lizard."

"No, it's not." Wes held an envelope aloft and said, "It's the pictures we took on our vacation with Jared last spring."

Instantly Emily came out of her chair. "It's about time! Were they good? Let's see them!"

Gail had come in with a platter full of golden pancakes, which she set on the table, then came over and stood behind the two as Wes opened the envelope.

The first picture was one of Emily and Jared walking along a grassy pathway.

"Why, that one was taken at Antietam," Emily said. "Look at Jared. Isn't he handsome?"

"Yes, he is," Gail said softly, and for a moment the three were silenced by the realization of how terribly far away he was now.

Wes finally broke the silence. "This next one I'm going to put on my wall. It's the best picture I ever took."

Emily looked as Wes held up the photo. It was a shot of her and Jared standing on the cannon at Gettysburg. He had his arms around her, keeping her steady, and they had just turned to look at each other. They were smiling, their faces clearly outlined against the fleecy white clouds in the sky. Somehow Wes had managed to catch a special moment, and now it was preserved for them for all time.

"It's a wonderful picture, son," Gail said, then turned away quickly. "Now you two had better eat your pancakes."

As Gail left the room dabbing at her eyes, Wes said, "She can't help crying over Jared."

Emily could not respond, for she was close to tears herself. That moment in Gettysburg had been vividly brought back to her, and she knew she would give anything in the world to bring

Jared back and stand with him like that just one more time. "Let me have this one. Please, Wes."

"Sure," Wes said huskily. "I can get another print made."

The two sat down, and as delicious as their mother's pancakes were, Emily had trouble eating. She only managed to get down one. Wes ate two, then said, "We're going to have to run or we'll be late."

★   ★   ★   ★

Emily had never adjusted very well to the new English teacher who had replaced Mr. Laurence at Richmond High. Mr. Clyde Clinton was not a handsome man, to say the least. He was so short that Emily stood two or three inches taller, depending on the heels she wore. He had apparently gone bald, because he wore a frightful-looking toupee. "He looks like he's wearing a squirrel on his head," Wes had whispered the first time he had met the teacher.

Indeed, the toupee did not improve his looks at all. Nor did the mustache, a definite mistake in Emily's opinion. He had fair hair, and she thought his mustache looked as though he'd been eating something, and morsels of food were left along his upper lip.

In all likelihood Emily would not have liked any man who had to follow after Ryan Laurence. It would have been better if a woman had taken his place. Every time she had English class, she could not help contrasting the two men, and Mr. Clinton always came out on the wrong end of her thoughts.

"All right, class. Quiet down," Mr. Clinton said loudly and unnecessarily one day in class.

No one was really talking, but the English teacher was afraid that someone would take advantage of him. Therefore, he adopted a rather abusive fashion toward the students. He did know his subject matter well, especially grammar. Emily had always been good at grammar, diagramming sentences, and punctuation, and she found no fault with that. She did feel, however, that he was much too harsh on those who were not so gifted in this aspect of English.

Emily's big disappointment in the man came when he handed her first theme back. It had been so marked up in red that she had suffered quite a shock. Mr. Laurence had also marked up her papers, but she seemed better able to accept his critiques of her writing. Mr. Clinton did not need to correct her spelling or punctuation, but he freely commented on issues such as style and content. Those, Emily was confident, had always been her strong suit, so she bristled at his criticisms. She began to read the comments while Mr. Clinton was passing out the rest of the papers, aware that muted groans were going up from the whole class. As far as she knew, no one had ever gotten an A on one of his assignments.

The more she read, the angrier she became. She waited until he had passed out all the papers and shot the usual challenge: "Are there any questions about your grade?"

Emily looked at the C+ pressed into her paper and raised her hand. "I have a question, Mr. Clinton."

"What is it, Emily?"

"I don't understand why I got a C+. This same paper would have gotten an A under Mr. Laurence."

A rich crimson suffused Mr. Clinton's face. He had never met Ryan Laurence, but everyone in the school revered the Englishman, not only for his heroism in joining the army, but for his teaching ability. Mr. Clinton knew better than to say anything detrimental about his predecessor, especially since the man had been killed so tragically. He pursed his lips and stroked his mustache, then said, "That may have been, Emily, but I felt there were some things in your paper that needed correction."

"You say here that I used too many concrete expressions." Emily looked up, and her eyes locked with those of the teacher. "The writing I like best is always full of concrete expression. I've always felt it was better to show someone something than simply to tell them. I say here that the Ford was painted a gruesome, sickening apple green, much like a birdhouse."

"That's overdone!" Mr. Clinton snapped.

"Well, what would you say, then?"

"I would simply say the car was green."

Emily stared at the short man and then proceeded to go down the paper point by point. She had not gotten halfway through when Mr. Clinton suddenly realized he was getting the worst of the exchange. "That'll be enough out of you, Emily!"

"But you asked if there were questions about our grade. That's what I'm doing. I don't think the grade was fair."

"You'll take the grade I gave you, and that's all there is to it!"

Emily had a reputation for being hot-tempered at times, and her red hair accentuated the accusation, even when it was unfounded. Now, however, a rage seemed to explode in her. She got up, gathered her books, and blurted, "I won't stay in a class with a teacher like you! You're not fair!"

"You sit down in that chair, Emily Winslow!"

"I will not!" Emily turned and walked out, ignoring the sputtering and threats that Mr. Clinton sent after her. She closed the door to the classroom more forcefully than necessary and stomped down the hall. She did not even stop at her locker but turned and walked out of the building, angry to the bone. When she stepped outside, she took a deep breath of the fresh air and headed down the sidewalk toward home. She hadn't gone five steps when she heard a window open behind her.

Mr. Clinton's voice shrilled out, "You'd better come back, young lady, or you'll be expelled!"

Emily turned and said, "Go ahead and expel me, then! See if I care!" And then she began to run. She ignored his continuing threats as they faded and found she did not care in the least what repercussions would follow her rebellion.

★　★　★　★

Aaron stepped outside the house and paused for a moment. Emily was sitting in one of the lawn chairs, looking down at the goldfish in the pond he had made. He pulled up another lawn chair beside her and sat down. Leaning forward, he watched a huge goldfish slowly waving his tattered, filmy fins. After watching the fish silently for a while, Aaron said, "Look. He's making an *O* with his mouth. I guess that's all a goldfish can say—*O*."

Emily looked at the goldfish, then toward her father. "You didn't come out here to talk about goldfish, Daddy."

"I just thought I'd come out and sit with you for a while."

"I guess Mom told you what happened at school today, huh?"

"She didn't have to. Your principal called me."

"Oh? And what did Mr. Hilliard have to say?" Emily asked.

"He said you got pretty upset and walked out of Mr. Clinton's classroom."

"Did he tell you what I yelled back at him?"

Aaron suddenly laughed. "Yes, he did. Is it true?"

"Yes, it is," Emily affirmed. She had always been a truth-teller, and she was still upset, even though hours had passed since she had staged her rebellion. "He was wrong, Daddy. I'll show you my paper. He doesn't know what he's talking about."

"That's possible. We all get a teacher like that from time to time. More than one usually."

"Why doesn't he go do something else? Why would he want to teach?"

"Maybe he can't do anything else."

"Well, he's icky!"

"Icky? What does that mean? I don't recall ever hearing such a word."

Emily turned to stare at her father reproachfully. "You know what 'icky' means."

"I can guess. It means you don't like him."

"That's not fair, Daddy."

"I know it's not, sweetheart." Aaron reached over and took her hand and held it. "You know," he said suddenly, "I remember the first time I ever held your hand. You were just a few minutes old, and you were in your mother's arms. I reached out and took your hand. It was so small, but I stared at it, and I remember saying to your mother, 'Look, she's got fingernails just like a real person.'" Aaron laughed. "Your mother got upset with me. She said, 'She *is* a real person, you idiot!'"

"Did she really say that? I mean, did she really call you an idiot?"

"She sure did, and she was right." Aaron looked down and said, "Look at that hand now. I've held it all the way through childhood and grade school, and now it's a woman's hand, and I'm so proud of my girl."

Tears came to Emily's eyes, and she said, "Oh, Daddy, I'm so terrible!"

"You're not terrible at all. Your temper's just a little bit on the warm side."

"I know it, and I'm trying to change."

"Did you know that Mr. Clinton has a little girl?"

"No, I don't know anything about his family."

"It's not a very happy story. She was born with Down's syndrome."

"Oh, Daddy, I didn't know that!"

"He loves that little girl. I think she's three now, and from what I hear, he pours his life into her. But I guess he brings some of his frustrations to class, which he shouldn't do."

Emily sat without speaking, and when Aaron turned to face her, he saw tears running down her cheeks. "Sometimes it helps to know what others are going through before we make a hasty judgment."

"I'll apologize to him tomorrow. I promise," Emily said as she wiped her tears away.

"I think that might be a good thing. And try to say something nice about him so that the class can hear it."

"I will. The Bible says that being kind to our enemies is like pouring hot coals on their head. I'll do just that and burn his brains out!"

Aaron suddenly reached out and grabbed her, laughing as he said, "You *would* say a thing like that! I hope you truly can say something kind to him tomorrow. We need to learn to be understanding of others."

"I will, Daddy. I promise."

★ ★ ★ ★

The next day at school, Mr. Clyde Clinton was shocked when Emily walked into his classroom and apologized before the entire class. She said, "It was all my fault, Mr. Clinton. I should never have challenged you, and I never will again. Whatever grade you put on my papers, that's what it will be. So please forgive me. I know I'm immature and haven't learned to control my temper. If you could help me with this, I would appreciate it."

It proved to be a turning point not only for Emily, but for her classmates as well, who became much more cooperative with their English teacher after her example.

Several days later, Wes was raking leaves after school, a job he did not particularly care for. He would much rather be developing pictures or taking them. Photography had become such a big interest in his life that he had been lectured sternly by both of his parents. It was true enough that he had let his grades slide, but now as he raked the leaves, he muttered, "I don't see why it does any good for a fellow to know algebra. Who says $x + y$ equals z? Doesn't make any sense."

Looking up, he saw a peculiar-shaped cloud drift across the horizon, and he at once dropped the rake. He raced into the house, ran up the stairs, and dashed into his room. Grabbing up his camera, he ran outside again and opened a small leather case. He selected a filter, put it over the lens, and grunted with satisfaction. "That'll bring that cloud out." He moved around, trying to find the right angle, for he had long since learned not just to point and shoot. His pictures had to be framed, composed, as a painter would compose a painting. Finding a bare tree that he could put at the side of the picture to give it balance, he held the camera still and, moving only his forefinger, pushed the shutter. He nodded at the satisfying click. "I bet that'll be a good one. Maybe win a prize."

"Hello, Wes." Mr. Jennings, the mailman, had approached and stood smiling while Wes took the picture.

"Hello, Mr. Jennings. You got some mail?"

"Sure do." Mr. Jennings was a tall, lanky man, who constantly complained about his feet. He did so now as he said, "My dogs are killin' me. Make sure you don't wind up being a postman."

"I'm going to be a photographer."

"I'll bet you are." Mr. Jennings sorted through his mail, and his mouth twisted in a grimace as he looked up. "Got a letter here from France, but it's not from Jared."

"How do you know? We don't know anybody else in France."

"Got Jared's name on the return, but it's not his writing. See?"

Wes went over and took the four letters Mr. Jennings held out. Quickly he studied the one on top and said, "I never saw that writing before. Maybe it's from one of Jared's friends over there."

"Hope so. Hope it's not bad news."

Wes looked up startled and shook his head but could not answer. "Thanks, Mr. Jennings," he said, then turned and ran toward the house.

He took the letter at once to his father, who was working in the study. "There's a letter here from France, but it's not from Jared—at least, it's not in his handwriting."

Instantly Aaron rose and said, "Let me see it." He took the letter, studied it carefully, then said, "Go get your mother and sister in here. We'll read it together."

"Sure, Dad."

Aaron stood staring at the envelope and felt a trace of fear. Ever since his son had left for Europe, he had not spoken of it, but every day he had to fight the fear down. He knew he must not show his grave concerns in front of the family. When they came in, Wes was explaining about the strange handwriting on the letter, and Aaron waited until he was finished.

"Well, we'll see who it's from." Using a letter opener, he slit the envelope and took out a single sheet of paper. He looked down and said, "It's signed by Jared, but it's not his handwriting."

"Read it, Daddy," Emily urged, her face somewhat pale, and her fists clenched tightly together.

"Dear Folks,

I know you will be surprised to get this letter not in my hand. This will be a short one. I will write more later. We went over the top a few days ago, and I took a bullet. More than one, really. One

*hit my right hand, so I can't write, but James Parker is writing for
me as I dictate."*

"How badly was he wounded? Does he say?" Emily broke in.
"Let him read, dear," Gail said quickly.
Aaron continued.

> *"It was a big push, and I made it all right for most of the way.
> But finally I was wounded. I couldn't walk, but I'll have to tell you
> how much James Parker has done for me. We were pinned down,
> and the call came to retreat, but I couldn't do it. James came and
> got me up on his back, and he carried me back with bullets flying
> all around. When we were just five yards away from the trench, he
> took a bullet, too, and both of us fell in.*
>
> *We're in the hospital together. His bed's next to mine. He's pro-
> testing right now, telling me not to say these things, but I must tell
> you, I think I owe my life to James.*
>
> *I will write later. The doctor is coming by again, and I'll know
> more about how serious he thinks my wound is. Keep on praying
> for me, and keep James in your prayers, too.*
>
> Love, Jared"

Aaron handed the letter to Gail, who read through it again.
"Thank God it wasn't worse," she said.
"I wish he had told us more," Wes said with a troubled ex-
pression. "He didn't even say where he got shot."
"I'm sure he'll say in the next letter," Aaron offered hopefully.
Gail handed the letter over to Emily, who also read it care-
fully. The handwriting was quite different from that of her
brother's. It was legible enough but not nearly so carefully done.
She mentioned this but said, "James was wounded, too, so I
shouldn't fuss about his handwriting."
"We owe James Parker a lot. I think we all ought to write to
Jared and include a letter to this friend of his."
"That's a good idea," Gail said. "Let's do it right now and get
them in the mail as quick as we can."
Emily went to her bedroom to write her letter, and Wes did
the same. Emily filled up one page, front and back, to Jared and
then wrote a briefer note to James Parker. She did not know exactly how to address him, but she said,

Dear James,

My name is Emily. I suppose Jared has told you about me. I'm his sister, and we were always best friends.

I can't tell you how deeply grateful we are to you for saving my brother. I'm sure not many men would have done such a brave act, so we all feel a deep debt of gratitude. I wish I could say this in person, but since that is impossible, I will just tell you that as long as I live, James, I will be grateful to you. If you'd like, I will write to you again.

She hesitated, not knowing how to end the letter. Finally she decided on "With warm regards." It seemed rather formal, but she could think of no other closing. She signed her name and then read what she had written again. It was not entirely what she wanted to say, for aside from her fear over Jared's welfare, she was also conscious of a depth of gratitude she had never known.

She did very poorly at school the next day, not able to concentrate in any of her subjects. When she got to English class, she smiled and said to her teacher politely, "Hello, Mr. Clinton. How are you today?"

At Emily's greeting, he gave her a shy smile. "I'm fine, Emily. And how are you?"

"I'm fine." She was the first one in the room, and somehow she felt compelled to say, "We got a letter yesterday. My brother's been wounded over in France."

"Oh, I'm so sorry!" Mr. Clinton said, and indeed he was. "I hope it's not serious."

"He couldn't write the letter himself, but a friend of his wrote it."

"So sad! I didn't know your brother for very long, but he seems to be a fine young man."

"Yes, he is. The best I know. How's your little girl?"

"She's fine."

"I'd like to meet her sometime. Perhaps I could take her for an ice cream cone."

Mr. Clinton swallowed hard. "That . . . that would be very nice, Emily. She would like it a lot."

"We'll do it, then. You let me know when, and I'll be there."

Emily took her seat, and the class began shortly. It amazed her how much Clyde Clinton had changed. She knew it had something to do with her rebellious behavior, but even more with her apology. Now as she sat there listening, she found herself ashamed of the opinions she had once held of the man. *I'll never judge anybody again*, she vowed. *Never.*

CHAPTER SIX

BUCK LEATHERWOOD

★ ★ ★ ★

Emily threw herself into the war effort with a grim ferocity. She always tended to go overboard with any new hobby or fad, but supporting the war any way she could was more important than collecting butterflies—an activity she had once done with a passion. Now she joined every drive to collect scrap material that would be used in the war, and she supported the Victory Bond Drive with every penny she could get and urged others to do so as well.

She also spearheaded a special assembly to encourage patriotism and to keep the boys in the trenches in everyone's minds. The school band played George M. Cohan's "Over There," a song the composer had written as soon as he'd read the newspaper headline that the United States had entered the fray. The thrilling melody and words held out the promise that the Yanks would soon put an end to the war, and it quickly became the nation's victory hymn.

The assembly was a rousing success with the Boy Scouts marching in with dozens of American flags flying, and the entire school belting out,

"Over there, over there,
Send the word, send the word, over there.

That the Yanks are coming, the Yanks are coming,
The drums rum-tumming everywhere.
So prepare, say a prayer,
Send the word, send the word to beware,
We'll be over, we're coming over,
And we won't come back till it's over over there!"

Emily also avidly read every book she could find on the war, both fiction and nonfiction. Among her favorite novels was H. G. Wells's bestselling *Mr. Britling Sees It Through*, which contrasted the nobility of the British to the barbarism of the Germans. The main character, an American, by observing the courageous Mr. Britling, chose to put aside his neutrality and enlist in the Canadian army. Emily loved Wells's book in particular and pestered everyone she knew to read it. Indeed, the bestseller was probably instrumental in changing the minds of many American isolationists. She also loved reading patriotic poetry, including *In Flander's Fields* by John McCrae, and the bestselling poem by Alan Seeger that began "I have a rendezvous with death..." It both entranced and frightened her, as did any poem about death on the battlefield.

★　★　★　★

Emily was gathering her schoolbooks together on a Friday in late October when Buck Leatherwood suddenly approached her. He was the bruising fullback for the Richmond High School football team, a roughly handsome young man with blond hair and blue eyes. His parents were well off, so he drove an Oldsmobile. He was one of the few high-school students who actually had a license and his own car.

"Hi, Emily," he said as he drew alongside her.

"Hello, Buck."

"Did you read about Mata Hari?"

"Mata who?"

"Mata Hari—you know, that Dutch dancer who was arrested by the French for spying. She was accused and put on trial for being a German secret agent. She gave them important military secrets on the construction of Allied tanks. The newspapers were full of stories on how she got those secrets, too."

"Oh, her," Emily said, picking up her last book and walking quickly away. "I don't really care." She had heard about the woman, but she wasn't interested in discussing the situation with Buck, since the whole ordeal had been an unsavory and scandalous story.

Buck grinned broadly and ran down the hall after her. Catching up, he continued anyway. "Well, she won't be stealing any more secrets. The French filled her full of lead this morning. A firing squad put an end to her."

Emily, who had a vivid imagination, felt suddenly queasy, the vision of a gruesome execution filling her mind. Not wanting to let on that she was shaken by the news of the woman's death, she said simply, "Well, I suppose she deserved it."

"You betcha!" Buck said. Then in almost the same breath, he asked, "Hey, how about you and me go out and do the town tonight, Emily?"

Most of the girls at Richmond High would have given their pinky fingers to have been Buck's girl. Emily, however, had never felt attracted to him, and now she replied offhandedly, "Oh, I don't think so, Buck. Thanks anyway."

Buck was not accustomed to being refused, and he immediately turned on the charm, such as it was. The more he talked, the more curious Emily became. She had heard so much about Buck that she started to wonder what it would be like to date him—not as a regular thing, but just once. Against her better judgment she finally agreed. "Oh, all right, Buck. Tonight, then."

"Hey, that's what I want to hear. Put on your best dress. You and me'll knock 'em dead. We'll take in a movie, then maybe go dancing at the Green Door."

"I'm not going to the Green Door. You can bet on that."

The Green Door was a dance hall in a neighboring town with a shady reputation. Emily had never been there, but she knew her parents would never allow her to step foot in a place like that. "The movie's all right, Buck, and maybe a soda, but that's it."

"Okay, doll. I'll be by about seven."

As soon as Emily got home, she found Wes in the front yard waiting for her.

"What do you say we go to the movies tonight, sis? It's William S. Hart's latest—*The Square-Deal Man*."

"Sorry, Wes. Got other plans."

Her little brother stared at her. "What other plans?"

"I'm going out with Buck Leatherwood."

"Buck Leatherwood! You can't do that!"

"Oh, yes I can," Emily said defensively.

"You know what he's like. Everybody knows."

"Oh, that's just gossip. I can take care of myself."

The argument continued into the supper hour, for Wes begged their parents to do something as soon as they had sat down to eat and asked the blessing.

"Do something about what?" Aaron said as he helped himself to a pork chop.

"About Emily. She's going out with Buck Leatherwood."

Emily had been dating for over a year, but at this announcement both her parents put their forks down and stared at her. Gail said at once, "I don't think that's a good idea, Emily."

"Oh, Mother, it'll be all right. Don't worry."

"He's no good," Wes insisted. "I think you ought to say no."

"Will you be quiet, Wes? I can take care of myself."

"No, you can't. You need a keeper," Wes said heatedly. "I told Jared I'd look out for you. If he were here, he wouldn't let you go out with Buck."

Emily knew her younger brother's words had some truth to them, but she was too far committed now to back out. Her stubborn streak arose as she defended herself against her parents and her brother. Finally she said forcefully, "Look, we're just going to a movie, and then we'll have a soda. That's all."

"Well, I'm against it," Aaron said. "But you're growing up, Emily, and we have to trust you to make your own judgments." He looked over at his wife, and something passed between them. "But as soon as that soda is over, right back home. Okay?"

"All right, Daddy. I'll probably be ready by that time anyway."

* * * *

Emily was not terribly excited about her date. As a matter of fact, she was more interested in the new outfit she was going to wear. She dressed carefully, first putting on the navy wool skirt over her cotton chemise. Metallic trimming was in vogue, and the belt and patch pocket had silk-and-silver thread embroidered into an elaborate design. She slipped on the waist she had chosen, a delicate pink garment of embroidered silk over a foundation of silk chiffon. As she tried it on, she muttered, "It's pretty, but it wasn't worth six dollars. I never paid so much for a garment in my whole life." She grabbed her coat, for it was cold outside, and left her room. Even as she did so, she heard a horn blow and went to the front door. Wes was standing there looking out.

"Look at him," Wes said. "Blowing his horn. He's nothing but a low-down thug!"

"Oh, be quiet, Wes!" Actually Emily was furious that Buck would simply blow the horn, expecting her to come running out. She had half a mind not to go, but gritting her teeth, she said, "I'll be in early."

"I'll go out with you," Wes volunteered. "I want to tell that big lug a thing or two."

"Wes, you stay out of it!"

"I will not!" Wes marched out to the car, circled to the driver's side, and said, "Hey, you! As soon as the movie's over and one soda later, you bring my sister home. You hear me?"

Leatherwood was astonished by the sudden attack, but it amused him. He reached out the open window and struck Wes's shoulder sharply, causing the boy to rock back on his heels. "Don't worry, kid. I got a sister myself. I know how to treat a lady."

Wes watched sullenly as Emily got in and the Oldsmobile roared off. "Big ape," he grunted. "He'd better get her back here early. That's all I've got to say."

Emily settled back in the car, but almost at once she became apprehensive. "The Rialto's that way, Buck. Where are you going?"

"Ah, we can see a dumb western anytime," Buck said, grinning at her. "We're going out to the Green Door."

"I told you I would never go to that place."

Leatherwood simply laughed. He reached over and pulled her close and said, "You aren't used to having a good time, are you? These milk-and-water kids you been goin' with don't know how to have fun."

Emily protested, angrily demanding that he stop the car and let her out, but Buck just laughed. They left the outskirts of Richmond and drove for twenty minutes before pulling up in front of the Green Door, a one-story white frame building, the parking lot filled with cars and trucks. "Come on," Buck said as he got out of the car. "I'll show you some real fun."

"I'm not getting out of this car."

Buck simply reached in, picked her up in his arms, and set her on the ground. "Now, you don't want me to leave you out here alone, do you?"

"I want you to take me back home."

"Tell you what. I'll make a bargain," Buck said. "We'll go in. We'll dance a couple of times. Then we'll do anything you say. But I bet you'll want to stay."

Emily argued but saw that there was no way out. She walked stiffly toward the door, and as soon as she stepped inside, she knew that she had made a terrible mistake.

The inside of the dance hall was dark and smoky, and a jazz band blasted music at such a high pitch that it hurt her ears. The dance floor was crowded with people doing all kinds of unseemly dancing that Emily had heard of but had never seen.

"Come on," Buck said. "We'll get a table." He practically pulled her across the room, where they sat down with a woman he introduced as Marilyn, then promptly ordered two drinks.

"I'm not drinking anything, thank you," Emily said primly.

Buck laughed boisterously, ignoring Emily's comment and waving to others in the crowd that he seemed to know. When the drinks arrived he said, "Come on. One drink never hurt anybody." When Emily refused he frowned but said, "Okay. That'll be two for me." He downed first his drink, then hers, and stood up—wobbling a bit as the liquor quickly rushed to his head.

Pulling Emily from her seat, he dragged her toward the dance floor. "Come on, toots. Let's dance."

Emily had never been treated so roughly, and she struggled free from his grasp. "I'm going home, Buck Leatherwood—one way or another."

Buck argued and grabbed her arm again, but she pulled away and started walking out, calling over her shoulder, "If you try to stop me I'll scream, and there's bound to be somebody in here who'll help me."

Cursing under his breath, Buck followed her outside. Emily got in the car, her back straight as a board, while he tried to crank the engine on the front of the car. After several unsuccessful attempts, it finally started. He slammed himself into the driver's seat and cursed again. "I'm giving you one more chance."

"Take me home."

Buck drove away from the Green Door at full speed, terrifying Emily as the car veered from one side of the road to the other, but she would do anything to get home. Five minutes later, however, he pulled off the main road back to Richmond onto a side road. He stopped the car, and Emily gasped in fear. "What are you doing?" she demanded.

"I'm gonna get something out of this date," Buck snarled. He grabbed her and pulled her over to him with his right arm, and with his left hand, he held her face so she couldn't move and tried to kiss her.

Emily was sick with fright, but in a rush of adrenaline she somehow had the strength to get her right hand free, double up her fist, and strike him right in the face. The blow caught him at that delicate spot just under the nose where the nerves are thick.

"Ow!" Buck cursed and grabbed his nose.

His stunned reaction was all Emily needed to make her escape. Opening the door, she tumbled out, momentarily losing her footing on the muddy ground, then running from the car as fast as she could.

Buck got out, screaming, "Get back in this car!"

"I won't! Not with you!"

"Get in or I'll leave you out here!"

"Go ahead!" She was already putting a fair distance between herself and her attacker.

Buck made no move to run after her. He just stared at her disappearing form as she headed back toward Richmond on foot, and he shouted, "All right, walk then! See if I care!" He got back in the car, spun the vehicle around, and roared away, throwing red mud all over the front of Emily's outfit.

She breathed a sigh of relief that he had let her go so easily, but then, as the pale lights of the Oldsmobile grew fainter and disappeared, she began to worry. Any car that came along this road would likely be going to the Green Door, and she could wind up with someone even worse than Buck Leatherwood. Guilt covered her like a suffocating blanket. "I never should have gone out with him. I knew all the time it wasn't right. Why did I do it?" she berated herself.

Her shoes were not designed for walking on muddy gravel roads, and soon her feet were covered in goo, looking like two blobs of red gumbo. She struggled along, stopping from time to time to rake the mud off with her fingers, when finally she heard a car approaching. Despite her fears, she knew she couldn't really walk all the way home, so she waited until the headlights hit her. Shielding her eyes from the glare, she started to wave. The car pulled to a halt, but she suddenly froze with panic. It was a dark night, and she was alone, and there was no telling who was in this car!

"Why, Emily, what are you doing out here?"

"Who is it?" Emily said.

"It's me, Noel Batterson."

Emily let out a cry of relief. Noel Batterson was a friend of her parents. He operated a cleaning establishment in Richmond, and she at once began to explain, "Oh, Mr. Batterson, I'm so glad to see you." She stumbled over toward the car, and Batterson got out, staring at her with astonishment. "What are you doing way out here in the middle of nowhere?"

Emily swallowed hard. "I went out with a boy from school. We were supposed to go to the movies in Richmond, but he drove me to the Green Door instead. I begged him to take me back, but he wouldn't stop."

"I hope you didn't go in that place."

"He made me go in, but then as soon as I got inside, I made him take me out. But on the way home he . . ." She couldn't finish, as she felt herself choking up with tears.

"Who was it?" Mr. Batterson demanded. "I'll take care of him!"

"No, please don't . . . it doesn't matter," Emily said quickly. "Would you take me home, Mr. Batterson?"

"Sure. Get in the car, Emily."

Emily trudged over and climbed into the passenger seat. She sat there miserably while Batterson turned the car around and started back for Richmond. He did not ask questions, and for that Emily was most grateful. She didn't feel like explaining this evening to anyone. When they pulled up in front of her house, he asked, "Do you want me to go in with you?"

"No, thank you, Mr. Batterson, but I'm going to tell my parents how you practically saved my life. I'm sure my dad will be calling you."

"Well, I'm glad it didn't turn out worse, Emily. Young women can't be too careful, you know."

"I was a fool tonight," Emily said. "But I won't be again."

"Good girl." Batterson reached over and patted her shoulder.

Emily whispered, "Thank you again," and got out of the car. She climbed up the steps hesitantly. It was only eight o'clock, and she knew her parents would not be in bed. She was tempted to simply wait until later to go in, but that would not do, for she knew neither one of them would go to bed until she got home. Taking a deep breath, she gingerly opened the front door and took off her mud-caked shoes in the entryway. Hearing voices, she walked toward them into the kitchen, where both parents, who were sitting at the table, turned to stare at her.

"Why, Emily!" her mother said. "What in the world—!"

Emily stood very still. "I made a mistake," she said.

"Are you all right?" Aaron asked, great concern in his voice as he rose and came over to her. He was joined by Gail, and they stood on either side of her waiting for her reply.

"Oh, I'm all right, except I've been an idiot." She went on to explain how Leatherwood had forced her to go with him to the

Green Door. She did not omit any of the details about how he tried to attack her. She saw her father's face harden and knew what was on his mind. "I'm so sorry, Dad. It was my fault for going with him. You and Mother were right, and Wes, too. I'll have to tell him when he gets home from the movie."

"You were very fortunate that Mr. Batterson came along," Gail said.

"I know it. I told him you'd call him and thank him."

"I'll do more than that. I'll have lunch with him tomorrow," Aaron said. "You sure you're all right?"

Emily laughed nervously. "I'm all right physically, but I never thought I could ever feel so dumb."

Aaron and Gail exchanged glances. "Well, we're all dumb at times, but maybe you've learned a lesson tonight that you'll never forget."

"I have," Emily said, shaking her head. "I'll never do a thing like that again."

"Go clean up, dear," Gail said. "Then come back, and we'll talk some more. No sermon," she said quickly.

"Thanks, Mom. Thanks, Dad." Emily turned and walked away, leaving her parents standing there looking after her.

"It could have been much worse," Aaron said. "I think I'd better have a talk with Leatherwood."

"Be careful, dear. Don't do anything rash."

"Oh, I won't—I'll just let him know in no uncertain terms that if I ever catch him near my daughter again, he'll wish he'd never met her!"

★   ★   ★   ★

Three days after Emily's disastrous date with Buck Leatherwood, a letter came from France. As usual Aaron waited until the rest of the family had gathered so they could all read it together. He was accustomed, as they all were by this time, to the writing of James Parker. He opened it and started to read:

"*Dear Mom and Dad and Wes and Emily,*

I can't dictate much. I'm not doing well at all, I'm sorry to report. My wounds have gotten infected, and the doctor's also afraid that I have pneumonia."

Aaron paused then, his eyes running ahead, and when he looked up, the other three saw that he was stricken with worry.

"What is it, Aaron?" Gail said, her voice trembling.

Aaron read in a voice that was unlike his own:

"I may not make it back home. Don't grieve over me if I don't come back. Think of me but don't grieve. And be kind to James. He's been my best friend."

Aaron went over to Gail and put his arm around her. "We'll have to pray that he will make it. God can do all things."

Gail could not speak. She turned and put her arms around Aaron, and he held her.

Wes was staring at the letter in disbelief. "I thought he was doing so well."

Emily saw that there was another sheet of paper. She could barely speak, but she said, "Dad, is that from James?"

"What . . . oh yes. You read it, Emily."

Emily took the sheet of paper and saw that it was very brief:

"I wrote Jared's words down. It took quite some time, for he is very weak.

I wish I had a better report, but I must say that the doctors are not hopeful. I have gotten very close to Jared while I've been here, and I would do anything in the world to help him. I would even give my life for him, but, of course, that's impossible.

From what Jared has told me, you are all praying people, and I think prayer is all that will help him now. I will write as often as I can.

Your faithful friend,
James Parker"

A silence fell over the room then, and Emily could stand it no longer. She turned and walked away. The thought of Jared not coming back was too overwhelming. When she got to her room, she fell onto the bed and began to weep silently, pressing her fists against her lips. She tried to pray, but it seemed that was impossible.

* * * *

The next letter came four days later. It was in a strange handwriting, and as soon as Aaron took it and saw the official seal, he knew the truth. His lips grew tight, and he opened it while the others waited. Emily held on to Wes's arm and watched her father's lips as he formed the words, "We regret to inform you that your son, Jared Winslow, died of his wounds in the hospital." Aaron stopped and bowed his head, and the letter fell to the kitchen floor. Gail cried out and started to sob. He reached for her to comfort her, but he could not say another word, for his own grief constricted his throat.

Emily watched the letter fall, and as it lay on the floor, she knew her life would never be the same again. The tears flowed down her parents' faces, and then she listened as her father picked the letter up and read the comments from Jared's commanding officer, Captain Clark Ramsay. He said that Jared was a fine soldier, and he told how all the men had respected him and admired his immovable faith in the face of death.

"But that doesn't matter now. He's dead." Emily stood there, her face pale, and she seemed to hear the beating of her own heart as a distant drum throbbing slowly. "Why did my brother have to die? God, why did you let it happen?" She waited for an answer but none came, and then she turned and walked out of the room, feeling more alone than she had ever felt in her entire life.

PART TWO

NOVEMBER 1918–JANUARY 1919

★ ★ ★ ★

CHAPTER SEVEN

AN UNEXPECTED VISITOR

★ ★ ★ ★

The year 1918 brought untold death and misery before the war finally culminated with the signing of the armistice on November the eleventh. Silence had fallen over the battlefields of Europe, and after the Germans signed the treaty at five in the morning, the cease-fire took effect six hours later. The Great War was finally over, but the massive loss of life and destruction had left devastating scars all across Europe.

For America the last year and a half had been like no other in her history. The strain of sending millions of American young men to fight in a war in Europe had drained the country of some of her confidence. After the first flush of excitement with all the parades and speeches containing flowery promises that America would save the world, the country settled down to the long haul of fighting a slow and agonizing war. No one knew how long it would take or how many young men would have to die before the goal was achieved.

Russia also turned a corner in her history during this year. The reigning Czar Nicholas II and his family were deposed by the revolutionary forces led by Vladimir Ilich Ulyanov, known to his followers as Lenin. The huge country, after having rid itself of the centuries-old monarchy, set up a government under Lenin. The new state quickly confiscated estates and nationalized land banks and industry, and in March of 1918 Russia withdrew from World War I. But there was no peace for the masses. Civil war swept the country, and in the struggle that ensued, the carnage cost the Motherland millions of lives and untold destruction.

To legitimize the authority of the new state, Lenin knew he must do more than simply depose the old order. On July the sixteenth, Nicholas, his wife, Alexandria, and their five children were ordered to the cellar of their house. The family went downstairs suspecting nothing but were met by a hail of bullets from a hastily assembled firing squad.

Throughout Europe, as family after family were informed of the deaths of their young men on the battlefield, a mysterious and virulent strain of influenza appeared without warning, creating a new and even deadlier enemy right in people's homes. America was struck by this same disease, now known as the Spanish flu—so called for the rapacity of its attack in Spain. It swept around the world, infecting six continents. In the United States, San Francisco passed ordinances mandating the wearing of surgical masks, and Chicago movie theaters refused to admit coughing patrons. Historians said grimly that half the world's population was touched by this terrible and virulent disease.

The Winslows did their part during this difficult time. They bought liberty bonds to support the war effort. They followed the newspaper accounts of the terrible battles that were taking place and rejoiced over the exploits of America's war heroes—men such as Alvin Cullum York, who led a successful attack on a German machine-gun emplacement. York captured one hundred thirty-two prisoners and thirty-five machine guns. He was awarded the Congressional Medal of Honor and the French Croix de Guerre. Eddie Rickenbacker clinched his title as America's number one flying ace.

And so the armistice finally came, but the nations of Europe were decimated. The kaiser fled to Holland, and Germany was heavily penalized, losing all lands she had sought to gain through force. No battle had destroyed Germany's fertile soil, but its economy was in shreds. More than ten million people had died in the war, including six million civilians. Even after all that carnage, no one was really sure why the war had begun. The world could only hope that the armistice would bring a lasting peace and that never again would they have to face another great war.

★　★　★　★

"Cap'n Brown, come on. You're not going to catch that squirrel. Don't you ever learn?"

Emily was tramping through the woods with Cap'n Brown by her side. Snow had fallen the previous day, and the temperature had dropped enough so that it remained on the ground. As always she enjoyed walking on an unbroken carpet of crystalline white and had left the house at four o'clock to take a walk before dark. The woods looked like a winter wonderland, and as Cap'n Brown rushed about in his hopeless quest to catch a squirrel, Emily lifted her head and looked up at the tops of the trees. The leaves were gone, and the oaks and hickories lifted their naked arms to the sky, almost as if they were in prayer. The sky itself was steel gray, a solid canopy without a single break in the color. The night would come soon now, and Emily walked faster. She had come far from home, and her feet made a crunching sound as they broke through the thin, frozen crust.

Finally she reached the pond she and Jared and Wes had enjoyed for so long. She paused at the side and then finally sat down on the old cedar tree that had fallen five years earlier. She knew it would lie there for many years, for the cedar did not rot as did the pines and hardwoods. The quietness that fell upon her from her surroundings was profound. From far away she could faintly hear the sound of a dog barking. For a long time Emily sat there, her heart and mind persistently dwelling on memories of Jared. It had been a year since his death, but she still thought about him almost every waking moment. When the letter had first come, starkly pronouncing his death, she had gone about her life almost in a trance. For a time she had cried herself to sleep every night and went through each day wishing it were already over. Even after all this time, she had not truly accepted his death. There had been no final good-bye beside a deathbed.

There had been no body to bury at his funeral. She could hardly bear the pain of knowing that he lay in some hastily dug grave somewhere in France. As the realization struck her again of how cheated she felt, she flung her arms wide and cried out into the cold evening air, "Oh, God, why did you have to take him? Why?"

Her impassioned cry shook the silence of the woods and brought Cap'n Brown to her side. He whined and poked her arm with his muzzle, looking up with troubled eyes.

Emily threw her arms around the large dog and held him. Suddenly into her mind came a poem by Christina Rossetti. It was one she had always loved and had memorized to recite once for her English class at school. The words forced their way through her mind as she buried her face in Cap'n Brown's thick fur:

> When I am dead, my dearest,
> Sing no sad songs for me;
> Plant thou no roses at my head,
> Nor shady cypress tree;
> Be the green grass above me
> With showers and dew drops wet;
> And if thou wilt, remember,
> And if thou wilt, forget.

> I shall not see the shadows,
> I shall not feel the rain;
> I shall not hear the nightingale
> Sing on, as if in pain;
> And dreaming through the twilight
> That doth not rise nor set,
> Haply I may remember,
> And haply may forget.

The words ran through Emily's mind, and the tears rose again. She held on to Cap'n Brown, who nuzzled her gently, and finally she cried out, "He's gone, Cap'n, he's gone!"

Emily rose to her feet and wiped her face with her sleeve, then started back home. Her somber mood made the woods seem grim and ominous now. The death of her brother had affected her more deeply than anything ever had in her whole life. She knew the whole family was still suffering from their loss, although she believed she had suffered the most. There was no reason for her to think this way, for she knew the deep love that her parents had always had for Jared. But Jared had been more than her brother. He had been her best friend and the only one who truly understood her.

To rid herself of the thought, she broke into a trot, and Cap'n Brown kept pace by her side. By the time she reached the edge of her neighborhood, the night had closed in so fast that the darkness seemed almost physical. As she reached her block she slowed down to a walk. When she was in front of the home of their next-door neighbors, the Carletons, she slowed her pace and stopped abruptly. There in the dim light she could see a man wearing a long overcoat and hobbling on a cane. He had come to the sidewalk that led to the front porch of her house, and she saw that he was peering in the darkness, apparently looking for the number.

Emily came to a full halt and suddenly her mouth felt very dry. Dark as it was, she could tell that he was wearing the khaki overcoat of a soldier of the American Expeditionary Force. She watched as he took a halting step, leaning on his cane. He took several such steps forward down the driveway. She was surprised when he halted, stared at the house for a moment, then turned and limped back toward the street. She hastened toward him as he started back in the direction of town. As she drew near him he turned to face her.

"Are you looking for someone?" Emily asked.

A short silence separated his reply, and then he said awkwardly, "I guess not."

Something about the man disturbed Emily. His hesitation as he approached her house, then his rapid turning away was strange. She took a step closer and leaned forward. "I'm Emily Winslow. Can I help you?"

The man was a little under six feet tall. In the glare of the streetlight she could make out that his eyes were gray, and he had a thin face, rather aristocratic, she thought. Suddenly she drew her breath up short and blurted out, "You're James Parker, aren't you?" She saw the face change, and then he nodded. "I'm so glad to meet you, James." She put out her hand, and awkwardly the soldier switched the cane to his left hand and took hers. His hand seemed thin and cold and somehow unsteady to her. "You were coming to see us, weren't you?"

"Well, yes I was, but—"

"Well, come on. This is the place."

"It's . . . not a convenient time, I'm afraid."

"Don't be silly," Emily smiled. She felt a warmth rise within her, a warmth she had not felt since Jared's death. Now she simply took his arm and turned him around. "It's cold out here. Come on in and meet the family."

Parker reluctantly moved forward, and Emily opened the door and turned to face him. "Come in." She let him enter, and then she called out, "Dad—!" When her mother appeared in the kitchen doorway at the end of the hall, Emily said, "Mom, look who's here! This is James Parker."

Gail at once came forward, her face exuberant. "Why, what a surprise. I'm so glad you've come, James! Here, take that coat off and come into the living room."

Parker said haltingly, "I don't want to be a bother."

"How could you be that?" Gail said. She took the coat and hung it on the hall tree. At that moment Aaron emerged from his study, and Gail said, "Look who's here, dear. It's James Parker."

Aaron's expression was one of disbelief and joy. He came forward and put his hand out. "I'm honored to finally meet you. Why, you're just in time for supper."

"Oh, I couldn't possibly—" James began.

But Aaron quickly interrupted. "No argument now." He turned to Gail and asked, "How long before we can feed this man, and me, too?"

"Give me another ten minutes, dear."

"Fine. Come on in by the fire, James. It's gotten pretty cold out there. When did you get in?"

Emily accompanied the two men into the living room and watched as Aaron practically forced the young man to take a seat in front of the fire and peppered him with questions. Studying James's face under a brighter light, she saw that he was a well-proportioned man with a wiry frame. He had tawny hair, longer than most men usually wore it, and she noted that it had a slight curl to it. His gray eyes were deep-set, and he had a short English nose and a slight cleft in his determined chin. His hands looked strong, but his fingers were long, like a musician's or a surgeon's. He was pale and drawn, and when she had a chance, she asked, "When did you get out of the hospital, James?"

Parker turned toward her, saying, "I was in the field hospital in France several months before they could ship me home. I've been recuperating and going through therapy ever since in an army hospital in Washington. I was released a couple of days ago."

"How are you feeling? Does the wound still give you much trouble?"

"Oh no, it's not painful. It has weakened my leg enough so that I'll probably always have to use a cane. But other than that I'm fine now."

"I'm so glad you came to pay us a visit," Aaron said. "Have you been back to your own home yet?"

Parker hesitated, then shook his head slightly. "Well, actually, I don't have any family. I've been wondering just what I'd do when I got out of the hospital, and my first thoughts were to come see you right away."

"Well, I'm glad you did," Aaron said. "Where was your home originally?"

"I grew up mostly in upstate New York, but I moved around a lot."

When James didn't offer any more information, Aaron wasn't sure how much else to ask about the young man's family. Just then Gail came in from the kitchen and said, "Come along. Supper's on the table."

Emily watched as Parker fumbled for his cane and stood to his feet. Her eyes met those of her father as he directed James to the dining room.

Gail pulled out a chair and said, "Now you sit right here, Mr. Parker."

"Just James, if you don't mind."

"Of course. And you can call me Gail, and you can call my husband Aaron."

They had just sat down when hurried footsteps sounded on the stairway, and Wes popped into the room. He stopped dead still at the first sight of the soldier, and Emily said quickly, "This is Jared's friend, James Parker. This is my brother Wes."

Wes went at once to the soldier and put out his hand. "I'm glad to see you, James."

"Are you still taking pictures, Wes? Your brother told me you were the best photographer in America."

Wes's face flushed with pleasure. "Not that good, I'm afraid."

"Well, sit down, son," Aaron said. "I'm starved to death." He waited until Wes had seated himself and then bowed his head. "Our Father, we thank you for bringing this young man to our home. We thank you that his life has been spared. We give you thanks for this food and for every blessing. In Jesus' name, amen."

Emily looked up quickly to see an odd expression on James's face. He was staring at Aaron in a most peculiar way, and she could not imagine what was troubling him. Quickly she said, "Here, have some of this roast, James. My mother makes the best roast in the world."

"Jared told me she was a fine cook." The soldier filled his plate with roast beef, mashed potatoes, and English peas as the dishes were passed around the table. The aroma of fresh bread filled the air in the dining room. "That smells so good," Parker said suddenly. "I understand you bake your own bread."

"Oh, most of the time," Gail smiled as she passed the butter across to him.

"Once you've tasted my wife's fresh-baked bread you'll never want any store-bought bread again," Aaron proclaimed.

"How did you get here, James?" Emily asked. "There's no train this late in the day."

"I rode a bus."

"In the snow? That must have been a rough ride!" Aaron exclaimed.

James Parker smiled, his eyes showing a trace of humor. "I've had worse rides," he murmured.

As the meal progressed, the others talked about a variety of issues, including the war, but Parker said very little. He listened to Wes talk about his photography, and finally he asked Emily about herself. "You graduated from high school this year, didn't you, Emily?"

"Yes. I was so glad to get out."

"Was it that bad?"

"Oh no, not really. But I wanted to do something different."

"And what would that be?" Parker asked. He was studying her thoughtfully, and his rather wide mouth turned upward in a smile. "Have you got the great American novel finished yet?"

Emily stared at him, then laughed shortly. "Jared told you I'm a writer, huh?"

"Yes, he did. He talked about you endlessly. I feel like I already know you, even though we've only just met." Parker looked around the table. "In fact, I feel like I know all of you. I saw all the pictures you sent to Jared, and, of course, he talked about you constantly."

Gail brought in an apple pie for dessert, and when Parker tasted it, he looked up and smiled at her. "I've never had pie this good."

"Why, thank you, James."

After the meal was over, Parker said rather nervously, "I'd like to tell you about Jared."

"Come on into the living room by the fire," Aaron said quickly. He got up and led the way, and for the next hour Parker spoke about Jared. With the Winslows eagerly hanging on to his every word, he told of Jared's courage, his cheerful acceptance of the hardship in the trenches, and how he had been the most popular man in his company.

Emily listened hungrily, and finally when Parker told of Jared's last days and hours, she struggled against the tears that came to her eyes.

Finally Parker looked around and said, "I didn't know whether to come and tell you all this or not. After a year I thought it might just be too painful. Some people don't want to hear about the details of the loved one they've lost."

"You did right to come, James," Aaron said at once. His voice was husky, and he was holding Gail's hand. "We're very grateful to you for coming."

"Indeed we are," Gail said.

Parker reached for his cane, which rested against the sofa, and stood up slowly. "Well, I've got to be getting along. I didn't mean to stay this late."

"Why, where are you going?" Emily said.

"Oh, I'll find a room somewhere. I left my suitcase at the bus station."

"You'll do no such thing," Gail Winslow said. "You're staying with us."

"Why, I couldn't do that!"

"Don't try to argue with my wife, James," Aaron smiled. "I've been arguing with her ever since we've been married and have never won yet."

"He can have Jared's room," Emily said quickly.

"Of course. You look tired, James. Emily, you go make sure that there are towels and fresh sheets on the bed."

Emily left with Wes at her side as Aaron picked up a log to add to the fire and invited Parker to sit down again. After Emily and her brother had made preparations, she came into the living room and said, "Your room's all made up, James. The bathroom's right down the hall there. There are plenty of fresh towels."

"I'll get you some of my pajamas," Aaron offered. "Then we'll pick up your suitcase tomorrow so you can have your own clothes."

James Parker had his head down staring at the carpet. Emily could not imagine what was going on in his mind. When he lifted his head, he simply said, "Thank you. Good night."

After he had gone into Jared's bedroom and closed the door, Emily took her father's arm and drew him away. "Daddy, I think he's sick. Did you see how his hands were trembling?"

"I'll have Doc Bradford come by and look him over tomorrow. Now I'll go get him some pajamas."

Emily went to the dining room and helped her mother clear the table and wash the dishes. As they were standing at the sink, Gail suddenly turned, and Emily saw tears in her eyes.

"Poor boy," Gail whispered.

Emily knew that the tears were not all for James Parker—her mother was thinking of Jared.

After the dishes were done, Emily went to her room. It was early yet, but somehow she did not want to go anywhere. Her thoughts were full of their unexpected visitor, and as she wrote in her journal, she found it difficult to keep her mind on it. She had pictured James Parker as being somewhat different, but now as she sat at her desk, she thought of what he had done for her brother, and gratitude filled her.

Finally she took a bath and put on her warmest pajamas, for the temperature outside was dropping. As usual she propped the pillows up behind her head and began reading. Usually she read a novel for a while and then a chapter from the Bible, but the novel held no interest for her, and she picked up the Bible. She was reading through the historical sections and had reached the sixteenth chapter of Second Samuel. She had been moved by the history in the previous chapters, which told of the rebellion of Absalom, the favorite son of King David. In truth she had been angry with Absalom because he was trying to kill his father. He had raised enough military forces to cause David to leave Jerusalem.

The last part of the fifteenth chapter told of the flight of David. There had been something prophetic in all this to Emily. David had always been an exciting character in the Bible. Indeed he was a man after God's own heart, and now to read about his betrayal by this child he loved best and his flight from his beloved Jerusalem had touched her heart. She read the sixteenth and seventeenth chapters, where she discovered a very noble action on the part of one of David's followers:

> And it came to pass, when David was come to Mahanaim, that Shobi, the son of Nahash of Rabbah of the children of Ammon, and Machir the son of Ammiel of Lodebar, and Barzillai the Gileadite of Rogelim, brought beds, and basins, and earthen vessels, and wheat, and barley, and flour, and parched corn, and beans, and lentils, and parched pulse, and honey, and butter, and sheep, and cheese of kine, for David, and for the people that were with him, to eat: for they said,

The people is hungry and weary, and thirsty, in the wilderness.

She kept coming back to these three verses and rereading them. For some reason this historical note to David's life moved her deeply. Finally she closed the Bible slowly and put it on the table. Turning out the light, she lay down and pulled the blankets up over her. Her mind was on James Parker, and she thought of how pale and weak he seemed. Though she did not yet know why he was alone in the world, she had been moved by his confession that he had no family and no place to call home, and finally she began to pray. As she prayed she thought of the people who had showed King David such devoted kindness. She finally whispered, "And can we do less for this man who risked his life to save my brother?"

CHAPTER EIGHT

"It's All Right to Cry...."

★ ★ ★ ★

Dr. Bradford came down the steps slowly. He was a heavy man in his late sixties and had suffered some heart trouble. He had been the family doctor for as long as the Winslows had lived in Richmond, and now as he reached the foot of the stairs, his face was rather pale as he said, "It ought to be against the law to build two-story houses—too hard on us fat men with weak hearts."

"Come into the kitchen, Dr. Bradford," Gail said quickly. "I've got some hot coffee and some fresh apple pie."

The doctor followed Gail into the kitchen and drank the scalding hot coffee as if it were cool ice water. "Ah," he said. "Now *that's* coffee!" He applied himself to the pie and devoured it quickly. "I'll have just another half cup of that coffee, Gail."

Gail quickly removed the pot, poured a half cup of the black liquid, and put the pot back on the stove. "How is he, Doctor?"

"Well, I think he needs to be back in the hospital. I'm not sure why they released him."

"Is it his wound?"

"No, that seems to be clearing up all right, but I don't like that cough. If it turns into pneumonia, I wouldn't like it at all."

"I hope it's not the flu. We missed all of that, but I don't see how. Every family in the neighborhood had a case except us."

"Well, I told him I thought he should go to the hospital here in town, but he said he didn't have any money."

"Don't worry about it, Doctor. We'll take care of him."

"He might be just as well off here as he would be in the hospital. They're so full, I doubt he would get a bed anyway. That Spanish flu is still taking a toll."

Dr. Bradford rose and picked up his bag. "Give me a call if he gets worse. I'll stop by day after tomorrow and check him again."

"Any special medicine he needs?"

"No. Just good home cooking. Keep him out of the cold and give him a lot of pampering."

"We'll do that, Dr. Bradford." Gail smiled. "We think he's special around here."

Bradford was close enough to the family to know of the circumstances surrounding James Parker. "Well," he said roughly, "he's in good hands. I can see that. Just keep me posted."

★ ★ ★ ★

Emily looked up when she heard the sound of faltering footsteps on the stairway. Quickly she ran halfway up and met James as he was coming down the steps. "Did you sleep well?" she said, smiling.

"Pretty well." Parker smiled back at her. "How about you?"

"Oh, well enough, I guess."

Emily slowed her pace to adjust to his halting gait, and when they reached the bottom of the stairs, she said, "Mother made pancakes this morning. I hope you like them."

"I'll like anything, I think. Your mother's a fine cook."

"I hope I'll be as good someday."

"I'm sure you will."

When they reached the dining room, Emily said, "Dad's already had breakfast, and Wes is gone, but I thought I'd join you."

"Sounds good to me."

Emily ran in and said, "Mom, James is up. He looks better and has some color in his cheeks."

"You go sit down. I'll bring the pancakes."

"No, I'll help you."

The two moved about the kitchen quickly, and soon James Parker was cutting a plate-sized pancake. He sliced it into small bites, and then Emily said, "We have honey, maple syrup, and sorghum. Which do you like best?"

"I'll have some of all of it." Parker smiled. He really had a good smile, and his gray eyes seemed to have more light in them. This was his third day with the Winslows, and the rest had done him good. He poured some of the sorghum over a portion of his pancakes, wolfed it down, then speared another morsel with his fork. He put it in his mouth, chewed it, and shook his head. "These cakes are delicious. They don't make them like this in restaurants."

Gail came in with a platter full of ham and set it on the table. Then she sat down and said, "I've already eaten with Aaron, but you two go ahead."

As Emily ate her pancakes she said, "You look much better, James. Your eyes are clearer, and your cheeks are filling out." She touched her own cheeks with her forefinger to illustrate her point.

"I feel like an intruder eating your food, and I hope I'm not making a nuisance out of myself."

"Don't be foolish!" Emily said.

After the two had downed all of the pancakes, Gail said, "I'll fix some more if you're still hungry."

"No, not for me," James said quickly. He shook his head. "No wonder I'm gaining weight. It's strange that your husband doesn't weigh three hundred pounds."

"He's one of those men who can eat whatever he wants and never seems to gain an ounce." Gail laughed ruefully. "I have to watch what I eat, but not him. Why don't you two go into the living room? I'll bring your coffee out there," Gail said.

Emily quickly rose, and the two went into the living room. She sat down beside James on the overstuffed couch, and Gail came in with two cups and a pot of coffee. "You'll have to wait on yourself. I have to go to the store."

"All right, Mom," Emily said. "I'll do the dishes."

Parker watched Gail as she left and shook his head. "You picked winners for parents. Jared always talked very highly of them."

James was wearing some of Jared's old clothes, since all he had been carrying in his suitcase were uniforms. It had given the family a bit of a shock when he had first appeared wearing one of Jared's favorite shirts. He was smaller than Jared was, the same height but not so well filled out, so that the clothes hung loosely on him. Now he reached down into his pocket and said, "I've got something for you." He had brought some of Jared's personal things, including his Bible and his watch that his father had given him. James held something in his hand and said, "He always kept this in his kit. Said it made him think of his baby sister." He opened his hand and smiled when Emily gave a cry of surprise.

"It's the bear!" She reached out and took a small ceramic bear sitting up in a comic position. "I gave him that for his birthday when I was only six. He always kept it on his dresser. Said he thought the bear looked like me."

"Not a bit of it," James said. "You're much prettier than that bear."

Emily held the smooth item in her hand, running her fingers over it. "Brings back old memories. We make a big thing of birthdays around here, and I looked everywhere to find something I thought he'd like." She held the bear against her cheek and turned to smile at James. "I don't know what was going on in my childish mind to think he might like a gift like this. But he did—or at least he always said so."

"You two were very close, weren't you?"

"Yes, we were. We were more like two brothers, I guess. Most brothers leave their little sisters out when they get to be a pest, but not Jared. He always took me with him on his hunting and fishing trips. We were very close."

The cadence of the grandfather clock ticking in the hall made a rhythmic beat as the two sat talking. Emily finally said, "We don't talk about it much, but I suppose you know how grateful we are to you, James, for what you did for Jared." She saw a slight flush touch his cheek, and he shook his head. "Don't say it was nothing, because it *was* something. It was so brave of you to go out and carry him off the field when he got wounded."

"That sort of thing happened a lot," James said.

Emily could see he was embarrassed by the remark and clearly wanted to change the subject.

"I won't pester you with gratitude," Emily said, then reached over and squeezed his arm. "But I'll never forget it."

"It didn't work out right, Emily. I wish I'd been the one to go instead of him. I didn't have any family to leave behind."

"We'll never know why tragedies happen as they do, but you're alive, James, and we'll never forget what you did for Jared in the hospital."

James shrugged his shoulders and ran his hands through his tawny hair. "I can't stay here forever," he said.

"Where will you go when you leave here?"

"I don't know."

"Stay with us, then. Mom and I will fatten you up like old Dr. Bradford."

James turned to face her, his gray eyes glowing with an enigmatic light. Emily felt embarrassed by the steadiness of his gaze, and then she laughed and said, "You want to hear some more of my stories?" She had been reading her short stories to James, stories she had been trying to get published in several women's magazines, but so far without success. Now she laughed in a half-embarrassed fashion. "But you probably don't."

"Nothing I'd like better," he assured her. "You're a fine writer, Emily."

The praise brought a flush to her cheeks, and she could not think of an answer.

"It must be nice to be able to do something like that," James said. "I could never think of a thing to say. One of these days you'll be writing books that bring a great deal of pleasure to people, and I'll be saying, 'Why, I knew Emily Winslow when she was just starting out. But I knew all the time she was going to be great.'"

"Oh, don't be silly!"

"I'm not being silly at all. You have a gift with words. You know, some people can do that."

James turned serious for a moment and chewed on his lower lip as he thought. It was a habit that Emily had noticed, and she was once again rather shocked at how well she had gotten to know this man who had come to their home a virtual stranger.

"Who do you like? Which writers?" she asked, and for a long time the two sat talking about writing.

Actually James had read more than Emily herself, a fact that surprised her. She had read the most fiction, but he had read by far the most nonfiction. The fire crackled in the fireplace, sending a rich aroma of woodsmoke through the room, and as the two sat sipping coffee, Parker studied the face of the young woman and noted the brightness of her eyes and her widow's peak. He had never seen anyone with eyes as blue as hers. They were almost electric when she got excited. He smiled as she read her stories, for she threw herself into the reading of them just as much as she threw herself into the writing.

When Gail came back from the store, she looked in and saw Emily standing by the fireplace, reading from a sheaf of papers, her voice animated. Gail shook her head and passed on into the kitchen.

★　★　★　★

"I don't think I need to carry this cane anymore."

"Yes, you do," Emily said bossily. "You know what Dr. Bradford said."

The two were out walking along the sidewalk, and indeed James was making much better progress under the loving care of his new family than he had in all those months in hospitals. He scarcely had a limp now and protested that his leg felt strong enough to support his weight. The coughing had dropped away until it was only on rare occasions that it still troubled him.

They stopped at the curb, waiting until a truck passed, and watched as the wind picked up a pile of leaves, whirled them into a funnel shape, then rolled them onto the curb. The leaves hissed as they scooted across the ground, and the smell of woodsmoke was in the air, for some people were still burning leaves.

"Is Wes driving you crazy yet, James? He has certainly latched on to you," Emily said.

"He's a fine kid. I never saw a better one. When he fills out, he'll be a big man."

"I think he's so cute," Emily said. "So tall and lanky now. He's not as good an athlete as Jared was, but he's very good at photography."

"I wish I knew more about photography so I could talk to him about it. He knows so much, it's hard to carry on an intelligent conversation."

Another bunch of leaves suddenly swirled by them, striking at them almost like a snake, and Emily looked up at the sky. "I think it might snow soon."

"It doesn't snow much here in Richmond, does it?"

"Hardly ever, but I love it. I'd like to live where the snow gets three and four feet deep."

"That's fine for the first day when it's coming down," James said. "Very pretty. But the next day it turns to slush, and you can't drive your car down the road, and everything is frozen up."

"Where did you experience cold and snow like that?"

"In upstate New York where I grew up. I went out many days when the pump was frozen, and we had to thaw it out."

Emily shot a curious glance at him, for he rarely spoke of his youth. She wanted to know more about his family and his growing-up years, but she had discovered that he was as good at evading talk on that subject as she was at eliciting it. "Do you feel like going to a high school football game this afternoon?" Emily offered instead. "Richmond High is playing their archrival, Petersburg."

"Yes, I'd like that," James said.

"Do you like sports?" she asked.

"Never had time for them much, but I could get addicted, I think."

"Jared was so good at everything. Everyone said he could

have been a professional baseball player, and he was good at football and basketball, too. Just any kind of sport."

"I remember once our company was sent back from the front line for a little rest. We got a baseball team together, and another company did the same. Jared was the pitcher. I don't think the other team got a hit that day, and it seemed he could hit everything they threw at him."

"Did you play, James?"

"They put me in the outfield where I couldn't do any damage." James smiled at the thought. "With Jared pitching, no balls ever came my way. I still remember that day. There weren't many like it."

"You didn't like the army, did you?"

"I hated every minute of it—except for a few times like that," James added quickly. "I wasn't a good soldier."

"I don't believe that," Emily protested.

"It's true enough. Some men were cut out to be good soldiers, and others, like me, just weren't."

Emily considered his words as the two walked along, and finally she said abruptly, "Have you had a lot of girlfriends, James?"

Her remark caught Parker off guard. He laughed aloud and shook his head. "What makes you ask a question like that?"

"Because that's the sort of thing girls are interested in, of course. Did you?"

"One or two," he said, shrugging his shoulders.

His offhand remark piqued Emily's curiosity even more, and she reached out impatiently and squeezed his arm. "Tell me. I want to know."

"I would think I had about the same number of girlfriends as you have boyfriends."

"Oh, that's no answer!"

"I don't think I had any girlfriends as charming as Buck Leatherwood." Parker suddenly laughed at the startled expression on her face. "Wes told me about it."

"That was awful! And he was awful."

"Why don't you tell me about it? I got the bare bones from Wes, but I like to hear you talk."

"Oh, I don't want to talk about that," Emily said. But when he insisted, she told him the whole story and ended by saying, "Dad should have taken a strap to me. I deserved it."

"I can't see your father doing that."

"Come on, let's go home. We'll want to get a big lunch if we're going to go to the game."

★ ★ ★ ★

Emily enjoyed the football game immensely. Since she had graduated, this was the first time she'd been back at her old school. It was fun being in the high school stadium again and showing off her date. James had worn some of Jared's clothes, and all of the girls in the senior class, and even younger ones, watched her and James avidly. Many of them came up to be introduced, but Emily managed to get rid of them rather efficiently.

"You're very popular with your girlfriends," James observed. He was sitting beside her in the stadium, wearing a blue wool jacket that Jared had been very fond of and a pair of gray flannel trousers. He turned to study her and saw that she had not appreciated the remark. "What's wrong?" he asked. "Did I say something out of order?"

"Oh no, but they're not coming because they like me. They just want to meet you."

"Me? Why, they're children."

"How old are you? I never asked."

"Twenty-three. An old man, Emily."

"Oh, you're decrepit all right. That's why all these silly girls keep flocking around hoping you'll notice them."

James shook his head. "I feel like I'm a hundred years old. They all look like babies to me. Of course," he said quickly, "you're much more grown-up than they are. How old are you now? Seventeen?"

"I'll be eighteen in January."

"An old, old lady." James reached over and took her gloved hand and squeezed it. "Some man's going to get a prize when he gets you. I hope you'll let me sing at your wedding."

"Oh, don't be foolish!" Emily laughed and turned her attention back to the game, not quite sure how to respond to James's remark.

As the game progressed they both cheered loudly when the home team made a good play and groaned when they made a bad one. Richmond finally lost the game in the last minute, and groans went up from everyone in the stands. "They lost!" Emily cried out. "They lost!"

"Well, it doesn't matter eternally, does it?"

Emily turned and saw he was smiling at her, and she had to laugh. "No, it doesn't matter eternally. I can't even remember who won when we played Petersburg last time."

"Sports are one of those aspects of life that are existential."

Emily liked James's use of big words. "I know what that means," she said.

"Of course you do. You're a smart girl."

"You mean," she pursued the thought, "that they are important while they're going on but not afterward."

"Like eating a steak. Nothing is more important than eating that steak, but the next day the steak's gone, and you've got to eat another one. Most things are like that."

"Not everything, though," Emily said. She took his arm as they left the stands and walked around the track. She was very much aware of the envious stares of her girlfriends and said, "Look, they're all positively green! Put your arm around me."

"What'd you say?"

"Put your arm around me," Emily whispered. She waited until James had done so, and when she looked at him, her eyes were bright with laughter. "That ought to do them!"

"Emily, you are something!" He kept his arm around her until they walked outside, and then they met Wes at the car.

"Let's go out and celebrate," Wes said at once. "Hey, you've got your arm around my sister."

"I made him do it," Emily said. "I wanted to make all the girls jealous of me."

"Well, let's go out and celebrate."

"But we lost," Emily protested.

"Then we'll celebrate losing."

They went out to a favorite diner and had hamburgers and sodas and donuts, then finally went home. Wes said, "Come on up, James. I want to develop some film." Wes had made his own darkroom in a small spare room in the attic, and he lured James up every chance he got.

"You go develop them and show them to me when you're done. I'll never learn that stuff. I'm not the scientific type," James grinned.

"All right, but I want you to see them. They're going to be great. I'm going to send them off to a contest."

"He's really crazy about photography, isn't he?" James said, turning to Emily.

"Yes," Emily said. "Oh, I hate to go in."

"Getting pretty late."

"I know, but I hate to go to bed."

"Are you afraid of the dark?"

"Oh no, don't be silly! Just afraid I'll miss something."

They were standing on the porch, and the twenty-watt bulb cast feeble shadows. He turned to study her face and said, "That's just like you, Emily. You're afraid you'll miss something. You enjoy life better than anybody I've ever known."

Emily felt warm at the praise. "What a nice thing to say!"

"It's the truth," James said.

"Let's not go in yet," she said. She laughed suddenly and asked, "What did you think of Frances Dalton this afternoon?"

"I don't remember her. Which one was she?"

"She was the one in the white coat who kept trying to get you to leave me and go with her."

"Oh yes. She was rather persistent."

"She's the prettiest girl in Richmond. She can get anybody she wants."

"No, she's not the prettiest girl in Richmond," James said. He grinned at her and said, "I think I'd argue that point."

He did not elaborate, but Emily knew he was paying her a compliment. "Oh, you're just being nice. I look at myself in the mirror every day. My face is too wide, and I have this dumb red hair."

"Jared told me you didn't like your red hair, but he loved it."

"Did he say that?"

"Sure did. Lots of times."

"He always told me that, too," Emily murmured. "But I thought he was just trying to make me feel better."

The two talked for a while, and James teased her mildly about her age. "Don't try to be old so quick. You've got the world in the palm of your hand, Emily. You're going to have a great life."

The two were standing in the yard, and the stars shone brightly overhead. It was one of those nights that brought out the stars like clusters of diamonds flung out across the sable background. Emily turned to him and said, "Sometimes I get—" She could not finish and had to bite her lips, and she looked down.

James suddenly understood her problem. "You're still grieving over Jared, aren't you?"

"I guess I always will."

"He was a good man. The best I ever saw." He hesitated, then said, "I haven't told you this, but I was with him when he died. And the last thing he said was, 'Tell Emily I love her.'"

The words seemed to break Emily Winslow apart. She began to tremble, and her body quaked. She leaned against James, and he put his arms around her.

"It's all right to cry. I do it myself sometimes."

Emily clung to him fiercely. The sobs racked her body, and he wrapped his arms around her, holding her in a protective fashion.

Finally the spasm of grief passed, and she stepped back. "Thanks, James," she whispered.

He watched her as she went inside, and he shook his head as if in reproach before he followed her through the front door. They quietly said good-night to each other and her parents before going to their separate rooms.

Emily went to bed at once after putting on her pajamas and reading her Bible. She lay in the darkness, and for a long time she thought about what James said were Jared's last words. The pain of her loss was still like a knife, and she wondered, *Will I ever get over this? Can I ever accept it?* And then she tried to sleep, but for a long time she lay awake. The last thing she remembered was James Parker holding her and comforting her.

CHAPTER NINE

A NEW JOB

★ ★ ★ ★

"How in the world did you get this shot, Wes?" James Parker held up an enlargement and considered it with something close to amazement. "I've never seen anything like this."

"Took me a long time to get that one, James." Wes moved closer and squinted at the photograph of a red-tailed hawk descending with widespread wings and claws. Beneath the raptor was a rabbit that had been caught in the act of making a desperate leap away from the death that awaited him. The details were so sharp that the markings on the hawk were clearly visible.

Wes leaned back and said with satisfaction, "I noticed that old hawk always hunted in the afternoon in a field out close to my grandparents' house. The place was full of rabbits, and I could see the hawk snagging them, but they were always too far away to get a picture." Wes's eyes glittered as he said, "What I did, James, was start putting out food for the rabbits—carrots and lettuce and stuff they like. I got them trained to come to that same spot almost anytime. Then I made me a little blind out of saplings and camouflaged it with leaves so that it'd look just like a bush to the hawk. Well, I sat there until I thought my rear end was going to get paralyzed." Wes grinned, and his warm brown eyes glowed. "I got him, though. At first I saw him circling overhead, and then he dove like a rock."

"Did he get the rabbit?"

"Why, shoot no. He missed. That rabbit jumped sideways, and the hawk missed by about a foot. To tell the truth, I was glad to see that. I'm always on the rabbit's side. I like to see 'em get away."

Parker studied the picture and shook his head. "It's a fine photograph."

"I entered it in a photographic contest in New York. Had to send in a ten-dollar entry fee, but if I win, the prize is the best camera made."

"Well, I can't imagine anyone else doing a better job than this."

Wes smiled back, and the two continued to talk. The walls of Wes's room were decorated with photographs, mostly his own. Many were of his family, but he had a number of wildlife photos as well—a deer, a bobcat, a wild pig, and a variety of birds that he had captured with his lens.

Finally Parker said, "It's nice to be good at something. You think you'll be able to make a living as a photographer?"

Wes's young face hardened with determination. "I'm going to do it or bust," he said. "You wait and see if I don't!" Then a grimace turned his lips upward. "I wish I was as good at my school-work as I am at taking pictures."

"You having trouble?"

"Sure am."

"What subjects are bothering you?"

"Well, all of them, to tell the truth. Emily helps me with English, so I scrape by there, but this bookkeeping course is giving me fits."

"Let me see what you've got. Maybe I can help."

Wes's eyes lit up. "You know something about bookkeeping?"

"Well, I worked as a bookkeeper for a while."

Wes immediately dug his books out, and soon the two were sitting close together at Wes's desk. They worked for a consider-able time, and finally Wes said, "Well, it's plum easy the way you explain it, James."

Parker smiled as he said, "I wouldn't think a bright young

fellow like you would have any trouble. I think you've just got your mind on other things."

"Guess you're right about that. Mostly on pictures and cameras and stuff like that."

Later on in the day Wes explained to Emily how good James was at bookkeeping. The two of them were sitting in Emily's room, where Wes had come to ask for help on his English lesson. "Why, he'd be a great teacher. Old Lady Simms talked for a solid hour about how to work this problem," he complained. "When she got through I didn't have an idea in the world what she was talking about. But James, why, he sat down there and in fifteen minutes made it just as clear as air."

"I wonder how he learned bookkeeping."

"He said he worked as a bookkeeper for a while."

Emily considered Wes for a moment, and then she tapped her chin thoughtfully. "A bookkeeper—that might be something we could use."

"Use for what?" Wes asked.

"Oh, nothing. Look, don't you see you've got a misplaced modifier here?"

"I don't even know what that is."

Emily suddenly giggled. "Well, look. You say, 'He was a tall man with gray hair and a mustache named Billy.' "

"What's wrong with that?"

"I never heard of a mustache being named Billy."

"I didn't mean that! I meant the man's name was Billy."

"That's right. So your modifier's in the wrong place."

"Shoot! If I can talk, I don't know why I have to take English. All right. Go over it one more time, Emily. I've got to pass this course or Dad will kill me!"

★   ★   ★   ★

On Sunday morning Emily talked James into going to church with them. She liked to sit as close to the front as she could. The rest of the family liked to sit farther back, but she insisted that James come with her to the third row center. He looked around uncomfortably and said, "Do you always sit so close to the front?"

"Yes, I like to sit up close. Don't you?"

James rubbed his chin. He was wearing a suit Aaron had bought for him. The two had gone shopping that week and had come back with a complete outfit. Emily thought he looked very handsome in the warm brown lightweight wool suit, shiny brown shoes, and a tasteful tie that showed against his white shirt. She was wearing an apple green taffeta dress that complemented her hair. The dress had a fine white Georgette collar and a stylish throw-tie belt that looped around and dangled in front. She had been pleased when James had told her how much he liked her dress.

"This is an old church," Emily said. "You see that line across the pews right in the middle?"

James leaned forward with interest and saw, indeed, that there was a faded streak in the center of each pew about four inches wide. "What made that?" he asked.

"There used to be a board across there. The men had to sit over on the right, the women on the left."

James suddenly turned to look at her and whispered, "I bet I know who was responsible for taking that board down. It was probably you."

"Don't be silly! My grandmother had something to do with it, I think. She was quite a rebel. Still is, for that matter."

The two sat there whispering, and then the choir came in, followed by the pastor, who was accompanied by his song leader. At the direction of the song leader, everyone stood up and sang the doxology. The pastor then led in a prayer, and the song leader said, "All right. We'll sing number twenty-three."

Emily was not sure what James thought about religion. She herself had been in church almost since the day she was born, as had Wes, so it was a natural environment for them. But she did notice during the song service that James knew most of the songs. Finally, when they sat down after a hymn, she whispered, "You have a fine voice, James, and I noticed you know most of the hymns."

James turned to look at her, not answering for a moment,

then shrugged. "I learned a few growing up."

"Were your family Christians?" she asked.

"No," James said rather shortly.

His curtness puzzled Emily, but she couldn't ask him any more questions, as it was time for the sermon.

"My message this morning," Pastor Ronald James said in a fine baritone voice, "concerns what many feel to be the most important element in our Christian life. And that is faith. My text is taken from the book of Hebrews, the eleventh chapter, and I'm sure that most of you have read this chapter many times. We will not take time to read the whole chapter, although I will be referring to it. We will center our thoughts around the sixth verse, which says, 'But without faith it is impossible to please him: for he that cometh to God must believe that he is, and that he is a rewarder of them that diligently seek him.'"

Emily had always liked Reverend James's sermons. They were timely and up-to-date, and they always had some humor in them. But he was also a man of great compassion, and she had seen him weep over the lost more than once. Now as he began to preach, she stole glances at James from time to time and noted that he was listening, but she could not imagine what was going on in his mind.

The first part of the sermon dealt with how Christians please God by having faith. The pastor said, "Faith is two empty hands held open to receive the Lord Jesus Christ."

Emily thought that was a fine statement, and she nodded her approval. She was aware that James had turned to look at her, but she did not dare turn her head at that time. The last five minutes of the sermon were a plea from the minister for those who had never expressed their faith in Jesus to do so now.

"I know some of you sitting out there who do not know Christ as your Savior are wondering how we can believe in anything that we cannot see. But faith is believing beyond what we can see with our eyes. Faith never knows where it's being led. If it knew, it would not be faith."

Finally Reverend James closed the message, saying, "I ask anyone here this morning who is not a Christian to give your heart to Jesus. Men have made salvation very complicated. Some

have said that you must go through many ordinances and ceremonies, but the thief on the cross is the classic example of faith."
He read the Scripture about the dying thief and then said, "What
could he do? Could he go out and do good works to prove to
God that he was earnest? Could he give money? No. He could
do absolutely nothing except look to Jesus. And he said, 'Lord,
remember me when you come into your kingdom.' And you all
know what Jesus said, 'This day thou shalt be with me in para-
dise.' "

The minister paused and then took a deep breath. "We're all
going to stand and sing a hymn that all of you know well. It was
written by a young woman who tried to please God. She had
tried everything she knew and then finally said, 'I'm going just
as I am without one plea.' So that is what you must say today—
'Just as I am without one plea.' Jesus saves."

During the hymn Emily noted that although James sang the
first stanza, he fell silent on the others. As several people went
to the front of the church during the invitation, she stole a glance
and saw that he was staring at the book but seemed to be obliv-
ious to what was going on about him. She almost asked him
what was wrong but then decided it was a private matter.

As they filed out of the church to meet with her family and
go home for Sunday dinner, Emily did have the courage to say,
"Your people weren't Christians, you say?"

"No."

"What about you, James?" she asked.

James looked directly at her for one moment, but she could
not interpret the look in his gray eyes.

He said rather shortly, "I guess whatever religion I might
have had was knocked out of me in the trenches."

Emily was disappointed but could make no answer. As the
two joined the rest of the family Emily felt sad, for all of the
family had become fond of this young man.

★　★　★　★

Christmas was still a week away, and Emily had asked her parents to go to a band concert in Edington, a town some fifteen miles away. Aaron had said, "I'd like to, Emily, but I can't. Why don't you get James to take you?"

"But how will we get there?"

"He can probably drive. You can use the Ford."

Eagerly Emily had asked James and discovered that indeed he could drive, and he readily agreed to take her.

"It's getting cold. You'd better wear your heaviest coat," Gail said as the two started out the door. "Someday they'll put a fire of some kind in a car to keep it warm."

"I'd be in favor of that," Emily said. "But we'll be all right, and we'll be home early."

James opened the door of the Model-T and climbed in. He used the right-hand door, for there was no left-hand door by the front seat. He reached over to the wheel and set the spark and throttle levers in position. Emily knew something about the car, for she had helped her father many times. "You set the throttle levers like the hands of a clock at ten minutes to three."

"Why don't you sit here and give me a hand, Emily?" James asked.

Willingly she went around to the driver's side and reached in. James went to the front, inserted the crank in his right hand, and put his forefinger through a loop of wire that controlled the choke. Pulling the wire, he turned the crank, and the engine roared. He ran around to the door, tossed the crank handle inside, and jumped in to move the spark. The engine ran noisily as Emily got in too and slammed the door.

"I hear some of these new Fords have self-starters in them," James said. "Anything would beat this. A lot of fellows get their arms broken by those cranks."

He released the emergency hand brake and shoved his left foot against the low-speed pedal. As the car swept out into the street, he released his left foot, and the car went into high gear.

It was cold inside the car, and Emily had pulled up a lap robe to cover her lower body.

They made the trip to Edington with no trouble and attended the concert. It was not a particularly good one, and Emily leaned over once and said, "That man can't sing as well as you can. Why don't you get up and challenge him?"

James looked at her and laughed as he shook his head. "No thanks. He's probably the mayor's uncle or something."

The concert lasted only an hour, and the sun was shining, despite the cold weather. As they drove along, Emily suddenly said, "Look, James, there's the Green Door."

James looked across to where she indicated. "What's that?"

"Oh, it's where I let that thug Buck Leatherwood drag me. I was such a fool to go out with him. Everybody knew what he was."

As the Ford sailed down the gravel road, James did not speak for a time. And then finally he said, "I guess we're all foolish at times."

Emily raised her voice over the noise of the motor to ask curiously, "What was your childhood like? You never talk about it."

"Not much to say. It wasn't good." James dodged a rabbit that darted out from the right side of the road, barely missing it. "That fellow must have a death wish," he murmured.

Emily thought he would say no more, but finally he shrugged slightly and went on.

"My father ran out on my mother and the family when I was born. I never saw him. My mother tried to keep the family together by taking in washing and scrubbing floors. I can't remember a whole lot about that. She died when I was four."

"Oh, how terrible for you!"

"I only remember that it was like the world had come to an end or the sun had gone out."

"What did you do?"

"Well, there were four of us kids, all pretty young, and somebody decided to parcel us out to uncles and aunts."

"What about you, James?" He turned to look at her, and for an instant she saw bitterness in his eyes.

"I guess we ran out of relatives. I wound up in an orphanage."

Compassion rose suddenly in Emily. "Was that hard?"

"It wasn't good. I ran away when I was fifteen. Didn't have anywhere to go, so I just bummed around. Became a hobo. Did all sorts of jobs, and, of course, I didn't have much of an educa-tion." He hesitated and then added, "When the war came I was glad to join up. I didn't have any responsibilities anyway, and I thought it would at least give me some square meals, some clothes to wear, and something to do. I was wrong about that."

"It's been hard on you, hasn't it?"

"Well, I'm alive."

The cryptic remark troubled Emily. "What will you do now?"

James Parker suddenly laughed and shrugged his shoulders. "Become a hobo again, I guess."

★   ★   ★   ★

Emily wasted no time in going to her father. He was working at his desk, and when he turned at the sound of her voice, Aaron could see the stubborn look on her face that meant she had some sort of plan that involved him. "Well, I can see I'm in for trou-ble," he said with a mock sigh. "What do you want me to do this time?"

"Dad, we've got to do something about James."

"Do something? Like what?"

"You don't know what a hard time he's had. He told me about it on the way back from the concert." Emily gave her fa-ther a brief summary of what James had told her and then said, "He's a young man. He's still got time to make something out of himself."

"I think he will."

"But, Dad, now that the war's over there are two million men coming home. Jobs are scarce now that there's no need for facto-ries to keep making war materials. You know that. It's going to be hard."

Aaron nodded, for he had thought much about this subject. "You're right. You have an idea?"

"Wes says that James is really good at accounting, and that he said he had a job once working as a bookkeeper. Can't we help him go to college?"

"Did he finish high school?"

"No, I don't think so. He says he was nothing but a hobo. But he is good at accounting, Dad. Couldn't you help him?"

Aaron Winslow nodded. "I think I might be able to do something about that. As a matter of fact, I've been thinking about James. I spend half my life in the library doing research for my writing projects and the other half studying the stock market. I could use an assistant around here."

"Oh, Daddy!" Emily's eyes were sparkling, and she threw her arms around him. "You're wonderful! I've got the best dad in the whole world."

Aaron was nearly pushed off balance by her sudden attack. He laughed and said, "Well, send him around, and we'll talk about it."

Aaron went back to his work as Emily left, but within five minutes he looked up to see James come in.

"Emily said you wanted to see me, sir?"

"That's right, James. Come in and sit down." He waited until the young man was seated and said, "If you don't have other plans, James, I could use an assistant."

Parker blinked with surprise and then shook his head. "I appreciate your offer, but I think you're doing this just to be nice. You really don't owe me anything."

"I'm not just being nice, James. I've been thinking about taking on a young man to help me with my research. You have no idea how boring it is to go to a library and look for a subject until you nearly go blind. You think you can handle that?"

James Parker looked across at the tall figure of Aaron Winslow. A smile touched his lips, and he said, "I think if you'd teach me, I could do it."

"Good. It's settled then. We'll start first thing after Christmas. You know we're going over to my mother's house for Christmas dinner."

"No, sir, I didn't know that."

"There'll be some other Winslows there. It'll be good for you to meet them."

CHAPTER TEN

CHRISTMAS AT BELLE MAISON

★ ★ ★ ★

"That's it right there, James—the old Winslow homeplace."

James Parker looked out the window as Aaron turned the Ford into a circular driveway. James took in the tall house with the white columns in front and said, "It's a beautiful place, sir."

"Yes, it is. Kind of a showplace around here. So many homes got burned down during the Civil War, but I'm glad this one lasted."

Aaron pulled the car up into a line of other vehicles that were parked on the east side of the house, and they all got out. "I feel a little out of place, like an intruder," James whispered to Emily as they approached the steps.

"Think nothing of it! Everyone will be glad to see you. We told them all so much about you. You'll like them, too. I don't know who all will be here, but the house is usually full on Christmas."

The door opened as they were climbing the front steps, and a slender woman with silver hair came forward to greet them, ignoring the cold. "Aaron," she said with a smile and a warm embrace.

"Sorry I couldn't get here earlier, Mother."

"Well, you're here now."

"I'd like for you to meet an addition to our family. This is

James Parker. James, this is my mother, Belle Winslow."

"I'm so happy to see you, sir. Aaron and Gail have told me so much about you."

Taking the woman's hand, James said with some hesitation, "I wasn't sure whether to come or not, Mrs. Winslow. It seems like such an imposition."

Belle Winslow tossed her head. Wearing a striking white dress with silver embroidery on the bodice, she was still a beautiful woman. "Always plenty of room and especially for you. I've wanted to tell you how grateful I am for what you did for Jared."

"I . . . it wasn't much, ma'am."

Suddenly the doorway was filled with people, making conversation difficult. James tried to remember the names, but he had difficulty. Aaron said, "You haven't met my brother, Lewis. This is his wife, Deborah. And these are his children, Hannah and Joshua."

James shook hands with each member of the family, and his face flushed as they all said something kind to him.

Belle Winslow insisted they all come in out of the cold, and soon they were all inside the lovely old house. She led them to an enormous drawing room, a lavishly furnished room but very warmly decorated. The light beige-and-blue wallpaper complemented the large area rug of rose, beige, blue, and green over darkly stained wooden floors. There was an overstuffed sofa, several cushioned chairs draped in fringed paisley shawls, large mahogany tables, and cabinets filled with porcelain, feminine laces, brocades, and delicate needlework. Dainty lamps with fringed silk lampshades adorned the tables in front of the large floor-length windows, and these were covered with chocolate brown velvet curtains.

James was staring at the high ceiling, admiring the delicate gilded detail along the edges of the molding, when Joshua and Hannah joined him and Emily. Joshua was a tall young man of sixteen, and Hannah was three years older.

After several minutes of conversation about the house and the Winslow family, James asked the pair about themselves.

"Hannah and I have been best friends," Joshua said. "We tell each other all our secrets, don't we, Hannah?"

Hannah Winslow was also tall with striking blue eyes. "Well, I've got one secret I haven't told you."

"What! You're holding out on me?" Joshua said in mock horror.

"What is it?" Emily asked.

"I'm going to New York," Hannah said.

"Really? What do you plan to do there?" James asked.

"I'm going to find a career there."

Joshua nodded. "So am I—just as soon as I'm old enough. I told Mom and Dad I could go now, but they wouldn't let me."

Hannah laughed. "I would imagine not. Not at sixteen. I'll go to prepare the way before you."

Joshua reached out and squeezed his sister's arm until she cried out, "Let go of me, you brute!" He dropped Hannah's arm, then turned to James and said more seriously, "I want to hear all about you and Jared, James. We've heard it secondhand, but I want to hear it from you."

Emily saw a painful expression cross James's face and immediately said, "I don't think James likes to talk about that time much."

Hannah said quickly, "But you will tell us sometime, won't you, when you feel you can?"

"If you'd like, Miss Winslow."

After Hannah and Joshua had moved away to talk to other family members, Emily said, "I know it hurts for you to talk about Jared, but my family will want to know."

James sighed and told her, "I'll do the best I can."

★　★　★　★

The house was filled with guests, and it was shortly before dinner was served that Emily was able to get James off to himself. "My grandmother wants to talk to you."

"What about?" James said with some alarm.

"Well, I'm sure she'll want to hear about Jared. They were very close. She loved him dearly."

"She's a very gracious woman. How old is she now?"

"She's seventy-five. Her husband died two years ago. He was a wonderful man. His name was Davis."

"Your grandmother's still very attractive." He smiled at Emily and said, "I can see where you get your good looks."

Emily shook her head. "She's the most beautiful woman I've ever seen, and Dad says I should have seen her when she was younger."

"So she and your grandfather lived here in this house?"

"They sure did, James. *And* she was a spy for the Confederacy."

"Really! That sounds like something out of a novel."

"Her life was like that. When she married her cousin Davis, he was in the Federal army. After the war he became a Methodist preacher, and they moved all over the country. They moved back to Belle Maison when my grandfather retired a few years ago. I just loved Grandfather. He was the most interesting man to talk to. Well, come on. You'll have to let Grandmother make up her own mind about you. She's very determined. I've always thought she could read my mind."

"I feel like I'm going on trial."

"Don't feel like that. She has such a good heart."

Emily then led James into a small room off of the main drawing room, where her grandmother was waiting for them. Belle stood up and thanked James for coming to speak with her. "This was our sewing room back when I was growing up," she said when they were all seated. "Of course there were no electric lights and no indoor plumbing in those days."

James smiled. "Things are better, I suppose, than they were then."

Belle considered the young man for a moment, then shrugged her shoulders. "I'm not sure about that. Of course I'm in favor of indoor plumbing, but I'm not at all convinced that the times or the people are any better. It seems to me that people were more neighborly in those days."

James listened attentively as Belle spoke about the Civil War and her childhood. Finally she said, "Did Emily tell you I was a spy?"

"Yes, it must have been very exciting."

"It was terrible," Belle said simply. Her face grew still as she remembered her life years ago. "I had to pretend to be something I wasn't, and I had to betray some people who were very dear to me in order to do my work. It almost killed me at the time, and I wanted to quit."

Emily reached out and took her grandmother's hand. "But you found your husband. That made it worthwhile, didn't it?"

"Yes, it did, but I can still remember incidents that happened so many years ago. Davis's father took me in when no one else would, and I had to betray him to be true to my work for the Confederacy." She looked at James and said, "I hope you never have to do anything like that."

Emily turned and saw that James's face was set.

"It must have been terrible for you," he finally managed to say.

Belle saw that the young man was uncomfortable and changed the subject. "Now," she said, "I know it's painful for you, but I want to hear about Jared."

James spoke quietly for the next fifteen minutes, substantially telling her the same story Emily had heard before. When he finished, his face was pale. "I wish I could have done more for him, Mrs. Winslow."

Belle had listened carefully, her eyes fixed on the young man's face. She said, "We can never understand God's way, why one is taken and one is left. But I thank you for telling me."

Emily said quickly, "James, you run along and talk to Lewis and his wife. They'd like to get to know you better. I want to talk to Grandmother a little longer."

James rose and nodded. "It's so good of you to have me in your home, Mrs. Winslow."

He left and at once Emily turned to face Belle. "What did you think of him, Grandmother?"

Belle did not answer at first. "He seems to be wound up tight," she remarked finally.

Emily nodded. "I think that's what happened to the men who stayed in the trenches a long time. I know such horrible memories must still trouble James a good deal."

Belle looked Emily squarely in the eye and asked, "What is

this young man to you, my dear?"

"Why . . . I don't know what you mean."

"You haven't taken your eyes off of him since the two of you came in here." Belle smiled slightly. "Are you in love with him?"

"Why, Grandmother, I haven't known him for very long."

"That's beside the point. How do you feel about him?"

Emily bit her lip and looked down at her hands. "I don't know. I guess I was so grateful to him for taking care of Jared."

"That's fitting and just. You should be grateful to him, but that's enough."

Emily looked up quickly. She saw that her grandmother had some reservations, and she smiled and said, "Don't worry, Grandmother. We're just good friends."

Belle was silent for a moment, and then she rose stiffly and said, "Come along. Let's go in with the others. It must be almost time for dinner."

★   ★   ★   ★

The Winslow tradition was to open presents just before dinnertime, and James Parker sat as far out of the mainstream as he could get. The room was crowded, big as it was, and the large tree glittered with a variety of fine ornaments. Presents were stacked high underneath it, and James soon gave up trying to keep track of the children and the grandchildren. Wes stopped by long enough to grin and say, "Are you gettin' all the names straight?"

"I don't think so, Wes."

"Well, there aren't as many here as there usually are."

James watched as some of the younger children tore open their presents, and then he was suddenly interrupted when Emily appeared with several packages in her hands. "These are for you, James. Merry Christmas!"

"Why, Emily, you shouldn't have done that! I couldn't get you anything."

"Next year you can," Emily said, smiling. "Open them up."

Somewhat reluctantly James began to open the presents.

They were small, inexpensive gifts—a tie from Aaron, a pen and pencil set from Gail, a half-dozen silk handkerchiefs from Wes. The last present he opened was from Emily. When he pulled the wrapping aside, there lay a fine leather billfold such as he had never seen.

"It's made of alligator," Emily explained.

"It's beautiful, Emily, but you shouldn't have done it."

"I wanted to," Emily said simply. "Now every time you take it out to put money in it, you'll think of me."

James rubbed the fine leather and said, "I will think of you, but I don't suppose I'll have much money to put in there."

"Yes, you will. You're going to have a successful career."

"I wish I had your faith."

Emily sat beside him, and the two watched until all the presents were opened. And then Aaron said, "Come along. Dinner's on the table."

Dinner was indeed on the table, the centerpiece being an enormous turkey. Aaron went to the head of the table, picked up a carving knife and fork, and said, "I wish I were a surgeon, but since I'm not, I'll hack this bird up the best I can."

The meal included ham as well as turkey, corn bread dressing, all sorts of vegetables, fried and mashed potatoes, and an array of pickles and other enticements. It was topped off by mince pie, and when James tasted it, he said, "This is the best pie I've ever had in my life."

"I'm glad you think so," Belle said. "It's my mother's recipe. I'll make you another one next week."

"I don't think I'll want to eat for a week."

"Yes, you will. You've got to put on some weight, James."

At that moment, Aaron rose and said, "Well, it's time for the Christmas Winslow speech." He looked at Belle and shook his head. "I was so used to Dad making this speech, and he always did it so well. I miss him, Mother. Indeed I do."

Belle smiled rather sadly. "Yes, but he's with the Lord now. That's where he always wanted to be. You go right ahead, son. Do him proud."

Aaron began to speak, and Emily whispered to James, "This is kind of a tradition. We talk about the Winslow family going all the way back to the *Mayflower*. I guess we're a little bit proud of that heritage."

"You should be," James said. "It's a wonderful tradition."

For the benefit of any newcomers to the family gathering, Aaron was explaining, "There are Winslows all over the world, but it all started with a man named Gilbert Winslow, who brought his family to the New World from England. I suppose many of you have read his journal." Nods went around the table. The first edition of Gilbert Winslow's journal had been published by none other than Benjamin Franklin. His journal was reprinted several times, mostly for the family, but historians also were interested, for it gave a firsthand view by an excellent writer of what life was like on the *Mayflower* and later on in the Colonies.

"Gilbert Winslow, according to his own words, was a scoundrel of sorts," Aaron went on. "We have had our heroes and our scoundrels, but if Gilbert could be here today, I think he would be proud of his family." Aaron picked up a book and said, "I want to read just a brief entry from Gilbert's journal. I think I have it memorized, and so have some of you. This particular entry was written when Gilbert was in prison at the Salem witchcraft trials."

James blinked his eyes and listened carefully as Aaron read the passage:

> "It seems as though we will not survive this place. Every day someone is taken out and executed. I think of how I got here and what God has done in my life, and I can't be sad, for God has been good. He gave me a wife and a family, and when a man has God and a family, he has everything there is to be treasured. I think of how I fought against God when I was a young man and wonder that He did not strike me dead. But as I read through the Scriptures, I find one thread: He is a merciful, long-suffering God filled with tender mercy. I praise His name even here in the shadows of the valley of death. I regret that others of my family may die at this time, but they all know the Lord Jesus, and if it is His time for us to be taken from this world, I praise and rejoice in His holy will."

Aaron closed the book and said, "I can't read that passage

without weeping. How I would love to have known Gilbert and Humility Cooper, his wife. I look at the genealogical tree of the Winslows, and I see men like Adam Winslow and his son Nathan, who fought under George Washington. I see men like Paul Winslow, who became an admiral, and men like Zack Winslow and his wife, Bronwen, whom some of you in this room remember. And Sky Winslow, my grandfather, who left a legacy I will always be proud of. We have the younger generation, such as Lewis, who fought so bravely on San Juan Hill."

"And you were there, too, brother," Lewis called out with a smile on his face.

"Yes, I was there, too." Aaron returned the smile, then said, "I have no speech to make except to say that I hope those of you who are younger will find Jesus Christ as Lord, as so many Winslows have. We've had our ups and downs, and some of us, including me, have run from God. But He has brought us all back, so I want us to bow our heads and give thanks this Christmas to a merciful God—for all that He has done in our family, and for sending His Son into the world to save us from our sins."

Everyone in the room closed their eyes except Emily. She glanced at James and saw that he had slowly bowed his head, but his eyes were wide open. She wondered what he was thinking, but there was no way to make it out, for his face was still. After Aaron said "Amen," James got up at once and left the room without a word.

Hannah came over to ask, "What's the matter with James?"

"I'm not sure," Emily said.

"He was listening so intently to Aaron," Hannah remarked. "I wonder if he got offended."

Emily could not imagine. She went to hunt for James but could not find him. Then she went into the kitchen to help with the dishes, but she was troubled over his reaction.

★ ★ ★ ★

That night Emily simply could not go to sleep. She had been assigned a room with Hannah, and the two girls had stayed awake a long time, talking about the family. Hannah was full of her plans to move to New York, and Emily listened with some envy. "I wish I could do something like that."

"What are you going to do now that you're out of school? Are you going to college?"

"I think I probably will next year. I'm going to become a writer if it kills me."

"I don't think it'll do that," Hannah said, and she reached over to pat Emily's arm. "But I don't think it pays very well for most people."

Hannah had finally gone off to sleep, but Emily tossed and turned until finally in desperation she realized she wasn't going to be able to sleep. Stealthily she got out of bed, pulled on her robe and slippers, then went downstairs. She knew that sometimes a glass of warm milk made her sleep, so she warmed some milk on the stove, stirred in a little honey, and drank it slowly. She washed the cup out and thought, *Well, I'm just as wide awake as I was. I think that's an old wives' tale anyway.* She started back toward her room, but as she passed by the double doorway that led to the drawing room where the Christmas tree was set up, she stopped suddenly, for James was standing at the window staring out. She hesitated, then entered the room and called out, "James, is that you?"

Turning toward her, James said, "Yes. What are you doing up this late?"

"I couldn't sleep. What about you?"

"Me neither. I've just been watching the stars."

Emily went to stand beside him and looked out the window. "They are beautiful, aren't they?"

"Makes a man feel pretty small, all those stars."

The sky was indeed adorned with glittering diamonds, so it seemed, and Emily said, "I've always loved that verse in the Bible that says, 'He calleth them all by their names.'"

"The Bible says God named all the stars?"

"That's what it says, and there are billions of them."

"Hard to believe there are that many names."

"I know. I thought the same thing. I tried to think about how many stars there are, and our little world is just one of them. But

134

I think it is the one that God is most interested in."

"You don't suppose anybody else is out there?" James asked rather idly. His mind seemed to be far away, and he simply was making conversation.

"There could be, I suppose, but I've come to believe that God made the earth for people, and all the rest of the stars are just an adornment for us to admire."

James turned toward the young woman and studied her. There was a single light on at the far end of the room that cast its glow on her. He studied her, taking in the well-formed face, wider than most women's, and her hair, which even in the dim light was red enough to almost give off a glow. He had never seen such red hair, and he thought it quite beautiful. "I don't think about such matters enough, I suppose. It always seemed to me to take a long time to create that many stars."

"I don't think it's like that. I think God just spoke, and they were there."

Her words caught at him, and he looked back out of the window. There was a troubled expression on his face, and she suddenly touched his arm. "Is there anything wrong, James?"

He turned to her and shook his head. "Nothing to trouble you with."

"It wouldn't be a trouble. Can't you tell me?"

"I've been thinking about what your dad said about the Winslows. I don't think any of you fully realize what a wonderful blessing it is to have a family like yours. Oh, I know you're proud of them and all that, but to someone who hasn't had any family at all, like me, it's the most wonderful thing in the world. I envy you."

Emily could not speak for a moment. His words had been kind and sincere, and she felt she had gotten a glimpse inside of him. There was a loneliness in him that she had sensed from the first, and now as they stood there in the darkness, she wanted to reach out and help him. She looked up suddenly, and then she touched his arm and pointed upward. "Look up there, James."

Looking up, James saw several sprigs of mistletoe bound together and dangling from the ceiling by a thread. He turned back to her and did not speak.

Finally she said, "That's mistletoe."

"I know it is."

"Don't you know what it means?"

He did not speak, and finally Emily whispered, "I wouldn't think a soldier who's been to war would be afraid of a little kiss."

Her words touched James, and he reached out suddenly and pulled her into an embrace. His lips touched hers, and she returned his kiss with a sweetness and softness. And yet as he held her, he felt some hesitation on her part—as though she were half giving herself and half refusing him. He drew his head back and studied her. "I shouldn't have done that, Emily."

"I've been kissed before." Indeed Emily had been kissed before, but she knew that this was the first time she had been stirred by a man's embrace. She was astonished at how she had responded to the touch of his lips and the pressure of his arms.

James could not speak for a moment, and finally he released her and took a short step back. "Jared would break my skull for this."

"For what? We've done nothing wrong." Her words seemed to trouble James, and as he straightened up, Emily was puzzled by the tortured expression on his face.

"I wish . . ." he said in a tone so low that she almost missed it, "I wish I were as good a man as Jared."

He turned and, without another word, left her in the darkness staring after him. She knew she would think about his kiss for days, and even as she made her way back to her room to go to bed, she wondered at the expression she had seen on his face. *It was just a kiss*, she thought. *Why was he so disturbed?*

CHAPTER ELEVEN

THE HEART IS DECEITFUL

★ ★ ★ ★

Gail looked up from the paper she had spread out on the kitchen table and interrupted Aaron, who was eating a piece of cherry pie. "You've got cherry syrup running all down your chin."

"Have I?" Aaron mopped ineffectually at his chin with a napkin, and Gail shook her head.

"No. There's some over here. It's going to be running down your neck. Aaron, your eating is disgusting."

The accusation seemed not to trouble Aaron. He had merely wiped the juice away with his napkin and stuffed another enormous bite into his mouth. "You shouldn't cook so good," he mumbled around the morsel.

"I declare. You're messier than Wes, and that's saying a lot!" She looked down at the paper and said, "There's a story in here about prohibition."

"What does it say?"

"This man says that the law against liquor is going to be harder to enforce than anyone thought."

"I think he's right," Aaron said after swallowing another large bite of his pie. He reached over and picked up a large white mug and drank half a cup of coffee without stopping and then studied her as he said, "I'm surprised the states ratified the

Eighteenth Amendment. People have been trying for years to get an amendment against alcohol."

Gail looked across at Aaron and said, "I rejoiced when the amendment was passed."

"I know you did, and so did almost everyone else. But I'm worried about some of the effects."

"Why, it'll mean that people won't drink as much."

"It may mean that some people won't drink as much—but other people will drink more."

"Why do you say that?"

"It's the old story," Aaron said. "Do you remember back at the high school when the administration passed a new rule that said no student could stand on top of the statue of Robert E. Lee?" He referred to a life-sized statue on the campus of Richmond High School, a large bronze piece that had become quite a symbol for the city.

"Yes, I remember that."

"How many people got up on that horse with General Lee before the rule was passed?"

"Why, I never heard of anybody doing it."

"That's right. And how many times did students have to be expelled for getting on that horse *after* the rule was passed?"

Gail thought for a time and shook her head, puzzlement in her eyes. "Quite a few. I don't remember how many."

"There were dozens of them. Maybe hundreds. Some were caught and some weren't. The old story of human nature, Gail. The forbidden fruit. You tell someone they can't do something, and a certain number of people are going to do it even if they hadn't intended to."

"So you think this will cause some people to drink who wouldn't have before?"

"We'll have to wait and see, but the country is going into this new era of prohibition with a pretty lighthearted attitude. I'm afraid we're going to see a problem of gigantic proportions." Aaron leaned forward and locked his hands together and studied them for a time. "You realize that we've got eighteen thousand, seventeen hundred miles of coastline? Just think about how hard it will be to patrol all of that. The Coast Guard is pitifully small, and the navy can't do it."

"Are you saying that prohibition won't work?"

"I'd like to think it would, but anytime there is a market, people rush into it. And there's going to be the biggest market in the United States—illegal alcohol. Every petty crook and gang warlord will be fighting for their share of it."

The two sat there talking for some time, and then Gail put the paper aside and said, "How is James working out as your assistant?"

"He's doing fine. He has a quick mind. I don't think I ever saw anyone quicker." He frowned then and said, "But he's a strange young man. It's like he was born the day he came to our door."

"What do you mean by that, Aaron?"

"I mean he has no past. He never talks about his childhood or his youth, about what he did before he went into the army."

"Well, he had a hard life from what I understand."

"Yes, he did. He was thrown into an orphanage, and a hard experience like that can be terrible. Not all of them, of course, but he never talks about those days. I've tried to get him to open up, but Emily says his childhood memories are so painful he just doesn't like to talk about them at all."

"He's gotten very close to Wes."

"Yes, he has." Gail nodded. "And that's a good thing. Wes needs encouragement."

"I'll agree with that, but James and Emily are together almost constantly. Going to ball games, movies. They've been out hunting a couple of times. Have you ever thought something might come of this?"

Gail gave him a startled look. "You mean like they'd be drawn together?"

"They *are* drawn together. I'm talking about if she falls in love with him. What would you think of that?"

"What would you think?" Gail countered.

"I don't know," Aaron said heavily. "We know so little about him."

"Well, Emily's too young to make that kind of a choice."

"You don't really think that. When you were her age you were already married!"

"Yes, I guess I was at that," Gail said, smiling. "I just have a hard time thinking of my little girl as that grown-up already." Then she shook her head. "I don't know. I like James, but I hope they don't rush into anything."

★   ★   ★   ★

"Look, Dad, have you seen this story in the paper?" Aaron looked at the newspaper Emily held up to him and read the caption aloud. "Gypsy Smith Holds Meeting in Evansville."

"No, I haven't seen that."

"The meeting starts tonight. I'd love to hear him."

"He's a fine preacher. I've read a little about him. He's a real gypsy from all I can pick up."

"Yes, he's giving his testimony tonight—the first night of the meeting. Could we all go?"

"Your mother and I have to go to a committee meeting at church tonight."

Emily said quickly, "Would it be all right if James and I and Wes go?"

"I suppose so. We could have the Donovans pick us up. They'll be at our meeting, but the weather's pretty bad. It's already snowed a little, and the forecast says there's more coming."

"Well, I think we'll be all right," Emily said, "if we can use the car."

"All right," Aaron said reluctantly. "But not if the weather gets any worse."

★   ★   ★   ★

James pulled the car up next to the curb, and when Emily got out he slid across the seat and followed her out. "It looks like they could put a door on the left-hand side. Ford's a smart man, but I don't think he thought this thing through."

"Oh, don't be so fussy!" Emily teased. "At least we didn't have to ride in a wagon like my grandmother did. She told me that she and Grandfather Davis went to many a meeting in a buggy."

"They were pioneer stock," James said as he walked beside her. "We're much weaker than they were." Then he added, "I admire your grandmother. She's not only a beautiful woman, but I can tell that she's tough."

"I guess all the Winslows have been tough except us modern generation. We're softies."

Wes had not been able to come, as he had a meeting at school. Now as the two walked along, they leaned into the wind. Dark had fallen and the snow was coming down harder. They joined the people who were headed toward the church, but James shook his head. "This weather is getting pretty bad, Emily. Don't you think maybe we should turn around and go back?"

"Oh, don't be such a worrywart!" Emily said. Her eyes sparkled, and she took his arm. "Come on. I wouldn't miss hearing Gypsy Smith for anything."

The two went inside the church, and a smiling usher took them to a seat midway up. "I wish we could go up closer," Emily said. "I like to get close enough to see everything."

"Well, we can see just fine from right here," James said. "And from the way this crowd's filing in, we were lucky to get a seat at all."

Fifteen minutes later the service started. A song leader led the congregation in several hymns, and then he introduced Gypsy Smith. Smith was a stocky man of an indeterminate age. He could have been thirty or sixty. His hair was black, and he had a swarthy complexion and a pair of soulful brown eyes. With his ready smile, he announced, "Before I preach I'd like to sing for you." He nodded at the pianist and the organist, and as they began to play he lifted his voice. He had a beautiful baritone voice that filled the auditorium.

James leaned over and whispered, "If he preaches as well as he sings, he'll be something."

Indeed, the famous evangelist did preach as well as he sang.

He had a warmth and a genuineness about him that drew the whole congregation. He spoke of how as a young boy he had been one of the numerous gypsies wandering around England in wagons. He did not minimize the hardships of that life but laid it out so dramatically that both Emily and James felt sympathy toward him. He went on to tell how he had been converted and had given his life to Jesus. "Since that time," he said, "I have attempted to preach the Gospel of Jesus, and I have done so around the world."

James was moved by the evangelist's testimony, after which Gypsy Smith announced his text—John 3:16. With a big smile, he said, "I'm sure that everyone in this building memorized that verse as a child. It was the first verse I ever memorized, and I've always called it the gospel in miniature. My prayer always is to make the gospel so simple that even a small child can understand it."

And, true to his word, Gypsy kept the sermon simple. He spoke of the need in everyone's heart for a Savior. He quoted scripture after scripture from the Old and New Testaments, stressing the sinfulness of man and every human being's need for God.

"I need not convince you that everyone in the world is a sinner, I'm sure, but somehow," Smith said earnestly, "we have the idea that there are big sins and little sins. But the book of James tells us that, 'Whosoever shall keep the whole law yet offend in one point, the same is guilty of all.' Do you see what that means? We think that murder is a much worse sin than gossip or telling a lie, but according to God, they are both offenses against His law, and we become offenders whether we commit murder or adultery, or tell what we think is a harmless lie. Jesus came because all of us have offended God the Father. He became a baby born in a manger and grew up to become the Lamb of God that would take away the sin of the world."

For some time James Parker sat there listening to the simple message, and he could not help but feel that the words were directed to him. He was not aware that Emily was covertly watching him. So engrossed was he in the message of the evangelist that he forgot her completely.

As for Emily, she had never heard a man imbued with the power of God more than Gypsy Smith. As she looked around the congregation, she saw that every individual there seemed to be riveted to their seats listening to Smith's stirring words. *This man has the power of the Holy Ghost*, she thought, and she uttered up a prayer for James. She knew that he needed God desperately, although he would not admit to that.

Gypsy Smith went on. "We've talked about man's need for salvation. Now I invite you to look on Jesus. He is God's answer to man's offenses." He went on then to speak of the Lord Jesus Christ in glowing terms. He had a poetic turn of mind, this Gypsy Smith, and Emily and James sat entranced.

Finally the evangelist ended his sermon in the customary way. "We give an invitation, but it isn't our invitation. It's not mine, and it's not the invitation of this church," he said softly but with a powerful intensity. "The invitation comes from the Lord Jesus Christ, and it is very simple. He said, 'Come unto me all ye that labor and are heavy laden, and I will give you rest.' If you are here this evening with a heavy heart, if you have a guilty secret, if you have a sin that has put you in bondage, and you're unable to break it—I hold up the Lord Jesus. No matter what the sin or what the bondage, He is stronger than all. You can't break it. You can't escape. You've already tried, haven't you? But Jesus can. He broke the bonds of death and came out of the tomb, and now He invites everyone who is tired and weary and sick to come that he may set you free from all of it. As we sing, will you come and give your heart and soul and body to the Lord Jesus Christ."

The organist played the familiar hymn "Just As I Am" as the congregation stood and joined in. Emily was aware that James was as rigid as a ramrod. She turned to him and saw that his face was contorted with tension, and she prayed, *Oh, God, move on his heart!*

After several verses were sung and many went forward to give their hearts to Christ, Emily said, "James, would you like me to go with you to speak with Brother Smith?"

James did not answer. She could see that his teeth were clenched, and he was staring down at his feet.

"Not now," he muttered.

Emily knew she could say no more.

The service ended, and the two made their way outside. James had not said a word, and after he cranked the car and jumped inside, Emily got in beside him and shut the door. He peered out through the windshield and shook his head. "We shouldn't have stayed," he said briefly. "The road is going to be terrible. I don't even know if we can see it."

"It's only fifteen miles."

James did not answer but pulled the car out into the street.

The snow was coming down in flakes as large as quarters, and as they made their way along the road, both peered out anxiously, for it was getting difficult to see. No traffic was out, and Emily was getting worried. "You may have been right, James. This is terrible!"

They moved on as fast as James dared drive, and after a while he said, "We must be halfway there, but it's getting even worse, I think. I can barely see the road."

Five minutes after he spoke, the road took a turn, but the snow was blowing so hard that he missed it. Emily let out a small cry as the Ford skidded, and then the whole car shuddered as the wheels went into a deep rut at the edge of the road.

James tried to gun his way out of it, but both right wheels were stuck in a deep trench. He shut the engine off and the two sat there in the darkness.

"Well, we're in for it now," he said tersely.

"What can we do?"

"We can sit here and wait until a car comes along. Then we can find a farmer who can pull us out with a team or, even better, a tractor."

The two huddled closer as the cold settled in. Emily felt terrible. "This was all my doing," she said.

Turning to her, James said, "I wanted to come, too. We'll get out of this jam. I've been in lots worse, but I think we might as well try to walk it. Nobody's going to be out driving on this road tonight unless they have to."

The two of them got out, and instantly their feet broke through the snow. "We're not exactly dressed for this," James said. "Come on. We'll do the best we can."

The two walked carefully along the road. Once Emily stumbled, and James reached out and caught her arm. "Are you all right?"

"Yes, I stepped in a hole. It's a good thing I have on lace-up shoes, or I would have lost them both by now."

"My feet are wet and yours are, too. We're gonna freeze out here. It must be close to zero."

The snow was still falling, although not so heavily now. The flakes came down in long, slanting lines, carpeting the earth with a pristine layer of white that gave a ghostly aspect to the landscape. The cloud cover was beginning to break up enough to allow the full moon to peek through at times, and by that light Emily could see the trees sculpted into beautiful snowy forms.

The beauty, however, was lost on her, for the cold struck like a blow as they staggered along the highway, stepping in ruts and chug holes.

"Look. I think there's a house over there."

"There are no lights in it," Emily hesitated. "They've probably all gone to bed."

"We'll have to wake them up, then. We've got to have help. We can't stay out in this weather. We'll freeze to death."

The two turned off the main road and followed a twisting lane that seemed to meander aimlessly, eventually coming to a stop in front of a two-story frame house. The snow was several inches deep now, and as they stepped onto the wraparound porch, Emily sighed with relief. She waited while James banged on the door. They both waited, but there was no sound. He tried several times and then turned to her. His face was tense. "Nobody's home. It may be a deserted house."

"What'll we do now?" Emily asked.

"We've got to find some shelter from this weather soon." James walked to the edge of the porch, looked around, and said, "There's a barn back there. We can get in there. I wish we had brought some blankets from the car."

They made their way, breaking through the crust of snow. When they reached the barn, James had some trouble opening the door, for it was blocked with a drift nearly a foot deep. He leaned his weight against it and managed to wedge it open enough so they could squeeze through. James pulled a box of matches from his inside pocket. He struck one and held it up in the darkness. By the feeble yellow that emanated from the single match, he walked around until he spotted what he was looking for. "Bingo. Here's a lantern. I hope it's got oil in it."

Emily watched while he fumbled with the lantern and heard his grunt of satisfaction. "There," he said. "That'll help a little bit."

He hung the lantern back up on the nail and blew the match out. He held it until it was cold and then dropped it in his pocket. Looking around, he said, "I think that people still live here. This barn's not deserted."

Emily shivered. "They may be gone on a trip."

"Well, we'll have to stay here until daylight, that's for sure. Let's see what we can find."

The search did not take long. He found plenty of hay in the loft. He climbed down and walked to one of the stalls and said, "Look, horse blankets! They may smell a little ripe, but they'll keep us warm." There were three of them, and James said, "Here, wrap up in this blanket. I'll throw down enough straw for a bed so we can cover up. At least we won't have to sleep on the ground."

"You think we'll have to stay here all night?" Emily said with alarm.

"The only other choice is to walk down the road until we find somebody. I may do that, but you can't. Let's get you fixed up first. Then I'll think about it."

James raked straw until he had made a large pile. "Wrap this blanket around you and lie down."

"There's no way to make a fire, I suppose."

"Not in here."

Emily wrapped the blanket around her and lay down. James put another one over her, covering her feet. "It smells horsy," she said.

"Not surprised." Wrapping the other blanket around him, James lay down beside her and felt her shivering. "It's cold in here. The blankets help a little bit, but I'm afraid it's going to be a cold night."

They lay there silently, and Emily was acutely aware of the rank odors of the hay and of the smell of manure. The wind seemed to be brushing against the outside of the barn, almost as if it were saying, "Let me in." Fear came over her, and she whispered, "I've never been in trouble quite like this before."

"I have," James said. He moved closer and threw his arm around her, sharing his blanket with her. "Three blankets are better than two," he said. His lips were close to her cheek, and he said, "I had to spend the night once in a boxcar in North Dakota. Now, that was cold. No hay, no blankets, nothing but a thin coat. I kept myself awake—afraid I'd freeze to death. I still remember how my teeth chattered. They sounded like dice clicking together."

"What were you doing there?"

"Oh, hoboing."

As they shared the warmth, Emily realized that she had no fear at all of James himself. The thought came to her, *What if this had happened with Buck Leatherwood or somebody like that? I'd be helpless*. Thankful for James's protection, she snuggled against him, feeling the warmth of his body. "I'm getting warmer," she said.

"Good. We'll make it. You're just not used to roughing it like this. We had a terrible cold spell once in the trenches. I thought we were all going to die. Jared and I wrapped up in whatever blankets we had, just about like this. We laughed about how close we'd become! But our kidding around was just to keep away the fear."

His story sobered Emily as she thought of her brother, and the two fell silent again. She was aware of the warmth of his breath on her cheek. He did not speak for a long time, and she finally asked, "What are you thinking?"

"I was just remembering a time once when I was in Tennessee. It was night, and I hadn't been able to get a ride, so I just kept on walking. It was summer. Warm, not like this, and I passed by some houses. All of them had lights on, and I kept looking in. Some of the people were eating supper, and I could see them. Others were in the living room just being together talking, I suppose. I remember thinking, 'Those people have everything.'"

Emily felt a rush of compassion. "Why haven't you ever married?"

"I've got nothing to offer a woman, Emily. You ought to know that."

"That's not true."

He turned his head suddenly to look at her, and by the yellow light of the lantern he saw that her eyes were wide open, and she was watching him carefully. His arm was around her, and she was pressed close against him. She was warmer now and not so afraid, and as he held her, he said, "I shouldn't have let us get in this kind of a mess."

"It's not your fault. I was the one who wanted to come."

James watched the small changes around her lips as she spoke. He remembered the sweetness of those lips when they had kissed under the mistletoe at her grandmother's house. The lantern caught the red tints in her hair, and he said without meaning to, "You're a beautiful woman, Emily."

She reached out and put her hand on the back of his neck. "I would be terrified with most men in a situation like this, but I'm not afraid of you."

"Maybe you should be."

"No, you'd never hurt me, James."

Her confidence warmed him, and he said, "I've never known anybody like you." He leaned forward and kissed her lightly, and then he drew his head back. "Could I ask you something, Emily?"

"Yes."

"I don't know how to say this. You've got your life planned out. You're going to college next year and you're going to become a writer."

He broke off suddenly, and Emily half gave him a shake. "What are you going to ask?"

"I've never felt about any woman as I do about you. When I first came here I thought you were just a kid, but you're not.

You're a fine woman. And I was wanting to ask you if I could court you."

The words sounded strange, even artificial, to Emily. "Court me? What do you mean?"

"I mean, could we just do some fun things together? Not be engaged or anything like that. Nothing serious."

Emily Winslow sensed a tremendous void of loneliness in this man. He was like no other man she had ever met. All of the men she had known had carried the full weight of a family history and of friendship, but James had no family. He had no family expectations to live up to, no future plans. He just wanted her companionship. She reached up and put her hand on his cheek and whispered, "Yes, you may court me, James."

★ ★ ★ ★

"I'm sorry if you were worried, Mom and Dad, but there was absolutely nothing we could do."

Emily stood beside James in the hallway. They had come in to find her parents waiting for her, and Aaron had spoken almost harshly. "Where have you two been?"

Emily had not allowed James to speak. She had quickly told about the car sliding into the ditch, but she did not tell them about the time in the barn. Instead she said hurriedly, "So we had to walk until we got help."

"I'm awfully sorry, too. I can't tell you both how bad I feel," James said.

"It wasn't his fault," Emily said. "He wanted to come home before the service, but I wouldn't let him."

"How'd you get out of the ditch?"

"James found a farmer, and he pulled us out with his tractor. But it took time and there was no telephone."

Gail knew that Aaron was angry, and she herself was concerned. "I'm afraid you were very unwise, Emily."

"I know it, Mother," Emily said contritely.

"Well, no harm came of it," Aaron said. He heaved a sigh of

relief and put his hand on Emily's shoulder. "You don't know how we worried."

"Yes I do, Dad," Emily said quickly. "I'm so sorry."

Gail watched Emily's face, and then her gaze shifted to James. She said nothing, but later when she was alone with Emily, she asked, "Were you very afraid when you were isolated out there?"

"Not for a minute, Mother." Emily knew what was on her mother's mind. "I thought to myself when we were stuck there, 'If this were anybody but James, I'd be in trouble. And I'd be afraid.' But I wasn't afraid for one moment. He did everything he could to take care of me, and I kept waiting for him to do something that, you know, was out of line. But he never did."

Gail studied her daughter's face, and then she said a strange thing. "Be careful with James."

"What do you mean, Mother?"

"I mean the heart is a deceitful thing."

"My heart?"

"Anyone's heart."

Emily did not answer. She felt her parents' disapproval, and it hurt her. But she did not know what to say that would change their minds. "I trust James," she said.

"Be careful," her mother said again, then turned and left Emily standing there wondering what her admonition meant.

CHAPTER TWELVE

BEHIND THE MASK

★ ★ ★ ★

Burrow's Jewelry Store was practically empty. Only one customer besides Aaron and James moved along the glass cases, and the two clerks looked bored stiff.

"I'd hate to be a jewelry salesman," Aaron remarked, taking in the expressions on the faces of the two clerks.

"Why's that?" James inquired.

"After the Christmas rush, all through the month of January, nobody's buying jewelry. They might as well close up. I can't imagine standing on my feet all day long trying to look busy when there is absolutely nothing to do."

It was the twenty-second day of January, and the two men had come shopping for gifts for Emily's birthday. Aaron had known that James had very little money, so he had approached him by saying, "I haven't been paying you much money for your apprenticeship, James." He had given him a check, and James had stared at it and then had shaken his head. "That's too much," he had said.

But Aaron had insisted, and now the two moved slowly along. Aaron had already bought his gift at Miner's Department Store, a beautiful brush and comb inlaid with ivory, but James had seen nothing that he particularly liked. They had wandered into several shops, and now James stopped before a line of pencils and pens. "That's a beautiful set," he said. "But it's out of my price range."

Aaron looked at the set and said, "Go ahead, if that's what you'd like to get Emily."

"No. I've got barely enough," James said.

The clerk, a short, heavyset man with a pale complexion and light blue eyes, approached them. "May I help you?" he asked.

"Would it be possible to get that set engraved?" James asked.

"Why, yes, sir. We can have it back tomorrow."

"I'm afraid it would have to be today. It's for a birthday gift, and I've waited until almost too late."

"Well, I think that can be arranged," the clerk said quickly. He pulled a card from his pocket and said, "Just write what you would like on here."

James wrote a few words and handed it to the man.

"Come back at five o'clock," the clerk said. "They'll both be ready by then. A beautiful set, I might say. The finest I've ever seen."

"That's a good gift for a writer," Aaron remarked as they left the store. "Emily is very serious about a writing career."

"Yes, she is. I don't know much about writing, but it seems to me she has a natural talent."

"Well, I know a little bit, and all prejudice aside," Aaron smiled, "I think she does. But it's a hard, competitive profession. It's like professional sports. Every young man wants to pitch for the Yankees or the Braves, but only a few of them will make it."

The two walked along the main street, and Aaron spoke of Wes and his desire to be a photographer. "I think that's even a more competitive field than writing. As a matter of fact, I don't think I can name one famous photographer."

"I can't either, but someone has to take those pictures. Wes does such a great job. You've got two fine children, Mr. Winslow." He hesitated, then said, "I've told you before, but I'll have to say again how much I appreciate all you've done for me."

"Don't speak of it. After what you did for my son, I'm pleased to be able to do anything I can." As Aaron said this, he noticed an odd expression cross the face of James Parker that he could not identify. It seemed to be a mix of tension and something very close to fear. He could not imagine what was going on in the young man's mind. As a rule Aaron was good at knowing people, but despite the openness that James often displayed, there was a side of him Aaron could not understand—a wall that he could not pass through. He had spoken of this to Gail, and she had agreed. It troubled both of them. Now as they headed for home, Aaron tried to put such thoughts behind him. "You'd better go by and get that gift early," he said to James as they arrived back at the house. "The party's at six o'clock."

"I'll do that, sir," James said.

"Gail is cooking up a monstrous meal. She always does for every one of our birthdays. We get so stuffed we can't even look at the presents."

"I'm looking forward to it," James said with a half smile. "Will there be anyone else there?"

"No, just the family. When the children were younger we used to have parties for them, but now we just want the time together."

★ ★ ★ ★

Emily pulled her petticoat over her head and then plucked her party dress from a hanger. It was a white knit frock with a square neck. It had ruffles on the sleeve and around the hem and was a little fancy for just an evening at home, but it was part of the Winslow tradition that they would all dress up in their best for their birthday celebrations. She slipped on her black kidskin slippers with the single strap and then went over to the vanity and began brushing her hair. As she ran the brush down her shining red hair she studied herself in the mirror, trying to decide if she looked any older. As soon as she finished, she got up and went downstairs.

Going into the kitchen she found her mother putting the finishing touches on the dinner.

"My goodness it smells good in here," she said, giving her mother a hug. "Can I help you with anything?"

"You might mash the potatoes. They're all cooked."

"All right, Mom." While she was beating the boiled potatoes, Emily was surprised when her mother asked rather cautiously, "How do you feel about James?"

Quickly Emily looked up. "Why, I like him very much." When her mother made no reply, she said, "Why do you ask?"

"I thought you might be attracted to him. You spend so much time with him."

Emily flushed slightly. "I . . . I've become very fond of him, Mom."

At that moment Wes burst into the room. He was wearing a pair of gray flannel slacks and a navy blue sweater over a white shirt. "Hey, what's holding the dinner up? I'm starved to death."

"I bet your very first words were 'I'm starved to death,'" Emily said. "I think we're almost ready, aren't we, Mom?"

"Yes. Wes, help get all of this food on the table."

Emily finished with the potatoes, scooped them into a china serving bowl, and carried them into the dining room. James and her father had already come in and taken a seat. She smiled as her father said, "Here's the birthday girl. You look beautiful."

"Thank you, Dad."

"A new dress?" James asked.

"No, I've had it almost a year. I guess I must be full-grown finally. For years now it seemed that every time I bought a dress I outgrew it the next day."

"You look very nice," James said warmly.

As the table began to fill up with steaming bowls and platters, the family was ready to eat. After Aaron said a prayer for God's blessings on Emily on this special day, they dove into the sumptuous meal of roast chicken with apple-and-walnut stuffing, mashed potatoes and gravy, green bean casserole, and fresh-baked bread. When they were almost finished, Gail said, "Save some room for cake and ice cream."

"I can't do that, Mom," Wes said. He puffed his cheeks out. "I'm about to explode right now."

"I imagine you'll be able to arm-wrestle some cake and ice cream down," Aaron said dryly.

Turning to James, he said, "Let's move on into the parlor. We always open presents there."

Leaving the dishes where they were, they all went into the parlor and took a seat, except Emily. She stood beside a table that was topped with several gaily colored packages.

"Open mine first, Emily," Wes urged.

Emily looked at the largest package wrapped in showy paper and topped with a huge bow. She started to pick it up, and then her eyes opened wide. "My goodness! What is it? An anvil?"

"Open it up," Wes urged. "If you don't like it, I'll shoot you."

Emily laughed and took the bow off. Inside was a box, and when she opened the lid, she exclaimed, "The works of Charles Dickens! All of them! Oh, what a wonderful gift, but you must have spent a fortune for it."

"If you like it, that's all that counts," Wes said. He stood up as Emily came over and gave him a hug.

"I can't think of anything I'd like better," Emily said. "I've checked out Dickens books so much from the library, they hate to see me coming."

Emily insisted on pulling out every volume. They were well bound, and she opened one, saying, "I love the smell of books— the paper and ink—and just holding them in my hands."

The books were dutifully admired, and then Emily picked up the smallest package. "I've always heard the best things come in small packages." She looked at the card and said, "Thank you, James."

"You haven't even opened it yet. You might hate it."

Emily shook her head and smiled, then removed the paper. Inside was a small plush felt-covered box, and when she opened it she did not speak for a moment. She looked up at James and then shook her head. "You shouldn't have done this, James. You shouldn't have."

"What is it?" Wes said. "Let me see."

Everyone crowded around, and Emily picked up the gold pen and read the inscription aloud. Written in beautiful script, it said, "To Emily Winslow—Proverbs 31:25."

"Proverbs 31:25? I don't know that one," Aaron said.

James quoted the verse with a smile. " 'Many daughters have done virtuously, but thou excellest them all.' "

"See if it writes," Wes urged.

"Well, it doesn't have any ink in it," James said quickly. "I didn't have time for that."

"It's the most beautiful set I've ever seen. I'll keep it always—and the inscription is beautiful!" Emily's eyes were bright as diamonds as she looked at James.

"Just win the Pulitzer Prize with it." He smiled back at her.

Emily moved toward him as if to embrace him but put her hand out instead, which he took. "Thank you so much," she said, squeezing his hand fiercely. Her eyes glistened as she ran her hands over the smooth surface of the gold pen.

Emily had opened several more packages when suddenly the doorbell rang. Aaron frowned. "Who could that be? I'll go see."

He left the parlor and turned down the hall. When he opened the front door, he saw a tall man wearing the insignia of a captain in the United States Army. "Mr. Winslow?"

"Yes, I'm Aaron Winslow."

"My name is Ramsey, Mr. Winslow. Clark Ramsey."

"Captain Ramsey? Why, Jared spoke of you so often."

"Yes, he was in my company in France." Captain Ramsey hesitated, then said, "I hate to barge in, but I was going to Washington, and I hoped I would catch you at home if I just stopped by. I have a little business with you."

Aaron looked puzzled. "Why, of course, Captain. Come in." When Ramsey stepped inside, Aaron said, "Come into the parlor. We're having a little family birthday celebration."

"I could come back later—"

"Oh no. We're about through. My family will want to meet you. You were such a good friend to Jared."

"Well, if you're certain it wouldn't be an imposition. But I think my business will please you."

Puzzled by the officer's appearance, Aaron led the way into the parlor. "We'll take a little break in the celebration, Emily. I want you all to meet Captain Clark Ramsey. This is my wife, Gail, my son, Wes, and my daughter, Emily. It's her birthday we're celebrating."

Momentarily he forgot James, who was sitting behind him in a chair.

"I'm glad to know all of you," Captain Ramsey said. "I won't take much of your time."

"We thank you so much for the beautiful letter you wrote about Jared, Captain," Gail said. "I put it with the rest of Jared's belongings that we're keeping."

Captain Ramsey reached into his inner pocket and pulled out a small box covered with felt. It looked a great deal like the box Emily's writing set had come in. "Nothing can ever take away the sacrifice you have made, but I wanted to bring you this myself." He opened the box and held it out toward Aaron and Gail. They stared at it, and the officer said softly, "It's the Medal of Honor, sir. I know you and your family couldn't be prouder of your son, but this medal is just a memorial from his country. I don't think I know of any Medal of Honor more richly deserved."

Aaron's hand was shaking as he reached out. He took the box and held it and put his arm around Gail. Wes and Emily came to either side of them, and they all stared down at the medal.

"I have the written citation here that gives the details of your son's heroism," Captain Ramsey said. He handed the letter to Gail, who took it and opened it, and they all read the details. By the time she finished, her hands were shaking, too.

"Your son was the best soldier I ever saw, and that's saying a lot," Captain Ramsey said. "I missed him terribly and I still do. It gives me such pleasure to present this medal to you."

At that moment Captain Ramsey was aware, for the first time, that another person was in the room. He turned and put his eyes on James Parker, and Emily saw his face change. He had been smiling, but the smile vanished instantly, a hard glint appeared in his eyes, and his lips grew tight.

"Parker! What are you doing here?"

Aaron was taken aback by the antagonism in Captain Ramsey's voice. "Well, you know James, of course."

"I know him," Ramsey said harshly. "What's he doing here?"

Gail said, "What's wrong, Captain? We have letters telling us how James went out on the battlefield to carry Jared off when he was wounded, and Jared asked us to show kindness to him if he ever came here."

Emily stared at Captain Ramsey and then turned to look at Parker. The blood had drained from Parker's face. He did not speak a word, but he looked as if he had been struck a terrible blow.

She turned to the officer. "Captain Ramsey, what's wrong?"

"I don't know the circumstances here," Ramsey said in a clipped voice, "but this man was no friend to your son, Mr. Winslow."

"What do you mean, Captain?"

"I mean James Parker was known in the company as a liar and a thief—and a coward. He never carried your son off the battlefield. Parker there ran away under fire and took a bullet. It was Jared who ran out to get him. He carried Parker back, and just as he got to the trench, he took the bullet that eventually killed him."

Emily stood immobile, her throat almost closed, unable to speak a word. She whispered, "James—" and then when she saw his face, the truth was written there. "Is this true?" she said.

"He'll never tell you the truth, Miss Winslow. He never told the truth a single time. I did a little looking into his background after he was dishonorably discharged, and the best I can tell is he's been a crook all his life. Several of Jared's friends tried to stop him from going out to get him, but Jared just shook his head and reportedly said, 'Maybe. But Christ died for him.' So he went out after him, and that's how he died. For a worthless cur."

Wes uttered a strangled cry, and then he threw himself at James, striking out at his face. His father stepped forward quickly and pulled him back. "Never mind, Wes," he said, his voice cold. He looked at Parker and said, "I want you out of my house. Get your things and leave immediately."

Everyone watched for one instant as James stood. His eyes went around to the faces of the family that had taken him in. Then he turned and moved swiftly out. As soon as he left the room, Captain Ramsey said quickly, "I'm sorry. I came here to give you something beautiful and wonderful. I didn't mean to—"

"It's not your fault, Captain. Would you mind sitting down and telling us more about all of what happened?"

"Certainly, sir. I wanted to give you more details."

They all sat down, and Captain Ramsey began to speak. He had talked for only a few moments about Jared when they all heard the front door close. To Emily it was like the clang of a steel door that was shutting something out but was also shutting something in. She forced herself to listen as Captain Ramsey spoke of her brother. Once she glanced across at Wes and saw the pain and disillusionment that marred his youthful expression. She saw her parents also and knew that James Parker had left a mark on their family that nothing would ever erase.

★ ★ ★ ★

Emily was standing at the window when a soft knock came at her door. She had half expected that one of her parents or both would come. "Come in," she said, and when she turned she saw her father enter.

He came over to stand beside her, and then he put his arm around her. "Are you all right?"

"No, I'm not, Dad. I don't think I ever will be."

Aaron studied her face. He would have done anything to protect his children from such an outrageous betrayal of trust, but there was nothing he could do about it. He did not speak for a while, then he murmured, "It's terribly hard now, but it will be better given time."

"No, it won't. I was a fool!"

"Don't talk like that!"

"Why not? I *was* a fool to fall for a man like that! I must have no sense at all!"

Aaron spoke softly. He could feel the tremor in Emily's body and knew that she was cut inside, as if with razors. "I don't want you to let James's deception ruin your spirit, Emily. Right now all of us are struggling with hatred."

"You too, Dad?"

"Of course. You weren't the only one he deceived. We all wanted to believe him. He was very good at making people believe whatever he said."

"I'll always hate him."

"If you do, you won't hurt him. He's gone forever. You'll never see him again, but you'll hurt yourself."

Emily leaned against her father. He put her head down on his chest as he turned to hold her in his arms, and for a long time the two stood there. Finally, with her voice muffled, she said, "I can't change how I feel. I don't think I'll ever change, Dad."

"You'll change, Emily, in time."

"I'll never be able to believe a man again."

"Now, now, that's foolish talk. Not all men are as deceitful as James Parker." Finally he kissed her cheek and said, "If you want to talk about it, I think it would be good. Especially if you'd talk to your mother."

"All right, Dad."

As soon as her father had left the room, Emily straightened and whispered fiercely, "I'll hate James Parker as long as I live! He killed my brother!"

PART THREE

MAY 1922–AUGUST 1923

★ ★ ★ ★

CHAPTER THIRTEEN

SUMMA CUM LAUDE

★   ★   ★   ★

Emily Winslow sat in a row of folding chairs in the gymnasium of Leighton College. The Class of 1922 had gathered there along with parents, grandparents, and friends to be thrust out into the world by the school president and the faculty. Emily had completed her four years of work in only three years by going to summer school and taking a full load. Now as she thought back over the past three years, it seemed to her that a different Emily Winslow rose when the dean asked all the graduates to rise. As she moved forward slowly listening to the dean call out the names, she had the feeling that the young woman of eighteen who began college had been metamorphosed into someone entirely different by the age of twenty-one. For some reason this thought disturbed her, yet at the same time she knew she could face the future with a determination that had not belonged to the younger Emily Winslow.

The names were reeled off until there were only three graduates in front of her. After those three moved forward, she then heard the dean announce, "Emily Winslow, summa cum laude."

As Emily stepped forward, she heard a shrill yipping sound, and Wes's voice seemed to echo through the entire gymnasium. "That's my sister!"

The audience had been asked to hold their applause until the end, but now, following Wes's shrill yell, the applause came in waves as Emily took her diploma and shook hands with Dr. Sanford. He said to her, "I'm proud of you, Emily. Very proud!" His words of praise gave her a warm feeling, and as she crossed the stage, she looked out in the audience and spotted her parents and Wes. They were all smiling, and Wes was holding his arms extended upward with both thumbs in the air. She returned their smiles, waved her diploma, and put her own thumb in the air.

Emily stepped down off the platform and took her seat alongside David Wayne and Sarah Wilton, clutching her diploma tightly. She was more proud of it than the articles and stories she had gotten published during her three years in college. Quickly she thought of how hard she had worked—all the late nights of study and few vacations as she churned out ream after ream of papers. Some had found their way to the wastebasket, but her father had warned her to never throw anything way. *"You never know when you're going to use it again. Maybe just one sentence or one idea. Keep it all."*

For the most part, she had taken his advice and had managed to get published in a number of magazines. Several women's magazines accepted her short stories, and she also published an article on the city of Richmond, accompanied by Wes's photographs, in a travel magazine. While in college she found she had the most success with her nonfiction work. None of the publications ever paid her a great deal of money, but she now had a thick résumé and proven success in getting published.

Her thoughts were interrupted when the president of the college said, "That concludes the list of graduates. Let's give a tremendous hand of applause to these fine young people."

Emily stood with her class as the applause rolled on, and for one instant she was slightly confused. *What comes next?* she wondered.

Her goal in life had always been to be a writer, and she was proud of her successes so far. But now that college was over she needed a full-time job. Where would she work? Who would hire her?

The college band began to play the recessional, and as Emily walked out of the gymnasium holding her head high, she was struck with the unpleasant memory of James Parker. A deep bitterness and anger welled up in her, searing her insides like a hot coal. For the first six months after Parker had left, her spirit would often be shaken, and she would grow almost frantic with bitterness. Throughout her years in college she had learned to forcibly shove those thoughts out of her mind, and sometimes she could go for months without thinking of him in such a way.

But now as she marched out, keeping pace with the other graduates, it all came sweeping back, draining away all the joy of her graduation. The struggle was fierce, but by the time her parents and brother had come to meet with her outside in the bright May sunlight, she had gotten ahold of herself, forcing the painful memory back into some deep recess. It felt like a demon that was kept under lock and key but managed to escape from time to time to torment her with a mocking smile and glinting eye.

"Well, congratulations, daughter."

Aaron Winslow put his arms around her and picked her up, squeezing her until she gasped, "Daddy, don't squeeze me to death!"

"I can't help it. I'm so proud of you I wanted to shout along with Wes. I almost did."

"I'm glad you restrained yourself," Gail laughed, "because I almost shouted, too. Wouldn't that have been something? The Winslow family losing it all."

"I still think we ought to do it," Wes said. He put his fingers in his mouth, preparing to let loose a shrill blast, but Emily reached out and jerked at his wrist.

"Don't you dare, Wes!" she admonished him.

"Aw, sis, I'm so proud of you! I just don't know how to tell you!"

"Thanks, Wes. I was just as proud of you at your high school graduation, and you'll put me to shame when you go to college."

"How am I going to do that?" Wes grinned. "You can't get higher than summa cum laude. Besides, I don't want to go to college."

"Let's not start that old argument," Gail said softly. "I think we ought to celebrate and buy the most expensive meal we can find."

"I was thinking we'd go get a hamburger down at Mom's Place," Aaron said, winking at Wes.

Wes, at the age of nineteen, was one inch taller than Aaron and resembled his father in a startling fashion. His mother had told him, "If you want to know what your father looked like at nineteen, just look in the mirror, son."

"I don't want to eat at Mom's Place," Wes complained. "I'm with you, Mom. Let's spend all of Dad's money and buy a steak at George's."

"That'll take my war pension," Aaron grinned, "but lead on, McDuff."

As Emily left with them she pulled off her mortarboard and ran her hand over her hair. She had finally adjusted to being called "Red" and brushing off remarks about the tempers of red-headed women. Now as she shook her hair down her back, she said, "I feel kind of empty."

"I guess that happens after you look forward to something for so long," her mother replied. "Then it's gone. But you'll always remember these years."

"And besides, big opportunities are coming up," Wes said. "You've got your first Pulitzer to look forward to." He grinned and reached over and put his arms around her, squeezing her hard. Then he shook his head and took her arm. "Come on, Summa Cum Laude. I'll show you how to put a steak away!"

★   ★   ★   ★

Donald Sutton leaned back in his chair and stared across his battered desk. The desk had become a joke at the *Richmond Daily News*. Everyone had urged Sutton to get rid of it and buy a new one, but he had stubbornly clung to it, despite its nicks and scrapes and cigarette burns. The drawers would not work half the time, but all that did not matter to Donald Sutton, for he was a conservative man who clung to tradition. He liked old things better than new.

Now as he studied the young woman on the other side of him, he gave the impression of solidity. He was a burly man with black hair that had a startling white streak running from front to back a half inch wide. His eyes were black as ink, and the cigar he held in his right hand was as much a part of him as were his fingers. His other arm had been left in France during the last days of war. Blue smoke curled around his head and permeated everything within a twenty-foot radius. His only extravagance, as far as Emily could tell, was expensive cigars.

Emily had learned to trust Sutton, but she was nervous now as she sat on the chair across from him. She had been working on the paper for only two months, but she was bored out of her skull with her job. She had expected that working on a newspaper would be exciting, and she had come with high hopes, but she had quickly learned that she was not to be trusted with any important stories. So far she had covered the Richmond flower show, City Council meetings, and the annual convention of the Daughters of the American Revolution. When she had arrived at work this very morning, she found she'd been assigned the local dog show. It had been the proverbial final straw. She had marched into Sutton's office and demanded to talk to him. At his gruff assent, she had sat down, and now as he looked at her with his ebony eyes, she knew her chances of getting anything out of this man were small. One reporter had told her he had worked for four years before Sutton had trusted him with anything significant. Nevertheless, Emily had drawn up her courage and now said, "Mr. Sutton, you know how much I appreciate your giving me a job, but—"

"But you're bored, and you want to cover the latest ax murder."

Emily had to laugh, and she was relieved to see Sutton's lips turn up in something close to a smile. "Exactly what I want. Is there an ax murder to report?"

"No, and if there were, I wouldn't put you on it."

"But, Mr. Sutton, give me a chance. How can I ever get anywhere unless I can write about something more exciting than the swine selection at the county fair?"

Sutton puffed on the cigar without touching it. He leaned forward, placing his single hand flat on the mats of paper before him, and studied the young woman. He had liked her spunk, for she had appeared at his office one day without preamble and said, "Mr. Sutton, you've got to hire me. I'll do anything you say. I've got to go to work. I've got to learn to write." Sutton had tried to dismiss her with a wave of his remaining hand, but she had stubbornly stayed before him arguing, not stridently, but with a stubbornness that pleased him. He was a stubborn man himself, and finally he had said, "I don't have time to argue with you. I'll try you for a week. After that I'll probably fire you."

The week had passed and several more, so that now Emily had come once more to beard the lion.

She began to speak, telling him it was not money, and she did not mind long hours, but she needed a challenge.

"I think the dog show's a challenge."

Emily stared at Sutton. "A challenge! Any high school sophomore could write that up."

"No, they couldn't. It's harder to write about dog shows than it is about ax murderers. Everybody wants to read about an ax murder. Who wants to read about a bunch of mangy mutts?"

Emily could not help smiling at the editor's opinion. "But I—"

"You do a good job on the mutts, and the next time something bigger comes up, I may give you a chance. If you can't write about mutts, you can't write about anything. Now, be off. I'm busy."

"All right, Mr. Sutton," Emily said, clenching her teeth. "And you're going to get a story about mutts like you've never read in your whole life."

"Good. Close the door on your way out."

★　★　★　★

Cap'n Brown met Emily with a rush. He reared up on her as he had done a million times, and when she said, "Down, Cap'n," he simply leaned forward and tried to lick her face. Nothing would break him of this habit. Upon the advice of a veterinarian, she had tried stepping on his paws, but the dog had merely howled so mournfully she could not stand it. Finally she shoved him aside and said, "If you don't leave me alone, I'm not going to give you any supper."

Cap'n Brown heard "supper." He had an amazing vocabulary, and any word connected with food was instantly recognized. He loosed a staccato symphony of short, happy barks and followed her into the house. When she went to the kitchen, she reached into the cabinet and pulled out a bag of dog biscuits. Taking several in her hand, she said, "Sit," and when he held his nose up in the air, she balanced one of the biscuits on his nose. He quivered with ecstasy but did not move. "Eat!" she commanded. The biscuit disappeared, and Cap'n Brown's tail thumped the floor. Emily fed him several more.

Her mother, who was sitting across the room, said, "You're going to fatten that dog too much. It's bad for him."

"I know it is, but I can't help it. When he looks at me with those mournful eyes, I think he's starving to death."

"He'd look at you with mournful eyes if he'd just eaten a thirty-two-ounce T-bone steak," Gail smiled. "Cap'n, you get out and go chase a squirrel." She went over to open the screen door, and Cap'n marched out with his tail between his legs, the picture of rejection.

Gail laughed. "If they gave awards for dog actors, Cap'n Brown would win. He'll try anything to get sympathy. Look at him now. You'd think he was going to his own funeral."

"I know it. He's just awful."

"How did it go at the office today?"

"You would have been proud of me, Mom." She picked an apple off of a dish and bit into it, then sat down on a high stool beside the kitchen counter. "I walked right in and demanded that Mr. Sutton give me a more important assignment." She took another bite and mumbled around it. "You should have seen me. I stood right up to him and his crummy old cigar."

"Did he give you a better assignment?"

"No, he didn't. He said that anybody could write about exciting events, but it took a real writer to make a dog show interesting."

Gail laughed, turned, and opened the oven door. Taking two potholders, she pulled out a deep dish and set it on the cabinet. "I guess you showed him."

Emily sighed and chewed on the apple slowly. "I don't know about that, but I'm going to write something about the dog show that'll make him pay attention."

"What can you say about a dog show?"

Emily nibbled at the apple for a time and then smiled. "I think I'll talk about how ugly the dogs are."

"Emily, you can't do that!"

"Sure I can. Mr. Sutton thinks they're ugly. He called them mutts."

"But the people who own the dogs will have your head on a platter."

"Well, they might, but Mr. Sutton will learn that I know how to stir people with my writing. Mom, let me help you with supper."

"No, you go on and lie down for a while. I know you're tired."

"I'm not tired, but I do need to work on that story that's giving me so much trouble."

"Oh, by the way, there were three letters for you in the mail. I put them out on the table in the hall."

"Thanks, Mom. I'll do the dishes tonight."

Leaving the kitchen, Emily took another bite of the apple and stopped to pick up the letters. The first one was from her cousin Hannah Winslow, who was making quite a career for herself in New York City. Joshua, her brother, was there now, too, and the pair of them were enjoying New York tremendously. They both urged Emily to come and join them.

The second letter she picked up was from a magazine, and she knew without opening it that it contained a rejection. She opened the envelope by splitting it with her fingernails and read the familiar words. "Thank you for sending us your work. We found it does not meet our needs at the present time. Please try us again."

Emily shook her head ruefully. She had not really counted on an acceptance, and suddenly she smiled. She had gotten one form letter like this that ended with the words, "Please try us again," but the editor had carefully crossed that out. It had crushed her for a time, but her father had found the letter vastly amusing. He still teased her about that.

She glanced down at the third letter, but suddenly a chill came over her.

"I know this writing—it's from James Parker."

She stood immobile, and the bitterness that she had kept carefully locked away for so long escaped. This time it was worse, for the very sight of his writing brought back memories of the letters that the family had received while Jared was in the hospital—those lying, deceitful letters she had believed so implicitly.

Her hands shook as she opened the envelope and took out a single sheet of paper. She stared at it, and then her lips pressed together, leaving a white line. She ground her teeth together and closed her eyes, struggling to control the fury that rose in her. She walked mechanically down the hall and went upstairs to her room and closed the door behind her.

★　★　★　★

"What's so great about this new camera you're interested in, son?" Aaron asked. He picked up a piece of fried chicken and nibbled at it.

"Why, Dad, it's a Kodak. It's the best camera in the world!"

"What does it do besides take pictures?"

Wes stared at his father. He could never be sure whether his father was serious or not. "Why, it takes better pictures."

"I don't see how some of your pictures could be any better than the ones you've already made."

Wes stared at his father and then laughed. "Why did you want to get an Oldsmobile instead of a Ford?"

"Because it's a better car," Gail said. "And I'm sure that Kodak camera you're talking about would enable you to take better pictures."

"It ought to for the price they're asking for it," Aaron said.

"Well, Dad, a man needs good tools. The competition's pretty tough in the world of professional photography."

The entire family was proud of Wes, for he had won a number of contests. He had also received commissions to photograph weddings and other events, and his pictures of Richmond had been published in *Travel America* along with Emily's article. Both Emily and her mother knew that Aaron would get the camera for Wes.

Emily had spoken very little during the meal, and when Gail brought out the dessert, she said, "None for me, Mom."

Aaron looked at her. "What's the matter? You love blackberry cobbler."

"I'm not very hungry, Dad."

Aaron then shot a glance at his wife. Both of them knew this young woman very well, and now they saw that she was upset. "What is it, Emily? Some trouble at the paper? Did you lose your job?"

"No, I didn't lose my job." She hesitated, then reached into the pocket of her skirt. "This letter came today." She hesitated for a moment, then shook her head. "It's from James Parker."

Instantly the other three Winslows stared at her as she opened it, pulled out the single sheet of paper, and read, " '*I have hesitated to write this letter, but I must. I've had a change come into my life and am now not the same man that you knew. I'm trying to build a new life for myself, and I would like to ask for your forgiveness. I know this will be difficult, and I will understand if you do not feel you can grant it. But I'm going to everyone that I hurt in the past. I know I hurt you more than anyone, so please forgive me if you can.*' "

Wes clamped his lips together, then shook his head. "He's got a nerve after what he did!"

Aaron was quiet for a moment, then looked over toward Gail. Something unseen passed between them, and he said, "I think we'll have to forgive him."

Emily's head snapped up. Her eyes seemed to blaze for a moment. "Forgive him! I'll never forgive him! He killed my brother!" She got up and threw the letter on the table, turned, and ran out of the dining room.

Wes got up to follow her, but his mother said, "Better leave her alone, Wes."

Wes was upset. "I can't believe that . . . that *thug* would write!"

"We all have to ask for forgiveness," Aaron said. "I did."

"So did I," Gail murmured. She reached over and took Wes's hand. "You were saved when you were sixteen, Wes. Didn't you have to ask God to forgive you?"

"Sure I did, but—"

"Well, it's the same thing. I think we don't have any choice. We'll have to forgive him."

"That's right. Unforgiveness will kill a man or a woman as surely as a bullet," Aaron said. "I know it's tough, son, but you don't know his heart. God does. It seems he's trying anyway."

Wes bowed his head and shrugged his shoulders. "I'll try," he said, "but it's not going to be easy."

★　★　★　★

Emily opened her dresser drawer and took out the small box. She opened it and stared down at the gold pen and pencil. She had put them away after Parker left, and now as she stared at them, the memories came flooding back. She thought of the kisses she had given him and how she had fallen in love with him. There was no other way to put it. She knew that now. That was why she could not forgive him. What he had done to Jared was horrific, and lying to her family was terrible, but he had deliberately set out to deceive her. Long ago she had decided he had cared nothing for her, and now as she stared at the golden writing set with the words "To Emily" engraved on the side, her hands began to tremble. A thought came to her, and she picked out the pen and went over to her desk. With hands not entirely steady, she filled the reservoir with ink. Taking out a sheet of paper, she had to wait until she could control her writing. When she did, she wrote a short note and then laid the pen down and read it: *I will never forgive you. You killed my brother as surely as if you'd shot him yourself. You came to this home, where we tried to show you love and acceptance, and you proved yourself to be a lying deceiver. I never want to see you again, and I don't want any more letters from you. God is your judge, and He may forgive you—but I never will!*

Emily picked up an envelope, and on it she wrote "James Parker" and the address he had given in his letter. Her hand trembled. She was embarrassed by the shaky handwriting, and when she had better control of herself, she addressed it firmly. She stuffed her letter inside, licked the flap, sealed it, and put a stamp on it. She stood looking at it for a moment, then tossed it on the table.

She stared at it as if it were a venomous reptile and then left the house and walked for over two hours. When she returned she avoided her parents and Wes and went to bed, still shaken and still struggling to control the anger that the very name of James Parker stirred within her.

CHAPTER FOURTEEN

AT THE END OF THE RAINBOW

★ ★ ★ ★

Donald Sutton chewed on his cigar, staring at the news copy in front of him and at the enlarged photograph that accompanied it. He did not move for so long that Emily finally demanded, "Well, what do you think of my story?"

Lifting his eyes, Sutton mouthed around his cigar, "What do I think of it? I think you're crazy, Emily."

The silence seemed to thicken in the room, and the only movement for a few seconds was the upward curling smoke of Sutton's cigar. Then Emily demanded, "What's wrong with it?"

"Everything! This is a family newspaper, Emily, not a trashy New York tabloid." He slapped his meaty hand down on the photograph, exclaiming, "If I ran that picture, I'd have every preacher in town and almost every mother of a teenage daughter down here demanding my head in a basket!" Removing the cigar, Sutton shook his head. "You've been here long enough, Emily, to know this news isn't fit to print!"

The story was one Emily had covered on her own time. She had gone to the bathing beach on the Potomac along with Wes. She had written a story about a beauty contest being held there, and Wes had taken a great many photographs of the contestants. Emily had captured the essence of the show and written about the prizewinners and what it was like to be a bathing beauty queen. Wes had captured the young women in their tunic bathing suits, their caps over their long curls, and their long stockings—except for one contestant who had daringly rolled her stockings below the knee. Wes had captured the bare knees and clingy bathing suits, with thousands of spectators looking on, mouths open, as they applauded the girls. Emily had interviewed Miss Washington, who was declared the most beautiful girl in America, and had ended the article by saying, "The one-piece bathing suit will become orthodox wear for bathing beauties. Promoters of seaside resorts will start having their own contests, and the tabloid editors will have a field day."

Emily stared at Sutton, and her face was flushed with anger. "Are you trying to tell me that this story is indecent?"

"I'm trying to tell you, Emily, that the preachers and the mamas will say it's indecent. Why, we'd lose a thousand subscribers if I printed this story."

"Donald, I think you're avoiding the times. This story is news. It's what's happening in America, and if you and the preachers and the mamas don't like it, at least they ought to know what's going on."

Sutton rose to his feet and came around to face Emily. "Emily, you're young. You haven't had to face irate subscribers. If you had, you'd know that this story won't do. And the photographs! Why, it looks like one of the Hearst papers from New York."

"Well, at least people are reading the Hearst papers."

"No, they're not! They're looking at the pictures. We're a newspaper, not scandal-mongering yellow journalism like those New York sheets!"

Emily argued for the next ten minutes, getting angrier all the time. She had learned, for the most part, to keep her anger under control, but from time to time it did slip out. And now she finally shook her finger in Donald Sutton's face, proclaiming, "If you don't print this story and use these pictures, I quit!"

Sutton had a temper of his own. "Fine! I think we'll manage to struggle along without you! We did a pretty fair job for quite a few years without your help."

"Good!" Emily snapped. She turned and walked out, her head high, and marched right to her desk.

Everyone had heard the conflict, for Sutton's door had been open. Now as Emily left with all of her belongings in a paper sack, Max Carter, the assistant editor, came into Sutton's office. He smiled, saying, "You made her pretty mad."

"She needed to be cut down."

"I don't know, boss," Max said. "She's the best writer we've got."

"I know she is." Sutton chewed on his cigar furiously, then took it out and dropped it in the brass cuspidor. Frustration was written across his broad features, and he shrugged his beefy shoulders. "She'll come back," he declared. "She gets mad once in a while, but she always gets over it."

"I hope so. If she doesn't, you'll have to hire two more reporters to fill her shoes."

★ ★ ★ ★

The house was strangely silent as Emily stepped inside, and she remembered that her parents had gone to visit friends in a neighboring town. Slowly she walked into her room and sat down on the bed. A state of depression had fallen on her, as it often did after she showed the tempestuous side of her nature. "Why did I have to lose my temper and fly off the handle?" she muttered, staring at the floor. "Donald Sutton has done nothing but try to help me since I've been on the paper, and now I've acted like an idiot!"

Emily Winslow was an emotional young woman—too much so for her own good when she was challenged and yet knew she was right about something. She instantly recognized the dark cloud that had now settled over her. In the past when this sort of emotional outbreak happened to her, it had sometimes taken her days to get over it. Now she dreaded telling her parents and Wes what she had done, and the thought crossed her mind that, perhaps, she might go back and apologize to Mr. Sutton. She finally knelt beside her bed and began to pray. Her prayer was very simple. "Lord, forgive me for showing that side of me that you must hate. You've said that the wrath of man worketh not the righteousness of God, and I certainly didn't show righteousness when I lost it with my boss. So, Lord, I ask you to forgive me. I'm ready to do anything you say. If you want me to go back and apologize, I'll do it. . . ."

Finally the cloud seemed to lift, and as Emily knelt there, she found herself smiling. "Thank you, Lord, for your forgiveness. I've about worn out First John 1:9, but I know I'll use that verse for the rest of my life." Indeed, the scripture was one of her favorites. " 'If we confess our sins, he is faithful and just to forgive us our sins, and to cleanse us from all unrighteousness.' "

Getting to her feet, Emily was thankful to God for removing the oppressive cloud that had hung over her. She left the room and went downstairs and began pulling out the ingredients for supper, for she had decided to surprise her mother and cook a full-scale meal. She was an excellent cook, and soon she had planned the meal and put the ingredients together. She decided to fix a chocolate pudding first so it would have time to set and cool. Taking the milk from the refrigerator, she poured it into a saucepan, added flour, cocoa, and sugar, brought this to a boil, and then, when it thickened, she set it off to the side and added a little vanilla to bring out the sweetness. When the pudding was done, she poured it into single serving dishes and popped these into the refrigerator. She decided to have mashed potatoes with the meal, and she quickly began peeling and dicing the potatoes into a pan of water, then put them on the stove to boil. Next she went to the refrigerator again and removed some pork chops, which she rinsed under cold water. She arranged the chops in a shallow baking dish, added a small amount of water, butter, and seasoning, covered it, and put it in the oven to bake. Smiling with satisfaction, Emily looked at the mess she had made and began cleaning up after herself.

Finally, with dinner under way, she went into the living room and sat down by the radio, turned it on, and began looking for a station to listen to. She and the rest of the family had fallen victim to the new national addiction that had been changing the habits of Americans. The two-year-old invention had caught on slowly at first, and amateur operators had objected to the stream of popular music that issued from the first radio station, operated by the Westinghouse Company.

Emily, along with Wes, had no such objections to the radio. They had delighted in being able at times to tune in stations as far away as Havana or Miami. Now Emily listened to several new tunes that flowed out of the speaker: "Ma, He's Makin' Eyes at Me," "There'll Be Some Changes Made," and "Toot, Toot, Tootsie, Good-Bye!"

She laughed when they played a nonsense song entitled "Yes, We Have No Bananas," and she felt the poignancy of a love spat when a quartet sang, "That Old Gang of Mine." For a long time she sat there enjoying the music and relaxing, and finally she heard a door slam. Wes came in and found her sitting beside the radio.

"There you go wasting your life." He plumped down beside her and listened for a few moments, too.

Emily decided she would break the news of what she'd done. "I've got to tell you something, Wes, but don't say anything to Mom and Dad."

Wes looked up at once, noting the seriousness in Emily's eyes. "What is it, sis? Is it trouble?"

"I think it is, but mostly it's with me. I've done a stupid thing."

Wes suddenly grinned. "I'm glad to hear it."

"Glad to hear it! Why?"

"Because I do so many dumb things it's nice to have a partner in stupidity. What have you done?"

"I've quit my job." Emily saw Wes's eyes fly open with surprise, and she went on to relate how she had given her boss an ultimatum. "So now I've asked God to help me do something. Somehow I feel like I've come to a fork in the road, but I don't see any other choice now but to go back and apologize to Sutton." Wes sat there listening as Emily poured her heart out, and finally she threw her hands up and said, "I just don't know what to do."

"I do," Wes said at once. "We'll pray. And while we're at it, let's pray that God will give us something to do together."

Emily stood up and went over to sit beside Wes. "I think

that's the best idea anyone could have. God's able to do all things."

The two sat there and prayed, first Wes and then Emily, and when the prayer was over she looked up, her eyes a little misty. "I'm glad you're here, Wes. I need you at times like this."

"I need you, too, sis. Now let's look forward to what God is going to do for us. Whatever it is, I know it'll be great!"

*   *   *   *

Emily discovered that they were out of milk, so she walked to the store to get some. Her parents would be home soon, and as she passed by her old high school, she thought suddenly of Mr. Laurence. She had often thought of him since he had given his life in the war effort, and now a sadness came over her, for when she thought of him, her thoughts always went to Jared as well. She had to struggle against the grief that would still well up at times, wounding her spirit, as sharp and cutting as a sword.

She stepped into the store, got the milk, and started home, and once again a vague memory came to her. She thought of Buck Leatherwood and the terrible evening she had spent with him. She grieved then, for Buck Leatherwood was now serving ten years in the penitentiary for armed robbery. He was a young man who had talent and a future but had blown it by one rash act. Feeling compassion for him over this tragedy, Emily had written to him in prison on a regular basis, and in each letter she managed to put in something about Jesus. At first Buck had been resentful, angry, and bitter, but she could tell from the tone of his letters that he was changing, and she found herself, as she entered the house, breathing a prayer for him.

As she opened the door, Wes said, "The mail's come, sis." Emily stopped at the table in the hall and, holding the milk in the crook of her arm, reached down and picked up the letters. There was only one for her, but her heart beat suddenly faster when she saw the *National Geographic* return address. She had flooded various magazines with submissions, hoping for a substantial project, but the rejections had come rapidly. Still, she could not help being excited as she set the milk down and carefully opened the envelope. She pulled it out, stared at it, and then screamed, "Wes! Wes!"

Wes came running in, alarm in his eyes. "What's wrong, sis?"

"It's an acceptance from *National Geographic!* I'm going to do a special story for them that will take several months at least. It's my door into a new writing career!"

Wes let out a loud yell, and the two embraced. He lifted her off her feet and danced around. She was laughing and almost crying, and finally she protested, "You're squeezing the life out of me! Put me down!"

"Sis, that's wonderful! That's just great!"

"Greater than you know, Wes." Emily put her hand on her chest and said, "We're, both of us, going to do this together."

Wes stared at her. "You mean I get to take pictures?"

"Yes, and I'll do the writing. It's going to be wonderful! Don't say anything to the folks. After supper I'll make the announcement."

"You won't have to announce much," Wes said. "When they look at you, and me, too, I guess, they'll know something's happened. Something good? No! Something *great!*"

★　★　★　★

"That was a fine supper, daughter. I don't think your mother could have done much better." Aaron winked at Emily, then reached over and squeezed Gail's hand. "You'd better stand to your laurels, sweetheart. That daughter of yours is a powerful good cook."

Emily had put the letter from *National Geographic* in her pocket. She pulled it out now and said, "I have an announcement to make."

"It sounds serious," Gail smiled.

"I can see it's not bad news because your eyes are sparkling. What is it?" Aaron said.

"I sent off a proposal to *National Geographic* a long time ago.

I'd just about forgotten about it, but I got the answer today. They've commissioned me to do the story and Wes to take the pictures."

There was rejoicing at the Winslow table, and finally Emily said, "Here's what it is. *Geographic* will accept a story done on a primitive tribe in the Amazon River basin."

Both her parents stared at her, and it was Gail who exclaimed, "You'll have to go to South America?"

"Yes, of course, and Wes, too. We'll live as close as we can to a tribe there—the most primitive one I could find. It's a tribe called the Guapi that have had almost no contact with civilization. That's where we're going, Wes and I."

The questions flowed quickly from both parents as they tried to understand what all this would involve. Finally Aaron leaned back and said, "So, if I have it right, you have to pay your own expenses, and it's possible they may not accept the story after it's finished."

"That's right, Dad, and it will cost money that I don't have. And it's possible I may fail. You know how high the standards are for that magazine. But here's my plan. If I can write this article for *National Geographic*, Wes and I can gather enough material while we're there to make a book out of it. And I just know that someone will print it."

Gail held her breath then, and Wes was silent. They knew that it would cost a great deal of money, and although Emily had not asked, she was hoping her father would volunteer to finance the expedition.

Aaron was smiling and finally said, "I'm as proud as punch of you, both of you. I'll gladly foot the bill. You can pay me back when you get paid. If you can't, it'll be a great experience for you. I don't think you'll fail."

Emily jumped up from her seat, ran around, and grabbed Aaron, falling into his lap with her arms around his neck. "Oh, Dad, thank you so much!"

"Here, here, don't strangle me!" Aaron protested.

He had no chance to say more, for Wes had come over and was beating him on the back, crying out, "Thanks, Dad. You'll be proud of us."

The rest of the evening was a time of excitement and planning. Everyone had to look at the globe and maps that Emily had collected of South America. Finally Gail looked at the clock and declared, "It's bedtime. Everybody to bed!"

Emily kissed her parents, struck Wes on the shoulder, and dodged as he made a grab at her. "Tomorrow we start the real work. It'll take a lot of doing!"

★　★　★　★

Emily's word proved to be prophetic. It did indeed take "a lot of doing" to plan such an expedition. The planning involved months of gathering equipment, making contacts with a missionary couple the Winslows knew through their church who worked in this area, applying for passports and visas, and getting shots for every imaginable disease, so that Wes had cried out, "If I have to take one more needle, I think I'll die." But the two of them had thrown themselves into this new adventure with all the energy of youth.

Finally on June the thirtieth the two stood at the dock in New York saying good-bye to their parents. The *Columbia* waited, and passengers were going aboard. Now that the moment to leave had come, Emily felt a sudden gust of fear, but she quickly brushed it aside and embraced her mother. She felt her mother clinging to her and whispered, "Don't worry, Mom. We'll be fine."

She moved over to Aaron, who put his arms around her and kissed her cheek. "I'll be praying for you every day, daughter."

"I know you will, Dad."

Wes said his good-byes to his parents, and then the shrill blast of the *Columbia*'s whistle rent the air.

"You two had better get on board," Aaron said. "You won't be able to mail letters much, but if the chance comes, we want to hear from you."

Aaron and Gail stood there watching as the two walked up the gangplank. Aaron put his arm around her, and they waited for the ship to move out. The rail was lined with travelers, and as the ship began to slowly pull away from the pier, Gail said, "It's dangerous. I'm really afraid for them."

"It's hard to let them go, honey, but we prayed, and it's time to trust God for their lives." He squeezed her and said, "I feel like an old mother bird letting her fledglings out of the nest. I don't know if they have strong enough wings to fly on such a treacherous journey, but God will guide and protect them."

The two parents stood there as the *Columbia* was pulled into position by the tugs. They waved toward their children and watched until the ship slowly wheeled about and left the harbor. Finally Aaron said quietly, "Well, there they go. They're in God's hands now."

CHAPTER FIFTEEN

THE DARK SIDE OF BRAZIL

★ ★ ★ ★

The *Columbia* had nosed its way into a quay and lowered a gangplank. Emily and Wes were alive with excitement as they scurried around getting ready to leave the ship. They had enjoyed their trip but were anxious to get to work. Their greatest concern was getting their luggage and equipment ashore, but they discovered quickly that South Americans are far less eager to keep their eye on the clock than Americans.

"Everyone seems to move in slow motion," Wes complained. He had been scurrying around collecting their luggage, but now as he gazed at the porters, he measured their pace and shook his head. "They act like they're half asleep."

"Well, the guide books all say that people from countries like this are not as time conscious as we are," Emily said. "We'll just have to be patient."

By the time they had gotten ashore, their patience was already fairly well tried. The ship had arrived early in the morning, and now the two needed to find transportation to the river town of Santarém, where they would find the missionary couple they had contacted. The Pettigrews did not know many of the details of their project, but they were very willing to help the young Americans however they could.

Emily and Wes discovered that a riverboat made the trip, following the tortured meanderings of the Amazon, but there seemed to be no schedule. They also encountered the language barrier, for neither of them had mastered enough Portuguese to be of service. Finally at a booking office they discovered that a ship might leave the next day headed for Santarém, but the olive-skinned manager smiled and put his hands out in a helpless gesture. "Who can say?" he said in very poor English. "Maybe tomorrow. Maybe next week. Come and see."

"We'll have to find someplace to stay," Wes said grimly. "Come on. There's bound to be a hotel."

But Belém, they discovered, was not overrun with hotels. It was the capital of Pará on the south bank of the Rio do Pará. Emily had read up on the place and discovered that the Portuguese had settled here in 1616, and it had been used as a gateway to the interior. It was the major trade center of the Amazon Valley. Most of the structures were low squat buildings, many of them built of blocks, and there was a squalid air about the entire city.

The two stored most of their luggage and equipment at the shipping office and then set out to find a place to stay for the night. The sound of the Portuguese tongue, soft and rather sibilant, was strange to their ears. They passed through an open meat market, and the stench almost caused Emily to turn back. "I never smelled anything like this. It's terrible!" she exclaimed.

Wes examined the carcasses of sheep, cattle, and birds, all of them covered with flies, and shook his head. "I wouldn't want to eat anything bought here."

"We may have to," Emily said. "We can't eat out of cans the whole time we're here."

Eventually the two found what passed for a hotel. They got two rooms and found that there was one bathroom for the whole floor, which they had to share with other lodgers. When Emily stepped inside her room, fatigued and ready for bed, she looked askance at the mattress. She could not see any bugs, but it was dirty, and the only covering was a single blanket. She undressed, lay down, and waited for morning, thinking, *I'll be glad to get out of this place. It can't be much more difficult living in a tent in the jungle. At least it'll be cleaner.*

★ ★ ★ ★

The small boat powered by a chugging steam engine pushed its way through the muddy waters. Fortunately the pair had found the boat waiting for them the next morning. They had paid the owner to wait until they got their luggage and equipment aboard, and now they were standing in the prow taking in the sights.

"I can't believe the size of this river!" Wes exclaimed. "Look, you can't even see to the other side of it!"

A small man with a bronze face and wearing a white linen suit and a broad-brimmed white straw hat had heard what Wes said. "Your first time on the river?" he said with a distinct accent.

"Yes, it is," Wes said. "It's huge, isn't it?"

"Indeed. As a matter of fact, it's the second-longest river in the world. The first is the Nile, of course, but the Amazon is king here. Some people call it Rio Mar, which means the 'river sea.'"

"Have you lived here a long time?" Wes asked the man.

"Yes, I was born upriver here. Where are you headed?"

"We're going to do a story for *National Geographic* on one of the native tribes."

"Which tribe is that, may I ask?"

"The Guapi."

A cloud passed over the man's face, and when he did not speak, Emily said, "What's wrong? We don't know much about this tribe."

"They are very isolated. I don't know if any white people have ever gone that far inland. You might be wise to choose another tribe more civilized."

Emily shook her head. "No, the story was sold to *National Geographic* on the basis of a tribe that was still living in the old ways."

"Well," the man smiled briefly, showing discolored teeth, "you'll find that all right. Just be careful they don't eat you."

Emily stared at him, trying to decide if he was joking. "You don't mean that, do you?"

"It's not unknown for these people. Not just the Guapi, but

others. Plenty of them are headhunters, and cannibalism was common in the old days. I don't know about the Guapi. I would just say you've taken on quite a task."

Their fellow traveler's words did not discourage either Emily or Wes. They enjoyed the trip up the river. The brown waters of the Amazon stretched out to infinity, it seemed. When they got close to the shore, they both delighted in the wildlife. Crocodiles were common enough, and once Emily said, "Look—there's a jaguar!"

She pointed, and Wes came quickly and saw a jaguar up in a tree, his paws dangling over a branch. He looked at them sleepily and without a great deal of interest. "I'd hate to meet him alone on his ground," Wes grinned.

They pulled into Santarém with only an hour's daylight left. The owner of the boat helped them get their luggage ashore, and then after they had paid him, he hopped back in the boat, speaking to his crew of two.

"Well, we've got to find the Pettigrews and quick. It's getting dark." The Pettigrews were the missionary couple whose names had been given to the Winslows by the pastor of their church. Emily had written to them several months earlier, and the Pettigrews were expecting them sometime during the month, but they couldn't know exactly when the young people would arrive.

Emily stopped a man who was walking along with a bundle on his head. "Pardon me," she said. "Do you speak English?"

The man stared at her and said something she did not understand. Emily said, "Pettigrew . . . Pettigrew."

Enlightenment came to the man, and he motioned, saying something to them.

"He wants us to follow him," Emily said quickly. "We'll have to carry this luggage ourselves."

"There's no telling how far it is, but we can make it," Wes answered.

They followed the short, muscular native into the center of the village. It was not so much a village as a collection of houses built of heavy reeds with thatch roofs. Finally they came to a building that had been built of lumber and was painted white.

There was a cross on top, and the Indian smiled and pointed at the building and said, "Jesus. Jesus."

"That's right. Jesus." Emily smiled. "Thank you very much."

The two moved toward the white building, but they noticed that a house was hidden behind it. "That must be where the missionaries live," Wes said.

"Let's try the church first," Emily suggested. The door of the church was open, so they went inside. It was a simple, bare building with benches having no backs and a pulpit of sorts in the front. "Nobody here. Let's go to the house," Emily said.

They left the church and walked around beside it, and as they did so, a man stepped outside. He came toward them, a smile on his face and said, "Good evening. My name is Pettigrew."

"Oh, Reverend Pettigrew," Emily said with relief. "I'm Emily Winslow, and this is my brother, Wes. We're so glad to find you!"

"Well, we've been expecting you two. Do come inside. These mosquitoes will carry you off. I'm surprised they haven't already."

In truth Emily had been fighting the mosquitoes, as had Wes. The pests seemed immune to the antimosquito lotion they had been using, and both Emily and Wes were glad to step inside. There was no electricity, but kerosene lamps lit the interior of the small, plain dwelling. Pettigrew called out, "Hazel, we have guests." He waited until a short woman with glasses came from another room. She was wearing an apron and wiped her hands on it as her husband made the introductions. "This is Miss Emily Winslow and her brother, Wes. This is my wife, Hazel."

Emily shook hands and then said, "We're so grateful for your invitation. We don't know what we would have done without your hospitality."

"Think nothing of it!" Mrs. Pettigrew said. "We're delighted to have visitors from the States. We don't get many, you know. You're just in time for supper." Hazel turned to her husband and said, "Roger, could you please show our guests where they can wash up?" Then to Emily and Wes, she said, "You can leave your things right over there in that room."

"As a matter of fact," Roger Pettigrew said, "we'd be happy for you to stay with us during your whole time here. There are no inns or hotels here in the jungle, you know."

"Oh, but that would be an imposition," Wes protested.

"Nonsense. It's what the room was built for," Pettigrew said cheerfully. He had a round face and a pair of merry blue eyes and a mustache of which he seemed inordinately fond, for he stroked it almost continually. "Come, I'll show you where to wash up, and as soon as you're ready, we'll sit down and have a fine meal. My wife's a wonderful cook."

Indeed Hazel Pettigrew was a wonderful cook. After the two visitors had washed up and sat down at the table, Roger Pettigrew asked a quick blessing, then waved his fork. "Now, you'd better eat all you can."

The meal was simple, a meat stew with some strange-tasting potatoes that neither Wes nor Emily recognized but found very good. Other items Mrs. Pettigrew had to identify for them.

After they had eaten, they sat back drinking tea, and Emily set out to explain their project. The Pettigrews listened with interest, but when Emily finally ended, he shook his head. "My dear, I think you'd better change your plan."

"Why's that, Reverend Pettigrew?"

"The Guapi people are too dangerous. Even the traders don't go into their area."

Emily had expected opposition, and she began at once to explain that the Guapi were just exactly the type of tribe that she had to write about and get pictures of. "You see, *Geographic* is interested in doing an article on a very primitive tribe as untouched by civilization as possible."

"Well, Emily, you'll certainly find them untouched," Mrs. Pettigrew said, smiling grimly. "When the traders won't go into an area, you can be sure there's a great deal of difficulty."

The four sat there talking for over two hours. Pettigrew got out maps and showed the location of the Guapi people, and both he and his wife argued firmly that it was not a wise move for the two visitors to try to go into their territory. But Emily and Wes would not be dissuaded.

"Well, who would take you in?" Reverend Pettigrew asked, spreading his hands wide. "You have to have a guide."

"Surely we can hire someone," Wes said.

"I'm not sure you could." The minister shook his head. "You just haven't been listening. People around here are afraid of those natives."

"It really might be better for you to find another tribe," Hazel said. "Now, there's a tribe not far from here that might do admirably." Mrs. Pettigrew went on to urge the two to stay with them and go out only during the daylight hours. "It's not over five miles from here," she urged. "And you wouldn't have to sleep outdoors. That in itself is dangerous."

"We expected danger," Emily said. "But—"

"There are jaguars that even come into this village—and snakes. Oh, my word!" Pettigrew threw his hands up. "There's a snake here called the fer-de-lance. It's one of the deadliest snakes in the world. It delivers more venom in a single bite than any other snake, I do believe. The Indians in their language call it the 'five-stepper.'"

"Why do they call it that?" Wes asked.

"Because after one bites you, you've got about five steps to get help. After that it's too late."

Emily shivered at the thought. "I never heard of poison acting that quickly." Emily saw that they were getting nowhere, and soon she said, "I'm very tired. Perhaps you wouldn't mind if we went to bed early."

"Of course not. The beds are all made. Sleep as late as you'd like tomorrow," Pettigrew said.

The two went to the guest room, which had been divided by a curtain hanging on a wire with a bed on either side. "These beds are better than what we had in Belém. It's very comfortable here," Emily said.

"The Pettigrews don't think we can make it out there in the jungle," Wes remarked.

"We've got to, Wes," Emily said fiercely. "We've just got to."

★   ★   ★   ★

"It looks pretty hopeless, Emily," Wes said.

The two were walking slowly along the main street of

Santarém, and both were perspiring from the oppressive heat and slapping at the mosquitoes that swarmed around them wherever they went. "We've tried everything I can think of."

Emily removed a handkerchief, which had become standard gear, from her pocket and mopped at her face. During their two days at the Pettigrews' she had bathed every day, but ten minutes after her bath she would find herself soaked with sweat. The heat was like a blanket pressing down, and now as she walked along, it almost seemed difficult to breathe, the day was so hot. Wes's comments caused her to shake her head violently. "We're going to do it, Wes. I don't know how," she said, gritting her teeth, "but we're going to get to the Guapi somehow."

The two of them had spent two days searching desperately for someone to guide them into the Guapi territory. The Pettigrews had done all they could, but they had had no luck whatsoever. Even the natives of other tribes refused to go, and in any case, as Pettigrew pointed out, "You can't put yourself in the hands of natives. They just don't understand the problems the white person has with this country."

Now as they approached the missionaries' residence, Wes said suddenly, "It looks like the Pettigrews have company." A vehicle was parked out front. "Probably a visiting missionary," Wes commented.

When the two entered the house, they were introduced at once by Roger Pettigrew to his guest. "This is Mr. Carl Schultz. Carl, may I introduce Wesley and Emily Winslow."

"I am happy to meet you." Schultz was a burly man with a broad sunburned face and a pair of light blue eyes that took the pair in carefully. His hair was blond, and he appeared to be somewhere in his late forties. He spoke with a thick German accent. "We were just speaking of you and your problem."

"Yes, Mr. Schultz," Emily said eagerly. "We're desperate for a guide."

"I've tried to persuade Carl to take you, but he's headed for the coast on urgent business."

"Perhaps when you come back," Emily said.

"That will not be for at least three weeks," the German replied. He saw the disappointment in the faces of the two young

Americans and shook his head. "Reverend Pettigrew has told you about the dangers. I'm not sure you are aware of them."

"Well, of course, we don't know the country," Emily said, "but we're desperate to go. Could you suggest anyone who could go with us?"

Schultz ran his thick fingers through his hair and thought deeply. Finally he shrugged. "There's always Marlowe."

"Nonsense! That won't do at all!" Pettigrew said sharply.

"Who is Marlowe?" Wes demanded eagerly.

"He will not do," Mr. Pettigrew said. "Don't even think about it."

Schultz shrugged his burly shoulders. "Well, I can't think of anyone else, but I will ask around when I get to the coast. I know a great many traders. None of them that I know of has ever entered Guapi country, but if they were well enough paid, it might be possible."

Schultz left soon after that, and Emily and Wes went in to have tea with the Pettigrews.

Mrs. Pettigrew served the tea and then sat down and said sympathetically, "I know you're discouraged. It seems like a closed door to me and to Roger."

"I think it is," her husband agreed. "Missionaries find out about closed doors. We see something that desperately needs doing, and we start out"—he sighed and shrugged his shoulders—"and then we find out it's impossible. So we have to make other plans."

"Really, there are tribes you could have easy access to," Hazel Pettigrew urged. She had become quite fond of the young people in a short time and was genuinely concerned about their safety. "Why don't you consider it?"

Emily hesitated. She was headstrong, and once she started a project, she hated to give it up. Still, she could see the difficulty was enormous. "Who is this Marlowe?" she asked quickly. "Is he a trader?"

"Marlowe," Hazel said. "You're not talking about Ian Marlowe?"

"Oh, Schultz brought his name up as a possible guide, but I

194

don't think that would work out," Roger said, shaking his head firmly.

"No, I don't think he would," Hazel agreed.

"But who is he?" Emily insisted.

"Oh, he calls himself a missionary." Roger Pettigrew shook his head.

Emily at once sensed the disapproving attitude in her host. Curiosity drove her to ask, "What sort of a missionary? What denomination is he?"

"Oh, he's nothing that I know of. That is, he's not sponsored by any denomination."

"What sort of a man is he?" Wes asked, leaning forward and putting his eyes on Pettigrew. "I have the feeling you don't approve of him."

"I think he's a foolhardy man. I don't say anything against his morals, you understand, but when he first came here, everyone tried to talk him out of going into the interior alone."

"Is that what he did?" Emily asked. "All by himself? Did he speak the language?"

"Certainly not. He just arrived one day and announced that he was going into the interior to preach the gospel to the natives," Hazel said. "I rather liked him, but he can't last."

"Has he gone to the Guapi tribe?" Emily wanted to know.

"Yes, I have heard that he has," Roger admitted. "He lives with an old man named Adriano Rey and his granddaughter on the edge of the Guapi country. Rey is a Christian man getting along in years now. We don't see much of him, but I know what Marlowe is doing is very dangerous."

Emily saw that Roger Pettigrew and his wife were clearly against using the man as a guide, so she said no more about it. However, that night when she and Wes were alone just before bedtime, she said, "Wes, we've got to look into this man Marlowe."

"I don't know. The Pettigrews are dead set against it."

"I know they are, but right now he's our only chance. Look, Wes, they talked about a door being closed and it has been. But what if God wants Marlowe to lead us to these people? Maybe that's the door that will be open."

"Maybe you're right, sis. At least we could talk to him."

"Let's pray about it and ask God to open the door. If He wants to use this man, then that's fine with me."

The two prayed together and then later Emily lay awake. She was grateful for the mosquito net that gave her some relief from their constant presence, and for a long time she lay seeking God's will. She went to sleep as she was praying, *Oh, God, give us a way to open the door!*

★　★　★　★

"I'm very sorry to hear of your decision," Roger Pettigrew said rather sadly. He and his wife had listened at breakfast as Emily told him that both she and Wes had prayed, and they wanted to at least talk to Marlowe. "I will take you to Adriano's house," Roger said.

"Oh, couldn't you just hire a native to take us? We hate to take you away from your work."

"Well, I think that might be possible. We have one fine man who knows the country well and is very trustworthy. He would charge you very little."

"Fine," Emily said. "When can we leave?"

"I'll see to it, but I think tomorrow morning might be possible."

★　★　★　★

The guide's name was Samuel, which was not his birth name but one that the missionaries had given to him. He was a well-built, wide-eyed, and alert individual with jet black hair and liquid brown eyes. He spoke English fairly well and had been willing to take the two to the house of Adriano Rey.

As he paddled their large dugout downstream, piled high with their tents and photographic equipment and gear, Samuel spoke incessantly of Jesus. He was a relatively new convert and would sing lustily the hymns that he had learned from the missionaries. His favorite was "Amazing Grace," and he made the jungles echo as he steered the dugout down the twisting, curving tributary.

"We got a good guide, I think," Wes smiled. "He sure is enthusiastic."

"Yes, he is. He's such a fine man." Emily smiled as Samuel's voice continued to boom, sending "Amazing Grace" up into the rain forest canopy. The river wound underneath trees so thickly woven together that they could not see the sky at times. Except for the gurgling of the river itself, there was mostly silence, broken once by a terrible scream the native identified as a monkey.

The trip was pleasant, for the canoe moved swiftly enough to avoid most of the bugs. Both Emily and Wes had smeared their faces with an ointment, which seemed to do a good job of driving the bugs away. The heat was quite oppressive, and yet with the gurgling of the river water, it did not seem so bad.

Finally Samuel pointed and said, "There is house. Adriano Rey."

Eagerly Emily looked forward and saw a house built on poles. It was made of what seemed to be bamboo or large reeds and had a thatch roof, as most native houses used. As soon as Samuel drove the prow of the dugout up on the bank, Wes leaped out, grabbed the rope, and pulled it half up over the bank. Emily scrambled out and turned to say, "Samuel, would you unload our things?"

"Yes. Praise God. Blessed be Jesus."

Emily hid her smile, for she had developed an affection for the man. "If American Christians were as excited as he is," she whispered to Wes, "we'd see the world evangelized quickly."

Even as they were unloading, a man and a young woman stepped out of the house on the small balcony and, after looking at them, came down the steps. The man was small but seemed strong and active. His hair was white, as was his mustache, and his eyes were black as ink. His face was smooth, and it was almost impossible to guess his age. He spoke to them in English, saying, "Welcome."

"Senhor Rey?"

"Yes. I am Adriano Rey. This is my granddaughter, Sarita."

Sarita was a full-figured beauty with olive skin and violet eyes such as Emily had not seen in any of the natives. "I'm sorry to intrude on you. My name is Emily Winslow. This is my brother, Wesley."

"You are welcome." Adriano looked up and said, "Hello, Samuel."

"Praise God and the Lamb forever," Samuel called out loudly. "Going to heaven."

"Yes. Going to heaven, Samuel. You must come in. We will have something to drink, and perhaps you're hungry."

"We are a little hungry. It was a longer trip than I thought."

"You came from Santarém?"

"Yes. We've been staying with the Reverend Pettigrew and his wife."

"And how is the good minister?"

"Very well. He sent this letter to you." Emily fished into her pocket and brought the letter out.

"Come in, and we will eat together. Samuel, you come, too."

"Praise God. I'll come, too."

The meal was simple. Sarita moved quickly and surely, with a native grace. Emily noticed that Wes watched her with unusual curiosity. *I'll have to be careful. She's a beautiful young woman, but the last thing Wes needs is a romance with a native beauty.*

Emily waited until the strong tea was served by the young woman. After sipping it, she said, "This is delicious."

"I must have my tea," Rey smiled, wiping his mustache. "One of the few items of civilization that I demand."

"I know you're wondering what we're doing out here," Emily said, "so let me tell you why we've come." She began to explain, and Adriano and his granddaughter listened carefully. Emily made the story as brief as possible, and she ended by saying, ". . . and so we were hoping that Mr. Marlowe would help us. We've been unable to find anybody who would take us into the Guapi country."

Sarita Rey shook her head. "It would be very dangerous. The Pettigrews are right. You should find a more civilized tribe."

"Are the Guapi so dangerous?" Wes asked the young woman.

"I think they are. My grandfather and I would not go into their country at all."

"But Mr. Marlowe has gone, and they haven't harmed him."

Adriano shrugged his shoulders. "He says God sent him— that God takes care of His own. He's a most unusual man."

"Have you known him long?"

"No. He simply appeared one day and asked the directions. Sarita and I tried our best to talk him out of it, but he simply smiled and said God was sending him."

"I fear for him," Sarita said suddenly. "The Guapi are not trustworthy."

"Well, I would like to at least talk to him. Is he here now?"

"You are fortunate. He is very punctual with his timetables. He gives us the time when he will be back, and he has never failed yet. He will be back either today or tomorrow."

Emily breathed a sigh of relief. "That is fortunate. Does he stay gone long at a time?"

"Sometimes several weeks. I think he lives pretty much as the Guapi live, although I don't know how."

Emily's mind worked quickly, and she said, "Would it be all right if we set our tents up outside on your property?"

"Of course, Miss Winslow. You would be most welcome to stay in our house."

"Actually," Emily smiled, "we're anxious to try our equipment out. This might be a good time."

"Then, at least, you must have dinner with us tonight. I expect Ian will come in late this afternoon."

★ ★ ★ ★

Emily and Wes enjoyed the meal. Sarita spoke excellent English, and when Wes insisted on helping her cook, she had laughed at him. "The men I know of our people do not cook."

"Probably just as well," Wes nodded. "I'm not much of a cook. How did you learn to speak English so well?"

"I stayed at the mission school with the Pettigrews." Sarita turned and looked at the tall young man. "How old are you?" she asked.

"Why, I'm twenty."

"Are you married?"

"No, not me," Wes said.

"Most of our men and women marry young here. One of my friends got married last week. She was only fourteen."

Wes laughed. "When I was fourteen I don't think I could even wave good-bye correctly."

"You take pictures?"

"Yes, I do. That's what I want to do. By the way, if you don't mind, I would like to take some pictures of you and your grand-father and of your house."

Sarita turned and smiled at him. "That would be very good. I have no picture of my grandfather."

"He's very handsome. I'll take some of him and some of you."

Emily was sitting at the table talking with Adriano. She had enjoyed the meal and had taken an instant liking to the old man. She saw that he had a great deal of wisdom, and there was a gentleness about him that she instinctively liked. "You have more family, senhor?"

"No, alas, Sarita is all. My son married her mother. She was a German woman. They were very happy, but both of them died of smallpox." His eyes went to the young woman, and wistfully he said, "I miss them very much, but I have Sarita to remind me of them."

"She's a very beautiful young woman."

"Yes, she is," he sighed and shook his head. "I do not know what she will do. She is better fitted to live in a town than out here on the bank of this river."

"Perhaps she will—" Emily broke off as Rey suddenly stood to his feet. She had heard nothing, but he said, "I hear someone coming. Probably Ian."

Eagerly Emily and Wes turned to the door, Emily rising to her feet. So much depended upon this man, and she could not help but pray again that God would give her and Wes favor with him.

"It's him. I know his step," Sarita said. She went over and

opened the door, and a figure filled it. "Come in, Ian. We have guests," Sarita said.

Emily stepped forward with a smile—but suddenly the smile faded. She heard Wes make a peculiar noise, a gasp of sorts, and then she clenched her hands into fists.

The man who stepped in the door was the man she had known as James Parker!

CHAPTER SIXTEEN

"CAN WE TRUST HIM?"

★ ★ ★ ★

As Emily stared at the face of the man who had paused in front of her, she was intensely aware of the small things that ordinarily would have passed her notice. A large fly was buzzing around her ears, making a droning sound as it circled and then lit on her cheek. Without consciously willing it, she brushed it away and was aware of its departure. From far off she heard the sound of some sort of bird. It was a shrill clicking sound that seemed to be saying, "*Jumpah! Jumpah! Jumpah!*"

For a single instant she shifted her gaze from the man she had known as James Parker and saw that Wes was transfixed. His eyes were open wide in a staring gaze, and his mouth dropped open. His back was stiff. *He's as shocked as I am.* The thought rushed through Emily's mind, and then she was aware that Adriano was talking.

". . . and these of your countrymen have come seeking help." Adriano turned and halted, for he saw the strained expression on Emily's face and noted also that there was a paleness about her that he had not noticed before. "Are you feeling ill, Miss Winslow?"

"No, I'm fine."

"Ah, well, the heat in this part of the world sometimes strikes visitors very hard. So this is my friend Ian Marlowe."

The man identified as Marlowe did not speak for a moment. He was wearing a pair of faded cotton drill trousers worn thin with many washings and a shirt equally worn. He had taken off a sun helmet, and the lower part of his face was tanned to a golden hue. His tawny hair was as Emily remembered it, but longer and slightly curly. He did not smile but said, "It's been a long time, Emily." Then turning to Wes, he nodded briefly. "You've grown up."

Adriano and Sarita were caught up by the little drama, and it was Sarita who exclaimed, "So you know each other!"

"A long time ago we did," Marlowe said. His face was thin, and he seemed to be, on the whole, planed down from the man that Emily and Wes remembered. He had no excess flesh, but he was the same.

"Perhaps you would like to have tea and something to eat," Adriano said. Turning to his granddaughter, he said, "Sarita, we will fix something. I know Ian is hungry."

Afterward Emily could not remember how she got through those first moments. She sat down and listened as best she could to the conversation that went on chiefly between Adriano and Ian Marlowe. Marlowe spoke quietly of his journey, minimizing the hardships, and even as she tried to pull herself together, she was aware that there was something different about this man who had so deeply wounded and deceived her and her family. She could not identify it, but there was something in his face, in his manner, even in his eyes that had changed. She saw that Wes was very quiet, and finally, after they had eaten a meal, Sarita and her grandfather left the room.

"This is awkward for you, I'm afraid," Marlowe said as he toyed with a cup half filled with tea. His hands were brown and hardened, and they appeared to be very strong.

"My real name is Ian Marlowe." The voice was quiet, and Marlowe took a sip of the tea, then set the cup down. "I was running from the law, and I changed it to James Parker. That was back when I was nineteen years old." He studied Emily carefully, then shook his head. "This must be a terrible shock for you."

"What are you doing here?" Emily whispered, her throat tight. "I never expected to see you again."

"I'm sure you didn't. Well, let me tell you all that's happened to me since I left your house. I remember when Captain Ramsey came, and I want to say at once that everything he told you was true. I did try to run away under fire, and I got shot in the leg and blinded by gas. Jared came out and carried me in. I don't remember much about that. I didn't even know who it was.

"I woke up in the hospital, and we were in the same ward. He was in poor shape, but the doctors thought he'd pull through." Something changed in Marlowe's voice, and he did not speak for a time.

Emily could hear Sarita and Adriano talking outside as she waited for him to continue.

"What Captain Ramsey said about me was true. I was a coward and everything that a man shouldn't be. That includes a drunk, a woman chaser, a liar, and a thief. I was all of that."

"You put on a pretty good act when you came to our house," Wes said, and bitterness tinged his tone. He was clasping his hands tightly together so that the knuckles were white, and as he stared at Ian Marlowe, his brown eyes were filled with animosity.

"I could always put on a pretty good act. That's what a confidence man and a crook does." Marlowe spoke of himself as if he were speaking of another person, and a sadness seemed to sweep across his features. He reached up and rubbed his forehead in an absent gesture, then shook his head. "That seems like a thousand years ago. Well, anyway, the doctors thought Jared would pull through. But it wasn't the wound that killed him. I don't know if Captain Ramsey told you or not."

"No, or if he did, I can't remember," Emily said.

"He had been sick before the battle started. He was one of those men who wouldn't give up. You probably know that."

"That's the way he was. What was wrong with him?"

"Could have been any one of half a dozen illnesses. You'll have to remember we were living like rats sleeping in the mud. Every kind of disease you can imagine plagued the troops. I know he had trench foot, but all of us did. I think it was pneumonia. He had lost so much weight even before the battle started. I know Captain Ramsey tried to get him to go to the hospital, but he wouldn't."

Emily was still half dazed by the sight of the man she had hoped never to see again. "What happened in the hospital?"

"When I woke up, and my eyes cleared up from the gas attack, I was in the bed across from Jared. He couldn't write, so I started writing the letters for him. Everything I said in the letters about him was just as he dictated them. The only lie in them was when I told about what a wonderful man James Parker was."

"Why did you do it?" Wes burst out. "Why would you do such a thing?"

"In those days I did anything that would help me. I built myself up. I was thinking of how I could use Jared. I found out pretty soon that your family had money, and I planned to show up and get what I could out of it."

"How . . . how did he die?"

For the first time Ian Marlowe seemed unable to speak. He looked down at his hands and studied them, letting the silence run on. Finally he said, "I know there's not a reason you should believe anything I say, but I've had a lot of time to think it over, and I think it was the way he died that I could never get away from. I still haven't." He looked up, and a strange grimace twisted his lips as he continued. "He failed a little bit every day. I saw enough in the hospital to be pretty sure that he wouldn't make it. As a matter of fact, I asked the doctor once, and I could tell that he had given up hope on Jared. He got weaker and weaker until finally he couldn't take much nourishment. We didn't have much nursing there, and I had to try to get a little food down him."

"Was he conscious when he died?"

"Oh yes. He had times when he would go into what was like a coma. But the night he died, he and I were alone. I heard him speak. It must have been about three o'clock in the morning, and it shocked me. He had been in a coma for over twenty-four hours, hadn't said a word, but his voice was clear. I crawled off of my cot and went over and sat down beside him and looked at him. There was enough light to see his face, and I saw that his eyes were open. His voice was stronger, too, but his breathing was very shallow. I said, 'Jared, do you want me to get the doctor?' And he just shook his head. And he said, 'No, I'm past all that.'

"I got some water, and he drank a sip or two, but I could tell he was failing. His breathing was very shallow, and I was afraid."

"What were you afraid of?" Emily demanded.

"I don't know. I'd seen enough death, so it wasn't that, but something about Jared had always frightened me a little bit. He was such a . . . such a different kind of man. All the men knew it. They all respected him and loved him."

"What did he do then?"

"He talked about all of you. You remember I put some of what he said in a letter, but I didn't put this part in," Marlowe said. "He reached out his hand, and as I took it, I was shocked at how frail it was. He had been such a strong man when I first knew him, but now there was nothing there. No strength, just bones under the skin. His eyes were sunken back in his head, as it happens with pneumonia, and I had to lean forward to catch his words."

"What did he say?" Wes asked hoarsely.

"He talked to me about what kind of man I was. He didn't accuse me or anything like that, but I knew what he was saying was true. I'd been a rotter all my life."

Here Marlowe swallowed and seemed to have difficulty finding the right words. "He told me," he said finally, "that Jesus was my only hope, and he begged me to turn from what I was and call out to Him to save me."

Emily started, for the shrill cry of a monkey very close to the house broke the silence of the room. She watched as Marlowe took a handkerchief out of his pocket and wiped his brow, and she saw that his face was paler.

Probably part of his act, she thought. *He's trying to look like a repentant sinner.*

"His last words were of his family. He whispered how much he loved you, and he asked me to write and tell you that he was thinking of you when he went home. 'Tell them I'll be waiting.' That's what he said."

Emily could not keep the tears back then. She turned to one side, groped in her pocket for a handkerchief, and valiantly struggled to contain herself.

Marlowe did not speak for a while but sat there loosely in the chair. He studied the two and finally shrugged, saying, "I planned to show up and get what I could out of you, and that's what I did."

"Didn't my brother's words have any effect on you at all?" Wes demanded.

"Not then, but I never forgot them. It's like I buried them somewhere deep down and shut the lid."

Emily felt a hardness growing in her, and she said bitterly, "You made a fool out of me!"

Ian Marlowe's face changed slightly. "I know you won't believe this, but after I got to your house, things began to happen to me. For one thing, I'd come there to get what I could out of you, but after I met you all, I began thinking of what Jared had said just before he died. It ate away at me, and I couldn't forget it. I tried to shut it out, but I couldn't." He broke off and hesitated, then he lifted his head and looked directly at Emily. "Not everything I said to you was a lie, Emily."

Emily blinked, for she knew he was referring to the feelings they had expressed toward each other. She had forced all of this out of her mind over the last few years, but now it came rushing back, so that she could remember the small things. She had never had this kind of response to any man before or since, and now she thought of those days with pain. "You'd have taken from us what you could if Captain Ramsey hadn't come and exposed you."

"I expect you're right about that, but something was beginning to change inside even back then because of what Jared had told me about his faith. You want to hear the rest?"

"All right. We might as well," Wes said evenly.

"After I left your house I went downhill—even for me, which is saying a lot. I went to New York and kept up my old ways. It wasn't long before I found myself sick and broke and ready to jump off a bridge." His voice changed, and just a fraction of a smile touched his lips. "I went to a men's rescue mission. It was

called the Water Street Mission. I went in just to get something
to eat, but I got more than that. Here is the part you won't believe, Emily, or you either, Wes. I found Jesus Christ during this
time. You don't know how it is with a derelict, but I reached the
bottom. One night I came in starving and sick just for the meal,
you understand, but the preacher got up, and he began to
preach. I'd heard it all before, but suddenly I knew that this was
my last chance." Marlowe brushed his hands across his face, and
his eyes dropped, and his voice lowered. "I don't know. He
preached on John 3:16. I'd heard it a lot, but for the first time I
suddenly knew in my heart that God did love sinners. And I was
a sinner. I began to cry, and when the preacher asked those who
wanted God to come down to the front, I stumbled forward. I
knelt down there, and he prayed with me. When I got up I was
a new man."

Emily struggled with Ian's words. They had had a visitor in
their church once whose ministry was to prisoners in jail, and he
had said, "A lot of men in prison get what they call *jailhouse religion*. It doesn't mean they know God. It simply means they pretend to so that they can gain favor with the warden and chap-
lain, the guards, and the parole board. It's hard to tell it from the
real thing, for some men are fine actors. They get that way in
prison."

As Emily recalled the evangelist's words, she was convinced
that Ian Marlowe was using her again. She stared at him, and he
met her gaze evenly.

"I don't expect you believe any of that, Emily, and you won't
believe the rest either."

"Go on. What happened then?" Emily said, her voice tense
and filled with strain.

"I stayed at the mission there, and I got a lot of help. I felt
God wanted me to do something, and the director of the mission, his name was Smith, helped me a lot. Finally I knew God
wanted me to be some kind of a preacher. That came as pretty
much of a shock." Ian smiled then and shook his head ruefully.
"It took a lot for God to convince me, but I finally began speaking mostly to small groups at the mission there. And then something happened. I knew God wanted me to carry the gospel in

some way to the world, but I didn't know how."

Emily listened skeptically as Ian Marlowe went on to tell that for a year he had done nothing but study the Bible and ask God to show him which way to go.

"Finally I was turning through a book. I saw a map of South America, and I knew that I would be here. The next thing I did was to learn Portuguese. Somehow I knew I'd be coming to this part of the world, and so I studied hard. I found out I was good at languages, and two years ago I decided to come to Brazil."

"Where did you get the money?" Emily asked sharply.

"I went around to all the mission boards I could find out about, but nobody would have me. Well, one of them said they would, but I'd have to go to seminary for years, and I didn't want to do that. So I got a job on the docks, saved all my money until I got enough to pay for my passage, and then I came. I got off the boat at Belém, just as you probably did, and started up the river. I had no idea where I was going, but God had told me I would preach the gospel to those who had never heard it. Finally," he concluded, "I arrived here. I was pretty sick, half starved, but Adriano and Sarita took me in. The first thing I did was get malaria, so I was helpless. I think I'd have died if it hadn't been for them."

Despite her grave distrust, Emily felt a strange interest in Ian's story. "When did you start going into the Guapi country?"

"As soon as I shook the malaria off," Marlowe said. "Everybody told me I was a fool, but I felt that it was God, so I just walked in. It's a wonder they didn't kill me. They are headhunters. I think they didn't know what to make of me." Marlowe looked down at the cup, drained the tea, then said, "It took me a year to get any kind of foothold, but I was able to be of some help to a relative of the chief's. He taught me the Guapi language, so that's what I do now. I go in, and I try to tell them about Jesus. They tolerate me, some of them that is, but they can be dangerous."

Emily did not know what to think. She was torn by the apparent sincerity of the man and the treachery that she had experienced by him in the past.

Finally she said, "You're probably wondering why we're here."

"The thought has crossed my mind." Marlowe smiled faintly. "After I wrote you the letter asking you to forgive me, I thought I'd never see you again."

Emily flushed slightly, for she remembered how harshly she had answered this man's plea for forgiveness. Then a flash of anger arose in her again as she realized that he had not been completely upfront with them even in that letter. "Why did you write to us using the name James Parker if you wanted to set everything straight?" She glared at him, waiting for him to form a response.

Ian put his head down and said nothing for a few moments. Then with a pained expression, he explained, "I've made so many bad choices in my life, Emily, and God is helping me rebuild my life based on truth now, not on lies. Believe me that it wasn't my intention to continue to deceive you, but I thought it would be too much of a shock to receive a communication from a complete stranger. I thought it best to broach the subject as the person you already knew—James Parker. I didn't want you to know where I was, so I had a friend from the mission forward my letter to you. I had planned to reveal my true identity to you if you had responded positively, but as it turned out, there was no need to say anything further. Again, I can only beg your forgiveness."

Now Emily felt more flustered than ever. "I honestly don't know what I can believe about you, Ian—if that is indeed your real name." Then to cover up her confusion and change to a more comfortable topic, she said, "The reason we're here is to work. We've been commissioned by *National Geographic* to do a story on a tribe, and we want to go to the Guapi."

"You'd better find another tribe."

"That's what everyone says, but that's not what I want to do."

"I wouldn't advise it," Marlowe said. He looked up suddenly and turned to his right, for Sarita had come in. "Sarita, we'll let Miss Winslow have my room. I can bunk outside."

"As you wish."

As Sarita went to stand close beside Marlowe, Emily saw a

possessiveness in the girl's attitude. Sarita's eyes were filled with mistrust, and Emily said quickly, "No, we brought tents. We'll sleep in those."

★ ★ ★ ★

"I don't know what to do, Wes," Emily said. The two had pitched their small tents outside, and now in the darkness they felt very small indeed. The jungle rose on both sides, swallowing them with its massive growth. Wes had come into Emily's tent, which was just large enough to hold the two of them. They had talked for some time about the strangeness of it all, and now Emily shook her head. "Can we trust him, Wes?"

"I don't know. From what he's said, he seems to have made an honest change, but he fooled us before." Wes slapped at a mosquito, then shook his head and said, "It's going to be tough, Emily. I just don't know if I want to put my life in his hands or not."

The two sat there talking quietly, and both were aware of the sounds outside the small tents. Adriano had vainly attempted to get them to stay in the room that Ian Marlowe occupied, but Emily had said, "No, we're going to be roughing it. Here's a good time to try out our equipment."

Now she shook her head and said, "We have to make a decision, Wes. We can either go find a more civilized tribe, or we can choose to trust that Ian has really changed and put ourselves into this man's hands. It's a hard thing, isn't it?"

"Yes, it is," Wes agreed.

The two sat there silently, and finally Wes said, "The decision has to be yours, Emily. This is your show."

Emily had known the final decision would be hers to make, and so she told Wes good-night and lay down to sleep. She tossed and turned for what seemed like hours, startled from time to time by the screams of howler monkeys and other strange noises that she could not identify. The Amazon was an alien world, and she knew their trip could become dangerous if they went farther into the interior. If one of them got hurt, there would be no running to the doctor, for there were no doctors. There were no grocery stores, no pharmacies, no policemen, just miles and miles of undisturbed rain forest. As she lay in the sultry heat of the night, she struggled with the problem of what to do. Finally she knew that she would have to do what she had come to Brazil to accomplish. She fell into a fitful sleep, and when she awoke the next morning, she went straightaway to Ian. He was sitting on the porch writing something in a book and greeted her quickly.

"Good morning, Emily. How did you sleep?"

"How do you think, with all those monkeys screaming all night!"

"After a while you'll get used to it and won't even notice," Ian said.

"I'm going to be very honest with you, Ian." It was difficult to call him that, for the name James leaped to her lips. "I don't know if I can ever forgive you for your deceit and for what happened to my brother. I realize it wasn't your fault that he had pneumonia, that he might have died anyway." She waited for him to answer and to make some sort of excuse for his behavior, but he simply stood there in the pale light of the dawn. The jungle was waking up about them, and the sun was mostly shielded in the east. But the pale rays were breaking through the tall trees onto the small house that occupied a microscopic niche in this huge rain forest. "I'm forced to ask a favor. Will you take us to the Guapi country?"

Marlowe studied Emily thoughtfully for a moment, then shrugged his shoulders. "I'm sure everyone's already told you that's not a good idea."

"We've already been told that by the Pettigrews back in Santarém, but I feel we need to go. I have to do this story," Emily insisted.

"Are you sure it's God's will?"

It was the kind of question that James Parker would never have asked. Emily suddenly remembered the spiritual struggles this man had gone through when he'd stayed with her family. She remembered being in a service with him when it appeared that he was moved by the gospel and was ready to give his life to Christ. The moment had passed, but now as she stood before him, she was aware how strange it was that he would be talking about God's will. For some reason it made her resentful, and she said quickly, "I sometimes have difficulty knowing God's will, but I'm going until I get a red light. Will you take us?"

Instead of answering, Marlowe turned and gazed out into the immensity of the jungle. She noted again his cleft chin and high cheekbones. He had evidently shaved, for his face was ruddy, and she noted a scar that she had never seen before that ran along his jawbone.

"The Guapi are killers and can be very dangerous, but you don't always see that. They can be very hospitable, very warm, but sometimes the smallest provocation can set them off, and they'll kill in an instant. You'll be risking your life, Emily, and I don't think your parents would approve."

"They knew we would be facing danger," Emily said quickly. "Will you take us?"

Reluctantly Marlowe nodded. "I don't like it, and I can't say yes or no. Let me pray about it, Emily, and you should pray, too. More than you've ever prayed about anything, perhaps."

At that moment Wes suddenly appeared, and the three went inside to eat breakfast.

The group seemed constrained, and Adriano could not understand it. He kept watching the face of Marlowe and then the faces of his guests. He waited until all three of them had left, then said, "Sarita, there's something going on with those three. Strange that they should come here and find Ian."

"They would be better off to go back. They have no place here," Sarita said.

"I think you are right, but that Emily seems to be a stubborn woman. I wonder what was between her and Ian back when they knew each other."

Sarita turned quickly. "What do you mean?" she demanded. "Between them."

"They have strong feelings for each other."

"She hates him. I could see that," Sarita said.

"That is very close to love. In all the time we have known him, Ian has never mentioned a woman, a wife or anyone. Perhaps this is why. This woman who comes out of nowhere from his past."

"I do not believe it. I wish they would go away."

Outside, Wes and Emily were discussing their plight. Wes began at once by saying, "Emily, I don't think we should go to the Guapi. From what everyone's been telling us, it's just too dangerous."

"Has Ian been talking to you?"

"Yes. He did tell me about some of the dangers that could happen out there. Maybe we should have listened to the Pettigrews and found a peaceful tribe near them."

"We've got to go to the Guapi, Wes. The assignment was to write a story on a tribe that has had hardly any contact with civilization," Emily said.

"Are you sure we can trust him? We trusted him once," Wes said grimly, "and we got burned. You more than the rest of us."

Emily flushed, for she knew Wes was referring to her attraction to this man. "I was a fool back then," she said.

"Well, he does seem different now."

"He seemed good to us when we first met him!" Emily said sharply. "But he's the only one who can take us. I'm going, Wes," she said abruptly.

"Then I'll go with you. I can't let you go alone."

They went to find Ian, and at once Emily said, "Have you made up your mind?"

Ian said, "Are you determined on going through with this?"

"Yes, we are," Emily returned stoutly.

"All right. I think it's a mistake, but I'll take you to the Guapi. It'll be up to God to keep you safe."

CHAPTER SEVENTEEN

A DANGEROUS TRIP

★ ★ ★ ★

"I'm afraid I'll have to check all of your gear."

Ian Marlowe was standing in front of the gear that Wes and Emily had laid out on the ground. He had told them the night before that it would be impossible to carry all that had been ferried in by the dugout. For the rest of their journey, they would have to carry all the supplies they would need on their backs.

Emily Winslow, over the years, had become a free spirit. She had always been a trifle headstrong, well able to control most circumstances and situations, but here in the bleak morning hours, when the feeble rays of the rising sun filled the clearing with a milky light, she felt intimidated and somewhat insulted.

"But these are just my personal belongings," she said quickly. "They couldn't be of any interest to you."

Ian looked down at the rather large package in Emily's pile of goods and shook his head. "I'm interested in our getting there," he said pleasantly and then smiled. "I know it may sound bossy to you, Emily, but every ounce is going to count on this trip."

Wes stood over to one side and could not restrain a grin. He listened as the two argued, and finally, with a furious gesture, Emily opened the bag and tossed out her "personal" items. For some reason it delighted Wes to hear Ian say, "I think you'd still better cut that pile in half, Emily."

Not accustomed to having her underwear viewed by strangers, Emily stared at Ian. It was in her mind that he was using her in some way, and she protested. "Well, I've got to have clean clothes."

"You'll just have to take fewer and wash them more often, I'm afraid." Ian's voice was firm, and he bent over to examine the rest of her gear. He put approximately half of it to one side, and Emily protested every decision. Finally Ian seemed satisfied.

Wes noticed that Ian had shifted at least a third of his gear, and Emily's also, to his own pack. Wes's gear consisted largely of photographic equipment, which proved to be the heaviest part of the load. When Ian came over and shook his head, Wes said, "I've got to have all of this, Ian. I need it to get the pictures we'll need for Emily's story."

"Well, you can try, but let me tell you, your shoulders are going to be pulling out of their sockets with all this gear before we're a day away from here."

"Aren't we taking any food?" Emily asked. She was still annoyed with Ian's rather domineering ways, for so she considered them, and she faced him with determination.

"I'm afraid all we'll be taking will be salt and whatever medicine you need. I'll be shooting game for the pot as we need it."

Suddenly he smiled, and Emily noted how much younger it made him look.

"You'll be eating some rather strange food," Ian said as he finished packing.

"What kind of strange food?" Emily asked.

"Well, I wouldn't be surprised if we ate an iguana every now and then."

"You mean one of those huge lizards? I wouldn't eat one of those things even if I was starving!" Emily said, shocked by the thought.

"They're not bad at all. They taste a little fishy, but there are worse things to eat."

"Worse things? What kind of things?" Wes inquired.

"I had a streak of bad luck and hadn't been able to shoot any game once. Hadn't been in the jungle too long, and I was starving to death. One of the tradesmen came along and wanted to know if I was hungry. When I told him yes, he reached down into a little leather bag and offered me what he had."

"What was it?" Wes asked.

"Live caterpillars."

Emily shuddered and made a face. "You didn't eat them, did you?"

"No. That was a bit too much for me. Oh, I thanked him and told him I wasn't hungry. It wasn't the truth, but you can't hurt these people's feelings. I'd better make that clear right now, Emily, and you too, Wes. They've got their own ways, and they don't like changes, so one of the biggest mistakes missionaries make, so I hear, is going in and trying to change everything."

Emily stared at Ian and then shook her head. "Well, I won't try to talk them out of eating caterpillars, but I don't think I could get one down."

Ian shrugged and said, "One of their favorite foods is monkeys. You'll have to face up to that. Do you think you can?"

Emily lifted her chin. "I can do whatever I have to do," she said with determination.

"That's the way to talk. Well, let's go in and eat breakfast."

The three of them went inside, where Adriano and Sarita joined them. Sarita had said little, Emily noticed, but her eyes went often to Ian Marlowe.

"This is good. What is it, Sarita?" Wes asked.

"That's turtle eggs."

"Not bad at all."

Sarita smiled at him. "My favorite is fish eggs, but they're hard to find."

"That's caviar," Emily remarked. "You wouldn't expect caviar here. I always think of that being in Russia or somewhere."

The rest of the meal consisted of fish, which was a staple of the Reys' diet. Emily suspected they would be eating plenty of fish during their expedition.

Sarita disappeared after serving their meal, not joining them. Ian got up as soon as he had finished and walked outside without a word. Emily watched him go, and her eyes met those of Wes. An understanding passed between them, but neither of them said anything. They turned to listen to Adriano, who was describing the trail they would be following through the jungle.

As Ian stepped outside, he noted that the weather seemed good, although it would probably rain. It always did, and he had grown to expect it. He moved along the Reys' porch to where Sarita stood leaning against the corner post. "You didn't eat anything, Sarita."

"I'm not hungry."

Ian leaned over and, seeing that she was avoiding his gaze, reached out and turned her face toward him. "What's wrong?" he asked. "You don't seem happy."

"There's nothing wrong with me. I just don't like to see you go."

"Well, I had planned to stay longer, but these folks need help. They'd never make it on their own."

"They're fools."

Ian reached out and pulled a lock of her jet black hair. "I expect they are—but so am I. At least that's what everyone around here has said about me for going into the Guapi country. To tell you the truth, I never expected to get out alive the first time I went in."

Sarita smiled and turned to face him fully. She was not tall, and as she looked up at him, there was a wistfulness in her voice as she said, "I remember when you first came. You were very sick."

"That's right." He touched her cheek and then shook his head. "I would have died if it hadn't been for you and your grandfather. I'll owe you my life for that."

"Those were good days, except for you being sick, of course. When you got well enough to leave, I thought you'd never come back. That happens to people that go into Guapi country."

"God had to take care of me. There's no other answer."

Sarita moved a fraction closer and reached out and put her hand on his chest. "How long will you be gone, Ian?"

"I guess until the Winslows get all their pictures and information they need." He could tell she was sad, and it troubled him. She had beautiful eyes; he had always admired them, but now he saw that they were filled with sadness. Wanting to cheer her up, he said, "I'll tell you what. As soon as I get back, you, your grandfather, and I will go down to the coast to Belém. I've been needing some supplies, and it'd be a good excuse. We'll go have a good time. See the sights."

"Really!"

"Sure. Now, don't be sad."

"I will try."

She withdrew her hand from his chest and stood regarding him with an expression he could not understand. She was always a puzzle to Ian, this girl or woman. Sometimes he had to remind himself that she was not a child, although she was very young. He suddenly asked, "What about that fellow Joaquin de Souza?"

"What about him?"

"Well, he's been hanging around a lot. I think he's interested in you."

"I don't care for him."

"Seems like a nice enough young fellow. And there was that other young fellow—Reginaldo something. You liked him, didn't you?"

Sarita did not answer. She turned away from him and stared out into the clearing. They were close enough to the river so that they could hear its pleasant murmuring, always the background against which all other sounds were measured. "Be careful, Ian."

Ian put his hands on her shoulders and turned her around. "I was born to be hanged. Don't worry about me. We'll all be all right, and you'd better watch out for that fellow Joaquin."

"He means nothing to me," Sarita said.

"Well, we'd better get started. I'll miss you."

Sarita took a quick breath. "I'll miss you, too, Ian."

Ian turned and went back into the house and said to Adriano, "I guess we'd better get moving. We have a long and difficult trip ahead of us."

Adriano rose at once and said, "God be with you and keep you safe."

"Thank you, Adriano," Emily said, smiling. She turned to Sarita, who had entered the room, and nodded. "Thank you for your hospitality, Sarita."

"You're welcome."

Moving out of the house, they descended the steps, and Ian picked up Emily's pack. "Here you are," he said. "Doesn't weigh much now, but it'll get heavier after we've been on the trail for a while."

Emily slipped her arms through the straps. She had already measured them and found that they were snug and comfortable. "It doesn't seem too heavy," she said. "I can carry it."

Ian did not answer. He had put, by far, the biggest load in his own knapsack. Now he swung it onto his shoulders and waited until Wes had strapped his knapsack on. "Good-bye, Adriano. You take good care of your grandfather, Sarita."

A strange feeling came over Emily as she followed behind Marlowe. Wes fell in step behind her, and as they left the clearing and entered a trail, she looked back suddenly and saw the Reys watching them. She was leaving civilization and going into a world that was totally foreign to anything she had ever known or experienced. Fear came to her for a moment, for despite her bold words she knew that the Amazon rain forest was a dangerous place to tread for the inexperienced. She forced the thought from her mind and focused on keeping up with Ian. She was very thankful that he had agreed to be their guide.

Soon they were out of sight of the Reys' house, and a strange sense of isolation crept over her. The jungle was dense, and a light rain began to fall. She was wearing a sun helmet, but the rain dripped down onto her neck and gave her an unpleasant sensation. The path was a narrow, endless tunnel that wound through emerald-colored foliage. The strangest feeling came to Emily as she looked up and saw the faraway treetops forming a dense canopy that shut out most of the sunlight. She had the feeling that she had been suddenly reduced to the size of an insect, so massive was the forest. Her eyes moved constantly, taking in all the strange sounds and sights of the jungle, which seemed to be a solid wall of vegetation. At times there appeared to be no path, but Ian always found a way. She was aware that she would be terribly lost if it were not for him. They were moving slowly, completely enveloped by the jungle. Her view was limited to a few feet, and she kept her eyes on Ian's back. From time to time she glanced up to the tops of the trees, where the pale rays of the sun peeped through from time to time. Finding herself falling behind, she gave herself up to the effort of keeping up with Ian.

The rain began in earnest thirty minutes later, and Emily turned to see Wes, who looked as miserable as she felt. *This is a rain forest.* Emily smiled briefly. *I guess we can expect showers.*

Ian turned and studied Wes and Emily. "All right?" he said.

"I'm fine," Emily said, but already the straps had begun to chafe her shoulders, and the load seemed much heavier.

On and on the three wound their way into the depths of the jungle under the tall trees. Overhead there was movement of various kinds, and Emily saw a group of monkeys once. What Ian had said floated back into her memory, and she shook her head involuntarily. *I don't think I could eat a monkey, but I may have to.*

By the time the sun was higher in the sky Emily was soaked. The rain had done its part, and then she had begun to perspire. The heat and humidity were overwhelmingly stifling, and she now had to keep her thumbs under the straps of her knapsack because the weight of the gear pulled at her. She had determined to avoid anything that would even sound like a complaint.

Finally Ian said, "We'll take a break here," and swung his knapsack to the ground. He kept his rifle in his hands, and his eyes moved constantly, sometimes high up in the trees and other times scanning the territory into which they were headed. Now he sat down and watched as his two companions did the same. "How are you making it?" he asked pleasantly.

"You were right," Wes said grimly. He took out a handkerchief that was already soaked and mopped his face. "This pack gets heavier as we go along."

"I expect you'll need to make a couple of pads. The straps are going to be cutting into your shoulders before long. I should have thought of that. You can use a pair of socks or any kind of garment."

As the three sat resting, Emily was again aware of the ominous setting in which they found themselves. Overhead the trees laced their branches together so that they almost made a solid canopy. But on the jungle floor, away from the river, the grass was thin, for there was not enough sunlight to support it.

"I always thought the Amazon River Basin had fertile soil," Wes finally remarked. "This ground seems pretty poor."

"It is poor. The rainfall carries the nutrients off so that they don't enrich the ground."

Emily sat listening as Ian spoke quietly of the Amazon. It was obvious he knew a great deal about the river.

"This river is not like any other in the world," Ian said. "It drains half of a continent. The Amazon Basin is about three-fourths the size of the United States."

"How deep is the river?" Wes asked.

"Well, at Obidos it's a mile and a half wide and two hundred feet deep."

"That's a big river," Wes said in awe.

"Yes, it is big. It handles about ten times the Mississippi's volume at Vicksburg. There the Mississippi's about a third of a mile wide and only seventy feet deep."

"Where does the Amazon start, Ian?" Emily asked.

"Well, it starts high up in the Andes in Peru. Just a trickle, but it goes for almost four thousand miles, and it's got a flow sixty times greater than the Nile River. Not quite as long as the Nile, but it's much bigger."

Finally Ian stood up and said, "We'd better head on. Let's see if we can make some sort of pads for those shoulders."

Emily searched through her bag and picked out her two shirts, which was all she had been allowed to bring. She fashioned two pads, and Ian came over to help her adjust them.

"That ought to be better," he smiled.

"Thank you," she said coldly.

Ian noticed her tone but said nothing about it. "We'd better get on our way."

They moved on down the pathway, and although Ian did not quicken the pace, Emily found that the heat and the humidity drained the strength out of her. She gritted her teeth and was thankful that she had padded the shoulder straps.

Once just before noon Ian suddenly lifted his rifle, and the echoes of the explosion seemed to roll through the jungle itself.

"What was it?" Emily said.

"A wild pig. A small one."

Ian moved out into the thickness of the jungle and cáme back with the carcass of a small pig. "I think we'll cook this up and eat it. It'll make us feel better."

"Can I help?" Emily said.

"I'll let you do the cooking. I'll clean it. Wes, see if you can find some dry wood."

Finding dry wood proved to be quite a problem, for everything seemed to be soaked. Nevertheless, by the time the meat was roasting over a crackling fire, Emily realized that she was hungry.

"I'm starved to death. I don't see how I could be after that breakfast," she protested.

"The jungle saps the strength out of you. You'll have a good appetite."

They had nothing to eat with the pork except a little salt, but Emily found the meat delicious. They took a two-hour break, and Emily suspected that Ian was pampering them a little bit.

"He never seems to get tired," Emily whispered to Wes once.

"No, he's used to it. But I'll tell you what, I'll be ready for bed tonight."

"So will I," Emily said.

★ ★ ★ ★

"This looks like a good place to camp," Ian said as he pulled off his knapsack. "Why don't you two take it easy? The first day's always the hardest."

"No, I want to help." Both Wes and Emily spoke up at once.

"Well then . . . Wes, you set up the tents, and I'll go see if I can find some fresh meat. Emily, you can gather some wood for a fire."

Emily busied herself making a fire as Wes struggled with the tents. He had to find saplings to use for braces and pegs, and once both of them looked up from their work when they heard a faint shot.

"Hope he doesn't come in with a monkey," Emily said.

Wes laughed. "So do I, but I expect we'll be eating monkey meat before this trip is over."

Emily discovered she was dead tired and was looking forward to going to bed in her tent. Ian came in with a small animal that looked like a deer, no more than two and a half feet high.

"Venison for supper. I'll dress it out."

It was an hour before they all sat down to eat. The tents were up, and Emily insisted on grilling the venison steaks. Once again they had nothing to go with the meat, but she found the taste of it delicious.

After they had eaten, they sat around the fire talking. All around them the jungle reached out and rose high in the air, so that she felt very small.

"What are the Guapi like, Ian?" Emily asked.

"Very unusual people. I don't really understand them a great deal."

"Do the men have more than one wife?"

"Oh yes. It is an accepted part of their tradition."

"What about their spiritual condition?" Wes said.

"It's hard to say about that. I tell them about God, and they tell me about their god. I think they're waiting to see if my God is stronger than theirs."

"Is the language hard?" Emily asked.

"Very hard. I learned Portuguese pretty easily. My teacher said I had a natural flair for it, but the Guapi language is terribly difficult. They make a few sounds that I can't possibly make."

Emily listened for a time, but soon she grew weary. She said, "I think I'll turn in, if you don't mind."

"I hope you sleep. Be sure to keep your net in place. These mosquitoes are fierce."

Indeed they were thick, and Emily arranged her netting carefully before she lay down on a blanket. She was lying on the earth with nothing but a small piece of rubberized cloth underneath, and she thought about how easily a snake could slither into her tent.

She had expected to fall asleep at once, but sleep came slowly. She was well aware that outside the small camp lurked jaguars and anacondas. Some of those snakes got to be thirty feet long, and according to some of the natives, anacondas were able to swallow a human being. Her exhaustion was so intense, however, that she had no time to be afraid, and she prayed, "Oh, God, keep us safe. That's all I can pray tonight. . . ."

The next day was a grueling repeat of the first. Emily kept up, despite chafed shoulders and a sense of weakness. By the time they camped for the night, she was totally exhausted and felt terrible.

Ian had shot some kind of bird that he had stewed in a pot, but Emily could eat little. Ian moved closer and said quickly, "Don't you feel well, Emily?"

"I think I'm just tired. I believe I'll go to bed early."

Emily practically crawled into her tent and fell down without rolling up in her blanket. She felt a chill and shivered as she drifted off into a restless sleep.

Sometime during the night she awoke, and her teeth were chattering. She was freezing to death, and then suddenly a light appeared. "What is it, Emily?"

She tried to sit up and found that she was too weak. "I . . . I'm freezing."

Ian said quickly, "You've got malaria."

Alarm ran through Emily. "What will we do?"

"We'll just have to stay here until you get over it."

Emily was aware that he had opened the fly to her tent and was putting another blanket over her. She opened her eyes but could see nothing in the murky light of the tent. "Will I die?" she whispered.

"God willing, you'll be well."

Emily remembered little of that night, except she would either burn up or freeze to death. She was conscious that Wes and Ian were there, and from time to time one of them would whisper encouragement to her.

Sometime near morning she knew that Ian was beside her, trying to get her to drink water. It was one of those times she was burning up and refused to keep the cover on. She sipped the water greedily, and then when he eased her back onto the blanket, she whispered, "I'm not much good, am I?"

"Malaria can get anybody."

"Have you had it?" she whispered.

"Oh yes." He reached out then and pulled the cover over her. "I know it's hot and it hurts, but you need to sweat it off."

Emily lay there, her mind wandering. She felt miserable and drained of all strength, drifting in and out of sleep. She was also aware that Ian was sitting there saying nothing, but his presence was a comfort.

CHAPTER EIGHTEEN

"I CAN'T FORGIVE HIM!"

★ ★ ★ ★

"I don't know what to think, Ian," Wes said, shaking his head in despair. "I've never seen Emily so sick like this."

"She'll be all right," Ian said.

Ian was standing beside Wes some fifteen feet away from where the two tents had been erected. It was the third day of Emily's fever, and Wes's face was pale and drawn with worry. He gnawed on his lower lip nervously and ran his hand through his brown hair, now lank with the heat.

"I've never been where there was no doctor available," Wes muttered. "I don't mind telling you, Ian, I'm pretty scared."

"God knows our future, and I believe He's going to pull her through this."

Wes searched the face of the other man and finally shook his head. "I wish we had never come to this place! We must have been crazy."

Ian put his hand on the young man's shoulder and said, "I know it doesn't mean much to say 'don't worry,' but I've seen God do wonderful things, even for people who don't believe." He turned then, removing his hand, and stared at the tent where Emily lay. There was no breeze at all on the floor of the forest, and the only sounds came from a far-off troop of monkeys as they made their way through the canopy and the shrill cry of a bird. "Your sister's a believer, and you're a believer, and so am I. So you and I will just have to pray for her."

Wes looked up with a glimmer of hope in his eyes. He had lost weight even over the short period of time he had been under the hot sun of Brazil. Now, however, he seemed to hold fast to Ian's words and nodded. "All right. We'll do that, then. She's got to make it, Ian—she's just got to!"

★　★　★　★

The fever at times seemed to be hotter than Emily could bear, while at other times the cold came with a shaking, teeth-chattering force. The voices would fade in and out, and some-times she felt a touch of a hand. But during those times she could not distinguish who was wiping her face with a cool cloth, al-though she knew there were two individuals close by.

Sometimes the darkness would surround her, holding her in an ebony canopy, and at other times the light would filter through. And when she would open her eyes, she would see faces that seemed to swim and waver as she tried to focus. Some-times the dreams would come, and she would know that they were dreams, and yet they were so very real. Once she saw her-self and Jared and Wes as clearly as if it were a photograph. They were swimming in the pond, and they were very young. She could hear, she thought, the sounds of the squealing and the screaming and the laughter. She could almost feel the refreshing waters as the vision of fond childhood memories filled her mind.

Consciousness came back with a rush as she seemed to emerge from a dark tunnel. Her eyes opened, and for a moment she could not understand what she saw, and then she saw a face.

"Wes—?" Her lips were dry, so dry she could scarcely speak. She licked them in an effort to speak more clearly. "Wes, is that you?"

"No. It's Ian. Wes is asleep. How do you feel?"

Emily knew that she was wringing wet, but the dullness of mind and the abyss that had tried to hold her captive were now gone. "I'm thirsty," she whispered.

"I'll get you some water."

Emily lay there, her bones aching. She saw the outline of the jungle through the door of her tent and attempted to sit up.

"Here, let me help you," Ian said.

A strong arm came around her shoulders, and she was lifted as if she were a child. Then she felt the touch of the tin cup against her lips. She grasped at the hand that held it, choking the water down.

"Take it easy, now. Very small sips. You can have all you want, but slowly."

"That's so good," Emily said, licking her dry lips.

"I know," Ian said.

His voice was low, but she focused on his face. He had not shaved, and the bristles of his reddish whiskers covered his face.

"Here. Have a little more. Just a sip."

Emily forced herself to sip the tepid water slowly. It was the best drink she had ever had in her life. She felt the liquid soaking down her parched throat and into her dehydrated body. He did not move his arms, so as she sat there in his embrace, the weakness was more frightening than anything she had ever known. For a long time he gave her small sips of water, and finally she said, "How long have I been sick?"

"This is the third day, but your fever's broken now. You'll be all right."

"Can I get up?"

"Not for a while. I want you to drink water in small sips, and I'm going to make a broth. You've eaten practically nothing. Can I trust you to take the water slowly if I leave it?"

"Yes." Emily took the cup, and she felt him lower her back. He pulled her knapsack under her head.

"There. Now you can sip the water. I'll go start stewing something for you."

Emily lay there, careful only to take small sips of water. By the time she had finished the cup, Wes had come into her tent, his eyes eager. "How do you feel, sis?"

"Much better."

"What a relief! You gave me quite a scare." Wes reached over and brushed her damp hair back off her forehead. "I didn't bargain for your getting so sick when we came out here."

"I hope you never get malaria."

"Ian says I probably will if I stay here long enough. He says everybody gets it sooner or later."

Wes sat down, and when she asked him, he helped her get into a sitting position. He held her braced against his arm and said, "I don't ever remember being so scared. There's no doctor around to help when somebody gets hurt or sick this far in the interior."

"I'm sorry to be such a trouble."

"Don't be silly!"

He sat there holding her and then said, "I don't think Ian has slept more than three or four hours a night. I just fall over sometimes. This heat drains me, but he seems to be used to it. He's quite a nurse. And he sure knows how to pray, sis. He's done a lot of that for you."

Emily took a sip of the water and suddenly caught an odor of something that smelled heavenly. "I'm so hungry," she said.

"That's good. You've got to eat to get your strength back."

Thirty minutes later Ian stooped and came into the small tent. "Kind of crowded, but you hold her up, Wes, and I'll feed her."

"I can feed myself," Emily protested.

"No, let me do it." Ian dipped a spoonful of the stew, blew on it, then held it out as he would to a child. "Open wide," he grinned.

Emily opened her mouth, feeling rather foolish. The stew was delicious, and she smacked her lips. "That's so good."

"I won't tell you what's in it," Ian smiled.

"It's not monkey, is it?"

"No, it's not monkey. It's a bird that lives around here. They're about the size of doves. It takes several of them to make a meal, but it's the best thing in Brazil, I think."

Emily ate as fast as he could put the stew in her mouth, and as soon as he was finished feeding her, an irresistible fatigue and urge for sleep overtook her. "Thank you. That was . . . good. . . ."

Wes stared at her. "She fainted."

"She's just worn out. Lay her back down. She won't need all these blankets. She'll be better now."

The two men moved outside the tent, and Ian said, "We can go back if you'd like, Wes. We can make a stretcher, of sorts, and carry her."

"I don't know, Ian. You know Emily. She's pretty stubborn. You think she'll be all right if we go on?"

"We'll have to stay here for a couple of days and keep her fed and let her get a little exercise. She won't be able to carry much, so you and I'll have to double up."

"I don't mind that."

"All right. We'll see what she says in the morning. But like you say, she's a stubborn woman. I think she'll want to go on."

★   ★   ★   ★

Emily stretched and said, "I feel so dirty. If I could just take a bath, I'd feel so much better." She had washed her clothes during the three days they had waited and had done little else except eat the meat, wild fruits, and berries Ian brought into camp. Now, however, she ran her hand through her hair, which was stiff and lank. She had washed her face, but that didn't feel like enough.

"No reason why you can't," Ian said. "There's the river."

Emily stared at him. "I'd be afraid to get in that. I've heard of piranha."

"I was scared to get in the rivers myself when I first came, but I found out that not all piranhas are vicious, only certain ones. They've got a bad reputation, but they don't attack a large animal unless the scent of blood is already in the water. We can find you a nice open space, and I'll check it out."

"That would be wonderful."

"I'll see what I can find."

Emily waited for fifteen minutes; then Ian came back to say, "There's a good place down here that's cut off from the main stream. No fish in it at all. You have soap?"

"Yes, but no towels. You wouldn't let me bring any," she said accusingly.

"Well, you can use a couple of your shirts and mine, too, if you need to. Come along. Wes, we've got to give the patient a bath."

Emily stared at him and flushed. "Never mind that," she muttered.

She followed Ian down to the stream that was less than two hundred yards away. It was much wider than she thought and shielded on both banks by vegetation.

"There's a nice sandy bottom right here. The water's clear."

"What about snakes?" Wes said.

"Well, I didn't see any. I was taking a bath once, and an anaconda went swimming by. He looked like he was thirty feet long."

"Did he see you?"

"I don't know. I stayed mighty still, so he went on. Wes and I'll wait within hollering distance. If you see a snake, give me a call."

Emily waited until the two men disappeared, then slipped out of her clothes. With her bar of soap in her hand, she stepped into the stream, which was deliciously cool, and sat down. She washed her hair first, soaped herself all over, rinsed off, then did it all again.

From time to time she would look around cautiously but saw no sign of snakes or any other dangerous creatures. She did see a frog such as she had never seen before, a brilliant crimson color.

Finally she got out of the pool, dried herself off, and climbed into dry clothes. Slipping on her socks and her boots, she let her hair hang down and walked over to where she could hear the voices of the two men speaking quietly. "I'm ready," she said.

Ian stepped out, still holding the rifle, and she said, "There was a red frog in there. I never saw a red frog before."

"It's probably a poison dart frog."

"He's poisonous?"

"The Indians make a pretty powerful poison out of him, so I wouldn't pick one up if I were you."

At that instant Wes said, "Look at that!"

Emily turned and blinked with surprise. She could not believe what she was seeing. "Is that a lizard?" she whispered.

Ian was smiling. "That's a basilisk," he said.

"What's it doing? It's running on top of the water on its hind legs!" Wes gasped. "I never saw anything like that!"

Emily stared at the lizard that was, indeed, skimming across the water bolt upright with his small legs held in front of him. "How does he do that?"

"Just sheer speed, I think. He doesn't weigh much." Ian suddenly laughed. "The natives call him the Jesus Christ lizard."

"Why in the world do they call him that?"

"I preached a sermon shortly after I got here. I didn't have much of their language yet. I was preaching about Jesus walking on the water, and when I said that, all the natives began to murmur in surprise. One of them told me about this lizard that walks on water. I thought they were kidding me until I saw my first one. That's what they call it now—the Jesus Christ lizard. Made a pretty effective illustration."

Emily watched as the lizard went back and forth over the water and then said, "I never saw anything like that."

★   ★   ★   ★

Emily's strength came back quickly with a few days of rest and nourishment, and soon she was ready to continue their journey to the Guapi tribe. She informed Ian, and he agreed, that if she felt strong enough, they would start the next morning.

The night before they continued on their trip, Emily lay in her tent. She was so accustomed now to the jungle night sounds, they no longer frightened her. She began to pray but found it a struggle. For some reason she felt far away from God. This had happened to her before, of course, so she simply waited and finally asked God, "What's wrong, Lord? Why can't I feel your presence?"

There was no answer in her spirit, not for a long time. But finally Emily began to think of Ian Marlowe, and she knew then what the problem was.

I still haven't forgiven him.

The thought leaped into her mind, and she knew instantly

that God was trying to tell her something. Emily knew her Bible well, and nothing was clearer than the New Testament teaching embodied in the Lord's Prayer: "Forgive us our debts as we forgive our debtors."

The words seemed to be burned on Emily's mind and in her spirit. She lay awake that night struggling with her feelings. Seeing Ian Marlowe, the man she had known as James Parker, had brought back all the memories of those times. She knew that she felt humiliated as a woman, for he had deceived her and caused her to fall in love with him. Then, when she had found out what kind of man he truly was, she had felt shamed. Even now, after these years of trying to forget what he'd done, she did not really know whether she had grown angrier with the man called James Parker for his deceit about her brother, or for his misleading her into feelings for him that she now regretted.

Emily Winslow struggled with all those thoughts for a long time that night, and finally in desperation she prayed, "Oh, God, I can't forgive him!" The silence seemed to be almost deafening, and finally she turned over and managed to go to sleep. She had, however, just before she dropped off, a sudden thought: *I've got to settle this matter, or I can't go on with God.*

PART FOUR

SUMMER–AUTUMN 1923

★ ★ ★ ★

CHAPTER NINETEEN

"I NEVER LOVED ANYONE...."

★ ★ ★ ★

Emily sat with her back against a towering tree, notebook in hand, and pencil scrolling across the page. She had decided to use pencils instead of pens, since the dampness would be apt to spoil the ink. She had been awakened earlier by Wes and had joined the men at breakfast. Now while they were packing the gear, she put her thoughts down in writing:

> The malaria did something to me mentally, I think, as well as physically. Naturally it was a miserable time with aches, pains, and fevers. I was either freezing to death or burning up. Ian says that it may come back when I least expect it. I feel much stronger this morning, but I still am not as well as I would like to be. We will be leaving in a few minutes, and Ian says we will reach the Guapi village sometime late this afternoon. I am anxious to get there so I can start my work.

Emily looked up and noted that Wes was laughing at something Ian had said. For some reason Wes's amusement caused a resentment she could not define. She knew it was tied up somehow with her feelings toward Ian, and as she began writing again, she let her thoughts flow freely onto the paper.

> My sickness showed me how weak and frail I really am. I could

easily have died and been buried here, and everything would have been over for me. For a time I thought I would die, and curiously enough I was not so much afraid as disappointed. I kept thinking, "But, God, I've got to live! There are so many things I need to do." Maybe everyone who dies thinks of everything they wished they could have finished. I remember those were the words my grandmother said when she died. She hated to leave things undone. That's exactly how I felt when I thought that death was imminent.

I might as well put down on paper what I feel and hope that no one ever reads it. I've been struggling for so long over my feelings toward Ian. Perhaps I should say toward James Parker. I have trouble at times remembering that Ian Marlowe and James Parker are one and the same man. I've harbored such bitterness for the man who deceived my family and me for so long, but now I'm confused. I remember Mom and Dad urged me to forgive James, but when I received his letter I didn't do that. And now there's something deep down inside of me, sort of like a cancer, I suppose, that keeps eating away at my spirit. I've known for a long time that I couldn't pray as I could before I developed this bitterness. Now it seems to be with me constantly.

Emily broke off when Wes came over and said, "All ready to head out, sis."

Scrambling to her feet, Emily folded the cover of the notebook and stuck the pencil in her pocket. "I'm ready."

Ian came over and handed her a knapsack that could not have weighed over fifteen pounds. "I can carry more than this," Emily protested.

"I don't want you to push too hard," Ian said. "Wes and I can handle the rest of the gear." Ian looked up at the sunlight suffused through the canopy and said, "We'll take it easy today. If we don't reach the Guapi today, we'll make it tomorrow."

Emily nodded, although the words almost leaped to her lips, *You don't have to slow down for me.* She had always recognized the streak of stubbornness that lay in her, but she had always called it by a nobler name. Perseverance, perhaps. Determination. Here in the jungle, far from anything civilized, she realized this was no time to be stubborn. Despite her feelings for Ian Marlowe, her life and Wes's were in his hands. "All right," she said. "You're the guide."

"Well, I must say, malaria has improved your disposition." Ian grinned at her and reached out and tugged a lock of hair that hung down her back. "You're getting absolutely tame."

Emily could not help returning his smile, but she pushed his hand away. "Never mind that. Let's get going."

They donned their knapsacks, and Ian, carrying the rifle as usual, was in the lead. Emily followed him, with Wes bringing up the rear. As they made their way through the jungle, Emily was conscious that her strength was limited. She, who had always been strong, now was at the mercy of her own frailty. Determined not to show it, she trekked along through the silent jungle all morning. She was thankful for the breaks Ian had taken during the morning so she could rest a bit.

Suddenly Ian said, "There's a snake over here, but it's harmless. Don't let it frighten you."

Emily turned quickly in the direction Ian was pointing the muzzle of his rifle. She took a deep breath, for there was a large snake with beautiful green and blue markings with white rings.

"You say it's harmless, Ian?"

"To us it is. I suppose it's dangerous to mice and rats. Beautiful, isn't it?"

Emily stared at the snake. "I've always been terrified of snakes. Do you really think he's beautiful?"

"God has made everything beautiful in its time."

"Is that in the Bible?"

"Why, yes it is. It's in Ecclesiastes 3:11, I believe."

Emily quickly turned from the serpent to study Ian's face. Even as she did, she realized this man was very different from the James Parker she remembered.

Wes had sat down to retie his boots. "What do you make of that scripture?"

"I don't really know." Ian smiled cheerfully. "I know that some of God's creations don't seem very beautiful to us—a warthog, for example—but I suppose to other warthogs one could be very handsome."

Emily looked back at the snake. "I can't separate what they *are* from what they look like. Maybe it's because a lot of them are so deadly—and I suppose I got the picture of the serpent in the

Garden of Eden bringing down all mankind."

"Most people don't like snakes. But there's a strange beauty about them. The same is true of a jaguar."

"Will we see one, do you think? We saw one up in a tree on our boat trip to Santarém."

"I hope not. They're very powerful creatures. If you meet one at the wrong time without a rifle, it wouldn't be much of a contest." Ian took his hat off and held it down by his side. He studied the snake and some thought possessed him. "Jaguars are beautiful in their own right. They're strong and powerful, and the coloring is like nothing else, but they are dangerous." Ian suddenly motioned with the rifle. "There he goes."

They both watched the serpent as he wound his way around the vegetation and disappeared with a flick of his tail. Ian turned to her and smiled. "That was a harmless one, but don't go making friends with any snakes. There're some pretty bad ones around here."

"You don't have to warn me about that," Emily said.

"Do you feel like going on now?"

"Yes, I'm fine."

"We'll take another break pretty soon. . . ."

★　★　★　★

The rest of the trek was hard on Emily, but she did not complain. They stopped for an hour at noon, and then on the latter part of their trip, Ian made it a point to stop every hour for at least ten minutes. Emily knew the rests were for her benefit, and several times she almost brought herself to argue over Ian's decision to stop repeatedly. But she refrained, and finally, as the setting sun was filtering through the trees in the west, Ian halted and pointed ahead.

"The village is right up there about a mile."

"They won't be expecting us."

"Oh, I expect they will," Ian countered. A strange smile moved the corners of his lips upward. "We've probably been watched all the way. These Guapi—they're magicians in the forest. They can become invisible, it seems. Are you ready for your first meeting with headhunters?"

Emily hesitated. "I wouldn't be if I were alone."

"Well, I believe we'll be all right, but you'll have to be prepared to change your ideas."

Emily did not question his words, but as they moved forward, a sense of excitement began rising in her. After so many months of planning and waiting, they were finally here. She knew somehow that God was in this whole expedition she and Wes had undertaken. He had opened the door for her and for Wes, and now after great effort and a bad sickness, she was about to embark on what would be the most important event of her life.

She walked closely behind Ian and heard him murmur in a soft whisper, "There's the village."

Looking ahead she saw a clearing and reed huts with grass roofs. Some of them had no walls and were mere shelters from the sun, which beat down on the open space. Smoke rose from fires and slowly spiraled upward in the almost breathless air. She saw dogs and birds moving in the open space and imagined that they were pets.

They passed by the side of the river, which flowed some hundred yards around the camp, catching it as in the crook of an elbow. Canoes were drawn up on the bank, and she saw rows of wooden tripods rising out of the water.

"What are those, Ian?"

"Fish traps."

"Where are all the people?"

"They're here. They're very shy. No matter what happens, both of you, don't show any fear. These people respect courage more than you would think."

And then Emily did see the people, for they seemed to materialize from nowhere. They were small, Emily saw, and copper-colored with jet black hair. As they walked closer a shock ran through her because they were practically naked.

Both Emily and Wes had known that natives of the Amazon rain forest wore few clothes. Some, she had read, went absolutely naked, and now the younger children that hung back beside the adults, even those approaching adolescence, wore not a stitch. The man that came forward was flanked by three women, all naked from the waist up. Emily was embarrassed by the sight.

Don't be a fool! she cautioned herself. *What did you expect— party dresses in the Amazon rain forest?*

She was aware of the drowsy sounds of a clucking hen, and what sounded like doves calling in the forest. She heard the rising pitch of cicadas and knew that they would soon begin their evening concert. Her nostrils burned with the rank smell that Ian had warned her about. *"There are no sweet-smelling villages,"* he had said—and she steeled herself against the odor.

The man who stepped forward had an air of authority about him. He was not tall, but he was strongly built and wore only a loincloth made of some sort of bark or closely woven fiber. His cheeks were tattooed in an intricate pattern, and his dark eyes, so black they were like obsidian, were taking in the visitors calmly enough. He spoke and waited until Ian greeted him. Ian smiled and turned to wave his hand toward the two visitors and said something else. The chief smiled and made a remark while looking at Emily.

When Ian did not respond at first, Emily looked at him. "What did he say?"

Ian gave a small negative shake of his head, and then he suddenly smiled. "He asked if you were my wife, and said if you were, I needed two or three more. He said you'd be too weak, that you'd wear out too soon."

Wes suddenly smothered a laugh, which made Emily shoot a furious glance in his direction. She knew her face was flushed from the long walk and saw that all the women were moving to where they could get a better glimpse of her.

"What did you tell him?" Emily demanded swiftly.

"I told him that I had no woman. That you and Wes are mighty important folks."

Emily said, "I have gifts. Would it be good to give them the gifts now?"

"Give the chief his. That'll help to put him in a good humor."

Emily pulled her knapsack off, unfastened it, and reached

down into the depths. She pulled out a razor sharp knife with a bone handle that she had bought for this occasion. She stepped forward, took the blade in her hand, and extended the handle to the chief. "Would you tell him please that I am honored to be here, and that I would like to make this small gift to him."

As Ian spoke the language, which sounded to her as if he had a mouth full of mush he was trying to talk around, Emily watched the chief. He simply stared at her and did not move. She was afraid he was going to refuse the gift, but then he reached out, took it from her, and held it carefully. He ran his fingers across the shining blade, tested the edge of it, and then said something.

"He said thank you very much, and he hopes you will enjoy your visit."

"Are these his wives?"

"I think so. They live pretty informally here, and I sometimes get the wives mixed up."

Having several wives seemed wrong to Emily, but she knew now was no time to argue about the marital customs of the Guapi. "Should I give his wives some presents?"

"It wouldn't hurt. He's a pretty stubborn man, but I know he listens to at least one of his wives. That one there on the end. The tall one. Her name is Domi. The chief is called Noki."

Emily pulled out several items from her bag and presented them to the three women, each of them with a child on her hip. The one called Domi took the red ribbon and studied it, then she tied it at once around her forehead and chattered excitedly to the other wives. One of the other wives had put on an inexpensive bracelet and the third a necklace of cheap beads. They all looked very proud, and when the chief said something, Emily said, "What did he say?"

"He said something about women being vain. Always having to have pretty things."

Emily could not resist it. "They don't have many pretty things."

"Never say that to them. Remember, God has made everything beautiful in its time."

Wes had pulled out his camera and asked, "Would it be all right if I take a picture?"

"I'd put that away for a while. Let them get used to you, Wes."

Disappointed, Wes plunked the camera back in his knapsack and waited.

Ian made a longer speech to the chief and listened to his reply, then said, "Come along. We'll get you settled in."

"Are we going to stay in the village?"

"I think it might be better if we put a little distance between us—just a few hundred yards. We'll go set up camp on the outskirts down by the river. It'll be handy for drinking water."

Emily and Wes followed, aware of the Guapi watching them. "Did that go all right?" she asked.

"Very well. Much better than my first visit. I thought then they were going to chop my head off right on the spot."

"How do these people choose their chief?" Wes asked.

"Well, it's a rather peculiar method." Ian walked easily down a path that led past the last of the huts. "He used to be a witch doctor, but he gave that up. He became chief, not because of his black magic, but because he was the man most able to understand the feelings of every other man in the tribe."

"Is that right?" Wes spoke up with surprise. "How does he do that?"

"I think God just put it in him. He's very sensitive. If you're around him enough, you'll think he's reading your mind. It's very difficult to know the feelings of the Guapi."

"Why is that?" Emily asked.

"Guapi don't express their feelings as we do. In fact, it's considered bad taste to show much emotion. You'll see it. Even young children pick it up early. I've seen a young native boy faint from pain rather than cry out. That's why they value the chief so much. They realize that he somehow knows what's going on inside of them."

"I'll have to include that in my story," Emily said.

"It wouldn't be a bad trait for American politicians to have. I think some presidents had it. Lincoln, for one, seemed to have been able to do that," Ian said.

They passed out of the immediate area where the village huts were located and came to one standing only a few yards from the jungle wall.

"This is mine," Ian said. "Some of the warriors helped me make it."

The structure was made out of bamboo uprights, some as much as six or eight inches in diameter, tied together with vines. The hut had a door but no windows, and it was thatched thickly with grasses. "You'll stay here, Emily. It's not much, but it'll give you some privacy. I'm glad you brought that little oil lamp. You may be able to work a little after dark."

Emily stepped inside and produced the lamp. When she lit it the darkness was driven away, and she saw that Ian had made a cot, a chair, and a table. "This will do fine, but I'll be putting you out."

"I'll sleep in your tent. Wes and I'll camp right here so we'll all be together."

Emily did not say anything, but she was happy that the two would be close.

"I'm anxious to get to work," she said.

"No work today," Ian said firmly.

"But there's so much I want to write down."

"You don't know malaria, Emily. You're still not as strong as you think." Ian suddenly grew very serious. "Out here, Emily, I'm the closest thing to a father you're going to have, and I hate to put it this way, but you'll have to do what I say, and I say— and right now—that you need to lie down and rest."

"Good for you, Ian! Make her mind." Wes grinned. "Here, sis, we'll unpack. You just sit down and let us pamper you a little bit."

Emily hesitated, about to make an argument out of it, but she suddenly smiled. "All right, Ian. I don't have to call you *Father*, do I?"

"Oh, I don't think that'll be necessary. Come on, Wes. Let's get those tents up. Then we'll think about cooking something."

Ian moved off and started putting the tent up, but Wes stayed behind. "I'm glad Ian sat down on you, sis. You don't need to push yourself. That malaria's bad stuff. Saps all the strength out of you."

Suddenly Emily was very glad that Wes had come along. She smiled ruefully. "You have a hard time raising me, don't you?"

"Not a bit of it. You've just got so much drive you think you have to bull your way through—but Ian's right. I'm glad he's with us."

Emily looked over to where Ian had already started putting up the tent and said, "So am I."

★　★　★　★

Emily woke after a brief nap, and when she stepped outside, she saw that the two tents were up and Wes and Ian were chatting. They both looked around, and Wes asked quickly, "Did you sleep?"

"Oh yes. I had a good nap."

"You feel like getting a little local color?" Ian said.

"Yes indeed. What is it?"

"Come along and I'll show you."

The three made their way past the village at a right angle, and Ian said, "They're robbing a bee tree today. The Guapi love honey. It's about the only natural sweet they have. I don't know what they'd think about a candy bar. Probably love it."

Leaving the open space of the village, they plunged into the rain forest again. There were no paths through here, none that Emily or Wes could see, but Ian soon led them to where a group of the Guapi were standing in front of a large tree trunk. Noki, the chief, was standing to one side, and he came over and spoke to Ian. Ian responded and then said, "He's glad that you're here to join in the celebration."

"Where are the bees?" Emily asked, staring at the tree. "Are they inside?"

"No. You see those big knots up there on the outside of the tree? Those are the nests of the bees. We want to stay back here. I don't like to get in the middle of a bunch of wild bees."

Emily and Wes watched fascinated as Noki directed the operation. He watched them make torches of dried leaves tied onto long, slender poles and set them afire. One of the warriors, a squat muscular man, had run under the nest and held the fire to it. The bees swarmed out at once. There was still enough light to see the angry bees as they swarmed around the men. Emily could hear the furious humming as the natives slapped themselves frantically. Often they had to retreat from the scene of the action.

The tree was then chopped down, and as soon as it fell, the fire was again applied to the nest, killing hundreds of bees.

"I don't see how they stand those bee stings," Wes said.

"They're not as bad as a hornet's, but bad enough. They'll get the honey now," Ian remarked.

The three watched as the warriors robbed the nests, putting the honey in some sort of containers that Emily could not see. "They make everything out of bark, even their containers. They haven't learned the art of pottery yet. Come on, let's go back. We'll have some of the honey even if we didn't get stung collecting it. . . ."

★ ★ ★ ★

The meal that night was very interesting. Emily kept a small pad, and from time to time she could not refrain from making notes. They sat down around the fire and listened to the laughter and the muted conversation of the Guapi. At one point the chief and the other warriors pulled out something that looked like huge cigars.

When one was offered to Wes, he took it and after one puff fell into a violent coughing fit, his face scarlet.

This amused all of the warriors, who laughed loudly, pointing at Wes.

"That's awful!" Wes gasped. "I don't smoke. But if I did, I wouldn't smoke that."

"I tried it once. It made my throat raw for a week."

When the food was offered it appeared to be some sort of

cake. "What is this, Ian?" Emily whispered as she took a portion of it in her hand.

"It's all right," he grinned. "No monkey in it. It's the closest thing to a pancake that the Guapi have."

"What's it made out of?" Wes said.

"Out of the manioc root."

Emily tasted it and said with surprise, "Why, it's very good, even without salt."

"The root contains a poison that has to be removed before it can be eaten. They get the poison out of it by peeling and grating the root into mush and then squeezing that mush into a sort of press. Once the juice is out of it, the mush is turned to flour. They call it *cassaba*, and it's one of their favorite foods."

Emily ate the food, and then one of the chief's wives offered her a drink in a cup made out of a shell.

"You'll have to take a sip of it. But if you can't stomach it, don't worry. Try to get rid of it as unobtrusively as you can."

Emily tasted the brew and knew instantly that she would not care for the drink. She found a moment when no one seemed to be watching and carefully let the rest fall to the ground beside her.

Wes drank all of his and said, "It's some kind of liquor, isn't it?"

"It's called *kasili*. It has about the same alcoholic content as a weak beer, I suppose."

"How do they make it?" Wes asked, taking a second cupful.

"Well, they boil the manioc in river water. That takes the poison out of it by evaporation, and then as the mash boils," Ian said with a straight face, "the women chew cassaba cakes, and they spit them into the pot so as to aid the fermentation process with their saliva."

Wes had been lifting his cup to taste the kasili again, but when he heard this, he swallowed hard.

Emily giggled as she said, "Go ahead, Wes. You like it, don't you?"

Wes looked at Ian and saw that he was drinking the kasili. "Doesn't that bother you?"

"No, not really. It shows good manners, though, to drink with them. They're very sensitive. Go ahead and drink it, Wes. You've probably had worse in your life."

★ ★ ★ ★

After the meal was over, the men pulled out some sort of musical instruments. They were, more or less, like flutes, only with several barrels all made out of reeds. They made a pleasant enough sound, and one of the men, a scrawny man, spoke for a considerable time.

"Who is that, Ian?" Emily whispered.

"That's their medicine man, or witch doctor you might call him. His name is Malu."

"What's he saying?"

"Why, he's the storyteller. Pretty much carries on the oral history of the tribe. Not very reliable, though."

Emily listened to Malu and then listened carefully as Ian interpreted it. "They've got a legend out of their past. It seems they were a large tribe of women who had only a few men. They were warriors and killed most of their enemies, but they kept a few men alive for husbands."

"That's what the Amazons were," Wes said with astonishment.

"About the same kind of legend."

"Do you believe that, Ian?" Emily whispered.

"I never tamper with another country's legends. We've got our Paul Bunyan and Johnny Appleseed. Anyway," he went on, "these women possessed magic flutes called *jakui*. But in time something happened. Malu's not real sure what, but the men wound up taking the flutes away from the women. Now no woman is ever allowed to see the jakui or be in the men's meetings where they play them. You look around and you don't see any women here except you."

"Why did they let me stay?" Emily questioned.

"I don't suppose they think you're important enough. Or maybe they think you're too important to ask to leave. I think they really look on us as another species. I don't count as a man, and you don't count as a woman. They believe in their own people."

The ceremonies went on for some time, and finally Emily felt herself growing very tired. She did not think that Ian was watching her, but he suddenly leaned over and said, "Time for bed, daughter."

She looked up and could not help but smile. "All right, Dad." She got up, bowed to the chief, and Wes rose also. They left the circle, and Wes went at once to his tent, saying, "I think I had too much Amazonian kasili. Good night."

When they got to the hut, Ian said, "Let me check it for snakes and scorpions."

"Gladly!" Emily said nervously.

Ian lit the small lamp, searched the hut, and put the lamp down on the table. He stepped out and smiled. "It's all clear."

Emily felt awkward, as always, when she was alone with Ian Marlowe, but she felt obligated to say, "Wes and I are very grateful for what you are doing for us, Ian, and I . . . I want to thank you for taking such good care of me when I was sick."

"Don't mention it. That's what I'm here for."

The cicadas were singing their song now. It made rather a peaceful sound to Emily. She was tired, but she leaned back against the doorframe and studied Ian. By the flickering light of the small lamp, she could see his features clearly, and a curiosity rose in her. "Why have you done all this for us, Ian?"

"Why, you asked me to."

"Do you do everything that anyone asks of you?"

He smiled and crossed his arms and stood looking down at her. "I don't know, Emily, why I do most things. It has something to do with the fact that I'm a Christian now."

Emily hesitated, then said, "What do you mean by that?"

"I mean all of my life I never loved anyone but myself. I don't think you'd know anything about that. You're not that kind of person. But it was the way I grew up, I suppose. It was the law of survival to take care of myself. I got used to it. I never loved anyone until—"

Ian broke off abruptly, and Emily leaned forward to see what was in his face. "I don't know what you mean by that. Until what?"

"I was going to say until I met you, but you don't want to hear about that." He dropped his head, then said, "I found out that I couldn't love anyone, and I thought I was a cripple emotionally. But then when I asked Christ to come into my life, He did. And when He came in, Emily, He brought something with Him."

"What was that, Ian?"

"He brought love with Him, and that's what I feel for these people here. That's what I want to feel for everyone." He suddenly laughed shortly and said, "It sounds like I'm preaching a sermon. Good night, Emily."

She watched him as he left and, stooping, entered the tent. For a long time she stood there, and then she walked over and sat down at the table. In the short time since they had arrived at the Guapi village, Emily had observed a number of interesting habits. For nearly an hour she covered page after page in her tablet, trying to write as carefully as possible. Outside, the cicadas made such a chorus that it was the only sound she heard.

Finishing a page, she turned to a new one, at the same time looking at the door of her tent—and her heart froze. A Guapi warrior was standing there watching her. At least she assumed that he was Guapi. His face was smeared with red like a mask. A feather-tufted tube of bamboo protruded from his earlobes, and a quiver of darts hung at his waist.

Emily could not move. His ebony eyes glittered as he watched her, and she saw that he had a blowpipe at his side. He was naked except for a loincloth and was as still as a human being could possibly be.

Emily could neither speak nor move, and she looked deep into his eyes, wondering what he would do.

And then suddenly with a smooth, liquid motion the warrior turned, and he was gone. He disappeared as silently as a wraith, and Emily blinked with shock. He seemed almost like a phantom to her, but he had been real enough.

She put the tablet down and noticed that her hands were trembling. She placed the pencil on top of the pad, went to the cot, and blew out the lamp. As she lay down, she thought, *There's no protection here, God, but you. . . !*

CHAPTER TWENTY

THE GUAPI WAY

★ ★ ★ ★

Wes was quietly taking pictures of a man named Yato, who was making a blowgun, while Emily sat on a log writing. Ian had gone hunting, and the two had been fascinated by the care that went into the construction of the weapon. It was slow, careful work, and Emily documented it as carefully as possible. It was this sort of specific information that *National Geographic* liked. The blowgun was made in two pieces, each equal halves of a long, straight-grained palm tree sapling. The trunk had been painstakingly split down the middle and separated into equal halves and then set aside for a week of drying. Now Yato was making an inch-deep groove down the exact center of each of the two halves. He finished cutting as Wes and Emily watched, and then he placed the two separate pieces together. Since Ian was not there to interpret, the two simply watched and recorded what they saw, trying to make the photographs and notes tell the story.

Yato was an older man, but his hair was still black. His face was marked with many creases, and his ears were pierced, as were those of all the men. Feathers and ornaments dangled from his earlobes. Yato wrapped bark strips around the two halves of the sapling to hold them snugly together and then poured a coating of liquid over the wrapping. The coating was very thin and served mostly to keep the gun airtight. After this process was done, Yato brought out some very fine sand, which he placed in a bowl of water and heated over a small fire. When the water was boiling, the sand was poured down into the blowgun's bore through a tiny funnel.

Emily watched this step repeated for what seemed to be countless times, and she finally said to Wes, "I guess he's making the inside smooth."

The afternoon went along slowly, for time seemed to have no meaning in this place. Over and over, Yato poured the sand down the barrel. The sound of children playing and screaming with pleasure came from the river, where they were bathing, and the women laughed softly as they went about doing their work.

"It's funny, Wes, how time seems so different out here in the jungle."

"That's right," Wes said, trying to get a closeup shot of Yato's hands as he worked. "At home we're always rushing around trying to get somewhere. I don't think these people are ever in a hurry."

"Might be a good idea if we could adopt that custom."

Time went on, and finally the mouthpiece was constructed to act as a small funnel.

"Look at that, Emily. That mouthpiece is specially made to fit Yato's mouth so that no air escapes, I would guess."

"I don't see how they ever hit anything more than five feet away," Emily observed. "It just looks impossible."

Wes moved over and started to pick up one of the darts, but Yato immediately turned and held his hand up with a warning frown. He said something, and Emily said, "I don't think he wants you to touch those darts. They probably have poison on the tips."

"I guess you're right." Wes smiled and stepped back to show that he was harmless, and Yato returned his smile and went back to working on the blowgun.

Half an hour later the two were still there when Ian appeared. He nodded at them and then stood looking down at Yato and made some remark. Two of the women who had been working nearby came over, and one of them reached out and pulled at the top of Emily's shirt, trying to pull it away from her body. Startled, Emily grabbed the front of her shirt and said, "What does she want?"

Ian said something to the woman, and when she replied, he could not help smiling. "Faces get pretty bronzed out here, like mine. Once I took my shirt off, and it frightened everybody."

"Why were they scared?" Emily asked.

"Because my face and neck were one color, kind of a reddish hue, and the rest of me was white. That lady there wants to see if you're white all over."

Emily giggled suddenly. "Well, you can tell her that I am." She waited until Ian translated, and the two women went away, their curiosity satisfied.

"I thought you might like to go on a hunt," Ian said.

"Hey, that'd be swell!" Wes agreed enthusiastically. "Let me make sure I've got plenty of film. The light's pretty good."

Emily rose and closed her notebook. "I'd like that."

"An old friend of yours will be doing the hunting. Omala."

"Omala? Do I know him?"

"He's the one who frightened you by looking in your door."

Emily felt rather foolish. "I was scared that time," she admitted. "I turned around, and there he was just watching me."

"You should have seen me the first time I saw one of these people when I wasn't expecting him. I was on my way here, stumbling around, and then I fell down. When I looked up I saw him. Not Omala, but someone who looked like him. I thought my time had come. Talk about scared!"

Emily felt better after hearing Ian's story, and she suspected that he had told her this to help put her at ease. "Well, I'm ready," she said.

"Better put on some bug juice. The bugs are bad today. These people call them *piums*—tiny black bloodsucking critters."

Emily nodded at once. "I'll put it on an inch thick."

As the two walked back to her tent, Ian remarked, "These people don't like the piums any better than we do. They leave swellings that itch like blazes and sometimes turn black."

When they reached the hut they found Wes there, and Ian instructed them carefully. "You've got to tie your shirt sleeves around your wrists and your pants around your ankles. And soak your hands and face and neck in all the bug stuff you can bear."

The mosquito dope smelled terrible, but Emily slathered it on, as did Wes. Even Ian applied a liberal portion to his face and hands.

When Emily had finished that preparation she looked up, startled to see that Omala had approached silently. "How do these people move without making any noise?" she said. She smiled and nodded, and he studied her carefully, then nodded and said something.

"He says he'll get you a fine supper," Ian translated.

"Tell him I said thank you, and I appreciate it."

As Omala led them through the forest, Emily was fascinated by the variety of birds that flitted through the trees. She asked about a scarlet one, and Ian said, "That's a macaw." A few moments later, he said, "There's what they call a *pulsatrix*. It changes color when it matures."

They had not gone far when Omala stopped them and put his finger to his lips.

"I recognize that sign," Wes whispered. "It means *shut up*."

They stood there silently, and the breeze scarcely seemed to move. The vegetation was dense, and the flies swarmed around them. Finally Omala pulled out a poison dart. He wrapped what looked like cotton around it, Emily observed, and inserted it in the mouthpiece. He made a noise, a whistling sound, that Emily assumed was the call of a bird. She waited, holding herself perfectly still. The fronds of a large fern rustled in front of them, and suddenly a large black bird ran out of the underbrush. Emily heard a puffing sound. She did not see the flight of the dart, but she saw the bird stop abruptly and turn to make a run. It ran only two or three steps, however, then began shaking and fell over.

"That was a good shot, friend," Ian commented. He listened to the warrior speaking as he went to retrieve the bird, which had fallen some thirty feet away. Omala came back, plucked the dart out, replaced it in the blowgun, and put the bird in a sack by his side.

"What did he say?"

Ian smiled at Emily's question. "He said the bird came because he thought he had found a female. He says that men looking for females always get in trouble like this."

Emily was startled. She had not yet become completely aware of whether these people were witty or simply said what they thought. She saw Wes grinning and reached out to pinch him on the arm.

They became quiet and still again, and finally a peculiar noise came floating to them. Emily saw Omala stiffen and hold himself perfectly still. For some reason his attitude frightened her, and Omala turned to Ian, whispering, "*Onca.*"

"A jaguar—somewhere close," Ian whispered to his two companions.

Omala stayed still and so did the others. Finally a bird made another call, and Ian nodded and lowered his rifle to a more relaxed position. "The jaguar's gone. That particular bird makes that call when a jaguar's around."

"Convenient for us," Wes said wryly.

For what seemed like a long time then, they stood still, and finally Omala looked upward to their right. Emily followed his gaze, and high in the canopy she saw a monkey, which must have been seventy-five yards away. It seemed impossible that anyone could hit that monkey with a blowgun, and she made a bet with herself that Omala wouldn't do it.

Once again she heard the puffing sound and caught a flash of the dart as it flew through the air.

"Did he hit the monkey?" Wes asked with astonishment.

"Yes, he'll be falling soon," Ian replied.

The four waited and soon the monkey fell to the ground. Omala ran over, picked it up, and held it by its hind legs. He pulled the dart out and then stopped. He looked upward and said something.

"There's a baby monkey up there," Ian translated.

"Oh, the poor thing! It'll die!" Emily cried.

"Would you like to have it for a pet?"

Emily said instantly, "Yes! But how will you get it?"

Ian smiled and turned to Omala. He said something, and the

native laid aside his blowgun. He climbed the tree easily and soon was back, holding a tiny ball of fur in his hand. Emily reached out, and the tiny creature, so small she could easily hold it in her palm, began to make a heartrending, whimpering cry. She held it to her chest and soon it grew quiet.

"Now you've done it," Wes grinned. "She'll want to make a pet out of everything. We kept our house full of stray cats, and once we had to raise a whole litter of coons."

Ian was watching Emily as she held the tiny animal. Her lips had a broad, maternal cast, and he was thinking he had rarely seen a prettier picture. "Plenty of pets around here. They're no trouble. But when you go back, what will you do with it?"

"I'll take it with me."

"Pretty strict laws about that. You'll probably have to give it to one of the people."

"All right," Emily said, stroking the soft fur. "At least I'll know she has a home."

★   ★   ★   ★

The hunt was successful, and they arrived back at the village with two fat woolly monkeys, enough to feed more than one family.

Omala invited them all to stay for dinner, and Emily said, "I don't think I can eat one of those monkeys."

"They'll have something else. You can fake it. This is what you came for, isn't it?" Ian asked. "To see what the people are really like."

"Well, yes it is. I'll stay if you will, Wes. You can eat all the monkey meat."

★   ★   ★   ★

Omala's family situation was interesting to both Wes and Emily, and they seemed to be accepted there. The house was open, for the most part, and five families shared it, all of them blood relatives. Hammocks hung everywhere, and Emily discovered that children usually slept with their mothers until they grew too large, and then they had hammocks of their own. When a bachelor stayed with a family, he kept a night fire blazing to drive away the chill. Some of the men were smoking their cigars as the women cooked, and finally Emily asked, "I never hear them call you by your name, Ian. Why is that?"

"If they did that, according to their beliefs," he said, "that would allow a *yolok* to attack me."

"What's a yolok?"

"It's an evil spirit, and it can only attack those whose name it knows. So these people put a lot of stock in names. I never call them by their names either. I either call them by a title such as 'the chief' or 'the chief's wife' or 'the head man's mother.' Something like that. Sometimes I just say 'the one who's with me.' "

"How odd," Emily breathed. She looked around at the peaceful scene and said, "Are they really cannibals, Ian?"

"I don't think these people are. I stayed with another group downriver on my way here. They fed me stew, and I fished a human finger bone out of it."

"My word!" Wes exclaimed, his eyes staring. "What did you do?"

"Well, I didn't eat any more stew! As a matter of fact, I went out in the jungle and threw up. I didn't tell them why, but I didn't linger for long. I don't think the Guapi are cannibals, though. They never talk about it. As a matter of fact, they get upset when they hear about other tribes that have that practice."

Emily had watched as the women prepared the monkeys. Omala had gutted them, then turned them over to the women. They had stirred the fires and gotten the flames burning high, then they singed and scraped off the fur, which left the skin to be eaten with the meat. Ian told them with a smile, "The tail goes to the lucky hunter. It's supposed to bring good luck."

When the meal was served, Emily very carefully chose a piece of the bird that Omala had shot and killed rather than monkey meat. The women had also roasted ears of corn in the embers and offered her something that looked like a banana.

Emily and Wes made out very well and noticed that Ian also avoided the monkey meat.

"Have you ever tasted monkey?" Wes asked Ian.

"Sure, it's not bad," Ian said with a straight face. "Tastes a little bit like a fox."

Wes stared at him. "When did you ever eat a fox?"

Ian laughed. "I never did. I was just teasing."

After the meal the three of them expressed their thanks, which Ian, of course, translated. Then they left to go back to their camp to sleep for the night.

It was early, so Ian built up a small fire to drive away the insects with the smoke, and they sat around and talked for a time. It was a peaceful night, and once something grunted out in the jungle.

"Is that a jaguar?" Emily said nervously.

"I think it's probably a pig. How's your story coming?"

"I don't know. I'm making hundreds of notes, but I'll have to wait until I get home to put it together."

"Same way with pictures. I can't really develop them here, so I don't know what I'm getting. The only thing is to take as many as I can."

"These people seem so gentle," Emily said. "Are they really as violent as you say?"

"They take a different view of life," Ian said. He thought for a moment, and then he said, "When I first came here I didn't know the language too well, of course. I was learning it. One warrior made advances toward his neighbor's wives while he was away hunting. Somehow it got around, and the husband made a deadly poison out of jungle shrubs. That night at a hunting feast, the man who had done the deed joined them. He didn't see any expression on the husband's face, so he thought he was safe. He drank some of that thick, souplike drink, the native beer, and everybody else drank, too. But a few minutes later . . ." Ian slowly picked up a stick and poked at the fire. It sent golden sparks high in the air, and then he tossed the stick in and continued, "A few minutes later he was on the ground doubled up with pain. The men just looked at him casually, and he died right there. The corpse was dragged away and left in the jungle."

"How awful!" Emily shuddered.

"You've heard it before. Remember the old song 'Frankie and Johnny'—how he was her man, but he done her wrong. So she shot him."

"That's just a song."

"No, it's not," Wes broke in. "It happens all the time."

Emily was glad for the blazing fire. It made a burning, golden point in the darkness that surrounded the hut and the two tents.

Finally she said, "I think I'll go make a few notes. Good night."

As soon as Emily was gone, Ian said, "I've never known a woman like her."

"Neither have I," Wes said. He was watching Ian carefully and started to speak, but then he changed his mind. "Good night," he said. "I think I'll turn in."

Ian Marlowe sat staring into the fire for a long time. He seemed fascinated by the leaping flames and made a lonely, solitary object there in the middle of the jungle. Finally he arose and put out the fire and went to his tent.

★ ★ ★ ★

The following day Emily rose early, had a quick breakfast that she cooked herself, and walked to the village. She planned to spend the whole day taking notes on what happened and what the people did that day in their daily routines. As she walked around, she noticed that the men and boys were lying in their hammocks with their feet dangling over the sides. Hunters were out already, so nothing seemed to be happening. Some of the women had begun to roast meat over fires, and she wrote down descriptions of the various members of one of the families. One was a very beautiful young girl, no more than ten or twelve, with liquid black eyes and a ready smile. Her teeth were white and would be the envy of any girl in America. Emily did not know her name, but the girl followed her around all morning. Emily also kept the baby monkey with her. She had named him Woodrow Wilson, and when Ian asked why, she had said, "Look at that long face. He looks like Woodrow Wilson."

Ian found this amusing, but the Indian girl begged to hold the animal, and Emily surrendered her. She had noticed that the Guapi had an enormous number of pets, including many birds that had been trained to come at the owner's call. One of them, a small black-and-yellow bird, came when the girl whistled, perched on her shoulder, and pecked gently at the girl's lips. The child held the monkey in one hand and stroked the bird. The little girl wore only a cord, and Emily could not get over how nakedness was the rule of the day.

"Would you like to have the monkey?" Emily asked her.

The girl nodded with a smile when Ian translated the question, and then he said, "You've made a friend there."

The day went quickly for her, but later in the afternoon Emily was startled by what sounded like a quarrel. Ian had returned from his hunt and came to stand beside her. "What's happening?" he asked.

"I don't know. It sounds like they're having a domestic quarrel."

Ian watched for a while and listened and then nodded his head. "You see that woman over there? The tall one. She's one of Etor's three wives. She feels she didn't get an equal share of the game that the hunters brought in."

Emily watched and expected to see a shouting match, but instead the tall woman moved out of the cooking hut and built up a fire outside.

"What's she doing, Ian?"

"She's showing that she's all alone. You watch. She'll keep her back to the others."

Emily was amused at the woman, who did keep her back turned. The others paid her absolutely no attention. "She's like the old story of an ostrich poking his head in the sand and thinking the hunters can't see."

"It's the way they have around here. No one would think of disturbing another person's privacy. It'd be nice if we had that kind of system in the States."

"I think many of these people's customs are wonderful. That's one of them. You love these people, don't you, Ian?"

Ian turned to look at her. "I told you once that I could only love myself before I met Jesus. Now, strangely enough, I can love these people and even those who are unkind to me."

Emily blinked, for although he had said no more, she felt that he was speaking of her own bitterness toward him. She could not answer but turned and walked slowly away.

Ian watched her and then turned away himself, wondering what was in her mind.

CHAPTER TWENTY-ONE

SARITA

★ ★ ★ ★

The morning sun brought a red glow to the waters of the Amazon. Emily stood back beside Ian while Wes moved closer to the still figure of Omala, who stood ankle-deep in the brown waters that curled around him. Emily and Wes had come to watch how the Guapi were able to hunt fish with a bow and arrow, and now all of them stood still, as if frozen in a tableau. Emily glanced toward Ian, who stood quietly beside her, his eyes fixed on the hunter, and through her mind came thoughts of the earlier days she had had with him back in Richmond. The memory troubled her, and she shook her head slightly and stared at the still figure of Omala.

The air was full of the spongy odors of the jungle—the smell of decaying vegetation but also of exotic flowering plants of all sizes and shapes, a rich aroma that surrounded the Guapi as water surrounds a fish.

Suddenly Omala drew the bow back and aimed at a pool at least thirty feet away. Emily squinted her eyes, trying to see something, but she could not even see a shadow among the rocks. But apparently Omala did. He loosed the arrow, which skimmed low across the water, so low that Emily thought it might flatten out and skim across the surface as a flat stone. But somehow a flash of silver stirred the pool. The water splashed, and Omala rushed forward to grab the arrow and lift up a foot-long fish that was skewered on it. Wading back, he jerked the arrow out, and putting the fish to his mouth, he crushed its back-bone with his teeth, and the fish grew still.

"That was incredible!" Emily exclaimed. She nodded and smiled at Omala, who smiled back and said something.

"He says that he'd like to share the fish with you."

"What kind is it?" Emily asked, moving closer.

"It's called an *acara-acu*."

It was a colorful fish, brown and orange, with shiny scales.

"It looks like an ocean fish—something you would see in the Gulf of Mexico."

"It does, doesn't it?" Wes had come up and snapped a picture of Omala holding the fish in his hand. "Ask him to bite it again so I can get a better shot," Wes urged.

He waited until Ian had translated his words, and then Omala dutifully raised the fish to his lips. Wes snapped the picture and grinned. "That'll be a good one," he said.

"I don't see how he speared that fish. I couldn't even see it," Emily remarked.

"Neither could I. I think you have to be born here to acquire these skills. Have you got enough shots, Wes?"

"I think so."

"Come along, and we'll see a few more interesting sights," Ian said.

As they walked along the riverbank, Wes asked, "What's the biggest fish in the Amazon River?"

"It's what the people here call a *piraiba*. It's a catfish, but bigger than any you've ever seen."

"How big do they get?" Wes inquired.

"They can grow over ten feet long and weigh more than five hundred pounds."

"Five hundred pounds! That's a monster!"

"They eat dogs that get careless and swim across streams. Some of the natives have claimed they even take small children who are bathing."

Emily shivered at the thought. "I don't even like to think about a thing like that!"

"Neither do I," Ian said. "Death comes easily out here in the Amazon."

They had reached the group of women catching small fish in basket traps. The party stopped and watched as the women waded out in the deep mud, dragging small baskets through the muddy waters. From time to time they would pull them up and pitch the fish shoreward. When they landed, small girls would collect them and crack their spines with their teeth to kill them as Omala had the larger fish. Then they would make a cut just below the gills, and with one motion the entrails were ripped out and discarded.

Wes took pictures of the girls as they wrapped the fish in green banana leaves to cook them. Emily had tried them and found them to be delicious.

A young man had been standing staring at the river. Suddenly he let out a cry and plunged below the surface.

"What's he doing?" Emily asked.

"Going after something," Wes said. He got his camera ready, and after what seemed like a long time, the boy came out holding a turtle overhead.

"Those are good," Ian remarked. "I think they're my favorite food."

Emily took notes as rapidly as she could on the various kinds of fish, including a spotted catfish that Ian said was called a *pintado*. They also saw a man coming in with a fish that weighed over seventy pounds. This was the *paiche*, the most common fish in the river.

Wes stayed to take more pictures, but Emily and Ian walked back toward the village. For some reason it had grown very difficult for Emily to carry on a conversation with Ian. She knew that somehow she would have to resolve the wall she had put up between her and Ian, but so far she had not been able to. At the root of it, she knew, lay the bitterness that she had carried for years. Just the night before a realization had come to her with a shock. In the darkness of her small hut, she had knelt beside her bed and struggled with her own thoughts. Prayer seemed impossible, and finally she had cried out, "Oh, God, I don't know what to do! I don't know if he's really changed or not, and I'm afraid to trust him!"

As she knelt there, something had come to her that she had never dreamed of. There was no audible voice, and she could not be certain that it was something the Lord was saying to her. The thought that rose in her was like a faint whisper in her spirit. It was not in words, however, but just an impression, and it amounted to a bitter truth. *I don't want to find out that Ian has really changed.* The thought had come to her so sharply and with such force that she had knelt for a long time struggling with it—and then came another impression. She suddenly felt that she was taking some sort of awful pleasure in harboring her bitterness against Ian!

"No, that's not true." She had spoken the words out loud, but the thoughts and the impressions had remained with her. Now as she walked along beside Ian, she tried to shove those thoughts away. It couldn't be true that she was enjoying the bitter thoughts that she still held against him! It just couldn't be!

Ian did not appear to be aware that she was having a struggle. He spoke easily about the life of the village. Indeed, he had been most helpful in assisting her to gather material for the article she was going to write. If there was any discomfort in their conversation, it was not on his part.

A voice caught the attention of the pair, and they turned to see Noki, the chief, striding toward them. Ian greeted him and listened as Noki spoke at length. When he paused, Emily asked, "What is it?"

"He says his wife is sick."

"What's wrong with her?"

"He doesn't know, but he wants me to come pray for her." Ian turned and studied Emily. "Would you come with me?"

"I . . . I suppose so, but I've never had much experience with praying for someone who is sick like this."

"I've had some, but you never know what's going on. Come along. We'll see if we can help."

The two followed Noki until they reached his house, and when they went inside, they found the woman, whose name was Peor, lying pale and motionless in her hammock. Ian began to ask questions, and Noki answered them in short phrases. Ian put his hand on the sick woman's brow and then took her pulse. He turned and there was a humor in his eyes. "It's not serious," he said.

"What is it?" Emily asked quickly.

"It amounts to the fact that Noki has been paying more attention to one of his other wives than to Peor. It's really all in her head."

"You mean she's not really sick?"

"She thinks she is—and sometimes that's about as bad as being sick. I think she's making a scene to get his attention." A grin swept across his lips, and he said innocently, "Women do that from time to time."

Emily shot an angry glance at him, but she did not answer for a moment. "Men do the same thing."

"I suppose you're right."

"Well, what will you do?"

"Well, we'll pray for her, of course, but the chief's not really a believer. I keep telling him about Jesus, and he says he's got to see a miracle of some kind."

Emily was rather shocked at this. "What kind of miracle?"

"He hasn't been very specific."

The conversation went on for some time and was interrupted when Malu, the witch doctor, came in. Emily listened as the witch doctor and the chief talked and noted that the witch doctor was quite friendly with Ian.

"Isn't he suspicious of you and your religion?"

"I don't think so. He's a pretty sharp old fellow. He's like doctors in the States who sometimes know that they can't do anything, but they go through the motions anyway. We'll watch him. It'll be something for you to include in your story."

Emily stood back and watched as Malu rubbed some sort of ointment on the patient's stomach and palms and feet. He tied a cotton thread around her elbows, wrists, ankles, and toes, and then Malu turned and muttered some words.

"He wants us to leave the room. Come along," Ian said as he moved outside. "He doesn't want to give away trade secrets. What he'll do is exorcise the yolok."

"An evil spirit?"

"I'm not exactly sure. It's part of what they call their magic around here. Somehow a yolok gets into people and brings an evil spirit."

Soon loud cries from the sick woman began to rent the air, and Emily shifted her feet nervously. She waited for Ian to speak, but he stood there quietly leaning against the side of the house and said nothing.

Finally Malu came outside, and his dark eyes glinted. He held out something in his palm, and Emily leaned forward to see a small black pebble. She listened as the witch doctor explained, apparently, his powers to Ian and then left.

"Well, that black pebble was the yolok. Now, let's go back, and we can pray for Peor."

Emily followed him inside and found Peor sitting up. She seemed to be better and sat still as Ian prayed for her. She smiled then and reached up and took his hand and said a few words.

"She's grateful for the prayer," Ian said. He turned and nodded to Noki, who smiled, and then the two left the hut.

"I wish Wes could have taken some pictures of that," Emily said.

"He'll have plenty of chances. This sort of ritual by the witch doctor goes on all the time. These are very spiritual people," Ian remarked as the two walked along between the huts that were scattered at random across the open space. The children, as usual, were playing games, some of them with their pets, while others kicked a ball made out of what appeared to be cotton.

"Spiritual? What do you mean by that?"

"Oh, I don't mean about our God. They haven't made up their mind yet about the true God. What I mean is they live in a world inhabited by spirits, so they think, some good and some evil. When someone gets sick, they say an evil spirit's there. When good fortune comes, the good spirits are there. So they are ready to receive just about anything."

"Have any of them accepted Jesus yet?"

"Not yet."

"Aren't you discouraged, Ian?"

"Oh, a little, I suppose." The two had reached the edge of the village, and he stopped and looked up at a strange-looking bird, a fearsome creature called a harpy eagle. He had explained before that the eagle was, more or less, the mascot of the village. These fierce-looking birds were called "winged wolves" by the natives, due to the ferocity of their attacks on monkeys.

Ian studied the bird, then shook his head. "No, I promised God I'd be faithful to declare the Lord Jesus to these people. I've tried to do that. I read of one missionary who stayed in India and preached for twelve years before he had a single convert."

Emily was impressed. She bit her lip and shook her head in denial. "I don't think I'd have the patience for that."

"I think God has to give that to you. I don't think any of us have it by nature."

"How long will you stay here?"

"I have no idea. I've been asking the Pettigrews to send a real missionary here, but there are no volunteers."

Emily at that moment found herself feeling admiration for Ian Marlowe. For that instant she was able to put aside the past. He had come without help or financial support to a strange country, had mastered a difficult unwritten language, and despite his lack of success in making converts, he was determined to be faithful. *But why do I still doubt him?* she thought. Then a call came that took the attention of both of them.

Ian squinted his eyes at the couple that had suddenly appeared, emerging from the jungle. "Why, it's Adriano and Sarita!" He left Emily standing there and hurried to meet the Reys.

Emily followed at a slower rate and watched Ian grasp the hand of the older man.

"Adriano, what in the world are you doing here?" Then he turned and gave Sarita a hug and laughed. "I didn't expect to see you here, Sarita."

"We brought the rest of your supplies. See, we persuaded two bearers to come with us," Sarita said, motioning at two husky young men who were carrying tremendous loads on their backs.

Emily saw that they seemed wary or even fearful, and Adriano said something to them in Portuguese. His words did not seem to reassure the bearers, and Adriano smiled.

"They were afraid, but I promised them double pay. They're

anxious to be on their way. Where will they put the supplies?"

"Over this way," Ian said quickly. He led the way to the tents and the small hut, and the bearers put their burdens down. They waited only until Adriano gave them some coins, and then they turned and ran away quickly, as if a jaguar were after them.

"You shouldn't have come all the way out here to the village," Ian said. "We could have gotten along."

"Perhaps you could, but I thought our two young friends here would be hungry for some real coffee."

"Coffee! Did you bring coffee?" Emily exclaimed.

"Yes, and a few other good items to eat. I thought you'd be tired of living on monkey meat."

Emily laughed and shook her head. "Right about now I could eat anything."

Ian said quickly, "Emily, would it be all right if Sarita shared the hut with you?"

"Of course," Emily said. "I'd be glad to have the company."

"I can sleep outside," Sarita said at once.

"No, of course not," Emily said. "Could you rig up another bed, Ian?"

"No trouble at all." He smiled down at Sarita and said, "I'm glad you're here." Then he slapped Adriano on the shoulders and said, "Come along. Noki will want to talk with you."

Sarita stood stiffly as the two men left. "I don't want to get in your way," she said cautiously.

"Why, it's good to have you, Sarita. Come along. We'll get your things separated and we'll make coffee. I'm dying for a cup," Emily said.

Wes came in shortly and went at once to Sarita. "Hello," he said. "When did you get here?"

"We came just a few moments ago," Sarita said.

She had a smile for him that she had not given Emily, and the two fell into a conversation. Emily watched them and somehow felt that Sarita had built a wall around herself. She had seen this earlier, back at the Rey home. Clearly Sarita had a special feeling for Ian. For some reason this troubled Emily, but she shook her head and thought, *It's none of my business*, and began at once making provision for the younger woman to share the hut.

★ ★ ★ ★

"Sarita, I'm going down to the river to take a bath. Would you like to come with me?"

Sarita had been arranging her gear, and now she looked up and studied Emily. "Yes," she said. "I think I would."

Emily grabbed the soap that Sarita had brought and several shirts that she could use to dry off on. "I wish I had a towel," she said.

The two women made their way down to the river where Ian had shown them a quiet pool that was free of piranha and apparently fairly safe from prowling jaguars. For twenty minutes they stayed in, letting the water cool them off. Finally, when they got out and dried themselves as best they could, Sarita said, "How long have you known Ian?"

"Oh, several years."

"Were you ever his woman?"

Emily suddenly flushed, for the question had taken her aback. In a way she had been his woman, at least had felt attracted to him and had fancied herself in love with him, but she knew that Sarita's question went deeper than this.

"No, not really."

"Do you want to be?"

"Of course not!" The answer popped out before Emily could even think. She saw a look of disbelief in Sarita's eyes.

"Do you have another man somewhere?" Sarita demanded.

Emily suddenly recognized then that Sarita had come with her simply to find out how she felt about Ian. "No," she said. "I don't."

Sarita pondered Emily's terse answer. She ran her hands down her coal black hair and then asked, "How old are you?"

"I'm twenty-two."

Sarita shook her head in disbelief. "You're twenty-two, and you have no man? Is something wrong with you?"

"No, there's nothing wrong with me. I'm going back."

Emily was angry and upset as she headed back along the trail toward her hut. She disliked being cross-examined, and now she had no doubt in her mind about Sarita's feelings for Ian. The young woman was in love with him and had seen Emily as a rival.

Sarita took her time getting back to the village. She walked along the riverbank and soon came upon Wes, who was taking pictures of the young people splashing about and enjoying themselves.

"Hello, Sarita," he said.

"What are you doing?"

"Taking pictures as usual."

Sarita sat down on the bank, and eventually Wes came over and sat down beside her. He talked enthusiastically about all the pictures he had taken so far of the Guapi, but Sarita did not seem to hear.

"Wes, why does your sister have no man?"

Surprised, Wes turned to her. "I guess she hasn't found anybody."

"She's old."

"Old! She's not old! She's only twenty-two."

"All the women I know who are that old are married, and most of them already have babies."

"I think it's different in our country. Some women don't marry sometimes until they're older than my sister."

"Why do they wait so long? Don't they want a family?"

"I don't know, Sarita," Wes said. He shook his head and then turned to look at her. "Why are you asking?"

She was a very direct young woman, and now she said evenly, "I thought she might be in love with Ian."

"Well, she was at one time."

Sarita's eyes narrowed. "She didn't tell me that."

"It wasn't a very happy matter."

Sarita studied Wes for a moment, then got up and left without another word. "What was that all about?" Wes muttered. "I'll have to ask Emily about it."

★ ★ ★ ★

274

Ian had taken his rifle apart and was cleaning it. Metal objects rusted quickly in the wet climate, and he hummed under his breath as he rubbed the barrel with an oily rag. He looked up to see Emily emerge from her hut, and when she came over, he said, "Hello. About ready to start supper?"

"Yes, I suppose so."

"I shot some birds today. Might be a change from red meat."

"What kind are they?"

"I don't know what they are. They look like pigeons, but they're not really. I plucked and cleaned them for you." He stood up and went over and picked up a bag. "I think there's enough for all of us. I had good luck. Where's Sarita?"

"I don't know," Emily said sharply.

Ian looked at Emily, for she seemed upset. "Did you two have a falling out?"

"What makes you ask that?"

"Something she said. She's got a temper."

"So have I."

Ian laughed. "Yes, I know. What's wrong between you two?"

"Nothing!"

"Well, as Shakespeare said, 'Methinks the lady doth protest too much.' Don't be upset with her. She's very young. Just a child really."

"She's not a child!" Emily actually had been agitated ever since her brief conversation with Sarita down at the river, and now she turned to him and said, "You know she's in love with you."

"Don't be foolish, Emily."

"I'm not foolish."

"Did she tell you this?"

"Not exactly."

"Well, I think you're imagining things. I'm fond of her, of course. When I stumbled into the Reys' house, she and her grandfather just about saved my life. I was pretty sick, so I'm grateful to her."

Emily turned to face him squarely. "She believes it's more than that."

"I think you're wrong." Ian studied her, and his mind went

back to the time when they had been closer. He had thought of those days often, and even through the years, he had never forgotten holding her in his arms and the kisses she gave him. Even now as she stood before him, he was aware of the attraction he still had for her. He admired her physical beauty—her glossy red hair that hung all the way down to her slim waist, her smooth skin, and her gentle feminine curves. Her face was quick to express her thoughts, and now he saw that she was disturbed. He said quickly, "She's a fine young woman, but there's nothing to what you say."

"You're a fool if you think that!" Emily snapped.

Ian blinked. "Well, that's speaking right out."

Ian fell silent, and Emily moved her shoulders in a restless motion. "I didn't mean to be so rough. It's just my nature."

"Yes, it is."

Suddenly Emily began speaking, saying things she had not planned but which had been bottled up within her. She was not even aware of how the words poured out of her. "When I got your letter asking for forgiveness, I was so angry. I have been for a long time. Mom and Dad said they were willing to forgive you, but I never was."

Ian nodded. "They wrote me a letter saying they'd forgiven me. I still have it."

Emily had not known her parents had corresponded with him, and now she shook her head. "I think Wes has forgiven you, but I've never been able to. I've hated you for a long time, Ian. My . . . my pride was hurt. I can't seem to get over it, and since then I've discovered some bad things about myself."

Ian waited for her to speak, but she did not. "What is it?" he said finally. "I found out a lot of bad things about myself, too. Sometimes it helps to say it out loud."

"All right, I'll say it then," Emily said, her voice husky. "I don't *want* to forgive you. I . . . I didn't know that about myself until last night."

"I can't blame you. What I did to you was terrible. No woman likes to be deceived."

Emily wanted to speak, but it was difficult for her. Finally she managed to say, "I don't want to hate you. The anger and bitterness I've held inside has brought me nothing but misery."

"I can't help you with that. I don't think anybody can—only God. But for your sake, I wish you could forgive me."

Emily stared at him. "For my sake?"

"Yes," Ian nodded. "Forgiveness brings freedom from what has wounded us. I know you think I was nothing but a scoundrel, and I've told you every way I know that you were right." He hesitated, and then suddenly he reached out and took her by the shoulders and held her firmly in his grasp. "I remember the times we had. I've never forgotten them, Emily. I remember the stream where we went and fished. I remember the time we slid off in the ditch and had to spend the night in that cold barn. And I remember sitting beside you while Gypsy Smith preached. His message went right to my heart, but for some reason I couldn't give myself to God. I remember those times, Emily, and what I felt for you was real. It wasn't part of the act."

His voice was soft, and his eyes contained something that Emily could not read, but she knew that he was speaking the truth. "I remember them, too," Emily said. She lowered her head, aware of his hands holding her shoulders. His hands were strong, and she felt a weakness but forced herself to look up. "I was falling in love with you, Ian, and I blame myself for it."

Ian suddenly reached out with one hand and laid it on her cheek in a gentle gesture. He held it there and waited for her to push him away, but she did not. She simply stood there, and the two of them seemed to be caught in some sort of spell that they could not break.

Finally Ian took a deep breath. He dropped his hands and locked them behind him. For a long moment he seemed unable to come up with words, or so it seemed to Emily. She did not know what he would say, but she found herself breathing rapidly, knowing that somehow she would have to resolve this matter between herself and Ian Marlowe.

"A man sees beauty in the world, Emily," Ian finally said, his voice soft as the summer breeze. "Sometimes he sees it in a woman." His lips drew together into a thin line, and then he said almost harshly, "Tough on me . . . but the only woman I've ever seen it in . . . is you." He turned and walked away quickly, leaving Emily to stare after him in disbelief.

CHAPTER TWENTY-TWO

"LOVE CAN BE PAINFUL"

★ ★ ★ ★

The days dragged slowly by for Emily after Ian's confession that he found beauty only in her. Time back in the States was a rushing river, and one was either caught up in it or left behind. Here in the Amazon rain forest, however, time was more like a still pond, broken only occasionally by the gentle circling of concentric rings. A soporific quality in the air brought a drowsiness to the spirit, and Emily found herself thinking more and more of the feelings she'd had for Ian years before, when she knew him as James Parker.

In the midst of these thoughts and feelings, Emily found each day with the Guapi full of new challenges to understand their ways. She was grateful for Ian's presence here. She knew that only God could have arranged such a miracle, and that without Ian as their guide, she and her brother would never have had this opportunity to live among the Guapi safely and learn from them.

Several times she had awakened to hear odd sounds coming from the village, and finally one morning after breakfast she asked Ian, "What are those strange noises I hear every morning?"

Ian looked at her and shrugged. "It's not very nice. That's the sound of retching you hear. The Guapi believe that a good clearing of the stomach starts the day off right. They get up and drink as much as they can of *wayus*—that's a tealike stimulant and a pretty effective emetic."

Emily was startled by his explanation but found a great compassion for these people welling up in her. "They don't live long, do they?"

"No, their lives are hard and they succumb to many illnesses. The death rate among their infants is pretty high, too."

"Do the witch doctors know anything at all about useful medicines?"

"If they do, they're pretty secretive about them," Ian said.

Emily noticed that Ian seemed to have drawn a line between them. He did not have the same openness he had shown before he had told her how he felt. She assumed he was afraid of a rebuff and was shielding himself by keeping a proper distance. He spoke evenly as he continued to talk about the medical care among the Guapi.

"They've been treating malaria with quinine for years, and they use cocoa as a painkiller. I read somewhere that our own doctors have discovered that *curare*—that's the poison the Guapi use on their darts and arrows—is good for controlling spasms."

"Before I came here I read that leprosy was pretty bad in this country," Emily said.

"It is bad. Only two cases of it I know of among the Guapi, though, and they're not very far advanced." He stood up suddenly, saying, "I'm going to go see a woman who's been bitten by a *shou*."

"What's that, a snake?"

"No, it's a spider."

"Will she die?"

"No, but this spider bite is very painful. When these people are hurting or ill, they want me to pray for them. It's one of the few things I can see where I've made a difference."

Emily stood up and asked, "May I go with you?"

"Sure, come along."

As the two walked toward the woman's hut, Ian kept carefully to neutral subjects. He told her of a man who lived downriver from the Reys who had leprosy. He had lost his fingers, and his feet were going, but he still loved to hunt. "He strapped sandals to his stumps, wired a shotgun to his shoulder, and then went out in the jungle alone. He came back with some pretty good specimens."

"That's real courage, I think," Emily said.

"He had that. Most of us would have given up."

They reached the hut and were admitted by a daughter. They found the sick woman lying in a hammock. Her face was drenched in sweat. A witch doctor had applied a poultice to her leg to treat the spider bite.

Emily said nothing but knew that Ian had mentioned her coming. Finally he said, "Emily, why don't you join me in prayer for this woman?"

Emily was startled. She started to protest but felt that would be wrong. She watched as Ian put his hands on the woman's head, and then she leaned forward and took up the woman's hand. She bowed her head, and as Ian prayed in the woman's own language, she began to pray. She had always had great faith in prayer, but she had difficulty praying about anything lately. Suddenly she found herself praying freely and knowing that she was in the presence of God. She almost lost the sense of where she was, the sense of place and time, and instead of praying silently as she normally did, the prayer burst from her lips. Passionately she prayed for the woman's release from pain and felt the woman squeeze her hand. Finally Emily ceased, and when she opened her eyes, she saw that both Ian and the woman were staring at her.

"That was a pretty potent prayer," Ian said quietly. He listened as the woman spoke and then turned to Emily. "She says the pain is all gone—that the flame-haired woman is close to God."

Emily was unable to speak for a moment, and then she smiled at the woman. "Tell her I'm glad she feels better." She listened as Ian translated, and then when the woman spoke, Ian turned to her. "She says may you have a good husband and many fine children."

Emily could not meet his eyes but nodded. "Tell her I thank her for her kindness."

They left the hut, and as they walked outside, the bright sunlight glittered so that it hurt Emily's eyes. She walked slowly down the path that led to her small hut, and Ian finally asked, "How's your work coming along?"

"Very well. You've been such a great help, Ian. I couldn't have done it without you."

"Do you think *National Geographic* will take your story?"

"I'm sure they will. There's been nothing like it written before."

The two reached the hut, and as they approached, Sarita was standing beside the door. Her eyes were on them, and she did not speak.

"Sarita, I think I'll go see if I can catch a fish for supper. Care to come along?"

"Yes, I will," Sarita said quickly.

Emily watched as the two walked off together. She did not miss the fact that Sarita reached out and touched Ian to draw his attention. When he spoke to her, she smiled up at him, and then her laughter floated back to Emily. Sarita's infatuation with Ian troubled Emily, but she could not say why.

She saw Adriano sitting in the shade of one of the small trees and walked over and sat down on the ground beside him. Adriano nodded pleasantly and asked about her work. When he heard her report, he nodded.

"You will be finished soon, no?"

"Yes, I don't know exactly when, but it won't be too long."

"And then you will go back home."

"Yes, we will."

Adriano did not speak for a time. His eyes were half hooded, and he was smoking a cigar—not one that the natives had made, but of a much finer quality. The light blue smoke curled upward into the air unbroken by a breeze, and finally he said, "What will you do then? When you get home, that is."

"Oh, write another story, I suppose."

Adriano studied her thoughtfully. He was a good student of human nature, and during the past two weeks, he had watched Emily carefully. Now he said, "Will Ian go back to the States with you?"

Emily was startled. "No. There's been no talk of that. What makes you ask?"

Adriano did not answer. He shrugged his shoulders in a curiously eloquent gesture, and finally after a time he said, "I am worried about Sarita."

Instantly Emily sat up straighter, and her eyes met those of the old man. "Because of Ian?"

"You're very perceptive. You see, of course, that she is in love with him."

"It's pretty obvious, although I'm not sure he knows it."

Adriano shook his head with a faint despair. "I do not think he does, but it is true."

"Do you think he cares for her at all?"

"Oh yes. He is a very warmhearted man, and he's very grateful to her for the way she cared for him when he was ill."

"But that is not enough for Sarita," Emily ventured.

"You are right. A woman would see that. Ian is very quick in some ways but very slow in the ways of the heart, I think." He puffed on the cigar for a moment, took it out of his mouth, and stared at it thoughtfully, as if it held some great enigmatic secret. Finally he put it back in his mouth and puffed gently, then removed it again. "There is something in your eyes when you look at Ian. Is it something from the old time when you first knew him?"

Emily felt her face glow. "I was very fond of him at one time—but that's all over."

"I do not think it is. The eyes are the window to the soul, and when you look at him I can see your heart."

"No, you're mistaken!"

Adriano did not argue. He simply sat there and finally said in the softest possible tone, "Love can be painful."

Emily felt uncomfortable around this old man. It seemed he could look right into her mind, even into her heart, so she rose and, making an excuse, slipped away.

"Yes, love can be very painful," Adriano murmured, "but where would we be without it?"

★　★　★　★

The same day that Emily had spoken with Adriano, Ian came to her and said, "Something is happening that you might use for your story."

"What is it?"

"It's something called *marake*."

"Marake? What is that?"

"It means 'the ant test.' Come along. You'll find it interesting. And get Wes with his camera. He'll want pictures."

The three of them went to the center of the village, where quite a few of the natives had gathered. For a long time there was singing and dancing, and it seemed to be a rather festive occasion.

Finally Ian whispered to the pair of them, "Get your camera ready, Wes, and your pencil, Emily."

"What's going to happen?" Wes asked.

"This is a test that's given to children at puberty."

Emily had brought a small notebook, and she jotted down as well as she could what went on. She watched as a child was brought forward and given kasili to drink.

"Why is that young girl drinking that?"

"It's the closest thing to a pain-killer they have," Ian said. "You probably won't like this ritual, but it's very important to these people."

Emily watched as the young girl, who was no more than thirteen, was brought to stand in the center of a group of elders. One man stood behind her and held her wrist out at arm's length. "That's her father," Ian whispered.

Malu, the witch doctor, approached with a wicker frame in his hand.

Wes snapped a picture, and the snapping of the camera was made inaudible by the singing that was going on, a chant with a hypnotic rhythm to it.

"What's in that wicker?" Wes asked.

"Ants," Ian replied briefly.

A chill went over Emily, and she watched as the wicker frame was applied to the body of the young girl. She saw the ants swarm out, crawling over the girl's face and over her entire naked body. The girl shut her eyes, and from time to time her lips would tighten, but other than that she showed no response as the ants swarmed all over her. She did not struggle or try to get away. Emily could see her father's face, stern but somehow pleased at the bravery and stoicism of his child as she endured the ritual.

Finally the music rose to a crescendo, and Malu pulled the wicker away. The girl's mother came, brushing the ants off of her body, and then the singing broke into a glad chant.

"She's grown up now according to marake," Ian said.

Wes was excited. "I got some good shots. This will be great, Emily! Be sure you put it in the story."

Emily and Wes joined Ian as he went to congratulate the family. She found herself wondering if it would not be better for American youth if they were bred to endure some hardships such as this puberty ritual. Not ants, perhaps, but something that would teach them that life can be hard. This thought passed through her mind as she smiled, and the young girl smiled shyly back at her.

As they left, Wes said, "I don't know if I could stand that or not."

"You could if you were a Guapi. You would have been brought up to expect it," Ian remarked, "from the time you were born. These people have learned one thing, that life is hard. So I think customs like marake give them a small taste of it, so when the hard challenges in life come, they're more ready for it."

"Not a bad idea," Wes nodded soberly. "I think the American Indians did somewhat the same. But we're a pretty spoiled bunch. Our parents try to protect us as much as they can, which I guess, maybe, is not the best idea."

Ian did not speak, nor did he look at Emily. He seemed preoccupied, and after talking to a few of the Guapi, he made his excuses and left. He had not gone far, however, before he found himself joined by Adriano.

"Did you go to the ceremony, Adriano?"

"Yes. Very impressive."

Ian would have passed on, but Adriano fell into step beside him. "I must speak to you, Ian."

Instantly Ian turned toward the man. He had great trust in Adriano Rey, and now he said, "What is it? Is there trouble?"

"Yes, come along. We will find a quiet place."

Ian followed Adriano down one of the jungle paths that led to the river. They stopped beside the brown waters that swept the bank with a sibilant sound, and Adriano motioned toward a trunk, then sat down himself beside Ian. "There's trouble," he said quietly.

"Something I can do to help?" Ian asked quickly.

"I think you must help if there is help at all."

"Tell me. Are you sick?"

"No, I am not."

Adriano did not answer for a while, and Ian knew that his silence was part of a ritual with him. Adriano Rey did not speak quickly but allowed thoughts to be born in him, and after a long time they would be birthed in a quiet voice. He waited until the older man lit his cigar and then started talking. Ian had also learned that Adriano often clothed his wisdom, which was considerable, in the form of a parable. It was the old way teachers used, even Jesus himself.

"My son, if you take a good-natured animal, say a dog, and you chain him up, then you often show him food but do not give him any, in time he will become very ill-tempered."

Adriano continued to speak of how an animal could become almost vicious if he were treated in this way, and finally he fell silent.

Ian waited, then said, "This is true. I would probably be the same."

Adriano turned and faced Ian and spoke clearly, though his voice was gentle. "You must know that Sarita cares for you."

Suddenly Ian Marlowe was embarrassed. He looked down at his hands for a time and then shook his head. "I didn't mean for this to happen."

"I know that. You are a good man, and you would not misuse any woman."

"Has she told you this, my friend?"

"Not in words, but I am not blind. Her eyes follow you wherever you go. Have you not seen it?"

Ian shifted nervously and ran his hand through his tawny hair. "At times I have thought she had an affection for me."

"I did not know whether you had seen that, but you must have if you are not totally blind." Adriano puffed on his cigar, then shook his head. "You are a fine man, Ian Marlowe, but you are not for Sarita." He let his words sink slowly into silence and then added, "You will leave this place one day and go back to your homeland. Sarita would be very unhappy there. She would be a stranger in a very different world. It must not happen."

"I'm very fond of Sarita," Ian said carefully. He was like a man picking his way through a dangerous minefield, for he did not want to hurt Adriano, and he certainly did not want to hurt Sarita. "What must I do, Adriano?"

The answer came quickly. "You must tell her that you can never care for her. Not in the way she wants you to."

"Why, I can't do that!"

"Why not?"

"It would be cruel to say such a thing."

"And do you think," Adriano spoke quickly and with more force, "that it is kinder to let her continue to think of you in this way when you know in your heart that nothing will ever come of it? She will become bitter and angry."

Ian sat on the log, misery reflected in every aspect of his body and features. He had vaguely felt this coming on, and more than once had tried to think of a way to let Sarita know that there could never be anything like love between the two of them. Not the kind of love she wanted, as Adriano put it. Finally he looked up and said, "I'm sorry about all this, Adriano. I never meant for it to happen."

"I know you did not. But unfortunate situations like this do happen, and when they do, we have to use great wisdom to resolve them. The greatest kindness you could show to Sarita would be to speak directly to her. Tell her your heart and make it clear that she should begin trying to put you out of her mind and heart and look for another."

Ian rose to his feet. He stood silently gazing off into the distance for a long moment, then he shook his head and said, "It will be very hard, but I will do it."

"Do it quickly. When she knows you do not love her as she had hoped, she will want to leave, and the quicker she gets away from you, the quicker she will be able to deal with her wounded feelings." Adriano watched as the tall man walked slowly away. He felt grief in his heart, for he loved Ian Marlowe as a son, but he had known with an ancient wisdom that this had to be. For a time he had hoped that the two would marry, but something told him that such a marriage would never work. They were from two different worlds and would each have to find their happiness with someone else.

★   ★   ★   ★

"Sarita, I need to talk to you."

Instantly Sarita put down the root she was cleaning with a knife and stood to her feet. "Yes, Ian?"

Ian stood silently for a moment. He had come into the hut and found Sarita alone. He knew that Adriano had taken Wes and Emily to watch a ceremony among the young men of the Guapi. He stood there uncertainly, and yet he knew what he must do. "Sit down, Sarita."

Sarita instantly sat down on her cot, and Ian took the one that Emily used. Never had he felt so unable to say clearly what he must say, but finally he looked up and said, "Sarita, I think you know how much I care for you and your father."

"Yes," Sarita said.

"I see something happening between us that I wish were different."

"What is that, Ian?"

Ian shook his head and had to force the words out. "It seems you have formed an affection for me—" At this point he saw hope blaze in her eyes and quickly he said, "But it must not be, Sarita. It can't be." He saw her draw back as if he had struck her and knew that being honest with her was going to be hard on her, more than he had thought. "In my country, before a man and a woman become married, there must be equal feeling on both sides, and—"

"And you do not care for me!" Sarita said. She stood up suddenly, and Ian rose with her. Her back was stiff, and she stared at him, all joy and hope gone from her face.

"I do care for you—as a dear sister. I could never forget what you did for me when I was sick, but that's not enough."

"Perhaps it will be enough for me!"

"It wouldn't be in time to come. A woman deserves to have all of a man, and it must be a special kind of love." Knowing that he must make his feelings almost brutally clear, he said, "I love you like a sister, not like a man should love a woman he wants for his wife."

He hesitated, then said, "You must have seen the affection Wes has for Emily. That's what I feel for you. I always will care for you in this way, but—"

"Don't say any more!" Sarita snapped. For a moment she looked away, then she looked up at him and said, "My grandfather and I will leave at once."

"You don't have to go, Sarita—"

She did not answer but turned and walked out of the hut. Ian suddenly felt a trembling in his knees and saw that his hands were not steady. He wiped his hand across his face and shook his head. "This is bad," he muttered. "Very bad." He left the hut and looked for Sarita, but she seemed to have disappeared. He walked slowly toward the tent and found Adriano there. He stopped and looked down and said in a voice of pure misery, "Well, I did as you suggested, Adriano, and I feel like shooting myself."

Adriano rose and came over to put his hand on the tall man's shoulder. "You must not blame yourself. You have been honorable in telling her the truth."

"She's hurt and angry, and I can't blame her."

"Yes, she is, but time will make a difference." He paused, then said, "We will leave tomorrow."

Ian nodded and walked away. He could not remember feeling so miserable, not for a long time at least, and he wondered how long such a feeling would last.

★ ★ ★ ★

"I haven't seen much of Ian since Adriano and Sarita left," Wes said. "How long has it been now—three days?" He nodded, then looked over at Emily. "You think he's angry about something?"

"I don't know, Wes." Emily was writing, and she paused and stared down blankly at the sheet. She was well aware of the truth of what Wes had said, for she too had noticed a difference in Ian but didn't know what to make of it.

Finally she rose and left, taking her tablet with her, making notes of interesting aspects about the Guapi that she had observed in the last few days. She had reams of notes, more than she would ever need for a magazine article but enough, perhaps, for a book, which was her goal.

Thirty minutes later she came upon Ian. She saw him come out of the chief's hut and hesitated. He glanced at her and would have turned away, but with determination she said, "Ian, would you walk with me awhile?"

"Of course."

Emily began to speak of a particular custom of the Guapi life she had noticed, ostensibly for putting in her notebook. The two walked for some fifteen minutes, and she did take a few notes. In truth, she was concerned at the cloud that seemed to have settled over him. His face was drawn, and the happiness that he normally displayed was now gone. They had reached the point where the harpy eagle looked down at them from his roost with his fierce gaze. Emily saw no joy in Ian's expression. His eyes appeared almost dead, and his voice had lost its usual vibrancy. Staring up at the eagle, she said, "Ian, is something wrong?"

He turned his face away from her and seemed to be studying the vegetation in the jungle that made a wall fifty yards away. "Things haven't been going too well," he said finally.

"Would you like to talk about it?" Emily asked quietly.

Still with his head turned, Ian said, "I've had to give a pretty hard jolt to a good friend of mine."

Emily knew then how bad it was with him. "Sometimes it helps to talk about what's bothering us. Sometimes it doesn't, but I'd be glad to listen."

Ian glanced at the eagle and then shook his head. "Come along," he said. "I might as well tell you."

Emily followed, and the two reached the edge of the jungle. She saw a brightly colored bird, all red and yellow and green, as it made its way, weaving between the trees. Soon Ian began to talk, and his voice was low and sad. "It's Sarita," he said. "She'd gotten too fond of me in the wrong way. I've always had an affection for her. She's been so kind to me, but I let it get out of hand. And I had to tell her that there would never be anything between us."

"That must have been very hard for her. I could see she cared for you."

And then something happened that Emily Winslow would never forget. She had known this man when he was no more than a common crook, out to serve himself at all costs. She had refused to forgive him because she could not believe he could ever change. Now, as he turned, she was shocked to see tears in his eyes. She could only stare at him and wonder at how much he had changed. She sensed how bad he felt for having hurt Sarita deeply without meaning to.

"I feel worse than I can tell you, Emily," he said. His voice was unsteady. "She's such a fine young woman, and I'd literally rather cut my arm off than hurt her. But I had to tell her how I honestly felt."

Emily wanted to put her arms around Ian and comfort him, but she did not move. Finally she said in a soft, consoling tone, "I know it's terrible, but time will make a difference. She will find someone to love her the way she needs."

Ian blinked his eyes, stiffened his back, then turned and walked away without another word. As Emily watched him go, she thought, *James Parker would never have cared for a woman's feelings like that.* She stood there at the edge of the jungle knowing that she had received a revelation of some kind. She knew she would never forget the tears in Ian Marlowe's eyes over the feelings of another—and she knew he was not the man she had hated for so long. A deep transformation had happened to him, and now she knew it full well.

CHAPTER TWENTY-THREE

PRISON DOORS OPEN

★ ★ ★ ★

Wes came in shortly after daybreak, happy, even though he was clawing at the mosquito bites he had collected. As he entered their camping area, he found Emily cooking pancakes over the open fire. "Hi, sis," he said. "Better throw an extra pancake or two on the griddle for me."

Waving the smoke away from her face, Emily looked up from where she was sitting on a stump. "Did you get some good shots?"

"First class!" Wes turned to his tent, stored his equipment, then came back and sat down across from Emily. "Those look good," he said.

"You never taste anything anyway. You gobble your food down so fast you don't have a chance to taste it," Emily teased.

She had no spatula, but using a broad-bladed kitchen knife, she lifted one edge of a pancake. "They don't rise as much as I'd like. When we get home I'll fix you some good ones. I really miss Mom's cooking."

"So do I," Wes said. "This trip has been a great time for me, but I'm looking forward now to going home and putting this story all together."

"How long do you think it will take you to get the pictures all developed and arranged?"

"It depends on what you want. You're the boss. I'll make the pictures fit the story."

"I'm not sure about that," Emily said. She lifted a pancake, put it on a tin plate, and handed it to Wes. "You go ahead and start. There's honey in that little jar there."

Wes bowed his head and said a quick grace, then, taking out his pocketknife, cut the pancake into small pieces. He poured the honey over it and laughed. "Look. There are three dead bees in this honey."

Emily smiled. "Just fish them out."

Wes did as she suggested, speared a bite-sized morsel of the pancake with the tip of his knife blade, and put it in his mouth. "Really good," he mumbled, nodding vigorously.

He continued to eat while Emily cooked another pancake and put it on her own plate, then poured out some more batter for the next one. As she cut her pancake up and began to eat, the two talked about how they would compile the book about their adventure here in the Amazon when they got home.

"This is the last of the coffee that Adriano brought. Enjoy it. I saved a little bit for you and Ian."

Wes took the tin cup, poured a little honey in it, and stirred it with the tip of his knife blade. "Manners go to pot around here, don't they? But we've made out fine. You've really taken good care of me, sis."

"No more than you've taken of me."

"Where is Ian?"

"I don't know."

Wes was sipping his coffee, and he looked up on noting the rather terse edge to his sister's voice. He studied her carefully, for he knew her quite well. Something was obviously troubling her, and he struggled as to whether he should inquire. Finally, knowing that there was no one else for her to talk to, he said, "What's the matter, sis? You've been so subdued lately—not like yourself at all."

"Oh, it's nothing. I'm just tired, I suppose."

Wes shook his head and sipped the strong black coffee again. "It's more than that," he said. "You're like a candle that's burned out. I've been worried about you for a while. Do you think it's still the effects of the malaria or something else getting you down?"

"No, nothing like that." Emily suddenly put down her tin plate and turned the pancake over in the pan with the knife. She did not pick up her plate again but sat on the log, a strange expression on her face.

"I wish you'd tell me what's bothering you." A thought suddenly came to Wes, and he said quietly, "It has something to do with Ian, doesn't it?"

Startled, Emily shot a glance at Wes. This brother of hers knew her too well! He was watching her expectantly, and she shrugged her shoulders. "I suppose it does."

"You've had quite a struggle with your feelings about Ian since we got here," Wes observed. "It's been eating at you a long time."

Suddenly Emily began to speak. In truth she had kept her thoughts bottled up. She couldn't talk to Ian about what was bothering her, but with Wes it was different. The two had grown very close since Jared's death, and now alone, with no other person to share her true feelings with, she suddenly knew she had to unburden herself. "I'm having a terrible time," she confessed. "You know how I felt about Ian when he called himself James Parker. I've hated him for years for what he did to me."

"I know you have, sis, and I think you've been wrong."

"You're probably right," Emily said. She shook her head and fell silent for a moment. The morning sun was rising, throwing its pale gleam over her face.

Wes noticed that there was a seriousness in her that went very deep. He had seen her upset before but never like this. "How do you feel about Ian now?" he asked. "I can't even think of him as James Parker anymore. That man seems to be dead and buried."

"You're wise to think of it like that, but . . ." Emily hesitated, then ran her hand down her hair in a gesture of dismay. "The two come together in my mind, James Parker and Ian Marlowe. Yet I haven't been able to really think of them as the same person. They seem so different."

"I think, sis, your pride is getting in the way here."

Emily lifted her head and stared at Wes. "What do you mean by that?"

"I mean, in effect, James Parker deceived you by making you fall in love with him."

Emily's face flushed. "I'm not sure that's true."

"Everyone else thinks it is. I know Mom and Dad do."

"You talked about it with them?"

"Why, of course. What did you think?"

"I don't know," Emily said wearily. She saw that the pancake was done and reached over to take it off the fire. "Here. Have another pancake." She put it on Wes's plate, but he merely held the plate in his hand and continued to watch her with an expectant light in his eye.

"Who was it that said, 'Hell hath no fury like a woman scorned'? I don't remember, but that's pretty well what happened. In a way he used you, and I can guess that no woman could go through that without some pretty strong feelings."

Emily did not answer for a time, but finally she said quietly, "I think you're right, Wes. My pride was hurt, so I've kept this anger and bitterness smoldering inside me all these years. I just haven't been able to shake it off. I've got these two men," she said almost in despair. "One is a coward who was responsible for the death of my brother, the man I thought I was in love with—but when I look at Ian, I can't see that man at all. I'm all mixed-up, Wes."

Wes put his plate down and came over to sit beside Emily. He put his arm around her and drew her close. His voice was warm as he said, "I've seen this coming on and wanted to help you with it, but I didn't know how. But I think you need to understand, Emily, that people can change. That's what the gospel is all about."

Emily listened as Wes spoke. She was thankful for his arm around her, for she needed someone to encourage her and to hold her. Then suddenly as Wes spoke on, she realized that if she had not been thrown into this situation and found Ian after all these years, she would never have gotten rid of that bitterness. She probably would have gone to her grave hating James Parker and ruining her own spirit.

Wes said, "Ian did a terrible thing back in his youth, but there's something good in him now. I think you've seen it since we've been here. I surely have. How he lied and deceived us all was terrible, but if the Bible is true, Christ can wipe all the past away. Don't you think?"

Emily nodded, unable to speak. Her throat was tight, and she could only whisper, "That's right, of course."

"I didn't trust Ian when we first met him," Wes said gently. "But after watching him serve these people out in the middle of the jungle, I've seen that he's really changed." He tightened his grip on her and said, "Emily, you've got to let go of the past. I know it has hurt you for years, but it's time to forgive and to get on with your life." He squeezed her hard, then got up and went back and began eating his pancake.

Emily had lost all of her appetite, for his words had cut deeply. She was confused, but she recognized the truth when she saw it, and now she quickly got up, saying, "Would you wash the dishes? I think I'll walk around a little bit."

"Sure, sis. You go right ahead."

Emily moved away from their campsite and walked slowly toward the village. As she did, her brother's words echoed in her mind, and the truth loomed as large as a mountain. Yet even now it was difficult for her to put away all of her bitterness for the man she had held a grudge against for so long.

She passed by two Guapi mothers who had seated themselves near cooking fires. She noted absently that they were using green twigs to turn over the ears of corn. Each of them was suckling a baby riding in a swing at her hip. Emily moved on and observed that two young men and several young boys were just beginning to stir in their hammocks. She smiled at them as they came out, and one of the youngest boys waved at her. She did not know their names, but their faces were familiar. They were a family that never missed the services Ian held every Sunday. She walked past another hut and noticed that a baby was crawling across the dirt floor. He snatched up a puppy and held it, laughing and pulling its ears.

A young girl who was cooking alongside her mother picked up a morsel of meat sizzling on a stick and took it over to her father. He reached out, took it with one hand, and patted her head with the other, smiling at her as he did so.

Emily wandered around the village speaking to many of the people and was greeted as Lomisah, which Ian told her meant "the fire-headed woman." When he had told her the name the Guapi had given her, she had laughed and said, "Redheads can't get away from teasing even in the midst of the Amazon jungle."

Finally she completed her tour of the village and came to herself with a start. Ian had appeared, and the natives were beginning to gather. She had not realized she had been there so long and almost turned to go away. But she had vowed she would attend every service, and she saw Wes entering the village, so she waited for him, and then the two went to where the small crowd had gathered.

Ian smiled at them and said, "Welcome to church."

"A good crowd this morning," Wes said. "Maybe we ought to take up a collection."

Ian laughed. "These people wouldn't understand that at all."

Emily did not enter into the discussion, and Ian almost at once moved to one of the huts to his back. The villagers spread out, some sitting on the ground, some standing, and Ian began to speak. Since he spoke in the Guapi language, neither Emily nor Wes understood what he was saying. He had offered once to translate into English, but Emily had said quickly, "No, that won't be necessary. We can worship even if we don't know what you're saying."

Ordinarily Ian sang a hymn, and many of the villagers had learned the tunes of several, enough to hum along, although, of course, they did not know the words.

Ian bowed his head, and Emily, before she bowed her own, saw that the natives did the same. She wondered what went on in their hearts. Even if they did not understand all that Ian was trying to teach them, they still obviously respected and even loved Ian Marlowe.

After Ian's brief prayer, he sang two songs that he had translated into the Guapi language, one, "The Old Rugged Cross" and the other, "What a Friend We Have in Jesus." The Guapi joined in with these.

Emily was taken off guard when suddenly Ian said, "It would be nice if you would sing for us, Emily."

Emily started to refuse but knew she must not. "What would you like for me to sing?"

"Anything. I remember you have a good singing voice. These people like singing of any kind."

Emily thought quickly and decided to sing one of her favorite songs, "Take My Life and Let It Be."

She had sung this hymn many times in her life, but at this moment the words took on new meaning for her as she lifted her clear alto voice and began:

> *"Take my life, and let it be*
> *Consecrated, Lord, to thee;*
> *Take my moments and my days,*
> *Let them flow in ceaseless praise.*
>
> *Take my hands and let them move*
> *At the impulse of thy love:*
> *Take my feet and let them be*
> *Swift and beautiful for thee.*
>
> *Take my voice and let me sing*
> *Always, only, for my King;*
> *Take my lips and let them be*
> *Filled with messages from thee.*
>
> *Take my will and make it thine,*
> *It shall be no longer mine;*
> *Take my heart; it is thine own,*
> *It shall be thy royal throne.*
>
> *Take my love, my Lord, I pour*
> *At thy feet its treasure store;*
> *Take myself, and I will be*
> *Ever, only, all for thee."*

A murmur went around the crowd, and she noticed that her song was well received. Wes whispered, "That was great, sis. I never heard you sing better."

Emily sat down beside Wes and listened as Ian preached. He

said, "I am preaching on Jesus this morning. John 3:16 is the text."

Emily sat quietly listening, intrigued by the sound of the words as they fell from Ian's lips. His face was alight, and his eyes sparkled as he spoke, and from time to time he lifted his right hand while holding the Bible up toward the sky with his left in a strange gesture of surrender. Even though she could not understand the words, Emily Winslow knew that this man was speaking the truth as he saw it. His bronzed face was fixed in an expression of joy, and his voice showed the eagerness in his heart to give the message of salvation to these who sat in darkness.

As the service progressed, Emily became uncomfortably aware that she felt very strange. It would have been difficult for her to put it into words, but she felt . . . guilty. A dark sense of what could only be shame came to her, and as she listened, the feeling seemed to grow more intense. Emily Winslow had been guilty of sin in the past, and she recognized conviction when it came to her. She knew that God was laying this burden upon her heart. And now as the voice of Ian Marlowe sounded in her ears, she heard beyond that voice, and in her spirit she knew that God was placing her in judgment.

Emily let none of what she was feeling show. She kept her eyes fixed on Ian, aware of the congregation and of Wes sitting beside her, but her heart was crushed in a way she had never known. Thinking it would pass away, that it was a mere mental attitude, she endured. But as time passed, there was no doubt at all. God was bringing her to judgment for the anger and bitterness she had actually cherished in her heart for so long, refusing to let it go and extend forgiveness!

The service closed, and as usual, Ian was surrounded by the villagers who wanted to ask questions about this God of his. Emily slipped away unobtrusively and made her way out of the village. She did not want to return to her hut, for she did not want to speak with anyone, and she knew Wes would return soon and probably Ian as well. Instead, she turned and took the familiar path that led down to the river. The yellow-and-scarlet bird made a rattling sound over her head, and then a howler monkey a little farther out in the jungle loosed his startling scream.

When she reached the river, she turned and walked slowly along the bank. She saw several natives fishing who did not choose to go to the service. For the most part the riverbank was deserted. She passed a naked young child, a boy no more than five or six, and she thought of the folk legend that one of the storytellers of the tribe had told one evening. Ian had translated it for her. The story was about the *curupira*, a demon that appeared as a small child, and whose feet were always turned backward. White men had cut off his feet, and a god had sewn them on backward. Some of the villagers believed they could solicit curupira's help for hunting and crop failures, and they brought him offerings of matches and sometimes liquor. But if they ever told anyone, curupira would hunt them down and stab them to death with his long, sharp fingernails.

The memory of the folklore passed swiftly through Emily's mind, and she prayed that the truth of the gospel would replace their fears of the curupira. She had recorded it in her notes and knew that many of these aspects of the Guapi way of life would be in the book that she planned to write.

Only once did she see anyone else. Two men had lassoed a caiman, which inhabited the Amazon in large numbers. These crocodiles sometimes caught the dogs of the tribe.

Emily watched as the two men dragged the scaly monster to the bank and killed it after some difficulty. Then she walked on. Finally she reached a place that was quiet and sat down beside a large tree that arched over the riverbank. She looked carefully for ants and snakes before sitting down, but she saw none.

Although the setting was a peaceful and quiet one, she felt no peace in her heart, for the conviction that something was terribly wrong with her intensified. She bowed her head and tried to pray but could not seem to get through to God. She had learned by experience that when God did not answer her, it meant something in her own life had broken the fellowship between them.

One verse of the hymn she had sung at the service came back to her memory:

Take my will and make it thine,
It shall be no longer mine;
Take my heart; it is thine own,
It shall be thy royal throne.

As the river rolled along gently in front of her, Emily sat thinking of that hymn, then began to pray, "Oh, God, I haven't let you have my will! You know my heart—how bitter I have been because of the wrong that was done to my family—and to me. I've tried to forgive, but I can't. But now, Lord, I've gone as far as I can go. I must have peace!"

The peace that she sought did not come easily. For a long time she sat there, her face at times buried in her hands as tears rose to her eyes. She wiped them away and prayed, even more determined to settle the matter once and for all.

She never knew how long she had sat there on that riverbank, but finally there came a time when she felt completely drained. Weakness seized her, and she cried out, "Lord, I give all my bitterness to you. Jesus died for my sins, and I claim your forgiveness—not because I deserve it, but because Jesus died for this sin on the cross. Forgive me, Lord, in the name of Jesus. . . ."

★　★　★　★

Ian looked up with a startled expression. He had not known that Emily was near, for he had been reading in the shade of one of the large trees close to his tent. He got up at once and started to speak, but then he saw something in Emily's face that silenced him. He had noted that for the past three days she seemed different, but he could not tell what was going on in her heart. Now he waited and was shocked when she said quickly, "Ian, I've come to ask your forgiveness."

Ian stared at her. "Why, Emily—"

"No, let me finish." Emily's face was pale, and tears began to gather in her eyes. "I've hated you for years for what you did to me and what you did to my family, and it's torn me to pieces. Last Sunday after the service I went down to the river, and it took a long time, but I asked God for His forgiveness—and, Ian, He gave it to me." Tears ran down her cheeks, and she wiped them away. "For the first time in years I feel free. The prison door has opened. So I've come to ask you to forgive me for my bitterness and the hatred I had for you."

Ian suddenly smiled and put out his hands, and Emily took them. "Of course, I forgive you," he said quietly.

Emily felt her hands held so tightly that it pained her, but she did not care. She knew she had closed the door on something wicked—a plague of her own heart that had almost destroyed her, and her voice was tremulous as she said, "Thank you, Ian. . . !

That night Emily wrote a letter to her parents. She had been writing all along, waiting for an opportunity to send the letters home. She knew they might not arrive before she did, but she wanted to record her experiences and feelings as they were happening. Now it was paramount to explain to her parents the miracle of forgiveness that had just taken place in her heart.

For a long time she tried to begin to explain what had happened during her time of prayer down by the river, but she could find no way that satisfied her. Finally she put down the facts, telling them how the man they had known as James Parker had appeared. She did not spare herself, but set down how the bitterness she'd had for years had leaped out and nearly consumed her. But then she wrote about how Ian Marlowe had been honorable in every way since she'd encountered him. Finally she described how he'd behaved toward Sarita—including the moment when she'd seen tears in his eyes.

"I've been wrong all this years," she said as she closed the letter. "People can change—and Ian is a changed man. His heart is open and honest, and I believe he's a fine Christian. No man could weep over a woman's feelings as he did without having a good and pure heart. I know God has forgiven me for my bitterness toward Ian, and I want you to know what an honorable man he's become."

She sealed the letter and put it with the others, hoping that she would soon find a way to send them home to her parents when they returned to Santarém or Belém.

CHAPTER TWENTY-FOUR

No Greater Love

★ ★ ★ ★

Three days passed, during which Emily sensed that Ian had grown more distant. Since her surrender to God out on the riverbank after Ian's sermon, she had kept to herself, seeking God, for the peace that had come upon her was marvelous indeed. She had not realized how bound her life had been with the bitterness she had carried for years. Now that it was gone, she sensed a freedom in her spirit she had never experienced before. She spent many hours reading the Scriptures and walking down by the riverside, giving thanks to God and asking for guidance.

But somehow she had not been able to find a way to communicate to Ian what had really happened to her. True enough she had asked his forgiveness, but she had expected that after her honest talk with him, the two of them would—well, she was not quite sure what she thought. But certainly she hadn't expected to be ignored!

Finally late one afternoon she finished her writing and noted that the material for the article was more than complete and that a book could certainly be made out of all that she had gathered, along with the pictures Wes had taken. Leaving her hut, she moved over to where Wes was sitting outside his tent simply staring out at the village. She sat down beside him and said, "What are you doing, Wes?"

"Thinking."

Emily found his answer slightly amusing. "That's a little bit unusual for you."

Wes grinned at her and turned his head to face her. "I guess it is. This trip has affected me in a way I never thought it would, sis."

"I know what you mean. I think every spoiled American should have to make a trip to a place like this to see what the real world is like. We're living in a fairy-tale world over there," she added. "Everyone has enough to eat. They can call the police if there's trouble. They ought to live in a village out here in the Amazon for a month. I think we all need to appreciate all the blessings God's given us in America."

The two chatted for a while, and finally Emily said rather cautiously, "Wes, something has been bothering me."

"What's that, sis?"

"It's Ian. He . . . he doesn't seem . . ." Her voice broke in confusion, and she brushed her hand down the back of her hair. "I don't know how to say it. He's cut me off, and I don't know why."

Wes turned to face Emily squarely. "I'm surprised you don't see it. I do."

"What is it?" She had told Wes all about apologizing to Ian and reminded him of it now. "I thought when I told him how God had changed me, we would—well, we'd get closer together."

"You know what I think? I think you're still in love with him. I think you always were."

"I don't know about that," Emily said defensively. "I certainly admire him now."

"I think it's more than that, Emily. There's something in your eyes when you look at him. Even when we first got here, I could see you hadn't really forgotten how much he meant to you at one time."

Emily shook her head and said, "We won't talk about that, but why won't he have anything to do with me now?"

"You're supposed to be smart, Emily. I'm just a dumb photographer."

"But I just don't see it. What is it, Wes?"

"Why, he's still in love with you, of course."

Emily stared at Wes in shock for a moment. "How . . . how do you know?"

"The way he looks at you. The way he treats you. I don't think he ever got over you. And since we came out here, I think it's all come back to him."

"Well, he doesn't treat me like he loves me!" Emily said almost petulantly.

"And you don't know why?"

"No. And I don't think you do either."

"Yes, I do." Wes thought for a moment, then said, "Look, what's he going to say to you? That he loves you? When a fellow says that to a girl, the next thing is 'Will you marry me?' But do you think he could say that?"

"I don't see why not."

"That's because you haven't thought about it. What does he have to offer you? He doesn't have any money. God brought him out to this wild place where no American woman could live forever. Oh, you've roughed it out here for a while, but all the time you knew you were going home again to a comfortable way of life."

Emily sat there quietly drinking in what Wes had just told her. "Do you really think that's it, Wes?"

"I'm pretty sure it is. I've talked with him a lot since we've been out here, and I really admire him, Emily. He's really straight this time. He had a bad beginning, but now he loves God more than any man I've ever seen. And faith. Wow, has he got faith! To come out here with no money, not speaking the language, no mission board behind him to support him. Just to walk into this jungle alone among dangerous tribesmen. I don't know how he did it. I know I couldn't."

Emily rose slowly, and her eyes were strangely thoughtful. "Thanks, Wes. It's good to have a brother like you."

"Anytime. Wes Winslow's Courtship Bureau. We never close."

Emily tried to smile, but her mind was filled with thoughts and questions about what Wes had said. *Could he still be interested in me?* she thought as she turned to leave. She moved away from

Wes and walked along the path to the village, where she spent two hours watching the women as they worked. She wished she knew the language so that she could get to know them better, but what she did know of the Guapi had come simply by watching them day after day.

All the time, however, she was thinking about what Wes had said, and being the determined young woman she was, she finally came to one conclusion. *I'll have to talk to Ian. I don't know what I'll say, but I've got to say something.*

★ ★ ★ ★

Emily's intention to talk to Ian was never fulfilled. She tried several times to work up her courage, but never once was she able to do so. *What would I say to him if he asked me to marry him?* she thought. *My life isn't here and his is.*

The following day after her conversation with Wes, she borrowed one of Wes's cameras, saying, "I'm going to get some shots of those orchids and whatever else I can find."

"Don't get lost," Wes said.

"No, I won't. I won't be going far."

The sun was high in the sky, but Emily was shielded by the canopy overhead as she walked along between the huge trees. Some of the trees had knees that came up nearly as high as her head, and she felt like a pigmy as she walked along. Dwarfed as she was by the gigantic trees, she took a wrong turn and could not find the orchids. The briars began to catch at her clothes, and she had to extract herself carefully to keep from tearing them, for she had so few clothes to wear.

Finally she decided to give up her search and started back. She was startled to meet Ian, who came from another direction, evidently having been on some business of his own. "Hello, Ian," she said with some restraint.

"Emily, what are you doing out here alone?" Ian was wearing his faded khakis and the sun helmet that had been used to drink out of so many times it was almost past redemption. He pushed it back on his head and added, "You taking pictures for Wes now?"

"Oh, I just wanted to get a few shots of my own."

"Maybe I can help you. What are you looking for?"

"Trying to find the orchids I saw the other day."

"Well, they're over there about three hundred yards. Come along."

Emily followed Ian, envying him as he seemed to be able to find an easy path through the lush vegetation. As always she kept her eyes open for spiders and snakes and jaguars, although she had never seen a jaguar or a poisonous serpent since they had arrived at the Guapi village.

Finally Ian stopped and pointed. "How about those?"

"Oh, those are just right!" Emily exclaimed. She moved past Ian and began taking pictures. She noted that Ian did not speak but waited silently, and she wished she could come up with the words she needed to say to him.

After getting several shots, she turned and said, "This will be—"

"Look out!"

She looked down at her feet and saw a green serpent coiled and in the process of striking. She tried to move but did not seem to be able to. At once she knew that this was a poisonous snake or Ian would not have shouted.

The snake struck, but Emily, at that same moment, was shoved aside. Ian had leaped at her and given her a tremendous shove that sent her reeling backward.

She fell down flat on her back, her hair caught in some thorns, and saw that Ian was thrashing at the snake with a stick.

Getting to her feet, she whispered, "Was it a poisonous one, Ian?"

"Fer-de-lance."

The very name sent a chill through Emily. This was the snake that the natives called in their language "a five-stepper," because five steps was about all anyone got before they died. She looked at Ian and saw his face was pale.

"What's wrong?"

"He got me—here on the leg." Ian raised his pants leg and was fumbling in his pocket.

"Oh, Ian, we've got to get help."

"Too late." Ian sat down and pulled a knife out. It was only a small penknife, but it had a keen edge. Emily saw him cut two crosses across the fang marks, small red dots, and the blood began to pour freely.

"I must get help, Ian."

"There's no help for this," Ian said. He sat down and watched the blood as it gushed from the gashes he had cut in his leg.

He looked up at Emily, and his lips were in a straight line. "It's not likely I'll make it through this. This poison is really bad. I'll start having trouble pretty soon, and then I'll probably die. I can feel it working on me now."

Emily felt as if she were going to faint. She moved forward and knelt beside him, and she leaned against him, and the feeling of helplessness seemed to drain her of all strength. She felt light-headed and wanted to scream out, but she knew that would be useless.

Ian took his eyes off of the wounds he had made and said steadily, "Emily, if I don't make it, there's one thing I want you to know. I love you, Emily. I did long ago—and I still do."

"Oh—Ian!" Holding on to his arm, she could not speak for a moment, then she whispered, "I love you, too, Ian."

"Do you? I never thought you would. I never thought you could really."

Emily saw that his breathing was becoming more labored, and his face was growing more pallid. His eyes fluttered, and he closed them, and he would have fallen, but she held him up, putting her arms around him. She held on to him with both arms and began to cry out, "Oh, God, let him live! Please, Lord, don't let him die!"

She could feel the labored breathing, and only her strength of will kept her from passing out herself. She had never been so frightened in her life. She put her hand over his chest and thought she could feel his heart laboring. All time seemed to have stopped, and she knew that Ian Marlowe was dying in her arms!

Afterward it seemed like a dream, but at the time it did not. She was holding Ian, trying to will her life into him and crying out to God both in her heart and aloud in a gasping prayer that came from the deepest part of her soul. And then, even as she prayed, she had the strongest impression she had ever had of God's presence. She saw nothing, for her eyes were tightly shut, and she was certain she could not have heard anything with her ears. But inside her spirit there was something almost like a voice that said very plainly, *I will heal him, Emily. Only trust me.*

Emily cried out, "I do trust you, Lord! I do! Only don't let him die. . . !"

For how long Emily sat there she did not know. Ian's body arched and went into spasms, and he seemed to struggle for breath. His eyes rolled up backward into his head.

All this time Emily clung to him and did not cease crying out to God. Finally she felt his body go limp, and fear flooded her heart. "Lord, don't let him die!" She collapsed against his lifeless body, sobbing.

Ian's limp body remained still for what seemed like a long time. Emily's weeping began to subside as she felt God's presence strongly with her again, and she found herself speaking out words of trust and faith, reminding God of His power to heal. Even as she uttered the words aloud, a belief stronger than she had ever known before rose up within her, and she spoke out with a calm assurance. "You can save him, Lord," she said. "Even if he's dead, you can bring him back. In the name of Jesus take away this poison!"

Right then Emily felt Ian give a faint jerking motion. She opened her eyes and saw that his eyes were fluttering. She cried out, "Ian, you're alive!"

Ian did not answer but took in a sudden deep breath and then exhaled it with a gusty sigh. He lay panting almost like a dog—but he was alive, and he was breathing.

Finally Emily saw his eyes open, and she cried, "Ian, can you hear me?"

"Yes." Ian's body was drenched with perspiration, and he could hardly speak, for he was struggling for breath. But the breathing was becoming more regular, and he reached out a hand almost blindly and touched her face. "How long—" he started to say but could not finish.

Emily suddenly took him in her arms and held him as she would a child. She began to weep and cried out over and over, "You're alive, Ian! You're alive! God has kept you alive!"

She released him, and Ian raised a hand that trembled badly to wipe his face. "I don't understand it," he muttered. "I never... knew anybody getting over one of those bites... from a fer-de-lance."

Emily was still holding his arm, and she squeezed it hard. "After you passed out I began crying to God, and the Lord came to me, Ian. He really did. And He told me that He'd heal you, and that I was simply to trust Him." She looked into his eyes and saw that he was watching her intently. "And I promised Him," she whispered, "that I would."

Suddenly Ian reached out and touched her hair and then her cheek. "Did I dream it?" he whispered. "Or did you say you loved me... when you thought I was dying?"

And then Emily knew the truth. "Yes, I said it, and I do love you, Ian!" She put her arms around him then, and the two of them clung together, neither of them speaking. The silence seemed to surround them, but as her head lay on his chest, she could feel his heart beating strongly, and she whispered, "I do love you, Ian... and now I know you love me, too!"

CHAPTER TWENTY-FIVE

FAREWELLS

★ ★ ★ ★

Emily was overwhelmed with mixed emotions as she said good-bye to the Guapi. Noki, the chief, had gathered all the people together and had made a speech, which Ian had translated. It had, in effect, said that the flame-haired woman and her brother were good—for people with pale skins. As Ian had said dryly, "That's about as good a compliment as you're likely to get out of Noki."

Omala, who had stayed close to Emily and Wes during their entire stay after nearly frightening her to death that first time he had appeared at the door of her hut, was all smiles. Emily had given the warrior her wristwatch and taught him how to wind it, and although he could not tell time, he was proud of his new acquisition. He was wearing it around his neck on a leather thong as he said his good-byes.

"This is quite a farewell party," Wes said as he looked over the food that the women had prepared and set out for them.

They had gathered Brazil nuts and thrown them into the fire after divesting them of their outer husk. Then they had fished the blackened shells out of the glowing embers, crushed them between two rocks, and picked out the nuts with sharp slivers of wood. The nuts were delicious, as were the berries that the women and young girls had gathered early in the cool of the morning.

Emily found herself enjoying foods now that she once thought she'd never be able to stomach, including the iguana eggs, which she had been taught to gather by poking a stick into the river's sandy beaches. She still tactfully avoided, however, the juicy grubs and crunchy large ants that were eaten either alive or cooked by the Guapi.

After eating with the whole tribe, they listened to more speeches and to the native music that filled the jungle air. When Emily, Wes, and Ian finally donned their knapsacks, Noki came forward and began to speak again. Emily noticed that Ian paid very close attention to the chief, and when the Guapi warrior had ended, Ian turned and said, "He says you are good people. That if all of the Jesus people are like you and your brother, it makes him believe that Jesus is strong medicine."

Emily was touched and moved by the chief's words. "Tell him for me that I hope he takes Jesus into his heart and that all of his people find peace in Him."

Ian translated this, and Noki's dark eyes glowed. He spoke some more and finally lifted his hand in a gesture of farewell.

"Time to go, I guess," Wes murmured. "You know, I hate to leave this place in a way."

"So do I," Emily said. She turned to follow Ian, who led the way into the rain forest. As she followed him, she felt the warmth of their closeness the day he had been bitten by the fer-de-lance. That had been only a week ago, but now he seemed to be fully recovered. Those days had been precious indeed to Emily, for she had discovered that she and Ian could talk for hours and that all of the old animosity and hatred and bitterness she had allowed to come into her heart was completely gone.

They trekked all morning, pausing briefly for one short rest and then for another longer one at noon. They ate sparingly and then went on until they made their camp for the night.

For supper they roasted a small deer that Ian had shot, and they sat around the campfire for a time listening to the noises of the night. Emily sat close to Ian and listened as he spoke with energy about the plans for evangelizing the Guapi. "I think they're ready now," he said, "for a real missionary."

"But you are a real missionary," Wes spoke up. The fire threw reflecting shadows on his face as he sat cross-legged on the ground. He studied Ian carefully, then said, "What are you thinking about? Leaving here?"

"I think I might be finished here. I want to do some more work on the language, but if real missionaries would come for a long term, I think that might be best."

Emily said nothing until after Wes had rolled up in his blanket beside the fire. He fell asleep at once, and she said quietly to Ian, "I didn't know you were thinking of leaving."

"I'm not sure about it, Emily. I don't really know what I'm going to do. I love to work with the Guapi, but for some reason I feel God pulling at me. I'll just have to wait and see what He has for me next."

She leaned against him, and the two sat there silently. Emily had noticed that there was a companionship, even when they did not talk, that she had never felt with another man. Ian, at times, fell into long silences, and she had learned to adjust to these times. Her own propensity toward talking made up for some of his silences, and now as the fire crackled and the smell of woodsmoke filled her senses, she was content to enjoy his silent companionship.

★   ★   ★   ★

Adriano came out of the house, his face wreathed in smiles. "You are back, my friends! Come in—come in!"

Emily took his greeting and stepped aside as he went to shake Wes's hand and embrace Ian. She saw Sarita, who had come out of the house, and rather dreaded the meeting. She went forward at once, however, and put her hand out. "Hello, Sarita. It's good to see you again."

"You are welcome in our house," Sarita said.

Her voice was neutral, and Emily could not read the expression in her dark eyes.

Adriano hustled them all inside and insisted at once on preparing a meal for them. He and Sarita moved around the stove and the table, and soon they had eggs from the chickens he was so proud of and a hen fried for the occasion.

As Emily ate, savoring the feel of a chair under her and a table to hold her plate, she glanced once or twice at Sarita, who was seated beside her grandfather. She said almost nothing, but her eyes went often to Ian.

After they had finished the main meal and were eating some fruit and berries that Sarita had gathered, Adriano listened as Ian told him about the work he had done among the Guapi. When Ian spoke of the possibility of leaving, Emily saw Sarita's head suddenly lift and her eyes narrow.

"You're leaving, Ian?" Sarita asked.

"Yes, I think it's possible. I'm going to talk to the Pettigrews about sending a missionary, perhaps a couple. They've always been anxious to send somebody to the Guapi, but there was nobody who could come. But that may have changed by now."

Emily was tired and chose to go to bed early, but before she did, Ian called her outside. "I need to talk to you," he said.

Emily walked outside. The stars overhead were glittering by the millions, it seemed. She could not remember such a display of the immensity of the heavens. The stars threw their pale light down on the small house and the clearing, and she stopped and turned to him. "What is it, Ian?"

"I'm going back to the States with you."

Emily blinked with surprise. "I thought you were just going to the Pettigrews."

"No, I'm going all the way home. That is, if you tell me that I can."

"Why, Ian, you don't have to ask me if you can go home!"

"In truth, I don't really have a home, Emily," Ian said quietly.

The white of the full moon cast contrasting shadows and light on his face. It made his features look stronger. He was planed down to the bare essentials, and both his face and his body were trim and lean. He reached out suddenly and put his arms around her and pulled her close. Without speaking he drew her in and lowered his head, and Emily lifted her face for his kiss.

For her the kiss was something old—and yet something new.

She had never forgotten his caresses, not completely, and now she knew that nothing had changed. The old wild sweetness was here, and she put her arms around his neck and held him closely. She was conscious that the years, the empty years, were now being filled, and all that had passed in her life and in her spirit was being transformed. The years of waiting were finished, and she once again had the only man she had loved.

Ian lifted his lips and seemed to savor the moment. This woman had a power over him, a way of lifting him up to some height that he would never reach with another woman, and he whispered, "I wish I could think of some way to tell you how much I love you, Emily."

"Just say it, Ian."

"All right. I love you."

He kissed her again, and she clung to him and put her hands on his chest. When he lifted his head again, she said, "Can you believe that this is a beginning and not something that happened a long time ago?"

"I think it's both," Ian said slowly. "I would never have met you if I hadn't been what I was. But I hope we never speak of that dark time in my life again."

"We won't have to. You're a new man now, Ian. God has done something wonderful for both of us through all of it. I have you, and you have me."

Ian suddenly stepped back, and a reserve of some sort came into his face. "I don't know how it's going to work out, Emily."

"Why not?"

"I can't ask anything of you."

"Why not? If you love me and I love you, then we can face whatever comes our way."

"No, there are other things to consider. I . . . I mean our lives are so different."

His voice was quiet, and she sensed a restraint of the spirit that had flamed out in him a moment earlier.

"I don't know what I'm going to do. You're going to be a successful writer. I know that. But I'm not entirely sure what the future holds for me. I may come back to Brazil. God may send me to the Guapi for the rest of my life. I couldn't ask a woman to share a difficult life like that."

"If that's what God tells you to do, and I'm your wife, then I'll go with you."

The two stood there for a moment, and then she put her hand on his cheek. "When I thought you were dying, I asked God to heal you. And He told me that He would, and that I should trust Him. God gave you back to me, Ian, and if He can do that, I can trust Him in anything. So if marrying you means going back to the Guapi, then I'll go back with you, Ian."

He kissed her again and then said, "I won't let you make a decision now. Come along. We'd better go inside."

★   ★   ★   ★

Sarita had been silent, but now that the two guests and her grandfather were in bed, she came to Ian, who was sitting at the table reading by the oil lamp. He lifted his head and stood up. "I've been thinking about you so much, Sarita. I know I hurt you terribly."

"You're going back to America?"

"Yes. There's something about me that you don't know. Years ago I was not a good man, and I did something very evil to Emily and Wes's family. I've got to go face their parents and try to make it right."

Sarita's lips trembled slightly, but she kept her composure. "It is not them altogether, is it?"

"What do you mean?"

"It is Emily. You're going back for her."

"If she'll have me."

"I think she will."

And then Ian reached out and took one of her hands and held it in both of his. He studied her face and met her gaze for a long moment. "You're such a lovely girl, Sarita. There's some man who will be just right for you, and he'll be getting a jewel."

"Do you really think so, Ian?"

"Of course. You're young, but God is getting a man ready for you, and you'll be very happy."

★ ★ ★ ★

The *Polaris* wallowed in the waves, throwing Emily slightly off balance. Ian reached out and pulled her back, holding her tight. The spray rose up and over the rail, half soaking them, but neither of them cared.

"You're soaking wet, Emily."

"So are you! And what's more, I don't care. We're going home, and I always did love storms."

Ian held her, conscious of her warmth against him. The two stood there and finally Ian said, "That was good news we got from the Pettigrews." They had been told by the missionaries that a couple had volunteered to take up work with the Guapi. "I think they'll do fine," he said. "Looks like my work there is ended."

They watched the horizon for a long time, then he added, "I'm going to do something that frightens me."

"I don't think anything could scare you."

"You're wrong about that."

"What is it?"

"I don't think I have the nerve to ask your father and mother if they'll let me marry you. I think I'd lose my voice. It seems like asking such a lot."

The wind whipped through the air and brought the spray, drenching them again. Emily's hair was wet and plastered to her skull, but her eyes danced. She put her arms around his neck and said, "I can. Leave it up to me."

"What if your father says no?"

"Then I'll do what I did when I was a little girl. I'll sit on his lap and tell him how handsome he is and how wonderful he is, and the first thing you know his *no* will turn into a *yes*!"

Ian suddenly laughed. "All right, I'll let you have it your way. As a matter of fact, I think that's going to be the story of you and me—my making decisions and your changing them to suit yourself."

"You'll get used to it soon. You'll even like it after a while." Emily laughed and then put her arms around him and held him close. "It's going to be just perfect, Ian."

★　★　★　★

Ian felt terribly out of place as the door opened and Aaron and Gail dashed out to embrace their children. He stood back and for one instant had the absurd idea of turning and running. *That won't do*, he thought. *Just face up to it.*

"Ian," Gail said and came forward. She put her hands out, and when he took them, she put her face up to be kissed. "I'm so glad you decided to come."

"Right! Somebody had to bring these two wayward children home. I wouldn't trust 'em to go to the grocery store." Aaron winked as he said this and came forward, putting his hand out and shaking Ian's. "Come on in. I've been helping Gail cook supper."

"No, you haven't. You've been getting in the way," Gail laughed.

At that moment a huge dog came sailing out of the door. He leaped up on Emily, who would have been pushed back if Ian had not grabbed her.

"Cap'n Brown, you monster!" Emily cried and got down on her knees to hug him. Cap'n Brown ecstatically licked her in the face, and then she turned and said, "Come on and greet the Cap'n, Ian."

Ian went forward rather hesitantly, but Cap'n Brown barked sharply in a staccato series of yelps and promptly licked Ian's face.

"Never mind that mangy dog," Aaron protested. "Let's go inside. We want to hear everything."

Twenty minutes later the family was all seated around the table, and as usual Emily did most of the talking. Her eyes danced, and words tumbled out of her mouth as she told them event after event that had taken place in the Amazon.

"What about your magazine article?"

"It's all ready to send off. I worked on it on the voyage home."

"And I fixed up a darkroom on the ship, and all the pictures are developed now. It's just a matter of enlarging some and cutting others. They came out great. I can't wait for you to see them."

Aaron sat back smiling, and he noticed how often Emily's eyes went to Ian. He noticed also that she often could not help reaching out to touch his arm or his hand, and once when a lock of hair fell over his forehead, she reached up and pushed it back. *Something in that*, Aaron thought. *And I can guess what. . . .*

Later that evening, when Emily and Wes went to their rooms to unpack and change, Ian came and stood before Emily's parents and said, "There's something I must say to you."

"What is it, Ian?" Gail said. She glanced at Aaron, and a look of understanding passed between them. They had talked about this moment since receiving Emily's batch of letters just a few days before the travelers themselves returned home, and now they waited until Ian spoke.

"I needed to ask your forgiveness in person. I'm so sorry for having deceived you."

"That's all over, Ian. We forgave you long ago," Aaron said.

Relief washed across Ian's face, but then he seemed to set his jaw. "I need to say something else." He had difficulty speaking, but finally he got it out. "I love Emily. I don't have much to offer her, for I'm a man with nothing. But I wanted you to know how I feel about your daughter, and I wanted to promise you that I won't take advantage of her or of you."

Gail went at once to him and reached out and put her hand on his shoulder. "We know you wouldn't, Ian. It's obvious to us that you've changed, and if Emily loves you, that's all we need to know."

Aaron nodded and then asked, "What has she said?"

"We love each other, but I can't marry her until some things are settled."

"That's probably wise," Aaron said. "But you're a young man. You can do anything you set your mind to."

★ ★ ★ ★

Two weeks and one day after the arrival home of the trio, the mail came late. Emily and Ian were sitting on the front porch swinging back and forth. "I never had a swing when I was growing up. I used to pass houses," Ian said mildly, "and I would see people sitting on the porches swinging. And I'd think to myself, 'They've got everything.'"

Emily took his hand and held it. She knew his terrible childhood had left a mark, and she was determined to get it out of his mind as much as possible. "When we have our house, the one thing we'll have is a swing," she promised. "We may not have any furniture to sit on, but we'll have a swing. And we'll sit on it, and people will walk by, and we'll wave at them. And they'll think, 'My, what a beautiful couple and how happy they are.'"

Ian smiled and said, "Do you really think so?"

"Yes, we can do anything we want to, Ian."

At that moment the postman appeared, walking past the Wilsons' house, and Emily sighed. "I'll never hear from *National Geographic*. If they had wanted the story, they would have written by now."

"They're a big firm. Takes time to process these things. It's not a decision that they could make lightly."

Emily watched as the postman came up the walk and rose to meet him.

"Why, hello, Emily. How's it feel to be back out of the jungles?"

"Just fine. You have some mail?"

"Only one. And it's for you."

Emily's hand trembled as she took the envelope. She stared at the face of it and then looked across at Ian. "It's . . . it's from *National Geographic*."

The postman turned and walked away, but Emily could not move.

"Open it," Ian urged.

"But what if it's bad news?" Emily said.

"If they don't take the story, we'll take it somewhere else. And then you have your book to write. Go on. Open it."

With unsteady fingers, Emily opened the envelope. She took out a single sheet of paper and then with despair cried, "I can't read it. If it's a rejection, I'll die!"

Ian smiled. "You won't die. Now, what does it say?"

"Here. You read it." Emily handed the single sheet to Ian. He opened it at once and scanned it. Then he looked up, and he was all smiles. "They've taken the story. Congratulations!"

Emily grabbed the paper and read it. When she looked at him, her eyes were bright with tears. "I was beginning to think they didn't want my story."

He put his arms around her and said, "I never doubted it for a moment."

Emily grew very still. "I don't know what I'll be doing after this, and I don't know what you'll be doing—but can we do it together, Ian?"

Ian Marlowe put his arms around Emily and drew her close. To her it was like coming home to harbor after a long voyage, and when he whispered, "Yes, we'll do it together," she could do no more than hold him tightly and thank God for the remarkable way He had worked in her life.

Be the first *to know*

Want to be the first to know
what's new from
your favorite authors?

Want to know all about
exciting new writers?
